P9-BYJ-238

TWENTY THOUSAND LEAGUES
UNDER THE SEA

JULES VERNE

TWENTY THOUSAND LEAGUES UNDER THE SEA

KÖNEMANN

🐿 Notes (on pp. 427 to 455)
are keyed thus in the margin

Editor's acknowledgement

Editors have to appear omniscient.
This appearance is contrived with the
aid of well-informed others. I should
like to thank the Bodleian Librarians,
Dr. Stephen Harrison, Dr. Alan Forey,
Professor Owen Dudley Edwards, and
(as usual) Dr. Wes Williams.

C.M.

© 1997 for this edition
Könemann Verlagsgesellschaft mbH
Bonner Straße 126, D–50968 Köln

Series editor: Michael Hulse
Volume editor: Chris Miller
Cover design: Peter Feierabend
Layout and typesetting: Birgit Beyer
Printed in Hungary
ISBN 3-89508-462-X

CONTENTS

Chapter   Page

Part I

Chapter		Page

Part II

Chapter		Page

CHAPTER I

A Floating Reef

In the year 1866 the whole maritime population of Europe and America was excited by a mysterious and inexplicable phenomenon. This excitement was not confined to merchants, common sailors, sea-captains, shippers, and naval officers of all countries, but the governments of many states on the two continents were deeply interested.

The excitement was caused by an enormous "something" that ships were often meeting. It was a long, spindle-shaped, and sometimes phosphorescent object, much larger and more rapid than a whale.

The different accounts that were written of this object in various log-books agreed generally as to its structure, wonderful speed, and the peculiar life with which it appeared endowed. If it was a cetacean it surpassed in bulk all those that had hitherto been classified; neither Cuvier, Lacépède, M. Dumeril, nor M. de Quatrefages would have admitted the existence of such a monster, unless he had seen it with his own scientific eyes.

By taking the average of observations made at different times—rejecting the timid estimates that assigned to this object a length of 200 feet, as well as the exaggerated opinions which made it out to be a mile in width and three in length—we may fairly affirm that it surpassed all the dimensions allowed by the ichthyologists of the day, if it existed at all. It did exist, that was undeniable, and with that leaning towards the marvellous that characterises humanity, we cannot wonder at the excitement it produced in the entire world.

On the 20th of July, 1866, the steamer *Governor Higgenson*, of the Calcutta and Burnach Steam Navigation Company, met this moving mass five miles off the east coast of Australia. Captain Baker thought at first that he was in presence of an unknown reef; he was preparing to take its exact position, when two columns of water, projected by the inexplicable object, went hissing up a hundred and fifty feet into the air. Unless there was an intermittent geyser on the reef, the *Governor Higgenson* had to do with some aquatic mammal, unknown till then, which threw out columns of water mixed with air and vapour from its blowholes.

A similar occurrence happened on the 23rd of July in the same year to the *Columbus*, of the West India and Pacific Steam Navigation Company, in the Pacific Ocean. It was, therefore, evident that this extraordinary cetaceous creature could transport itself from one place to another with surprising velocity, seeing there was but an interval of three days between the two observations, separated by a distance of more than 700 nautical leagues.

Fifteen days later, two thousand leagues from the last place it was seen at, the *Helvetia*, of the *Compagnie Nationale*, and the *Shannon*, of the Royal Mail Steamship Company, sailing on opposite courses in that part of the Atlantic between the United States and Europe, each signalled the monster to the other in 42° 15' N. lat. and 60° 35' W. long. As the *Shannon* and *Helvetia* were of smaller dimensions than the object, though they measured 300 feet over all, the minimum length of the mammal was estimated at more than 350 feet. Now the largest whales, those that are found in the seas round the Aleutian, Kulammak, and Umgullich Islands, are never more than sixty yards long, if so long.

These accounts arrived one after another; fresh observations made on board the transatlantic ship *Le Pereire*, the running foul of the monster by the *Etna*, of the Inman line; a report drawn up by the officers of the French frigate *La Normandie*; a very grave statement made by the ship's officers of Commodore FitzJames on board the *Lord Clyde*, deeply stirred public opinion. In light-hearted countries jokes were made on the subject; but in grave and practical countries like England, America, and Germany, much attention was paid to it.

In all the great centres the monster became the fashion; it was sung about in the cafés, scoffed at in the newspapers, and represented at all the theatres. It gave opportunity for hoaxes of every description. In all newspapers short of copy imaginary beings reappeared, from the white whale, the terrible *"Moby Dick"* of the Northern regions, to the inordinate *"kraken"*, whose tentacles could fold round a vessel of 500 tons burden and drag it down to the depths of the ocean. The accounts of ancient times were reproduced: the opinions of Aristotle and Pliny, who admitted the existence of these monsters, and the Norwegian tales of Bishop Pontoppidan, those of Paul Heggede, and lastly the report of Mr. Harrington, whose good faith could not be put in question when he affirmed that, being on board the *Castilian*, in 1857, he saw this enormous serpent which until then had only frequented the seas of the old *Constitutionnel* newspaper.

Then broke out the interminable polemics of believers and disbelievers in learned societies and scientific journals. The "question of the monster" inflamed all minds. The journalists who professed to be scientific, at strife with those who professed to be witty, poured out streams of ink during this memorable controversy; some even two or three drops of blood, for they wandered from the sea serpent to the most offensive personalities.

For six months the war went on with different success. To the leading articles of the Geographical Institute of Brazil, the Berlin Royal Academy of Science, the British Association, the Washington Smithsonian Institution, to the discussions of *The Indian Archipelago*, to the *Cosmos* of the Abbé Moigno, Petermann's *Mitheilungen*, the scientific chronicles of the best newspapers of the civilised world, the smaller newspapers answered with great animation. Their witty writers, parodying a saying of Linnæus, quoted by the adversaries of the monster, sustained that, in fact, "Nature did not make fools," and adjured their contemporaries not to give the lie to Nature by admitting the existence of "krakens," sea serpents, "Moby Dicks," and other elucubrations of delirious sailors. Lastly, in an article of a much-dreaded satirical journal, the most liked of its contributors hurried over the whole ground, reached the monster, like Hippolytus gave him his finishing blow, and killed him in the midst of a universal burst of laughter. Wit had conquered science.

During the first months of the year 1867 the question seemed to be buried out of sight and mind, when some fresh facts brought it again before the notice of the public. It had then changed from a scientific problem to be solved to a real and serious danger to be avoided. The question took another phase. The monster again became an island or rock. On the 5th of March, 1867, the *Moravian*, of the Montreal Ocean Company, being, during the night, in 27° 36' lat. and 72° 15' long., struck her starboard quarter on a rock which no chart gave in that point. She was then going at the rate of thirteen knots under the combined efforts of the wind and her 400 horse power. Had it not been for the more than ordinary strength of the hull in the *Moravian* she would have been broken by the shock, and have gone down with the 237 passengers she was bringing from Canada.

The accident happened about 5 a.m. at daybreak. The officers on watch hurried aft and looked at the sea with the most scrupulous attention. They saw nothing except what looked like a strong eddy, three cables' length off, as if the waves had been violently agitated. The bearings of the place were taken exactly, and the *Moravian* went on her way without apparent damage. Had she struck on a submarine rock or some enormous fragment of wreck? They could not find out, but during the examination made of the ship's bottom when under repair it was found that part of her keel was broken.

This fact, extremely grave in itself, would perhaps have been forgotten, like so many others, if three weeks afterwards it had not happened again under identical circumstances, only, thanks to the nationality of the ship that was this time victim of the shock, and the reputation of the company to which the vessel belonged, the circumstance was immensely commented upon.

Everyone knows the name of the celebrated shipowners Cunard and Co. This intelligent company founded, in 1840, a postal service between Liverpool and Halifax, with three wooden vessels and an engine of 400 horse power, gauging 1,162 tons. Eight years afterwards the stock of the company increased to four vessels of 650 horse power and 1,820 tons, and two years later they had two more boats, superior in power and tonnage. In 1853 the Cunard Company, whose privilege of carrying the mails had just been renewed, added successively to their stock the *Arabia, Persia, China, Scotia, Java*, and *Russia*, all vessels of first-rate speed, and the largest which, next to the *Great Eastern*, had ever ploughed the seas. Thus, then, in 1867 the company possessed twelve vessels, eight with paddles and four with screws.

I give these brief details to show the importance of this maritime transport company, known in the entire world by its intelligent administration. No enterprise of transmarine navigation has been conducted with more skill; no business affair has been crowned with more success. During the last twenty-six years the Cunard vessels have crossed the Atlantic more than two thousand times, and no voyage has ever failed, no letter, man, nor vessel has ever been lost. Notwithstanding the powerful competition of France, passengers still choose the Cunard route in preference to every other, as is apparent from an examination of the official documents of late years. This understood, no one will be astonished at the commotion caused by the accident that happened to one of its finest steamers.

On the 13th of April, 1867, by a smooth sea and favourable breeze, the Cunard steamer *Scotia* was in 15° 12' long. and 45° 37' lat. She was going at the rate of thirteen knots an hour under the pressure of her 1,000 horse power.

At 4.17 p.m., as the passengers were assembled at dinner in the great saloon, a slight shock was felt on the hull of the *Scotia*, on her quarter a little aft of the paddle.

The *Scotia* had not struck anything, but had been struck by some sharp and penetrating rather than blunt surface. The shock was so slight that no one on board would have been uneasy at it had it not been for the carpenter's watch, who rushed upon deck, calling out—"She is sinking! she is sinking!"

At first the passengers were much alarmed, but Captain Anderson hastened to reassure them by telling them the danger could not be imminent, as the ship was divided into seven compartments by strong divisions, and could with impunity brave any leak.

Captain Anderson went down immediately into the hold and found that a leak had sprung in the fifth compartment, and the sea was rushing in rapidly. Happily there were no boilers in this compartment, or the fires would have been at once put out. Captain Anderson ordered the engines to be immediately stopped, and one of the sailors dived to ascertain the extent of the damage. Some minutes after it was ascertained that there was a large hole about two yards in diameter in the ship's bottom. Such a leak could not be stopped, and the Scotia, with her paddles half submerged, was obliged to continue her voyage. She was then 300 miles from Cape Clear, and after three days' delay, which caused great anxiety in Liverpool, she entered the company's docks.

The engineers then proceeded to examine her in the dry dock, where she had been placed. They could scarcely believe their eyes; at two yards and a half below water-mark was a regular rent in the shape of an isosceles triangle. The place where the piece had been taken out of the iron plates was so sharply defined that it could not have been done more neatly by a punch. The perforating instrument that had done the work was of no common stamp, for after having been driven with prodigious force, and piercing an iron plate one and three-eighths of an inch thick, it had been withdrawn by some wonderful retrograde movement.

Such was the last fact, and it again awakened public opinion on the subject. After that all maritime disasters which could not be satisfactorily accounted for were put down to the account of the monster. All the responsibility of the numerous wrecks annually recorded at Lloyd's was laid to the charge of this fantastic animal, and they usually amount to 3,000, of which 200 are lost by unknown causes.

Thanks to the "monster," communication between the two continents became more and more difficult; the public loudly demanded that the seas should be rid of the formidable cetacean at any price.

CHAPTER II

For and Against

At the period when these events were happening I was returning from a scientific expedition into the disagreeable region of Nebraska, in the United States. In my quality of Assistant Professor in the Paris Museum of Natural History, the French Government had attached me to that expedition. I arrived at New York, loaded with precious collections made during six months in Nebraska, at the end of March. My departure from France was fixed for the beginning of May. Whilst I waited and was occupying myself with classifying my mineralogical, botanical, and zoological riches, the incident happened to the *Scotia.*

I was perfectly acquainted with the subject which was the question of the day, and it would have been strange had I not been. I had repeatedly read all the American and European papers without being any the wiser as to the cause. The mystery puzzled me, and I hesitated to form any conclusion.

When I arrived at New York the subject was hot. The hypothesis of a floating island or reef, which was supported by incompetent opinion, was quite abandoned, for unless the shoal had a machine in its stomach, how could it change its position with such marvellous rapidity? For the same reason the idea of a floating hull or gigantic wreck was given up.

There remained, therefore, two possible solutions of the enigma which created two distinct parties; one was that the object was a colossal monster, the other that it was a submarine vessel of enormous motive power. This last hypothesis, which, after all, was admissible, could not stand against inquiries made in the two hemispheres. It was hardly probable that a private individual should possess such a machine. Where and when had he caused it to be built, and how could he have kept its construction secret? Certainly a government might possess such a destructive engine, and it was possible in these disastrous times, when the power of weapons of war has been multiplied, that, without the knowledge of others, a state might possess so formidable a weapon. After the chassepots came the torpedoes, and after the torpedoes the submarine rams, and after them—the reaction. At least, I hope so.

But the hypothesis of a war machine fell before the declaration of different governments, and as the public interest suffered from the difficulty of transatlantic communication, their veracity could not be doubted. Besides, secrecy would be even more difficult to a government than to a private individual. After inquiries made in England, France, Russia, Prussia, Spain, Italy, America, and even Turkey, the hypothesis of a submarine monitor was definitely rejected.

On my arrival at New York, several persons did me the honour of consulting me about the phenomenon in question. I had published in France a quarto work in two volumes, called *The Mysteries of the Ocean Depths*. This book made some sensation in the scientific world, and gained me a special reputation in this rather obscure branch of Natural History. As long as I could deny the reality of the fact I kept to a decided negative, but I was soon driven into a corner, and was obliged to explain myself categorically. The Honourable Pierre Aronnax, Professor in the Paris Museum, was asked by the *New York Herald* to give his opinion on the matter. I subjoin an extract from the article which I published on the 30th of April:—

"After having examined the different hypotheses one by one, and all other suppositions being rejected, the existence of a marine animal of excessive strength must be admitted.

"The greatest depths of the ocean are totally unknown to us. What happens there? What beings can live twelve or fifteen miles below the surface of the sea? We can scarcely conjecture what the organisation of these animals is. However the solution of the problem submitted to me may affect the form of the dilemma, we either know all the varieties of beings that people our planet or we do not. If we do not know them all—if there are still secrets of ichthyology for us—nothing is more reasonable than to admit the existence of fishes or cetaceans of an organisation suitable to the strata inaccessible to soundings, which for some reason or other come up to the surface at intervals.

"If, on the contrary, we do know all living species, we must of course look for the animal in question amongst the already classified marine animals, and in that case I should be disposed to admit the existence of a gigantic narwhal.

"The common narwhal, or sea-unicorn, is often sixty feet long. This size increased five or tenfold, and a strength in proportion to its size being given to the cetacean, and its offensive arms being increased in the same proportion, you obtain the animal required. It will have the proportions given by the officers of the *Shannon*, the instrument that perforated the *Scotia*, and the strength necessary to pierce the hull of the steamer.

"In fact, the narwhal is armed with a kind of ivory sword or halberd, as some naturalists call it. It is the principal tusk, and is as hard as steel. Some of these tusks have been found imbedded in the bodies of whales, which the narwhal always attacks with success. Others have been with difficulty taken out of ships' bottoms, which they pierced through and through like a gimlet in a barrel. The Museum of the Paris Faculty of Medicine contains one of these weapons, two and a quarter yards in length and fifteen inches in diameter at the base.

"Now suppose this weapon to be ten times stronger, and its possessor ten times more powerful, hurl it at the rate of twenty miles an hour, and you obtain a shock that might produce the catastrophe required. Therefore, until I get fuller information, I shall suppose it to be a sea-unicorn of colossal dimensions, armed, not with a halberd, but with a spur like ironclads or battering rams, the massiveness and motive power of which it would possess at the same time. This inexplicable pheno-menon may be thus explained, unless something exists over and above anything ever conjectured, seen, or experienced, which is just possible."

The last words were cowardly on my part, but I wished up to a certain point to cover my dignity as professor, and not to give too much cause of laughter to the Americans, who laugh well when they do laugh. I reserved myself a loophole of escape, and, in fact, admitted the existence of the monster.

My article was well received, and provoked much discussion amongst the public. It rallied a certain number of partisans. The solution which it proposed left freedom to the imagination. The human mind likes these grand conceptions of supernatural beings. Now the sea is precisely their best instrument of transmission, the only medium in which these giants, by the side of which terrestrial animals, elephants or rhinoceri, are but dwarfs, can breed and develop. The liquid masses transport the largest known species of mammalia, and they perhaps contain molluscs of enormous size, crustaceans frightful to contemplate, such as lobsters more than a hundred yards long, or crabs weighing two hundred tons. Why should it not be so? Formerly, terrestrial animals, contemporaries of the geological epochs, quadrupeds, quadrumans, reptiles, and birds, were constructed in gigantic moulds. The Creator had thrown them into a colossal mould which time has gradually lessened. Why should not the sea in its unknown depths have kept there vast specimens of the life of another age—the sea which never changes, whilst the earth changes incessantly? Why should it not hide in its bosom the last varieties of these Titanic species, whose years are centuries, and whose centuries are millenniums?

But I am letting myself be carried away by reveries which are no longer such to me. A truce to chimeras which time has changed for me into terrible realities. I repeat, opinion was then made up as to the nature of the phenomenon, and the public admitted without contestation the existence of the prodigious animal which had nothing in common with the fabulous sea serpents.

But if some people saw in this nothing but a purely scientific problem to solve, others more positive, especially in America and England, were of opinion to purge the ocean of this formidable monster, in order to reassure transmarine communications.

The *Shipping and Mercantile Gazette, Lloyd's Lists*, the *Packet Boat*, and *Revue Maritime et Coloniale*, all papers devoted to insurance companies who threatened to raise their rate of premium, were unanimous on this point. Public opinion having declared its verdict, the United States were first in the field, and preparations, for an expedition to pursue the narwhal were at once begun in New York. A very fast frigate, the *Abraham Lincoln*, was put in commission, and the arsenals were opened to Captain Farragut, who actively hastened the arming of his frigate.

But, as generally happens, from the moment it was decided to pursue the monster, the monster was not heard of for two months. It seemed as if this unicorn knew about the plots that were being weaved for it. It had been so much talked of, even through the Atlantic Cable! Would-be wits pretended that the cunning fellow had stopped some telegram in its passage, and was now using the knowledge for his own benefit.

So when the frigate had been prepared for a long campaign, and furnished with formidable fishing apparatus, they did not know where to send her to. Impatience was increasing with the delay, when on July 2nd it was reported that a steamer of the San Francisco line, from California to Shanghai, had met with the animal three weeks before in the North Pacific Ocean.

The emotion caused by the news was extreme, and twenty-four hours only were granted to Captain Farragut before he sailed. The ship was already victualled and well stocked with coal. The crew were there to a man, and there was nothing to do but to light the fires.

Three hours before the *Abraham Lincoln* left Brooklyn Pier I received the following letter:—

"To M. Aronnax, Professor of the Paris Museum,

"Fifth Avenue Hotel,

"New York.

"Sir,—If you would like to join the expedition of the *Abraham Lincoln*, the United States Government will have great pleasure in seeing France represented by you in the enterprise. Captain Farragut has a cabin at your disposition.

"Faithfully yours,

"J. B. Hobson,

"Secretary of Marine."

CHAPTER III

As Monsieur Pleases

Three seconds before the arrival of J. B. Hobson's letter I had no more idea of pursuing the unicorn than of attempting the North-West Passage. Three seconds after having read the secretary's letter I had made up my mind that ridding the world of this monster was my veritable vocation and the single aim of my life.

But I had just returned from a fatiguing journey, and was longing for rest in my own little place in the Jardin des Plantes amongst my dear and precious collections. But I forgot all fatigue, repose and collections, and accepted without further reflection the offer of the American Government.

"Besides," I said to myself, "all roads lead back to Europe, and the unicorn may be amiable enough to draw me towards the French coast. This worthy animal may allow itself to be caught in European seas for my especial benefit, and I will not take back less than half a yard of its halberd to the Natural History Museum."

But in the meantime the narwhal was taking me to the North Pacific Ocean, which was going to the antipodes on the road to France.

"Conseil!" I called in an impatient tone. "Conseil!"

Conseil was my servant, a faithful fellow who accompanied me in all my journeys, a brave Dutchman I had great confidence in; he was phlegmatic by nature, regular from principle, zealous from habit, showing little astonishment at the varied surprises of life, very skilful with his hands, apt at any service, and, in spite of his name, never giving any counsel, even when not asked for it.

By dint of contact with the world of *savants* in our Jardin des Plantes, Conseil had succeeded in knowing something. He was a specialist, well up in the classification of Natural History, but his science stopped there. As far as practice was concerned, I do not think he could have distinguished a cachalot from a whale. And yet what a brave fellow he was!

Conseil had followed me during the last ten years wherever science had directed my steps. He never complained of the length or fatigue of a journey, or of having to pack his trunk for any country, however remote, whether China or Congo. He went there or elsewhere without questioning the wherefore. His health defied all illness, and he had solid muscles, but no nerves—not the least appearance of nerves—of course I mean in his mental faculties. He was thirty years old, and his age to that of his master was as fifteen is to twenty. May I be excused for thus saying that I was forty?

But Conseil had one fault. He was intensely formal, and would never speak to me except in the third person, which was sometimes irritating.

"Conseil!" I repeated, beginning my preparations for departure with a feverish hand.

Certainly, I was certain of this faithful fellow. Usually I did not ask him if it was or was not convenient for him accompany me on my travels; but this time an expedition was in question which might be a very long and hazardous one, in pursuit of an animal capable of sinking a frigate like a nutshell. There was matter for reflection even to the most impassive man in the world. What would Conseil say?

"Conseil!" I called for the third time.

Conseil appeared.

"Did monsieur call me?" said he on entering.

"Yes, my boy. Get yourself and me ready to start in two hours."

"As it pleases monsieur," answered Conseil calmly.

"There is not a minute to lose. Pack up all my travelling utensils, as many coats, shirts and socks as you can get in. Make haste!"

"And monsieur's collections?" asked Conseil.

"We will see to them presently."

"What, the archiotherium, the hyracotherium, the oreodons, the cheropotamus, and monsieur's other skins?"

"They will stay at the hotel."

"And the live babiroussa of monsieur's?"

"They will feed it during our absence. Besides, I will give orders to have our menagerie forwarded to France."

"We are not going back to Paris, then?" asked Conseil.

"Yes—certainly we are," answered I evasively; "but by making a curve."

"The curve that monsieur pleases."

"Oh, it is not much; not so direct a route, that's all. We are going in the *Abraham Lincoln*."

"As it may suit monsieur."

"You know about the monster, Conseil—the famous narwhal. We are going to rid the seas of it. The author of the *Great Ocean Depths* cannot do otherwise than embark with Commander Farragut. A glorious mission, but—dangerous too. We don't know where we are going to. Those animals may be very capricious! But we will go, whether or no! We have a captain who will keep his eyes open."

"As monsieur does I will do," answered Conseil.

"But think, for I will hide nothing from you. It is one of those voyages from which people do not always come back."

"As monsieur pleases."

A quarter of an hour afterwards our trunks were ready. Conseil had packed them by sleight of hand, and I was sure nothing would be missing, for the fellow classified shirts and clothes as well as he did birds or mammals.

The hotel lift deposited us in the large vestibule of the first floor. I went down the few stairs that led to the ground floor. I paid my bill at the vast counter, always besieged by a considerable crowd. I gave the order to send my cases of stuffed animals and dried plants to Paris (France). I opened a sufficient credit for the babiroussa, and, Conseil following me, I sprang into a vehicle.

The vehicle, at fifteen shillings the course, descended Broadway as far as Union Square, went along Fourth Avenue to its junction with Bowery Street, then along Katrin Street, and stopped at the thirty-fourth pier. There the Katrin ferry-boat transported us, men, horses, and vehicle, to Brooklyn, the great annex of New York, situated on the left bank of East River, and in a few minutes we arrived at the quay, opposite which the *Abraham Lincoln* was pouring forth clouds of black smoke from her two funnels.

Our luggage was at once sent on board, and we soon followed it. I asked for Captain Farragut. One of the sailors conducted me to the poop, where I found myself in the presence of a pleasant-looking officer, who held out his hand to me.

"Monsieur Pierre Aronnax?" he said.

"Himself," replied I. "Do I see Captain Farragut?"

"In person. You are welcome, professor. Your cabin is ready for you."

I bowed, and leaving the commander to his duties, went down to the cabin which had been prepared for me.

The *Abraham Lincoln* had been well chosen and equipped for her new destination. She was a frigate of great speed, furnished with overheating apparatus that allowed the tension of the steam to reach seven atmospheres. Under that pressure the *Abraham Lincoln* reached an average speed of eighteen miles and three-tenths an hour; good speed, but not enough to wrestle with the gigantic cetacean.

The interior arrangements of the frigate were in keeping with her nautical qualities. I was well satisfied with my cabin, which was situated aft, and opened on the wardroom.

"We shall be comfortable here," said I to Conseil.

"Yes, as comfortable as a hermit crab in a whelk-shell."

I left Conseil to stow our luggage away, and went up on deck in order to see the preparations for departure. Captain Farragut was just ordering the last moorings to be cast loose, so that had I been one quarter of an hour later the frigate would have started without me, and I should have missed this extraordinary, supernatural, and incredible expedition, the true account of which may well be received with some incredulity.

But Commander Farragut did not wish to lose either a day or an hour before scouring the seas in which the animal had just been signalled. He sent for his engineer.

"Is the steam full on?" asked the captain.

"Yes, captain," replied the engineer.

"Go ahead then," cried Farragut.

The *Abraham Lincoln* was soon moving majestically amongst a hundred ferry-boats and tenders loaded with spectators, past the Brooklyn quay, on which, as well as on all that part of New York bordering on the East River, crowds of spectators were assembled. Thousands of handkerchiefs were waved above the compact mass, and saluted the *Abraham Lincoln* until she reached the Hudson at the point of that elongated peninsula which forms the town of New York.

Then the frigate followed the coast of New Jersey, along the right bank of the beautiful river covered with villas, and passed between the forts, which saluted her with their largest guns. The *Abraham Lincoln* acknowledged the salutation by hoisting the American colours three times, their thirty-nine stars shining resplendent from the mizzen peak; then modifying her speed to take the narrow channel marked by buoys and formed by Sandy Hook Point, she coasted the long sandy shore, where several thousand spectators saluted her once more.

Her escort of boats and tenders followed her till she reached the lightboat, the two lights of which mark the entrance to the New York Channel.

Three o'clock was then striking. The pilot went down into his boat and rejoined the little schooner which was waiting under lee, the fires were made up, the screw beat the waves more rapidly, and the frigate coasted the low yellow shore of Long Island, and at 8 p.m., after having lost sight in the northwest of the lights on Fire Island, she ran at full steam on to the dark waters of the Atlantic.

CHAPTER IV

Ned Land

Captain Farragut was a good seaman, worthy of the frigate he was commanding. His ship and he were one. He was the soul of it. No doubt arose in his mind on the question of the cetacean, and he did not allow the existence of the animal to be disputed on board. He believed in it like certain simple souls believe in the Leviathan—by faith, not by sight. The monster existed, and he had sworn to deliver the seas from it. He was a sort of Knight of Rhodes, a second Dieudonné de Gozon going to meet the serpent which was desolating his island. Either Captain Farragut would kill the narwhal or the narwhal would kill Captain Farragut—there was no middle course.

The officers on board shared the opinion of their chief. It was amusing to hear them talking, arguing, disputing and calculating the different chances of meeting whilst they kept a sharp look-out over the vast extent of ocean. More than one took up his position on the crosstrees who would have cursed the duty as a nuisance at any other time. Whilst the sun described its diurnal circle the rigging was crowded with sailors who could not keep in place on deck. And nevertheless the *Abraham Lincoln* was not yet ploughing with her stern the suspected waters of the Pacific.

As to the crew, all they wanted was to meet the unicorn, harpoon it, haul it on board, and cut it up. Captain Farragut had offered a reward of 2,000 dollars to the first cabin-boy, sailor, or officer who should signal the animal. I have already said that Captain Farragut had carefully provided all the tackle necessary for taking the gigantic cetacean. A whaler would not have been better furnished. We had every known engine, from the hand harpoon to the barbed arrow of the blunderbuss and the explosive bullets of the deck-gun. On the forecastle lay a perfect breechloader very thick at the breech and narrow in the bore, the model of which had been in the Paris Exhibition of 1867. This precious weapon, of American make, could throw with ease a conical projectile, weighing nine pounds, to a mean distance of ten miles. Thus the *Abraham Lincoln* not only possessed every means of destruction, but better still, she had on board Ned Land, the king of harpooners.

Ned Land was a Canadian of uncommon skill, who had no equal in his perilous employment. He possessed ability, *sang-froid*, audacity, and subtleness to a remarkable degree, and it would have taken a sharp whale or a singularly wily cachalot to escape his harpoon. He was about forty years of age, tall (more than six feet high), strongly built, grave, and taciturn, sometimes violent, aud very passionate when put out. His person, and especially the power of his glance, which gave a singular expression to his face, attracted attention.

I believe that Captain Farragut had done wisely in engaging this man. He was worth all the rest of the ship's company as far as his eye and arm went. I could not compare him to anything better than a powerful telescope which would be a cannon always ready to fire as well.

Ned Land was a descendant of French Canadians, and although he was so little communicative, he took a sort of liking to me. My nationality, doubtless, attracted him. It was an occasion for him to speak and for me to hear that old language of Rabelais which is still in use in some Canadian provinces. The family of the harpooner came originally from Quebec, and already formed a tribe of hardy fishermen when that town belonged to France. Little by little Ned Land acquired a liking for talk, and I was delighted to hear the recital of his adventures in the Polar Seas. He related his fishing expeditions and combats with great natural poetry. It was like listening to an epic poem of the time of Homer, an Iliad about hyperborean regions.

I now depict this brave companion as I knew him afterwards, for we are old friends united in that unchangeable friendship which his born and cemented in mutual danger. Ah, brave Ned, I only hope I may live a hundred years more to remember you longer.

Now what was Ned Land's opinion on the subject of this marine monster? I must acknowledge that he hardly believed in the narwhal, and that he was the only one on board who did not share the universal conviction.

One magnificent evening, three weeks after our departure, on the 30th of July, the frigate was abreast of Cape Blanc, thirty miles to leeward of the Patagonian coast. We had crossed the tropic of Capricorn, and the Straits of Magellan lay less than 700 miles to the south. Another week and the *Abraham Lincoln* would be ploughing the waters of the Pacific.

Seated on the poop, Ned Land and I were talking on all sorts of subjects, looking at that mysterious sea whose greatest depths have remained till now inaccessible to the eye of man. I brought the conversation naturally to the subject of the giant unicorn, and discussed the different chances of success in our expedition. Then seeing that Ned Land let me go on talking without saying anything himself, I pressed him more closely.

"Well, Ned," I said to him, "are you not yet convinced of the existence of the cetacean we are pursuing? Have you any particular reasons for being so incredulous?"

The harpooner looked at me for some minutes before replying, struck his forehead with a gesture habitual to him, shut his eyes as if to collect himself, and said at last—

"Perhaps I have, M. Aronnax."

"Yet you, Ned, are a whaler by profession. You are familiar with the great marine mammalia, and your imagination ought easily to accept the hypothesis of enormous cetaceans. You ought to be the last to doubt in such circumstances."

"That is what deceives you, sir," answered Ned. "It is not strange that common people should believe in extraordinary comets, or the existence of antediluvian monsters peopling the interior of the globe, but no astronomer or geologist would believe in such chimeras. The whaler is the same. I have pursued many cetaceans, harpooned a great number, and killed some few; but however powerful or well armed they were, neither their tails nor their defences could ever have made an incision in the iron plates of a steamer."

"Yet, Ned, it is said that ships have been bored through by the tusk of a narwhal."

"Wooden ships, perhaps," answered the Canadian, "though I have never seen it, and until I get proof to the contrary I deny that whales, cachalots, or sea-unicorns could produce such an effect."

"Listen to me, Ned."

"No, sir, no; anything you like but that—a gigantic poulp, perhaps?"

"No, that can't be. The poulp is only a mollusc; its flesh has no more consistency than its name indicates."

"Then you really do believe in this cetacean, sir?" said Ned.

"Yes, Ned. I repeat it with a conviction resting on the logic of facts. I believe in the existence of a mammal, powerfully organised, belonging to the branch of vertebrata, like whales, cachalots, and dolphins, and furnished with a horn tusk, or which the force of penetration is extreme."

"Hum!" said the harpooner, shaking his head like a man who will not let himself be convinced.

"Remark, my worthy Canadian," I continued, "if such an animal exists and inhabits the depths of the ocean, it necessarily possesses and organisation the strength of which would defy all comparison."

"Why must it have such an organisation?" asked Ned.

"Because it requires an incalculable strength to keep in such deep water and resist its pressure. Admitting that the pressure of the atmosphere is represented by that of a column of water thirty-two feet high. In reality the column of water would not be so high, as it is sea-water that is in question, and its density is greater than that of fresh water. When you dive, Ned, as many times thirty-two feet of water as there are above you, so many times does your body support a pressure equal to that of the atmosphere—that is to say, 15lbs. for each square inch of its surface. It hence follows that at 320 feet this pressure equals that of 10 atmospheres; at 3,200 feet, 100 atmospheres; and at 32,000 feet, 1,000 atmospheres—that is, about six and a half miles, which is equivalent to saying that if you can reach this depth in the ocean, each square inch of the surface of your body would bear a pressure of 14,933 ⅓ lbs. Do you know how many square inches you have on the surface of your body?"

"I have no idea, Aronnax."

"About 6,500; and as in reality the atmospheric pressure is about 15lbs. to the square inch, your 6,500 square inches support at this minute a pressure of 97,500lbs."

"Without my perceiving it?"

"Yes; and if you are not crushed by such a pressure, it is because the air penetrates the interior of your body with equal pressure, and there is a perfect equilibrium between the interior and exterior pressure, which thus neutralise each other, and allow you to bear it without inconvenience. But it is another thing in water."

"Yes, I understand," answered Ned, becoming more attentive, "because I am in water, but it is not in me."

"Precisely, Ned; so that at 32 feet below the surface of the sea you would undergo a pressure of 97,500lbs.; at 320 feet, 975,000lbs.; and at 32,000 feet the pressure would be 97,500,000lbs.—that is to say, you would be crushed as flat as a pancake."

"The devil!" exclaimed Ned.

"If vertebrata can maintain themselves in such depths, especially those whose surface is represented by millions of square inches, it is by hundreds of millions of pounds we must estimate the pressure they bear. Calculate, then, what must be the resistance of their bony structure and the strength of their organisation to withstand such a pressure."

"They must be made of iron plate eight inches thick like the ironclads!" said Ned.

"Yes, and think what destruction such a mass could cause if hurled with the speed of an express against the hull of a ship."

Ned would not give in.

"Have I not convinced you?" I said.

"You have convinced me of one thing, sir, which is, that if such animals do exist at the bottom of the sea they must be as strong as you say."

"But if they do not exist, Mr. Obstinate, how do you account for the *Scotia's* accident?"

"Because it is——" began Ned hesitatingly.

"Go on!"

"Because—it is not true!" answered the Canadian, repeating, without knowing it, a celebrated answer of Arago.

But this answer proved the obstinacy of the harpooner and nothing else. That day I did not press him further. The accident to the *Scotia* was undeniable. The hole existed so really that they were obliged to stop it up, and I do not think that the existence of a hole can be more categorically demonstrated. Now the hole had not made itself, and since it had not been done by submarine rocks or submarine machines, it was certainly due to the perforating tool of an animal.

Now, in my opinion, and for all the reasons previously deduced, this animal belonged to the embranchment of the vertebrata, to the class of mammals, to the group of pisciforms, and, finally, to the order of cetaceans. As to the family in which it took rank, whale, cachalot, or dolphin, as to the genus of which it formed a part, as to the species in which it would be convenient to put it, that was a question to be elucidated subsequently. In order to solve it the unknown monster must be dissected; to dissect it, it must be taken, to take it, it must be harpooned—which was Ned Land's business—to harpoon it, it must be seen—which was the crew's business—and to see it, it must be encountered—which was the business of hazard.

CHAPTER V

At Random

The voyage of the *Abraham Lincoln* for some time was marked by no incident. At last a circumstance happened which showed off the wonderful skill of Ned Land and the confidence that might be placed in him.

On the 30th of June the frigate, being then off the Falkland Islands, spoke some American whalers, who told us they had not met with the narwhal. But one of them, the captain of the *Munroe*, knowing that Ned Land was on board the *Abraham Lincoln*, asked for his help in capturing a whale they had in sight. Captain Farragut, desirous of seeing Ned Land at work, allowed him to go on board the *Munroe*, and fortune favoured our Canadian so well, that instead of one whale he harpooned two with a double blow, striking one right in the heart, and capturing the other after a pursuit of some minutes.

Certainly if the monster ever had Ned Land to deal with I would not bet in its favour.

The frigate skirted the south-east coast of America with extraordinary rapidity. On the 3rd of July we were at the opening of the Straits of Magellan, off Cape Vierges. But Captain Farragut did not wish to take this sinuous passage, but worked the ship for the doubling of Cape Horn.

The crew agreed with him unanimously. And certainly it was not possible that we should meet the narwhal in so narrow a pass.

On the 6th of July, about 3 p.m., we doubled, fifteen miles to the south, the solitary island to which some Dutch sailors gave the name of their native town, Cape Horn. The next day the frigate was in the Pacific.

"Keep a sharp look-out!" cried all the sailors.

Both eyes and telescopes, a little dazzled certainly by the thought of 2,000 dollars, never had a minute's rest. Day and night they observed the surface of the ocean; and even nyctalops, whose faculty of seeing in the darkness increased their chances fifty per cent., would have had to keep a sharp look-out to win the prize.

I myself, who thought little about the money, was not, however, the least attentive on board. I was constantly on deck, giving but few minutes to my meals, and indifferent to either rain or sunshine. Now leaning over the sea on the forecastle, now on the taffrail, I devoured with greedy eyes the soft foam which whitened the sea as far as those eyes could reach! How many times have I shared the emotion of the officers and crew when some capricious whale raised its black back above the waves! The deck was crowded in a minute. The companion ladders poured forth a torrent of officers and sailors, each with heaving breast and troubled eye watching the cetacean. I looked and looked till I was nearly blind, whilst Conseil, always calm, kept saying to me—

"If monsieur did not keep his eyes open so much he would see more."

But vain excitement! The *Abraham Lincoln* would modify her speed, run down the animal signalled, which always turned out to be a simple whale or common cachalot, and disappeared amidst a storm of execration.

In the meantime the weather remained favourable. The voyage was being accomplished under the best conditions. It was then the bad season in the southern hemisphere, for the July of that zone corresponds with the January of Europe, yet the sea was so calm that the eye could scan a vast circumference.

Ned Land always showed the most tenacious incredulity; he even affected not to examine the seas except during his watch, unless a whale was in sight; and yet his marvellous power of vision might have been of great service. But eight hours out of the twelve the obstinate Canadian read or slept in his cabin.

"Bah!" he would answer; "there is nothing, M. Aronnax; and even if there is an animal, what chance have we of seeing it? Are we not going about at random? I will admit that the beast has been seen again in the North Pacific, but two months have already gone by since that meeting, and according to the temperament of your narwhal it does not like to stop long enough in the same quarter to grow mouldy. It is endowed with a prodigious faculty of moving about. Now, you know as well as I do, professor, that Nature makes nothing inconsistent, and would not give to a slow animal the faculty of moving rapidly if it did not want to use it. Therefore, if the beast exists, it is far enough off now."

I did not know what to answer to that. We were evidently going along blindly. But how were we to do otherwise? Our chances, too, were very limited. In the meantime no one yet doubted of our success, and there was not a sailor on board who would have bet against the narwhal and against its early apparition.

On the 20th of July the tropic of Capricorn was crossed at 105° longitude, and the 27th of the same month we crossed the equator on the 110th meridian. These bearings taken, the frigate took a more decided direction westward, and entered the central seas of the Pacific. Commander Farragut rightly thought that it was better to frequent the deep seas, and keep at a distance from continents or islands, which the animal had always seemed to avoid approaching. "Doubtless because there was not enough water for him there," said the boatswain. The frigate, therefore, passed at a good distance from the Society, Marquesas, and Sandwich Islands, crossed the tropic of Cancer by 132° longitude, and made for the seas of China.

We were at last on the scene of the last frolics of the monster; and the truth was, no one lived really on board. Hearts beat frightfully fast, and laid down the seeds of future aneurisms. The entire crew were under the influence of such nervous excitement as I could not give the idea of. They neither ate nor slept. Twenty times a day some error of estimation, or the optical delusion of a sailor perched on the yards, caused intolerable frights; and these emotions, twenty times repeated, kept us in a state of erethismus too violent not to cause an early reaction.

And, in fact, the reaction was not slow in coming. For three months—three months, each day of which lasted a century—the *Abraham Lincoln* ploughed all the waters of the North Pacific, running down all the whales signalled, making sharp deviations from her route, veering suddenly from one tack to another, and not leaving one point of the Chinese or Japanese coast unexplored. And yet nothing was seen but the immense waste of waters—nothing that resembled a gigantic narwhal, nor a submarine islet nor a wreck, nor a floating reef, nor anything at all supernatural.

The reaction, therefore, began. Discouragement took possession of all minds, and opened a breach for incredulity. A new sentiment was experienced on board, composed of three-tenths of shame and seven-tenths of rage. They called themselves fools for being taken in by a chimera, and were still more furious at it. The mountains of arguments piled up for a year fell down all at once, and all everyone thought of was to make up the hours of meals and sleep which they had so foolishly sacrificed.

With the mobility natural to the human mind, they threw themselves from one excess into another. The warmest partisans of the enterprise became finally its most ardent detracters. The reaction ascended from the depths of the vessel, from the coal-hole, to the officers' ward-room, and certainly, had it not been for very strong determination on the part of Captain Farragut, the head of the frigate would have been definitely turned southward.

However, this useless search could be no further prolonged. The *Abraham Lincoln* had nothing to reproach herself with, having done all she could to succeed. No crew of the American Navy had ever shown more patience or zeal; its want of success could not be imputed to it. There was nothing left to do but to return.

A representation in this sense was made to the commander. The commander kept his ground. The sailors did not hide their dissatisfaction, and the service suffered from it. I do not mean that there was revolt on board, but after a reasonable period of obstinacy the commander, Farragut, like Columbus before him, asked for three days' patience. If in the delay of three days the monster had not reappeared, the man at the helm should give three turns of the wheel and the *Abraham Lincoln* should make for the European seas.

This promise was made on the 2nd of November. Its first effect was to rally the spirits of the ship's company. The ocean was observed with renewed attention.

Two days passed. The frigate kept up steam at half-pressure. Large quantities of bacon were trailed in the wake of the ship, to the great satisfaction of the sharks. The frigate lay to, and her boats were sent in all directions, but the night of the 4th of November passed without unveiling the submarine mystery.

The next day, the 5th of November, was the last of the delay.

The frigate was then in 31° 15' N. latitude and 136° 42' E. longitude. Japan lay less than 200 miles to leeward. Eight bells had just struck as I was leaning over the starboard side. Conseil, standing near me, was looking straight in front of him. The crew, perched in the ratlins, were keeping a sharp look-out in the approaching darkness. Officers with their night-glasses swept the horizon.

Looking at Conseil, I saw that the brave fellow was feeling slightly the general influence—at least it seemed to me so. Perhaps for the first time, his nerves were vibrating under the action of a sentiment of curiosity.

"Well, Conseil," said I, "this is your last chance of pocketing 2,000 dollars."

"Will monsieur allow me to tell him that I never counted upon the reward, and if the Union had promised a hundred thousand dollars it would never be any the poorer."

"You are right, Conseil. It has been a stupid affair, after all. We have lost time and patience, and might just as well have been in France six months ago."

"Yes, in monsieur's little apartments, classifying monsieur's fossils, and monsieur's babiroussa would be in its cage in the Jardin des Plantes, attracting all the curious people in Paris."

"Yes, Conseil, and besides that we shall get well laughed at."

"Certainly," said Conseil tranquilly. "I think they will laugh at monsieur. And I must say——"

"What, Conseil?"

"That it will serve monsieur right! When one has the honour to be a *savant* like monsieur, one does not expose——"

Conseil did not finish his compliment. In the midst of general silence Ned Land's voice was heard calling out—

"Look out there! The thing we are looking for on our weather beam!"

CHAPTER VI

With all Steam on

At this cry the entire crew rushed towards the harpooner. Captain, officers, masters, sailors, and cabin-boys, even the engineers left their engines, and the stokers their fires. The order to stop her had been given, and the frigate was only moving by her own momentum. The darkness was then profound, and although I knew the Canadian's eyes were very good, I asked myself what he could have seen, and how he could have seen it. My heart beat violently.

But Ned Land was not mistaken, and we all saw the object he was pointing to.

At two cables' length from the *Abraham Lincoln* on her starboard quarter, the sea seemed to be illuminated below the surface. The monster lay some fathoms below the sea, and threw out the very intense but inexplicable light mentioned in the reports of several captains. This light described an immense and much-elongated oval, in the centre of which was condensed a focus the overpowering brilliancy of which died out by successive gradations.

"It is only an agglomeration of phosphoric particles," cried one of the officers.

"No, sir," I replied with conviction. "Never did pholas or salpæ produce such a light as that. That light is essentially electric. Besides—see! look out! It moves—forward—on to us!"

A general cry rose from the frigate.

"Silence!" called out the captain. "Up with the helm! Reverse the engines!"

The frigate thus tried to escape, but the supernatural animal approached her with a speed double her own.

Stupefaction, more than fear, kept us mute and motionless. The animal gained upon us. It made the round of the frigate, which was then going at the rate of fourteen knots, and enveloped her with its electric ring like luminous dust. Then it went two or three miles off, leaving a phosphoric trail like the steam of an express locomotive. All at once, from the dark limits of the horizon, where it went to gain its momentum, the monster rushed towards the frigate with frightful rapidity, stopped suddenly at a distance of twenty feet, and then went out, not diving, for its brilliancy did not die out by degrees, but all at once as if turned off. Then it reappeared on the other side of the ship, either going round her or gliding under her hull. A collision might have occurred at any moment, which might have been fatal to us.

I was astonished at the way the ship was worked. She was being attacked instead of attacking; and I asked Captain Farragut the reason. On the captain's generally impassive face was an expression of profound astonishment.

"M. Aronnax," he said, "I do not know with how formidable a being I have to deal, and I will not imprudently risk my frigate in the darkness. We must wait for daylight, and then we shall change parts."

"You have no longer any doubt, captain, of the nature of the animal?"

"No, sir. It is evidently a gigantic narwhal, and an electric one too."

"Perhaps," I added, "we can no more approach it than we could a gymnotus or a torpedo."

"It may possess as great blasting properties, and if it does it is the most terrible animal that ever was created. That is why I must keep on my guard."

All the crew remained up that night. No one thought of going to sleep. The *Abraham Lincoln*, not being able to compete in speed, was kept under half-steam. On its side the narwhal imitated the frigate, let the waves rock it at will, and seemed determined not to leave the scene of combat.

Towards midnight, however, it disappeared, dying out like a large glowworm. At seven minutes to one in the morning a deafening whistle was heard, like that produced by a column of water driven out with extreme violence.

The captain, Ned Land, and I were then on the poop, peering with eagerness through the profound darkness.

"Ned Land," asked the commander, "have you often heard whales roar?"

"Yes, captain, often; but never such a whale as I earned two thousand dollars by sighting."

"True, you have a right to the prize; but tell me, is it the same noise they make?"

"Yes, sir; but this one is incomparably louder. It is not to be mistaken. It is certainly a cetacean there in our seas. With your permission, sir, we will have a few words with him at day break."

"If he is in a humour to hear them, Mr. Land," said I, in an unconvinced tone.

"Let me get within a length of four harpoons," answered the Canadian, "and he will be obliged to listen to me."

"But in order to approach him," continued the captain, "I shall have to put a whaler at your disposition."

"Certainly, sir."

"But that will be risking the lives of my men."

"And mine too," answered the harpooner simply.

About 2 a.m. the luminous focus reappeared, no less intense, about five miles to the windward of the frigate. Notwithstanding the distance and the noise of the wind and sea, the loud strokes of the animal's tail were distinctly heard, and even its panting breathing. When the enormous narwhal came up to the surface to breathe, it seemed as if the air rushed into its lungs like steam in the vast cylinders of a 2,000 horse power engine.

"Hum!" thought I, "a whale with the strength of a cavalry regiment would be a pretty whale!"

Until daylight we were all on the *qui-vive*, and then the fishing-tackle was prepared. The first mate loaded the blunderbusses, which throw harpoons the distance of a mile, and long duck-guns with explosive bullets, which inflict mortal wounds even upon the most powerful animals. Ned Land contented himself with sharpening his harpoon—a terrible weapon in his hands.

At 6 a.m. day began to break, and with the first glimmer of dawn the electric light of the narwhal disappeared. At 7 a.m. a very thick sea-fog obscured the atmosphere, and the best glasses could not pierce it.

I climbed the mizzen-mast and found some officers already perched on the mast-heads.

At 8 a.m. the mist began to clear away. Suddenly, like the night before, Ned Land's voice was heard calling—

"The thing in question on the port quarter!"

All eyes were turned towards the point indicated. There, a mile and a half from the frigate, a large black body emerged more than a yard above the waves. Its tail, violently agitated, produced a considerable eddy. Never did caudal appendage beat the sea with such force. An immense track, dazzlingly white, marked the passage of the animal, and described a long curve.

The frigate approached the cetacean, and I could see it well. The accounts of it given by the *Shannon* and *Helvetia* had rather exaggerated its dimensions, and I estimated its length at 150 feet only. As to its other dimensions, I could only conceive them to be in proportion.

Whilst I was observing it, two jets of vapour and water sprang from its vent-holes and ascended to a height of fifty yards, thus fixing my opinion as to its way of breathing. I concluded definitely that it belonged to the vertebrate branch of mammalia, order of cetaceans, family. . . . Here I could not decide. The order of cetaceans comprehends three families— whales, cachalots, and dolphins—and it is in this last that narwhals are placed.

The crew were waiting impatiently for their captain's orders. Farragut, after attentively examining the animal, had the chief engineer called.

"Is your steam up, sir?" asked the captain.

"Yes, captain," answered the engineer.

"Then make up your fires and put on all steam."

Three cheers greeted this order. The hour of combat had struck. Some minutes afterwards the funnels of the frigate were giving out torrents of black smoke, and the deck shook under the trembling of the boilers.

The *Abraham Lincoln*, propelled by her powerful screw, went straight at the animal, who let her approach to within half a cable's length, and then, as if disdaining to dive, made a little attempt at flight, and contented itself with keeping its distance.

This pursuit lasted about three-quarters of an hour, without the frigate gaining four yards on the cetacean. It was quite evident she would never reach it at that rate.

The captain twisted his beard impatiently.

"Ned Land!" called the captain, "do you think I had better have the boats lowered?"

"No, sir," answered Ned Land, "for that animal won't be caught unless it chooses."

"What must be done, then?"

"Force steam if you can, captain, and I, with your permission, will post myself under the bowsprit, and if we get within a harpoon length I shall hurl one."

"Very well, Ned," said the captain. "Engineer, put on more pressure."

Ned Land went to his post, the fires were increased, the screw revolved forty-three times a minute, and the steam poured out of the valves. The log was heaved, and it was found that the frigate was going eighteen miles and five-tenths an hour. But the animal went eighteen and five-tenths an hour too.

During another hour the frigate kept up that speed without gaining a yard. It was humiliating for one of the quickest vessels in the American navy. The crew began to get very angry. The sailors swore at the animal, who did not deign to answer them. The captain not only twisted his beard, he began to gnaw it too. The engineer was called once more.

"Have you reached your maximum of pressure?" asked the captain.

"Yes, sir."

The captain ordered him to do all he could without absolutely blowing up the vessel, and coal was at once piled up on the fires. The speed of the frigate increased. Her masts shook again. The log was again heaved, and this time she was making nineteen miles and three-tenths.

"All steam on!" called out the captain.

The engineer obeyed. The manometer marked ten degrees. But the cetacean did the nineteen miles and three-tenths as easily as the eighteen and five-tenths.

What a chase! I cannot describe the emotion that made my whole being vibrate again. Ned Land kept at his post, harpoon in hand. The animal allowed itself to be approached several times. Sometimes it was so near that the Canadian raised his hand to hurl the harpoon, when the animal rushed away at a speed of at least thirty miles an hour, and even during our maximum of speed it bullied the frigate, going round and round it.

A cry of fury burst from all lips. We were not further advanced at twelve o'clock than we had been at eight. Captain Farragut then made up his mind to employ more direct means.

"Ah!" said he, "so that animal goes faster than my ship! Well, we'll see if he'll go faster than a conical bullet. Master, send your men to the forecastle."

The forecastle gun was immediately loaded and pointed. It was fired, but the ball passed some feet above the cetacean, which kept about half a mile off.

"Let someone else have a try!" called out the captain. "Five hundred dollars to whomsoever will hit the beast!"

An old gunner with a grey beard—I think I see now his calm face as he approached the gun—put it into position and took a long aim. A loud report followed and mingled with the cheers of the crew.

The bullet reached its destination; it struck the animal, but, gliding off the rounded surface, fell into the sea two miles off.

"Malediction!" cried the captain; "that animal must be clad in six-inch iron plates. But I'll catch it, if I have to blow up my frigate!"

It was to be hoped that the animal would be exhausted, and that it would not be indifferent to fatigue like a steam-engine. But the hours went on, and it showed no signs of exhaustion.

It must be said, in praise of the *Abraham Lincoln*, that she struggled on indefatigably. I cannot reckon the distance we made during this unfortunate day at less than 300 miles. But night came on and closed round the heaving ocean.

At that minute I believed our expedition to be at an end, and that we should see the fantastic animal no more.

I was mistaken, for at 10.50 p.m. the electric light reappeared, three miles windward to the frigate, as clear and intense as on the night before.

The narwhal seemed motionless. Perhaps, fatigued with its day's work, it was sleeping in its billowy cradle. That was a chance by which the captain resolved to profit.

He gave his orders. The *Abraham Lincoln* was kept up at half-steam, and advanced cautiously so as not to awaken her adversary. It is not rare to meet in open sea with whales fast asleep, and Ned Land had harpooned many a one in that condition. The Canadian went back to his post under the bowsprit.

The frigate noiselessly approached, and stopped at two cables' length from the animal. No one breathed. A profound silence reigned on deck. We were not 1,000 feet from the burning focus, the light of which increased and dazzled our eyes.

At that minute, leaning on the forecastle bulwark, I saw Ned Land below me, holding the martingale with one hand and with the other brandishing his terrible harpoon, scarcely twenty feet from the motionless animal.

All at once he threw the harpoon, and I heard the sonorous stroke of the weapon, which seemed to have struck a hard body.

The electric light suddenly went out, and two enormous waterspouts fell on the deck of the frigate, running like a torrent from fore to aft, upsetting men, and breaking the lashing of the spars.

A frightful shock followed. I was thrown over the rail before I had time to stop myself, and fell into the sea.

CHAPTER VII

A Whale of an Unknown Species

Although I was surprised by my unexpected fall, I still kept a very distinct impression of my sensations. I was at first dragged down to a depth of about twenty feet. I was a good swimmer without any pretensions to equal Byron or Edgar Poe, both masters in the art, and this plunge did not make me lose my presence of mind. Two vigorous kicks brought me back to the surface.

My first care was to look for the frigate. Had the crew seen me disappear? Had the *Abraham Lincoln* veered round? Would the captain have a boat lowered? Might I hope to be saved?

The darkness was profound. I perceived a black mass disappearing in the east, the beacon lights of which were dying out in the distance. It was the frigate. I gave myself up.

"Help! help!" cried I, swimming towards the frigate with desperate strokes.

My clothes embarrassed me. The water glued them to my body. They paralysed my movements. I was sinking.

"Help!" rang out again in the darkness.

This was the last cry I uttered. My mouth filled with water. I struggled not to be sucked into the abyss.

Suddenly my clothes were seized by a vigorous hand, and I felt myself brought back violently to the surface of the water, and I heard—yes, I heard these words uttered in my ear:—

"If monsieur will have the goodness to lean on my shoulder, monsieur will swim much better."

I seized the arm of my faithful Conseil.

"You!" I cried—"you!"

"Myself," answered Conseil, "at monsieur's service."

"Did the shock throw you into the sea too?"

"No; but being in the service of monsieur, I followed him."

The worthy fellow thought that quite natural.

"What about the frigate?" I asked.

"The frigate!" answered Conseil, turning on his back; "I think monsieur will do well not to count upon the frigate."

"Why?"

"Because, as I jumped into the sea, I heard the man at the helm call out, 'The screw and the rudder are broken.'"

"Broken?"

"Yes, by the monster's tusk. It is the only damage she has sustained, I think; but without a helm she can't do anything for us."

"Then we are lost!"

"Perhaps," answered Conseil tranquilly. "In the meantime we have still several hours before us, and in several hours many things may happen."

The imperturbable *sang-froid* of Conseil did me good. I swam more vigorously, but, encumbered by my garments, which dragged me down like a leaden weight, I found it extremely difficult to keep up. Conseil perceived it.

"Will monsieur allow me to make a slit?" said he. And, slipping an open knife under my clothes, he slit them rapidly from top to bottom. Then he quickly helped me off with them whilst I swam for both. I rendered him the same service, and we went on swimming near each other.

In the meantime our situation was none the less terrible. Perhaps our disappearance had not been remarked, and even if it had the frigate could not tack without her helm. Our only chance of safety was in the event of the boats being lowered.

The collision had happened about 11 p.m. About 1 a.m. I was taken with extreme fatigue, and all my limbs became stiff with cramp. Conseil was obliged to keep me up, and the care of our preservation depended upon him alone. I heard the poor fellow breathing hard, and knew he could not keep up much longer.

"Let me go! Leave me!" I cried.

"Leave monsieur? Never!" he answered. "I shall drown with him."

Just then the moon appeared through the fringe of a large cloud that the wind was driving eastward. The surface of the sea shone under her rays. I lifted my head and saw the frigate. She was five miles from us, and only looked like a dark mass, scarcely distinguishable. I saw no boats.

I tried to call out, but it was useless at that distance. My swollen lips would not utter a sound. Conseil could still speak, and I heard him call out "Help!" several times.

We suspended our movements for an instant and listened. It might be only a singing in our ears, but it seemed to me that a cry answered Conseil's.

"Did you hear?" I murmured.

"Yes, yes!"

And Conseil threw another despairing cry into space. This time there could be no mistake. A human voice answered ours. Was it the voice of some other victim of the shock, or a boat hailing us in the darkness? Conseil made a supreme effort, and, leaning on my shoulder whilst I made a last struggle for us both, he raised himself half out of the water, and I heard him shout. Then my strength was exhausted, my fingers slipped, my mouth filled with salt water, I went cold all over, raised my head for the last time, and began to sink.

At that moment I hit against something hard, and I clung to it in desperation. Then I felt myself lifted up out of the water, and I fainted—I soon came to, thanks to the vigorous friction that was being applied to my body, and I half-opened my eyes.

"Conseil!" I murmured.

"Did monsieur ring?" answered Conseil.

Just then, by the light of the moon that was getting lower on the horizon, I perceived a face that was not Conseil's, but which I immediately recognised.

"Ned!" I cried.

"The same, sir, looking after his prize," replied the Canadian.

"Were you thrown into the sea when the frigate was struck?"

"Yes, sir, but, luckier than you, I soon got upon a floating island."

"An island?"

"Yes, or if you like better, on our giant narwhal."

"What do you mean, Ned?"

"I mean that I understand now why my harpoon did not stick into the skin, but was blunted."

"Why, Ned, why?"

"Because the beast is made of sheet-iron plates."

I wriggled myself quickly to the top of the half-submerged being or object on which we had found refuge. I struck my foot against it. It was evidently a hard and impenetrable body, and not the soft substance which forms the mass of great marine mammalia. But this hard body could not be a bony carapace like that of antediluvian animals. I could not even class it amongst amphibious reptiles, such as tortoises and alligators, for the blackish back that supported me was not scaly but smooth and polished.

The blow produced a metallic sound, and, strange as it may appear, seemed caused by being struck on riveted plates. Doubt was no longer possible. The animal, monster, natural phenomenon that had puzzled the entire scientific world, and misled the imagination of sailors in the two hemispheres, was, it must be acknowledged, a still more astonishing phenomenon, a phenomenon of man's making. The discovery of the existence of the most fabulous and mythological being would not have astonished me in the same degree. It seems quite simple that anything prodigious should come from the hand of the Creator, but to find the impossible realised by the hand of man was enough to confound the imagination.

We were lying upon the top of a sort of submarine boat, which looked to me like an immense steel fish. Ned Land's mind was made up on that point, and Conseil and I could only agree with him.

"But then," said I, "this apparatus must have a locomotive machine, and a crew inside of it to work it."

"Evidently," replied the harpooner, "and yet for the three

hours that I have inhabited this floating island it has not given sign of life."

"The vessel has not moved?"

"No, M. Aronnax. It is cradled in the waves, but it does not move."

"We know, without the slightest doubt, however, that it is endowed with great speed, and as a machine is necessary to produce the speed, and a mechanician to guide it, I conclude from that that we are saved."

"Hum," said Ned Land in a reserved tone of voice.

At that moment, and as if to support my arguments, a boiling was heard at the back of the strange apparatus, the propeller of which was evidently a screw, and it began to move. We only had time to hold on to its upper part, which emerged about a yard out of the water. Happily its speed was not excessive.

"As long as it moves horizontally," murmured Ned Land, "I have nothing to say. But if it takes it into its head to plunge I would not give two dollars for my skin!"

The Canadian might have said less still. It therefore became urgent to communicate with whatever beings were shut up in the machine. I looked on its surface for an opening, a panel, a "man-hole," to use the technical expression; but the lines of bolts, solidly fastened down on the joints of the plates, were clear and uniform.

Besides, the moon then disappeared and left us in profound obscurity. We were obliged to wait till daybreak to decide upon the means of penetrating to the interior of this submarine boat.

Thus, then, our safety depended solely upon the caprice of the mysterious steersmen who directed this apparatus, and if they plunged we were lost! Unless that happened I did not doubt the possibility of entering into communication with them. And it was certain that unless they made their own air they must necessarily return from time to time to the surface of the ocean to renew their provision of breathable molecules. Therefore there must be an opening which put the interior of the boat into communication with the atmosphere.

As to the hope of being saved by Commander Farragut, that had to be completely renounced. We were dragged westward, and I estimated that our speed, relatively moderate, attained twelve miles an hour. The screw beat the waves with mathematical regularity, sometimes emerging and throwing the phosphorescent water to a great height.

About 4 a.m. the rapidity of the apparatus increased. We resisted with difficulty this vertiginous impulsion, when the waves beat upon us in all their fury. Happily Ned touched with his hand a wide balustrade fastened on to the upper part of the iron top, and we succeeded in holding on to it solidly.

At last this long night slipped away. My incomplete memory does not allow me to retrace all the impressions of it. A single detail returns to my mind. During certain lullings of the sea and wind, I thought several times I heard vague sounds, a sort of fugitive harmony produced by far-off chords. What, then, was the mystery of this submarine navigation, of which the entire world vainly sought the explanation? What beings lived in this strange boat? What mechanical agent allowed it to move with such prodigious speed?

When daylight appeared the morning mists enveloped us, but they soon rose, and I proceeded to make an attentive examination of the sort of horizontal platform we were on, when I felt myself gradually sinking.

"*Mille diables!*" cried Land, kicking against the sonorous metal, "open, inhospitable creatures!"

But it was difficult to make oneself heard amidst the deafening noise made by the screw. Happily the sinking ceased.

Suddenly a noise like iron bolts violently withdrawn was heard from the interior of the boat. One of the iron plates was raised, a man appeared, uttered a strange cry, and disappeared immediately.

Some moments after eight strong follows, with veiled faces, silently appeared, and dragged us down into their formidable machine.

CHAPTER VIII

Mobilis in Mobili

This abduction, so brutally executed, took place with the rapidity of lightning. I do not know what my companions felt at being introduced into this floating prison; but, for my own part, a rapid shudder froze my very veins. With whom had we to do? Doubtless with a new species of pirates, who made use of the sea in a way of their own.

The narrow panel had scarcely closed upon me when I was enveloped by profound darkness. My eyes, dazzled by the light outside, could distinguish nothing. I felt my naked feet touch the steps of an iron ladder. Ned Land and Conseil, firmly held, followed me. At the bottom of the ladder a door opened and closed again immediately with a sonorous bang.

We were alone. Where? I neither knew nor could I imagine. All was darkness, and such absolute darkness, that after some minutes I had not been able to make out even those faint glimmers of light which float in the darkest nights.

Meanwhile, Ned Land, furious at this manner of proceeding, gave free course to his indignation.

"The people here equal the Scotch in hospitality!" he cried. "They could not be worse if they were cannibals. I shouldn't be surprised if they were, but I declare they shan't eat me without my protesting!"

"Calm yourself, friend Ned; calm yourself," answered Conseil tranquilly. "Don't get into a rage beforehand. We aren't on the spit yet."

"No, but we're in the oven. This hole's as dark as one. Happily my 'bowie-knife' is still on me, and I shall see well enough to use it. The first of these rascals that lays his hand on me——"

"Don't get irritated, Ned," then said I to the harpooner, "and do not compromise yourself by useless violence. Who knows that we are not overheard? Let us rather try to make out where we are."

I groped my way about. When I had gone about five steps I came to an iron wall made of riveted plates. Then turning, I knocked against a wooden table, near which were several stools. The flooring of this prison was hidden under thick phormium matting, which deadened the noise of our footsteps. The walls revealed no traces of either door or window. Conseil, going round the reverse way, met me, and we returned to the centre of the room, which measured about twenty feet by ten. As to its height, Ned Land, notwithstanding his tall stature, could not measure it.

Half an hour passed away without bringing any change in our position, when from the extreme of obscurity our eyes passed suddenly to the most violent light. Our prison was lighted up all at once—that is to say, it was filled with a luminous matter so intense that at first I could not bear its brilliancy. I saw from its whiteness and intensity that it was the same electric light that shone around the submarine boat like a magnificent phosphoric phenomenon. After having involuntarily closed my eyes I opened them again, and saw that the luminous agent was escaping from a polished half-globe, which was shining in the top part of the room.

"Well, we can see at last!" cried Ned Land, who, with his knife in hand, held himself on the defensive.

"Yes," answered I, risking the anthithesis, "but the situation is none the less obscure."

"Let monsieur have patience," said the impassible Conseil.

The sudden lighting of the cabin had allowed me to examine its least details. It only contained the table and five stools. The invisible door seemed hermetically closed. No noise reached our ears. All seemed dead in the interior of this machine. Was it moving, or was it motionless on the surface of the ocean, or deep in its depths? I could not guess.

However, the luminous globe was not lighted without a reason. I hoped that the men of the crew would soon show themselves, and my hope was well founded. A noise of bolts and bars being withdrawn was heard, the door opened, and two men appeared. One was short in stature, vigorously muscular, with broad shoulders, robust limbs, large head, abundant black hair, thick moustache, and all his person imprinted with that southern vivacity which characterises the Provençal inhabitants of France.

The second deserves a more detailed description. I read at once his dominant qualities on his open face—self-confidence, because his head was firmly set on his shoulders, and his black eyes looked round with cold assurance—calmness, for his pale complexion announced the tranquillity of his blood—energy, demonstrated by the rapid contraction of his eyebrows; and lastly, courage, for his deep breathing denoted vast vital expansion. I felt involuntarily reassured in his presence, and augured good from it. He might be of any age from thirty-five to fifty. His tall stature, wide forehead, straight nose, clear-out mouth, magnificent teeth, taper hands, indicated a highly-nervous temperament. This man formed certainly the most admirable type I had ever met with. One strange detail was that his eyes, rather far from each other, could take in nearly a quarter of the horizon at once. This faculty—I verified it later on—was added to a power of vision superior even to that of Ned Land. When the unknown fixed an object he frowned, and his large eyelids closed round so as to contract the range of his vision, and the result was a look that penetrated your very soul. With it he pierced the liquid waves that looked so opaque to us as if he read to the very depths of the sea.

The two strangers had on caps made from the fur of the sea-otter, sealskin boots, and clothes of a peculiar texture, which allowed them great liberty of movement.

The taller of the two—evidently the chief on board—examined us with extreme attention without speaking a word. Then he turned towards his companion, and spoke to him in a language I could not understand. It was a sonorous, harmonious, and flexible idiom, of which the vowels seemed very variously accented.

The other answered by shaking his head and pronouncing two or three perfectly incomprehensible words. Then, from his looks, he seemed to be questioning me directly.

I answered in good French that I did not understand his language; but he did not seem to know French, and the situation became very embarrassing.

"If monsieur would relate his story," said Conseil, "these gentlemen may understand some words of it."

I began the recital of my adventures, articulating clearly all my syllables, without leaving out a single detail. I gave our names and qualities. The man with the soft, calm eyes listened to me calmly, and even politely, with remarkable attention. But nothing in his face indicated that he understood me. When I had done he did not speak a single word.

There still remained one resource—that of speaking English. Perhaps they would understand that almost universal language. I knew it, and German too, sufficiently to read it correctly, but not to speak it fluently.

"It is your turn now, Land," I said to the harpooner. "Make use of your best English, and try to be more fortunate than I."

Ned did not need urging, and began the same tale in English, and ended by saying what was perfectly true, that we were half-dead with hunger. To his great disgust, the harpooner did not seem more intelligible than I. Our visitors did not move a feature. It was evident that they neither knew the language of Arago nor Faraday. I was wondering what to do next, when Conseil said to me—

"If monsieur will allow me, I will tell them in German."

"What! do you know German?" I cried.

"Like a Dutchman, sir."

"Well, do your best, old fellow."

And Conseil, in his tranquil voice, told our story for the third time, but without success.

I then assembled all the Latin I had learnt at school, and told my adventures in that dead language. Cicero would have

56

stopped his ears and sent me to the kitchen, but I did the best I could with the same negative result.

After this last attempt the strangers exchanged a few words in their incomprehensible language, and went away without a gesture that could reassure us. The door closed upon them.

"It is infamous!" cried Ned Land, who broke out again for the twentieth time. "What! French, English, German, and Latin are spoken to those rascals, and not one of them has the politeness to answer."

"Calm yourself, Ned," said I to the enraged harpooner; "anger will do no good."

"But do you know, professor," continued our irascible companion, "that it is quite possible to die of hunger in this iron cage?"

"Bah!" exclaimed Conseil; "with exercising a little philosophy we can still hold out a long while."

"My friends," said I, "we must not despair. We have been in worse situations before now. Do me the pleasure of waiting before you form an opinion of the commander and crew of this vessel."

"My opinion is already formed," answered Ned Land. "They are rascals——"

"Well, and of what country?"

"Of Rascaldom!"

"My worthy Ned, that country is not yet sufficiently indicated on the map of the world, and I acknowledge that the nationality of those two men is difficult to determine. Neither English, French, nor German, that is all we can affirm. However, I should be tempted to admit that the commander and his second were born under low latitudes. There is something meridional in them. But are they Spaniards, Turks, Arabians, or Indians? Their physical type does not allow me to decide; as to their language, it is absolutely incomprehensible."

"That is the disadvantage of not knowing every language," answered Conseil, "or the disadvantage of not having a single language."

"That would be of no use," answered Ned Land. "Do you not see that those fellows have a language of their own—a language invented to make honest men who want their dinners despair? But in every country in the world, to open your mouth, move your jaws, snap your teeth and lips, is understood. Does it not mean in Quebec as well as the Society Islands, in Paris as well as the antipodes, 'I am hungry—give me something to eat?'"

"Oh," said Conseil, "there are people so unintelligent——"

As he was saying these words the door opened, and a steward entered. He brought us clothes similar to those worn by the two strangers, which we hastened to don.

Meanwhile the servant—dumb and deaf too in all appearance—had laid the cloth for three.

"This is something like," said Conseil, "and promises well."

"I'll bet anything there's nothing here fit to eat," said the harpooner. "Tortoise liver, fillets of shark, or beafsteak from a sea-dog, perhaps!"

"We shall soon see," said Conseil.

The dishes with their silver covers were symmetrically placed on the table. We had certainly civilised people to deal with, and had it not been for the electric light which inundated us I might have imagined myself in the Adelphi Hotel in Liverpool or the Grand Hotel in Paris. There was neither bread nor wine, nothing but pure fresh water, which was not at all to Ned Land's taste. Amongst the dishes that were placed before us I recognised several kinds of fish delicately cooked; but there were some that I knew nothing about, though they were delicious. I could not tell to what kingdom their contents belonged. The dinner service was elegant and in perfect taste; each piece was engraved with a letter and motto of which the following is a *facsimile:*—

Mobilis in Mobile.

N.

Mobile in a mobile element! The letter N was doubtless the initial of the enigmatical person who commanded at the bottom of the sea.

Ned and Conseil did not observe so much. They devoured all before them, and I ended by imitating them.

But at last even our appetite was satisfied, and we felt overcome with sleep. A natural reaction after the fatigue of the interminable night during which we had struggled with death.

My two companions lay down on the carpet, and were soon fast asleep. I did not go so soon, for too many thoughts filled my brain; too many insoluble questions asked me for a solution; too many images kept my eyes open. Where were we? What strange power was bearing us along? I felt, or rather I thought I felt, the strange machine sinking down to the lowest depths of the sea. Dreadful nightmares took possession of me. I saw a world of unknown animals in these mysterious asylums, amongst which the submarine boat seemed as living, moving, and formidable as they. Then my brain grew calmer, my imagination melted into dreaminess, and I fell into a deep sleep.

CHAPTER IX

Ned Land's Anger

I do not know how long our sleep lasted, but it must have been a long time, for it rested us completely from our fatigues. I awoke first. My companions had not yet moved.

I had scarcely risen from my rather hard couch when I felt all my faculties clear, and looked about me.

Nothing was changed in the room. The prison was still a prison, and the prisoners prisoners. The steward, profiting by our sleep, had cleared the supper-things away. Nothing indicated an approaching change in our position, and I asked myself seriously if we were destined to live indefinitely in that cage.

This prospect seemed to me the more painful because, though my head was clear, my chest was oppressed. The heavy air weighed upon my lungs. We had evidently consumed the larger part of the oxygen the cell contained, although it was large. One man consumes in one hour the oxygen contained in 176 pints of air, and this air, then loaded with an almost equal quantity of carbonic acid, becomes unbearable.

It was, therefore, urgent to renew the atmosphere of our prison, and most likely that of the submarine boat also. Thereupon a question came into my head, "How did the commander of this floating dwelling manage? Did he obtain air by chemical means, by evolving the heat of oxygen contained in chlorate of potassium, and by absorbing the carbonic acid with caustic potassium? In that case he must have kept up some relations with land in order to procure the materials necessary to this operation. Did he confine himself simply to storing up air under great pressure in reservoirs, and then let it out according to the needs of his crew? Perhaps. Or did he use the more convenient, economical, and con-sequently more probable means of contenting himself with returning to breathe on the surface of the water like a cetacean, and of renewing for twenty-four hours his provision of atmosphere? Whatever his method might be, it seemed to me prudent to employ it without delay.

I was reduced to multiplying my respirations to extract from our cell the small quantity of oxygen it contained, when, suddenly, I was refreshed by a current of fresh air, loaded with saline odours. It was a sea breeze, life-giving, and charged with iodine. I opened my mouth wide, and my lungs became saturated with fresh particles. At the same time I felt the boat roll, and the iron-plated monster had evidently just ascended to the surface of the ocean to breathe like the whales. When I had breathed fully, I looked for the ventilator which had brought us the beneficent breeze, and, before long, found it.

I was making these observations when my two companions awoke nearly at the same time, doubtless through the influence of the reviving air. They rubbed their eyes, stretched themselves, and were on foot instantly.

"Did monsieur sleep well?" Conseil asked me with his usual politeness.

"Very well, old fellow. And you, Mr. Land?"

"Profoundly, Mr. Professor. But if I am not mistaken, I am breathing a sea breeze."

A seaman could not be mistaken in that, and I told the Canadian what had happened while he was asleep.

"That accounts for the roarings we heard when the supposed narwhal was in sight of the *Abraham Lincoln*."

"Yes, Mr. Land, that is its breathing."

"I have not the least idea what time it can be, M. Aronnax, unless it be dinner time."

"Dinner time, Ned? Say breakfast time at least, for we have certainly slept something like twenty-four hours."

"I will not contradict you," answered Ned Land, "but dinner or breakfast, the steward would be welcome. I wish he would bring one or the other."

"The one and the other," said Conseil.

"Certainly," answered the Canadian, "we have right to two meals, and, for my own part, I shall do honour to both."

"Well, Ned, we must wait," I answered. "It is evident that those two men had no intention of leaving us to die of hunger, for in that case there would have been no reason to give us dinner yesterday."

"Unless it is to fatten us!" answered Ned.

"I protest," I answered. "We have not fallen into the hands of cannibals."

"One swallow does not make a summer," answered the Canadian seriously. "Who knows if those fellows have not been long deprived of fresh meat, and in that case these healthy and well-constituted individuals like the professor, his servant, and me——"

"Drive away such ideas, Mr. Land," I answered, "and above all do not act upon them to get into a rage with our hosts, for that would only make the situation worse."

"Anyway," said the harpooner, "I am devilishly hungry, and, dinner or breakfast, the meal does not arrive!"

"Mr. Land," I replied, "we must conform to the rule of the vessel, and I suppose that our stomachs are in advance of the steward's bell."

"Well, then, we must put them right," answered Conseil tranquilly.

"That is just like you, Conseil," answered the impatient Canadian. "You do not use up your bile or your nerves! Always calm, you would be capable of saying your grace before your Benedicite, and of dying of hunger before you complained."

"What is the use of complaining?" asked Conseil.

"It does one good to complain! It is something. And if these pirates—I say pirates not to vex the professor, who does not like to hear them called cannibals—and if these pirates think that they are going to keep me in this cage where I am stifled without hearing how I can swear, they are mistaken. Come, M. Aronnax, speak frankly. Do you think they will keep us long in this iron box?"

"To tell you the truth I know no more about it than you, friend Land."

"But what do you think about it?"

"I think that hazard has made us masters of an important secret. If it is the interest of the crew of this submarine vessel to keep it, and if this interest is of more consequence than the life of three men, I believe our existence to be in great danger. In the contrary case, on the first opportunity, the monster who has swallowed us will send us back to the world inhabited by our fellow-men."

"Unless he enrols us amongst his crew," said Conseil, "and he keeps us thus——"

"Until some frigate," replied Ned Land, "more rapid or more skilful than the *Abraham Lincoln*, masters this nest of plunderers, and sends its crew and us to breathe our last at the end of his mainyard."

"Well reasoned, Mr. Land," I replied. "But I believe no proposition of the sort has yet been made to us, so it is useless to discuss what we should do in that case. I repeat, we must wait, take counsel of circumstances, and do nothing, as there is nothing to do."

"On the contrary, Mr. Professor," answered the harpooner, who would not give up his point, "we must do something."

"What, then?"

"Escape."

"To escape from a terrestrial prison is often difficult, but from a submarine prison, that seems to me quite impracticable."

"Come, friend Ned," said Conseil, "what have you to say to master's objection? I do not believe an American is ever at the end of his resources."

The harpooner, visibly embarrassed, was silent, a flight under the conditions hazard had imposed upon us was absolutely impossible. But a Canadian is half a Frenchman, and Ned Land showed it by his answer.

"Then, M. Aronnax," he said, after some minutes' reflection, "you do not guess what men ought to do who cannot escape from prison?"

"No, my friend."

"It is very simple; they must make their arrangements to stop in it."

"I should think so," said Conseil; "it is much better to be inside than on the top or underneath."

"But after you have thrown your gaolers and keepers out?" added Ned Land.

"What, Ned? You seriously think of seizing this vessel?"

"Quite seriously," answered the Canadian.

"It is impossible."

"How so, sir? A favourable chance may occur, and I do not see what could prevent us profiting by it. If there are twenty men on board this machine they will not frighten two Frenchmen and a Canadian, I suppose."

It was better to admit the proposition of the harpooner than to discuss it. So I contented myself with answering—

"Let such circumstances come, Mr. Land, and we will see. But until they do I beg of you to contain your impatience. We can only act by stratagem, and you will not make yourself master of favourable chances by getting in a rage. Promise me, therefore, that you will accept the situation without too much anger."

"I promise you, professor," answered Ned Land in a not very assuring tone; "not a violent word shall leave my mouth, not an angry movement shall betray me, not even if we are not waited upon at table with desirable regularity."

"I have your word, Ned," I answered.

Then the conversation was suspended, and each of us began to reflect on his own account. I acknowledge that, for my own part, and notwithstanding the assurance of the harpooner, I kept no illusion. I did not admit the probability of the favourable occasions of which Ned Land had spoken. To be so well worked the submarine boat must have a numerous crew, and consequently, in case of a struggle, we should have to do with numbers too great. Besides, before aught else we must be free, and we were not. I did not even see any means of leaving this iron cell so hermetically closed. And should the strange commander of the boat have a secret to keep—which appeared at least probable—he would not allow us freedom of movement on board. Now, would he get rid of us by violence, or would he throw us upon some corner of earth? All that was the unknown. All these hypotheses seemed to me extremely plausible, and one must be a harpooner to hope to conquer liberty again.

I understood, though, that Ned Land should get more exasperated with the thoughts that took possession of his brain. I heard him swearing in a gruff undertone, and saw his looks again become threatening. He rose, moved about like a wild beast in a cage, and struck the wall with his fist and foot. Moreover, time was going, hunger was cruelly felt, and this time the steward did not appear. If they had really good intentions towards us they had too long forgotten our shipwrecked condition.

Ned Land, tormented by the twinges of his robust stomach, became more and more enraged, and notwithstanding his promise I really feared an explosion when he would again be in the presence of the men on board.

Two more hours rolled on, and Ned's anger increased; he cried and called at the top of his voice, but in vain. The iron walls were deaf. The boat seemed quite still. The silence became quite oppressive.

I dare no longer think how long our abandonment and isolation in this cell might last. The hopes that I had conceived after our interview with the commander of the vessel vanished one by one. The gentle look of this man, the generous expression of his face, the nobility of his carriage, all disappeared from my memory. I again saw this enigmatical personage such as he must necessarily be, pitiless and cruel. I felt him to be outside the pale of humanity, inaccessible to all sentiment of pity, the implacable enemy of his fellow-men, to whom he had vowed imperishable hatred.

But was the man going, then, to let us perish from inanition, shut up in this narrow prison, given up to the horrible temptations to which ferocious famine leads? This frightful thought took a terrible intensity in my mind, and imagination helping, I felt myself invaded by unreasoning fear. Conseil remained calm. Ned was roaring. At that moment a noise was heard outside. Steps clanged on the metal slabs. The bolts were withdrawn, the door opened, the steward appeared.

Before I could make a movement to prevent him the Canadian had rushed upon the unfortunate fellow, knocked him down, and fastened on his throat. The steward was choking under his powerful hand.

Conseil was trying to rescue his half-suffocated victim from the hands of the harpooner, and I was going to join my efforts to his, when, suddenly, I was riveted to my place by these words spoken in French:—

"Calm yourself, Mr. Land, and you, professor, please to listen to me."

CHAPTER X

Nemo

The man who spoke thus was the commander of the vessel.

When Ned Land heard these words he rose suddenly. The almost strangled steward went tottering out on a sign from his master; but such was the power of the commander on his vessel that not a gesture betrayed the resentment the man must have felt towards the Canadian. Conseil, interested in spite of himself, and I stupefied, awaited the result of this scene in silence.

The commander, leaning against the angle of the table, with his arms folded, looked at us with profound attention. After some minutes of a silence which none of us thought of interrupting, he said in a calm and penetrating voice—

"Gentlemen, I speak French, English, German, and Latin equally well. I might, therefore, have answered you at our last interview, but I wished to know you first, and afterwards to ponder on what you said. The stories told by each of you agreed in the main, and assured me of your identity. I know now that accident has brought me into the presence of M. Pierre Aronnax, Professor of Natural History in the Paris Museum, charged with a foreign scientific mission, his servant Conseil, and Ned Land, of Canadian origin, harpooner on board the frigate *Abraham Lincoln*, of the United States Navy."

I bent my head in sign of assent. There was no answer necessary. This man expressed himself with perfect ease, and without the least foreign accent. And yet I felt that he was not one of my countrymen. He continued the conversation in these terms:—

"I daresay you thought me a long time in coming to pay you this second visit. It was because, after once knowing your identity, I wished to ponder upon what to do with you. I hesitated long. The most unfortunate conjuncture of circumstances has brought you into the presence of a man who has broken all ties that bound him to humanity. You came here to trouble my existence——"

"Unintentionally," said I.

"Unintentionally," he repeated, raising his voice a little. "Is it unintentionally that the *Abraham Lincoln* pursues me in every sea? Was it unintentionally that you took passage on board her? Was it unintentionally that your bullets struck my vessel? Did Mr. Land throw his harpoon unintentionally?"

"You are doubtless unaware," I answered, "of the commotion you have caused in Europe and America. When the *Abraham Lincoln* pursued you on the high seas everyone on board believed they were pursuing a marine monster."

A slight smile curled round the commander's lips, then he went on in a calmer tone—

"Dare you affirm, M. Aronnax, that your frigate would not have pursued a submarine vessel as well as a marine monster?"

This question embarrassed me, for it was certain that Captain Farragut would not have hesitated. He would have thought it as much his duty to destroy such a machine as the gigantic narwhal he took it to be.

"You see, sir," continued the commander, "I have the right to treat you as enemies."

I answered nothing, and for a very good reason; the unknown had force on his side, and it can destroy the best arguments.

"I have long hesitated," continued the commander. "Nothing obliges me to give you hospitality. I could place you upon the platform of this vessel, upon which you took refuge; I might sink it beneath the waters and forget that you ever existed. I should only be using my right."

"The right of a savage, perhaps," I answered, "but not that of a civilised man."

"Professor," quickly answered the commander, "I am not what is called a civilised man. I have done with society entirely for reasons that seem to me good; therefore I do not obey its laws, and I desire you never to allude to them before me again."

This was uttered clearly. A flash of anger and contempt had kindled in the man's eyes, and I had a glimpse of a terrible past in his life. He had not only put himself out of the pale of human laws, but he had made himself independent of them, free, in the most rigorous sense of the word, entirely out of their reach. Who, then, would dare to pursue him in the depths of the sea, when on its surface he baffled all efforts attempted against him? What armour, however thick, could support the blows of his spur? No man could ask him for an account of his works. God, if he believed in Him, his conscience, if he had one, were the only judges he could depend upon.

These reflections rapidly crossed my mind, whilst the strange personage was silent, absorbed, withdrawn into himself. I looked at him with terror mingled with interest, doubtless as Œdipus considered the Sphinx.

After a rather long silence the commander went on speaking.

"I have hesitated, therefore," said he, "but I thought that my interest might be reconciled with that natural pity to which every human being has a right. You may remain on my vessel, since fate has brought you to it. You will be free, and in exchange for this liberty, which after all will be relative, I shall only impose one condition upon you. Your word of honour to submit to it will be sufficient."

"Speak, sir," I answered. "I suppose this condition is one that an honest man can accept?"

"Yes; it is this:—It is possible that certain unforeseen events may force me to consign you to your cabin for some hours, or even days. As I do not wish to use violence, I expect from you, in such a case, more than from all others, passive obedience. By acting thus I take all the responsibility; I acquit you entirely, by making it impossible for you to see what ought not to be seen. Do you accept the condition?"

So things took place on board which were, at least, singular and not to be seen by people who were not placed beyond the pale of social laws.

"We accept," I replied. "Only I ask your permission to address to you one question—only one. What degree of liberty do you intend giving us?"

"The liberty to move about freely and observe even all that passes here—except under rare circumstances—in short, the liberty that my companions and I enjoy ourselves."

It was evident that we did not understand each other.

"Pardon me, sir," I continued, "but this liberty is only that of every prisoner to pace his prison. It is not enough for us."

"You must make it enough."

"Do you mean to say we must for ever renounce the idea of seeing country, friends, and relations again?"

"Yes, sir. But to renounce the unendurable worldly yoke that men call liberty is not perhaps so painful as you think."

"I declare," said Ned Land, "I'll never give my word of honour not to try to escape."

"I did not ask for your word of honour, Mr. Land," answered the commander coldly.

"Sir," I replied, carried away in spite of myself, "you take advantage of your position towards us. It is cruel!"

"No, sir, it is kind. You are my prisoners of war. I keep you when I could, by a word, plunge you into the depths of the ocean. You attacked me. You came and surprised a secret that I mean no man inhabiting the world to penetrate—the secret of my whole existence. And you think that I am going to send you back to that world? Never! In retaining you it is not you I guard, it is myself!"

These words indicated that the commander's mind was made up, and that argument was useless.

"Then, sir," I answered, "you give us the simple choice between life and death?"

"As you say."

"My friends," said I, "to a question thus put there is nothing to answer. But no word of honour binds us to the master of this vessel."

"None, sir," answered the unknown.

Then in a gentler voice he went on—

"Now allow me to finish what I have to say to you. I know you, M. Aronnax. You, if not your companions, will not have so much to complain of in the chance that has bound you to my lot. You will find amongst the books which are my favourite study the work you have published on the *Great Ocean Depths*. I have often read it. You have carried your investigations as far as terrestrial science allowed you. But on board my vessel you will have an opportunity of seeing what no man has seen before. Thanks to me, our planet will give up her last secrets."

I cannot deny that these words had a great effect upon me. My weak point was touched, and I forgot for a moment that the contemplation of these divine things was not worth the loss of liberty. Besides, I counted upon the future to decide that grave question, and so contented myself with saying—

"What name am I to call you by, sir?"

"Captain Nemo," answered the commander. "That is all I am to you, and you and your companions are nothing to me but the passengers of the *Nautilus*."

The captain called, and a steward appeared. The captain gave him his orders in that foreign tongue which I could not understand. Then turning to the Canadian and Conseil—

"Your meal is prepared in your cabin," he said to them. "Be so good as to follow that man."

My two companions in misfortune left the cell where they had been confined for more than thirty hours.

"And now, M. Aronnax, our breakfast is ready. Allow me to lead the way."

I followed Captain Nemo into a sort of corridor lighted by electricity, similar to the waist of a ship. After going about a dozen yards a second door opened before me into a kind of dining-room, decorated and furnished with severe taste. High oaken sideboards, inlaid with ebony ornaments, stood at either end of the room, and on their shelves glittered china, porcelain, and glass of inestimable value. The plate that was on them sparkled in the light which shone from the ceiling, tempered and softened by fine painting. In the centre of the room was a table richly spread. Captain Nemo pointed to my seat.

"Sit down," said he, "and eat like a man who must be dying of hunger."

The breakfast consisted of a number of dishes, the contents of which were all furnished by the sea; of some I neither knew the nature nor mode of preparation. They were good, but had a peculiar flavour which I soon became accustomed to. They appeared to be rich in phosphorus.

Captain Nemo looked at me. I asked him no questions, but he guessed my thoughts, and said—

"Most of these dishes are unknown to you, but you can eat of them without fear. They are wholesome and nourishing. I have long renounced the food of the earth, and I am none the worse for it. My crew, who are healthy, have the same food."

"Then all these dishes are the produce of the sea?" said I.

"Yes, professor, the sea supplies all my needs. Sometimes I cast my nets in tow, and they are drawn in ready to break. Sometimes I go and hunt in the midst of this element, which seems inaccessible to man, and run down the game of submarine forests. My flocks, like those of Neptune's old shepherd, graze fearlessly the immense ocean meadows. I have a vast estate there, which I cultivate myself, and which is always stocked by the Creator of all things."

I looked at Captain Nemo with some astonishment, and answered—

"I can quite understand that your nets should furnish excellent fish for your table, and that you should pursue aquatic game in your submarine forests; but I do not understand how a particle of meat can find its way into your bill of fare."

"What you believe to be meat, professor, is nothing but fillet of turtle. Here also are dolphins' livers, which you might take for ragout of pork. My cook is a clever fellow, who excels in preparing these various products of the sea. Taste all these dishes. Here is a conserve of holothuria, which a Malay would declare to be unrivalled in the world; here is a cream furnished by the cetacea, and the sugar by the great fucus of the North Sea; and, lastly, allow me to offer you some anemone preserve, which equals that made from the most delicious fruits."

Whilst I was tasting, more from curiosity than as a gourmet, Captain Nemo enchanted me with extraordinary stories.

"Not only does the sea feed me," he continued, "but it clothes me too. These materials that clothe you are wrought from the byssus of certain shells; they are dyed with the purple of the ancients, and the violet shades which I extract from the aplysis of the Mediterranean. The perfumes you will find on the toilette of your cabin are produced from the distillation of marine plants. Your bed is made with the softest wrack-grass of the ocean. Your pen will be a whale's fin, your ink the liquor secreted by the calamary. Everything now comes to me from the sea, and everything will one day return to it!"

"You love the sea, captain?"

"Yes, I love it. The sea is everything. It covers seven-tenths of the terrestrial globe. Its breath is pure and healthy. It is an immense desert where man is never alone, for he feels life quivering around him on every side. The sea is only the medium of a preternatural and wonderful existence; it is only movement and love; it is the infinite with life breathed into it, as one of your poets has said. And in reality, professor, Nature is manifested in it by her three kingdoms—mineral, vegetable, and animal. This last is largely represented by the four groups of zoophytes, by three classes of vertebrates, mammals, reptiles, and those innumerable legions of fish, an infinite order of animals that counts more than 13,000 species, of which a tenth only belongs to fresh water. The sea is the vast reservoir of Nature. It is by the sea that the globe has, so to speak, commenced, and who knows if it will not end by it? There is supreme tranquillity. The sea does not belong to despots. On its surface iniquitous rights can still be exercised, men can fight there, devour each other there, and transport all

73

terrestrial horrors there. But at thirty feet below its level their power ceases, their influence dies out, their might disappears. Ah, sir, live in the bosom of the waters! There alone is independence! There I recognise no masters! There I am free!"

Captain Nemo stopped suddenly in the midst of this burst of enthusiasm which overflowed in him. Had he let himself be carried out of his habitual reserve? Had he said too much? During some moments he walked about much agitated. Then his nerves became calmer, his face regained its usual calm expression, and turning towards us—

"Now, professor," said he, "if you wish to visit the *Nautilus*, I am at your service."

CHAPTER XI

The Nautilus

Captain Nemo rose, and I followed him. A folding door, contrived at the back of the room, opened, and I entered a room about the same size as the one I had just left.

It was a library. High bookcases of black rosewood supported on their shelves a great number of books in uniform binding. They went round the room, terminating at their lower part in large divans, covered with brown leather, curved so as to afford the greatest comfort. Light movable desks, made to slide in and out at will, were there to rest one's book while reading. In the centre was a vast table, covered with pamphlets, amongst which appeared some newspapers, already old. The electric light flooded this harmonious whole, and was shed from four polished globes half sunk in the volutes of the ceiling. This room, so ingeniously fitted up, excited my admiration, and I could scarcely believe my eyes.

"Captain Nemo," said I to my host, who had just thrown himself on one of the divans, "you have a library here that would do honour to more than one continental palace, and I am lost in wonder when I think that it can follow you to the greatest depths of the ocean."

"Where could there be more solitude or more silence, professor?" answered Captain Nemo. "Did your study in the museum offer you as complete quiet?"

"No, and I must acknowledge it is a very poor one compared with yours. You must have from six to seven thousand volumes here."

"Twelve thousand, M. Aronnax. These are the only ties between me and the earth. But the day that my *Nautilus* plunged for the first time beneath the waters the world was at an end for me. That day I bought my last books, my last pamphlets, and my last newspapers; and since then I wish to believe that men no longer think nor write. These books, professor, are at your disposition, and you can use them freely."

I thanked Captain Nemo, and went up to the library shelves. Books of science, ethics, and literature—written in every language—were there in quantities; but I did not see a single work on political economy amongst them; they seemed to be severely prohibited on board. A curious detail was that all these books were classified indistinctly, in whatever language they were written, and this confusion showed that the captain of the *Nautilus* could read with the utmost facility any volume he might take up by chance.

Amongst these works I remarked the *chef d'œuvres* of the ancient and modern masters—that is to say, all the finest things that humanity has produced in history, poetry, romance, and science, from Homer to Victor Hugo; from Xenophon to Michelet; from Rabelais to Madame Sand. But science, more particularly, was represented in this library; books on mechanics, ballistics, hydrography, meteorology, geography, geology, &c., held a no less important place than the works on natural history; and I understood that they formed the principal study of the captain. I saw there all the works of Humboldt, Arago, Foucault, Henry Sainte-Claire Deville, Chasles, Milne Edwards, Quatrefages, Tyndall, Faraday, Berthelot, Abbé Secchi, Petermann, Commander Maury, Agassis, &c.; memoirs of the Académie des Sciences, the bulletins of different geographical societies, &c.; and, in a good place, the two volumes which had perhaps procured me the relatively charitable welcome of Captain Nemo. Amongst the works of Joseph Bertrand, his book, entitled, *Le Fondateur de l'Astronomie*, gave me a certain date; and as I knew that it had appeared during the course of 1865, I could conclude from that that the launching of the *Nautilus* did not take place at a later date. It was, therefore, three years, at the most, since Captain Nemo began his submarine existence. I hoped, besides, that more recent works would allow me to fix exactly the epoch; but I should have time to make that research, and I did not wish to delay any longer our inspection of the marvels of the *Nautilus*.

"Sir," said I to the captain, "I thank you for placing this library at my disposal. I see it contains treasures of science, and I shall profit by them."

"This room is not only a library," said Captain Nemo; "it is a smoking-room too."

"A smoking-room?" cried I. "Do you smoke here, then?"

"Certainly."

"Then, sir, I am forced to believe that you have kept up relations with Havannah?"

"No, I have not," answered the captain. "Accept this cigar, M. Aronnax; although it does not come from Havannah, you will be pleased with it if you are a connoisseur."

I took the cigar that was offered me; its shape was something like that of a *Londres*, but it seemed to be made of leaves of gold. I lighted it at a little brazier which was supported on an elegant bronze pedestal, and drew the first whiffs with the delight of an amateur who has not smoked for two days.

"It is excellent," said I, "but it is not tobacco."

"No," answered the captain. "This tobacco comes neither from Havannah nor the East. It is a sort of seaweed, rich in nicotine, with which the sea supplies me, but somewhat sparingly. If you do not regret the *Londres*, M. Aronnax, smoke these as much as you like."

As Captain Nemo spoke he opened the opposite door to the one by which we had entered the library, and I passed into an immense and brilliantly-lighted saloon. It was a vast four-sided room, with panelled walls, measuring thirty feet by eighteen, and about fifteen feet high. A luminous ceiling, decorated with light arabesques, distributed a soft, clear light over all the marvels collected in the museum. For it was, in fact, a museum in which an intelligent and prodigal hand had gathered together all the treasures of nature and art with the artistic confusion of a painter's studio.

About thirty pictures by the first artists, uniformly framed and separated by brilliant drapery, were hung on tapestry of severe design. I saw there works of great value, most of which I had admired in the special collections of Europe, and in exhibitions of paintings. The different schools of the old masters were represented by a Madonna by Raphael, a Virgin by Leonardo da Vinci, a nymph by Correggio, an Assumption by Murillo, a portrait by Holbein, &c. The amazement which the captain of the *Nautilus* had predicted had already begun to take possession of me.

"Professor," then said this strange man, "you must excuse the unceremonious way in which I receive you, and the disorder of this room."

"Sir," I answered, "without seeking to know who you are, may I be allowed to recognise in you an artist?"

"Only an amateur, sir. Formerly I liked to collect these works of art. I was a greedy collector and an indefatigable antiquary, and have been able to get together some objects of great value. These are my last gatherings from that world which is now dead to me. In my eyes your modern artists are already old; they have two or three thousand years of existence, and all masters are of the same age in my mind."

"And these musicians?" said I, pointing to the works of Weber, Rossini, Mozart, Beethoven, Haydn, Meyerbeer, Hérold, Wagner, Auber, Gounod, and many others, scattered over a large piano organ fixed in one of the panels of the room.

"These musicians," answered Captain Nemo, "are contemporaries of Orpheus, for all chronological differences are effaced in the memory of the dead; and I am dead, as much dead as those of your friends who are resting six feet under the earth!"

Captain Nemo ceased talking, and seemed lost in a profound reverie. I looked at him with great interest, analysing in silence the strange expressions of his face.

Leaning on the corner of a costly mosaic table, he no longer saw me, and forgot my presence.

I respected his meditation, and went on passing in review the curiosities that enriched the saloon. They consisted principally of marine plants, shells, and other productions of the ocean, which must have been found by Captain Nemo himself. In the centre of the saloon rose a jet of water lighted up by electricity, and falling into a basin formed of a single tridacne shell, measuring about seven yards in circumference; it, therefore, surpassed in size the beautiful tridacnes which were given to Francis I of France by the Venetian Republic, and that now form two basins for holy water in the church of Saint Sulpice in Paris.

All round this basin were elegant glass cases, fastened by copper rivets, in which were classed and labelled the most precious productions of the sea that had ever been presented to the eye of a naturalist. My delight as a professor may be imagined. The division that contained the zoophytes presented very curious specimens of the two groups of polypi and echinodermes. In the first group of the tubipores were gorgones arranged like a fan, soft Syrian sponges, Molucca ises, pennatules, superb varieties of coral, and, in short, every species of those curious polypi of which entire islands are formed, which will one day become continents.

A conchyliologist at all nervous would certainly have fainted before other more numerous cases in which the specimens of molluscs were classified. I saw there a collection of inestimable value. Amongst these specimens I will quote from memory the elegant royal hammer-fish of the Indian Ocean, with its regular white spots standing out brightly on a red and brown ground; an imperial spondyle, bright-coloured, and bristling with spikes, a rare specimen in the museums of Europe, and the value of which I estimated as £800; a common hammer-fish from the Australian seas, which is only procured with difficulty; exotic buccardia from Senegal; fragile white bivalve shells that a breath might blow away like a soap-bubble; several varieties of the Java aspirgillum, a sort of calcareous tube, edged with leafy folds, much prized by amateurs; a whole series of trochi, some a greenish yellow, found in the American seas; others of a reddish brown, natives of Australian waters; others from the Gulf of Mexico, remarkable for their imbricated shells; stellari, found in the southern seas; and, last and rarest of all, the magnificent New Zealand spur.

Apart and in special apartments were spread out chaplets of pearls of the greatest beauty, which the electric light pricked with points of fire; pink pearls, torn from the pinna-marina of the Red Sea; green pearls from the haliotyde iris; yellow, blue, and black pearls, the curious productions of different molluscs from every ocean, and certain mussels from the watercourses of the North; lastly, several specimens of priceless value, which had been gathered from the rarest pintadines. Some of these pearls were bigger than a pigeon's egg, and were worth more than the one which the traveller Tavernier sold to the Shah of Persia for 3,000,000 francs, and surpassed the one in the possession of the Imam of Muscat, which I had believed to be unrivalled in the world.

It was impossible to estimate the worth of this collection. Captain Nemo must have spent millions in acquiring these various specimens, and I was asking myself from whence he had drawn the money to gratify his fancy for collecting, when I was interrupted by these words:—

"You are examining my shells, professor. They certainly must be interesting to a naturalist, but for me they have a greater charm, for I have collected them all myself, and there is not a sea on the face of the globe that has escaped my search."

"I understand, captain—I understand the delight of moving amongst such riches. You are one of those people who lay up treasures for themselves. There is not a museum in Europe that possesses such a collection of marine products. But if I exhaust all my admiration upon it, I shall have none left for the vessel that carries it. I do not wish to penetrate into your secrets, but I must confess that this *Nautilus*, with the motive power she contains, the contrivances by which she is worked, the powerful agent which propels her, all excite my utmost curiosity. I see hung on the walls of this room instruments the use of which I ignore."

"When I told you that you were free on board my vessel, I meant that every portion of the *Nautilus* was open to your inspection. The instruments you will see in my room, professor, where I shall have much pleasure in explaining their use to you. But come and look at your own cabin."

I followed Captain Nemo, who, by one of the doors opening from each panel of the drawing-room, regained the waist of the vessel. He conducted me aft, and there I found, not a cabin, but an elegant room with a bed, toilette-table, and several other articles of furniture. I could only thank my host.

"Your room is next to mine," said he, opening a door: "and mine opens into the saloon we have just left."

I entered the captain's room; it had a severe, almost monkish aspect. A small iron bedstead, an office desk, some articles of toilet—all lighted by a strong light. There were no comforts, only the strictest necessaries.

Captain Nemo pointed to a seat.

"Pray sit down," he said.

I obeyed, and he began thus:—

CHAPTER XII

Everything by Electricity

"Sir," said Captain Nemo, showing me the instruments hung on the walls of the room, "here are the instruments necessary for the navigation of the *Nautilus*. Here, as in the saloon, I have them always before me, and they indicate my position and exact direction in the midst of the ocean. You are acquainted with some of them—the thermometer, for instance—which gives the internal temperature of the vessel; the barometer, indicating the weight of the air, and foretelling changes in the weather; the hygrometer, for indicating the degree of dryness in the atmosphere; the storm-glass, the contents of which decompose at the approach of tempests; the compass, for guiding our course; the sextant, for taking latitude; chronometers, for calculating longitude; and, lastly, the glasses for day and night, which I use to examine the horizon when the *Nautilus* rises to the surface of the waves."

"Yes," I answered; "I understand the usual nautical instruments. But I see others that doubtless answer the peculiar requirements of your vessel. That dial with a movable needle is a manometer, is it not?"

"Yes; by communication with the water it indicates the exterior pressure and gives our depth at the same time."

"And these sounding-lines of a novel kind?"

"They are thermometric, and give the temperature of the different depths of water."

"And these other instruments, the use of which I cannot guess?"

"Here I ought to give you some explanation, professor. There is a powerful, obedient, rapid, and easy agent which lends itself to all uses, and reigns supreme here. We do everything by its means. It is the light, warmth, and soul of my mechanical apparatus. This agent is electricity."

"Yet, captain, you possess an extreme rapidity of movement which does not well agree with the power of electricity. Until now its dynamic force has been very restricted, and has only produced little power."

"Professor," answered Captain Nemo, "my electricity is not everybody's, and you will permit me to withhold any further information."

"I will not insist, sir; I will content myself with being astonished at such wonderful results. A single question, however, I will ask, which you need not answer if it is an indiscreet one. The elements which you employ to produce this marvellous agent must necessarily be soon consumed. The zinc, for instance, that you use—how do you obtain a fresh supply? You now have no communication with the land?"

"I will answer your question," replied Captain Nemo. "In the first place I must inform you that there exist, at the bottom of the sea, mines of zinc, iron, silver, and gold, the working of which would most certainly be practicable; but I am not indebted to any of these terrestrial metals. I was determined to seek from the sea alone the means of producing my electricity."

"From the sea?"

"Yes, professor, and I was at no loss to find these means. It would have been possible, by establishing a circuit between wires plunged to different depths, to obtain electricity by the diversity of temperature to which they would have been exposed; but I preferred to employ a more practicable system."

"And what was that?"

"You know the composition of sea-water? In 1,000 grammes of sea-water you find $96\frac{1}{2}$ centigrammes of pure water, and about $2\frac{2}{3}$ centigrammes of chloride of sodium; in addition, small quantities of the chlorides of magnesium and potassium, bromide of magnesium, sulphate of magnesia, sulphate and carbonate of lime. You see, then, that chloride of sodium forms a notable proportion of it. Now it is this sodium that I extract from sea-water, and of which I compose my ingredients. Mixed with mercury it takes the place of zinc for the voltaic pile. The mercury is never exhausted; only the sodium is consumed, and the sea itself gives me that. Besides, the electric power of the sodium piles is double that of the zinc ones."

"I clearly understand, captain, the convenience of sodium in the circumstances in which you are placed. The sea contains it. Good. But you still have to make it, to extract it, in a word. And how do you do that? Your pile would evidently serve the purpose of extracting it; but unless I am mistaken, the consumption of sodium necessitated by the electrical apparatus would exceed the quantity extracted. The consequence would be that you would consume more of it than you would produce."

"That is why I do not extract it by the pile, my dear professor. I employ nothing but the heat of coal."

"Coal!" I urged.

"We will call it sea-coal if you like," replied Captain Nemo.

"And are you able to work submarine coal-mines?"

"You shall see me so employed, M. Aronnax. I only ask you for a little patience; you have time to be patient here. Only remember I get everything from the ocean. It produces electricity, and electricity supplies the *Nautilus* with light—in a word, with life."

"But not with the air you breathe."

"I could produce the air necessary for my consumption, but I do not, because I go up to the surface of the water when I please. But though electricity does not furnish me with the air to breathe, it works the powerful pumps which store it up in special reservoirs, and which enable me to prolong at need, and as long as I like, my stay in the depths of the sea."

"Captain," I replied, "I can do nothing but admire. You have evidently discovered what mankind at large will, no doubt, one day discover, the veritable dynamic power of electricity."

"Whether they will discover it I do not know," replied Captain Nemo coldly. "However that may be, you now know the first application that I have made of this precious agent. It is electricity that furnishes us with a light that surpasses in uniformity and continuity that of the sun itself. Look now at this clock! It is an electric one, and goes with a regularity that defies the best of chronometers. I have divided it into twenty-four hours, like the Italian clocks, because there exists for me neither night nor day, sun nor moon, only this factitious light that I take with me to the bottom of the sea. Look! just now it is ten a.m."

"Exactly so."

"This dial hanging in front of us indicates the speed of the *Nautilus*. An electric wire puts it into communication with the screw. Look! just now we are going along at the moderate speed of fifteen miles an hour. But we have not finished yet, M. Aronnax," continued Captain Nemo, rising, "if you will follow me we will visit the stern of the *Nautilus*."

I already knew all the anterior part of this submarine boat, of which the following is the exact division, starting from the centre to the prow:—The dining-room, 15 feet long, separated from the library by a water-tight partition; the library, 15 feet long; the large saloon, 30 feet long, separated from the captain's room by a second water-tight partition; the captain's room, 15 feet; mine, 9 feet; and lastly, a reservoir of air of 20 feet that reached to the prow; total, 104 feet. The partitions had doors that were shut hermetically by means of indiarubber, assuring the safety of the *Nautilus* in case of a leak.

I followed Captain Nemo across the waist, and in the centre of the boat came to a sort of well that opened between two water-tight partitions. An iron ladder, fastened by an iron hook to the partition, led to the upper end. I asked the captain what it was for.

"It leads to the boat," answered he.

"What! have you a boat?" I exclaimed in astonishment.

"Certainly, an excellent one, light and unsinkable, that serves either for fishing or pleasure trips."

"Then when you wish to embark you are obliged to go up to the surface of the water."

"Not at all. The boat is fixed on the top of the *Nautilus* in a cavity made for it. It has a deck, is quite water-tight, and fastened by solid bolts. This ladder leads to a man-hole in the hull of the *Nautilus*, corresponding to a similar hole in the boat. It is by this double opening that I get to the boat. The one is shut by my men in the vessel, I shut the one in the boat by means of screw pressure, I undo the bolts, and the little boat darts up to the surface of the sea with prodigious rapidity. I then open the panel of the deck, carefully closed before, I mast it, hoist my sail, take my oars, and am off."

"But how do you return?"

"I do not return to it; it comes to me."

"At your order?"

"At my order. An electric wire connects us. I telegraph my orders."

"Really," I said, intoxicated by such marvels, "nothing can be more simple!"

After having passed the companion-ladder that led to the platform I saw a cabin about twelve feet long, in which Conseil and Ned Land were devouring their meal. Then a door opened upon a kitchen nine feet long, situated between the vast store-rooms of the vessel. There electricity, better than gas itself, did all the cooking. The wires under the stoves communicated with platinum sponges, and gave out a heat which was regularly kept up and distributed. They also heated a distilling apparatus, which, by evaporation, furnished excellent drinking water. A bath-room, comfortably furnished with hot and cold water taps, opened out of this kitchen.

Next to the kitchen was the berth-room of the vessel, eighteen feet long. But the door was closed, and I could not see how it was furnished, which might have given me an idea of the number of men employed on board the *Nautilus*. At the far end was a fourth partition, which separated this room from the engine-room. A door opened, and I entered the compartment where Captain Nemo—certainly a first-rate engineer—had arranged his locomotive machinery. It was well lighted, and did not measure less than sixty-five feet. It was naturally divided into two parts; the first contained the materials for producing electricity, and the second the machinery that moved the screw. I was at first surprised at a smell which filled the compartment. The captain saw that I perceived it.

"It is only a slight escape of gas produced by the use of the sodium, and not much inconvenience, as every morning we purify the vessel by ventilating it in the open air."

In the meantime I was examining the machinery with great interest.

"You see," said the captain, "I use Bunsen's elements, not Ruhmkorff's—they would not have been powerful enough. Bunsen's are fewer in number, but strong and large, which experience proves to be the best. The electricity produced passes to the back, where it works by electro-magnets of great size on a peculiar system of levers and cog-wheels that transmit the movement to the axle of the screw. This one, with a diameter of nineteen feet and a thread twenty-three feet, performs about a hundred and twenty revolutions in a second."

"What speed do you obtain from it?"

"About fifty miles an hour."

Here was a mystery, but I did not press for a solution of it. How could electricity act with so much power? Where did this almost unlimited force originate? Was it in the excessive tension obtained by some new kind of spools? Was it by its transmission that a system of unknown levers could infinitely increase? (And by a remarkable coincidence, a discovery of this kind is talked of in which a new arrangement of levers produces considerable force. Can the inventor have met with Captain Nemo?)

"Captain Nemo," I replied, "I recognise the results, and do not seek to explain them. I saw the *Nautilus* worked in the presence of the *Abraham Lincoln*, and I know what to think of its speed. But it is not enough to be able to walk; you must see where you are going; you must be able to direct yourself to the right or left, above or below. How do you reach the great depths, where you find an increasing resistance, which is rated by hundreds of atmospheres? How do you return to the surface of the ocean, or maintain yourself at the proper depth? Am I indiscreet in asking you this question?"

"Not at all, professor," answered the captain, after a slight hesitation. "As you are never to leave this submarine boat, come into the saloon—it is our true study—and there you shall learn all you want to know about the *Nautilus*."

CHAPTER XIII

Figures

A moment afterwards we were seated on a divan in the saloon, with our cigars. The captain spread out a diagram that gave the plan of the *Nautilus*. Then he began his description in these terms:—

"Here, M. Aronnax, are the different dimensions of the vessel you are in. It is a very elongated cylinder, with conical ends, much like a cigar in shape—a shape already adopted in London for constructions of the same sort. The length of this cylinder, from one end to the other, is exactly 232 feet, and its maximum breadth is 26 feet. It is, therefore, not altogether constructed by tenths, like your quick steamers, but its lines are sufficiently long, and its slope lengthened out to allow the displaced water to escape easily, and opposes no obstacle to its speed. These two dimensions allow you to obtain, by a simple calculation, the surface and volume of the *Nautilus*. Its surface is 1,011 metres and 45 centimetres; its volume, 1,500 cubic metres and two-tenths, which is the same as saying that it is entirely immersed. It displaces 50,000 feet of water, or weighs 1,500 tons.

"When I made the plans for this vessel—destined for submarine navigation—I wished that when it was in equilibrium nine-tenths of it should be under water, and one-tenth only should emerge. Consequently, under these conditions, it only ought to displace nine-tenths of its volume, or 1,356 cubic metres and 48 centimetres—that is to say, it only ought to weigh the same number of tons. I therefore did not exceed this weight in constructing it according to the above-named dimensions.

"The *Nautilus* is composed of two hulls, one inside the other, and joined together by T-shaped irons, which make it very strong. Owing to this cellular arrangement it resists like a block, as if it were solid. Its sides cannot yield; they adhere spontaneously, and not by the closeness of their rivets; and the homogeneity of their construction, due to the perfect union of the materials, enables my vessel to defy the roughest seas.

"These two hulls are made of steel plates, the density of which is to water seven eight-tenths. The first is not less than five centimetres thick, and weighs 394.96 tons. The second envelope, the keel, is 50 centimetres high and 25 wide, weighing by itself 62 tons; the machine, ballast, different accessories, the interior partitions and props weigh 961 tons, which, added to the rest, form the required total of 1,356.48 tons. Do you follow me?"

"Yes," I replied.

"Then," continued the captain, "when the *Nautilus* is afloat in these conditions one-tenth is out of the water. I have placed reservoirs of a size equal to this tenth capable of holding 150.72 tons, and when I fill them with water the vessel becomes completely immersed. These reservoirs exist in the lowest parts of the *Nautilus*. I turn on taps, they fill, and the vessel sinks just below the surface of the water."

"Well, captain, but now we arrive at the real difficulty. I can understand your being able to keep just level with the surface of the ocean. But lower down, when you plunge below that surface, does not your submarine apparatus meet with a pressure from below, which must be equal to one atmosphere for every thirty feet of water, or one kilogramme for every square centimetre?"

"True, sir."

"Then unless you fill the *Nautilus* entirely I do not see how you can draw it down into the bosom of the liquid mass."

"Professor," answered Captain Nemo, "you must not confound statics with dynamics, or you will expose yourself to grave errors. There is very little work necessary to reach the lowest depths of the ocean, for bodies have a tendency 'to sink.' Follow my reasoning."

"I am listening to you, captain."

"When I wished to determine the increase of weight that must be given to the *Nautilus* to sink it, I had only to occupy myself with the reduction in volume which sea-water experiences as it becomes deeper and deeper."

"That is evident," said I.

"Now if water is not absolutely incompressible, it is, at least, very slightly compressible—in fact, according to the most recent calculations .0000436 in an atmosphere or in each thirty feet of depth. If I wish to go to the depth of 1,000 metres I take into account the reduction of volume under a pressure equivalent to that of a column of water of 1,000 metres—that is to say, under a pressure of 100 atmospheres. I ought, therefore, to increase the weight so as to weigh 1,513.79 tons instead of 1,507.2 tons. The augmentation will, consequently, only be 6.77 tons. Only that, Monsieur Aronnax, and the calculation is easy to verify. Now I have supplementary reservoirs capable of embarking 100 tons. I can, therefore, descend to considerable depths. When I wish to remount to the level of the surface, I have only to let out this water, and to entirely empty all the reservoirs, if I desire that the *Nautilus* should emerge one-tenth of its total capacity."

To this reasoning, founded upon figures, I had nothing to object.

"I admit your calculations, captain," I replied, "and I should be foolish to dispute them, as experience proves them every day, but I foresee a real difficulty."

"What is that, sir?"

"When you are at the depth of 1,000 yards the sides of the *Nautilus* support a pressure of 100 atmospheres. If, therefore, at this moment you wish to empty the supplementary reservoirs to lighten your vessel and ascend to the surface, the pumps must conquer this pressure of 100 atmospheres, which is that of 100 kilogrammes for every square centimetre. Hence a power——"

"Which electricity alone can give me," hastened to say Captain Nemo. "I repeat, sir, that the dynamic power of my machines is nearly infinite. The pumps of the *Nautilus* have prodigious force, which you must have seen when their columns of water were precipitated like a torrent over the *Abraham Lincoln*. Besides, I only use supplementary reservoirs to obtain middle depths of 1,500 to 2,000 metres, and that in order to save my apparatus. When the fancy takes me to visit the depths of the ocean at two or three leagues below its surface, I use longer means, but no less infallible."

"What are they, captain?" I asked.

"That involves my telling you how the *Nautilus* is worked."

"I am all impatience to hear it."

"In order to steer my vessel horizontally I use an ordinary rudder, worked by a wheel and tackle. But I can also move the *Nautilus* by a vertical movement, by means of two inclined planes fastened to the sides and at the centre of flotation, planes that can move in every direction, and are worked from the interior by means of powerful levers. When these planes are kept parallel with the boat it moves horizontally; when slanted, the *Nautilus*, according to their inclination, and under the influence of the screw, either sinks according to an elongated diagonal, or rises diagonally as it suits me. And even when I wish to rise more quickly to the surface I engage the screw, and the pressure of the water causes the *Nautilus* to rise vertically like a balloon into the air."

"Bravo! captain," I cried. "But how can the helmsman follow the route you give him in the midst of the waters?"

"The helmsman is placed in a glass cage jutting from the top of the *Nautilus* and furnished with lenses."

"Capable of resisting such pressure?"

"Perfectly. Glass, which a blow can break, offers, nevertheless, considerable resistance. During some fishing experiments we made in 1864, by electric light, in the Northern Seas, we saw plates less than a third of an inch thick resist a pressure of sixteen atmospheres. Now the glass that I use is not less than thirty times thicker."

"I see now. But, after all, it is dark under water; how do you see where you are going?"

"There is a powerful electric reflector placed behind the

helmsman's cage, the rays from which light up the sea for half a mile in front."

"Ah, now I can account for the phosphorescence in the supposed narwhal that puzzled me so. May I now ask you if the damage you did to the *Scotia* was due to an accident?"

"Yes, it was quite accidental. I was sailing only one fathom below the surface when the shock came. Had it any bad result?"

"None, sir. But how about the shock you gave the *Abraham Lincoln*?"

"Professor, it was a great pity for one of the best ships in the American navy; but they attacked me and I had to defend myself! Besides, I contented myself with putting it out of the power of the frigate to harm me; there will be no difficulty in getting her repaired at the nearest port."

"Ah, commander!" I cried with conviction, "your *Nautilus* is certainly a marvellous boat."

"Yes, professor," answered Captain Nemo with real emotion, "and I love it as if it were flesh of my flesh! Though all is danger on one of your ships in subjection to the hazards of the ocean, though on this sea the first impression is the sentiment of unfathomable depth, as the Dutchman Jansen has so well said, below and on board the *Nautilus* the heart of man has nothing to dread. There is no deformation to fear, for the double hull of this vessel is as rigid as iron; no rigging to be injured by rolling and pitching; no sails for the wind to carry away; no boilers for steam to blow up; no fire to dread, as the apparatus is made of iron and not of wood; no coal to get exhausted, as electricity is its mechanical agent; no collision to fear, as it is the only vessel in deep waters; no tempests to set at defiance, as there is perfect tranquillity at some yards below the surface of the sea! The *Nautilus* is the ship of ships, sir. And if it is true that the engineer has more confidence in the vessel than the constructor, and the constructor more than the captain himself, you will understand with what confidence I trust to my *Nautilus*, as I am at the same time captain, constructor, and engineer."

Captain Nemo spoke with captivating eloquence. His fiery look and passionate gestures transfigured him. Yes! he did love his vessel like a father loves his child!

But a question, perhaps an indiscreet one, came up naturally, and I could not help putting it.

"Then you are an engineer, Captain Nemo?"

"Yes, professor, I studied in London, Paris, and New York when I was still an inhabitant of the world's continents."

"But how could you construct this admirable *Nautilus* in secret?"

"I had each separate portion made in different parts of the globe, and it reached me through a disguised address. The keel was forged at Creuzot, the shaft of the screw at Penn and Co.'s, of London; the iron plates of the hull at Laird's, of Liverpool; the screw itself at Scott's, of Glasgow. Its reservoirs were made by Cail and Co., of Paris; the engine by the Prussian Krupp; the prow in Motala's workshop in Sweden; the mathematical instruments by Hart Brothers, of New York, &c.; all of these people had my orders under different names."

"But how did you get all the parts put together?"

"I set up a workshop upon a desert island in the ocean. There, my workmen—that is to say, my brave companions whom I instructed—and I put together our *Nautilus*. When the work was ended, fire destroyed all trace of our proceedings on the island, which I should have blown up if I could."

"It must have cost you a great deal."

"An iron vessel costs £45 a ton. The *Nautilus* weighs 1,500 tons. It came, therefore, to £67,500, and £80,000 more for fitting up; altogether, with the works of art and collections it contains, it cost about £200,000."

"One last question, Captain Nemo."

"Ask it, professor."

"You must be rich?"

"Immensely rich, sir; and I could, without missing it, pay the English National Debt."

I stared at the singular person who spoke thus. Was he taking advantage of my credulity? The future alone could decide.

CHAPTER XIV

The Black River

The portion of the terrestrial globe covered by water is estimated at 3,832,558 square myriametres, or 38,000,000 hectares. This liquid mass comprehends 2,250,000,000 of cubic miles, and would form a sphere of a diameter of sixty leagues, the weight of which would be three trillions of tons. To take in the idea of such a number we must remember that a trillion is to a thousand millions what a thousand millions are to unity—that is to say, there are as many thousand millions in a trillion as there are unities in a thousand millions. Now this liquid mass is about the quantity of water that all the rivers of the earth would pour out during forty thousand years. In the geological epochs, the period of water succeeded the period of fire. The ocean was at first universal. Then, by degrees, in the silurian epoch, the summits of mountains appeared, islands emerged, disappeared under partial deluges, again showed themselves, united together, formed continents, and at last lands were geographically placed as we see them now. Solid matter had conquered from liquid matter 37,657,000 square miles, or 12,916,000,000 of hectares.

The configuration of continents allows us to divide water into five great parts—the Arctic Frozen Ocean, the Antarctic Frozen Ocean, the Indian Ocean, the Atlantic Ocean, and the Pacific Ocean.

The Pacific Ocean extends from north to south between the two polar circles, and from west to east between Asia and America over an extent of 145° of longitude. It is the smoothest of all seas; its currents are wide and slow, its tides slight, its rains abundant. Such was the ocean that my destiny called upon me to go over under such strange conditions.

"Now, professor," said Captain Nemo, "we will, if you please, take our bearings and fix the starting-point of this voyage. It wants a quarter to twelve. I am going up to the surface of the water."

The captain pressed an electric bell three times. The pumps began to drive the water out of the reservoirs; the needle of the manometer marked by the different pressures the ascensional movement of the *Nautilus*, then it stopped.

"We have arrived," said the captain.

We went to the central staircase which led up to the platform, climbed the iron steps, and found ourselves on the top of the *Nautilus*.

The platform was only three feet out of the water. The front and back of the *Nautilus* were of that spindle shape which caused it justly to be compared to a cigar. I noticed that its iron plates slightly overlaid each other, like the scales on the body of our large terrestrial reptiles. I well understood how, in spite of the best glasses, this boat should have been taken for a marine animal.

Towards the middle of the platform, the boat, half sunk in the vessel, formed a slight excrescence. Fore and aft rose two cages of medium height, with inclined sides, and partly inclosed by thick lenticular glasses. In the one was the helmsman who directed the *Nautilus*; in the other a powerful electric lantern that lighted up his course.

The sea was beautiful, the sky pure. The long vessel could hardly feel the broad undulations of the ocean. A slight breeze from the east rippled the surface of the water. The horizon was quite clear, making observation easy. There was nothing in sight—not a rock nor an island, no *Abraham Lincoln*, nothing but a waste of waters.

Captain Nemo took the altitude of the sun with his sextant to get his latitude. He waited some minutes till the planet came on a level with the edge of the horizon. Whilst he was observing not one of his muscles moved, and the instrument would not have been more motionless in a hand of marble.

"It is noon. Professor, when you are ready——"

I cast a last look at the sea, slightly yellowed by the Japanese coast, and went down again to the saloon.

There the captain made his point, and calculated his longitude chronometrically, which he controlled by preceding observations of horary angles. Then he said to me—

"M. Aronnax, we are in west longitude 137° 15'."

"By what meridian?" I asked quickly, hoping that the captain's answer might indicate his nationality.

"Sir," he answered, "I have different chronometers regulated on the meridians of Paris, Greenwich, and Washington. But, in your honour, I will use the Paris one."

This answer taught me nothing. I bowed, and the commander continued—

"Thirty-seven degrees and fifteen minutes longitude west of the Paris meridian, and thirty degrees and seven minutes north latitude—that is to say, about three hundred miles from the coasts of Japan. Today, the 8th of November, at noon, our voyage of exploration under the waters begins."

"God preserve us!" I answered.

"And now, professor," added the captain, "I leave you to your studies. I have given E.N.E. as our route at a depth of fifty yards. Here are maps on a large scale on which you can follow it. The saloon is at your disposition, and I ask your permission to withdraw."

Captain Nemo bowed to me. I remained alone, absorbed in my thoughts. All of them referred to the commander of the *Nautilus*. Should I ever know to what nation belonged the strange man who boasted of belonging to none? This hatred which he had vowed to humanity—this hatred which perhaps sought terrible means of revenge, what had provoked it? Was he one of those misjudged *savants*, a genius to whom "*on a fait du chagrin*," according to an expression of Conseil's, a modern Galileo, or one of those scientific men like the American Maury, whose career has been broken by political revolutions? I could not yet say. I, whom hazard had just cast upon his vessel—I, whose life he held in his hands, he had received me coldly, but with hospitality. Only he had never taken the hand I had held out to him. He had never held out his to me.

For a whole hour I remained buried in these reflections, seeking to pierce the mystery that interested me so greatly. Then my eyes fell upon the vast planisphere on the table, and I placed my finger on the very spot where the given latitude and longitude crossed.

The sea has its large rivers like continents. They are special currents, known by their temperature and colour. The most remarkable is known under the name of the Gulf Stream. Science has found out the direction of five principal currents— one in the North Atlantic, a second in the South Atlantic, a third in the North Pacific, a fourth in the South Pacific, and a fifth in the South Indian Ocean. It is probable that a sixth current formerly existed in the North Indian Ocean, when the Caspian and Aral Seas, united to the great Asiatic lakes, only formed one vast sheet of water.

At the point on the planisphere where my finger lay, one of these currents was rolling—the Kuro-Scivo or Black River of the Japanese, which, leaving the Gulf of Bengal, where the perpendicular rays of a tropical sun warm it, crosses the Straits of Malacca, runs along the coast of Asia, turns into the North Pacific as far as the Aleutian Islands, carrying with it the trunks of camphor-trees and other indigenous productions, contrasting by the pure indigo of its warm waters with the waves of the ocean. It was this current that the *Nautilus* was going to follow. I saw that it lost itself in the immensity of the Pacific, and felt myself carried along by it. Just then Ned Land and Conseil appeared at the door of the saloon.

My two companions were petrified at the sight of the marvels spread out before their eyes.

"Where are we—where are we?" cried the Canadian. "At the Quebec Museum?"

"If monsieur allows me to say so," replied Conseil, "it is more like the Hôtel du Sommerard."

"My friends," said I, making them a sign to enter, "you are

neither in Canada nor France, but on board the *Nautilus*, and at more than twenty-five fathoms below the sea level."

"We must believe what monsieur says," replied Conseil, "but really this saloon is enough to astonish even a Dutchman like me."

"Marvel and look, Conseil, for there is enough for such a good classifier as you to do here."

There was no need for me to encourage Conseil. The worthy fellow, leaning over the cases, was already muttering words in the language of naturalists—Gasteropodes class, Buccinoides family, sea-snail genus, *Cypræa Madagascariensis* species, &c.

During this time Ned Land, who was not much interested in conchology, questioned me about my interview with Captain Nemo. Had I discovered who he was, from whence he came, whither he was going, to what depths he was dragging us?—in short, a thousand questions, to which I had not time to answer.

I told him all I knew, or rather all I did not know, and I asked him what he had heard or seen on his side.

"I have seen nothing, heard nothing," answered the Canadian. "I have not even perceived the ship's crew. Is it by chance, or can it be electric too?"

"Electric!"

"Faith, anyone would think so. But you, M. Aronnax," said Ned Land, who stuck to his idea, "can you tell me how many men there are on board? Are there ten, twenty, fifty, a hundred?"

"I know no more than you, Mr. Land; it is better to abandon at present all idea of either taking possession of the *Nautilus* or escaping from it. This vessel is a masterpiece of modern industry, and I should regret not to have seen it. Many people would accept our position only to move amidst such marvels. The only thing to do is to keep quiet and watch what passes around us."

"Watch!" exclaimed the harpooner, "but there's nothing to watch; we can't see anything in this iron prison. We are moving along blindfolded."

Ned Land had scarcely uttered these words when it became suddenly dark. The light in the ceiling went out, and so rapidly that my eyes ached with the change, in the same way as they do after passage from profound darkness to the most brilliant light.

We remained mute and did not stir, not knowing what surprise, agreeable or disagreeable, awaited us. But a sliding noise was heard. It was like as if panels were being drawn back in the sides of the *Nautilus*.

"It is the end of all things!" said Ned Land.

"Hydrometridæ family!" muttered Conseil.

Suddenly light appeared on either side of the saloon, through two oblong openings. The liquid mass appeared vividly lighted up by the electric effluence.

Two crystal panes separated us from the sea. At first I shuddered at the thought that this feeble partition might break, but strong copper bands bound it, giving an almost infinite power of resistance.

The sea was distinctly visible for a mile round the *Nautilus*. What a spectacle! What pen could describe it? Who could paint the effect of the light through those transparent sheets of water, and the softness of its successive gradations from the lower to the upper beds of the ocean?

The transparency of the sea is well known, and its limpidity is far greater than that of fresh water. The mineral and organic substances which it holds in suspension increase its transparency. In certain parts of the ocean at the Antilles, under seventy-five fathoms of water, the sandy bottom can be seen with surprising clearness, and the penetrating strength of the sun's rays only appears to stop at a depth of 150 fathoms. But in this fluid medium through which the *Nautilus* was travelling the electric light was produced in the very bosom of the waves. It was not luminous water, but liquid light.

If the hypothesis of Erhemberg, who believes in a phosphorescent illumination in the submarine depths, is admitted, Nature has certainly reserved to the inhabitants of the sea one of her most marvellous spectacles, and I could judge of it by the effect of the thousand rays of this light. On either side I had a window opening on these unexplored depths. The darkness in the saloon made the exterior light seem greater, and we could see the same as if the pure crystal had been the panes of an immense aquarium.

The *Nautilus* did not seem to be moving. It was because there were no landmarks. Sometimes, however, the lines of water, furrowed by her prow, flowed before our eyes with excessive speed.

Lost in wonder we stood before these windows, and none of us had broken this silence of astonishment when Conseil said—

"Well, friend Ned, you wanted to look; well, now you see!"

"It is curious!" exclaimed the Canadian, who, forgetting his anger and projects of flight, was under the influence of irresistible attraction. "Who wouldn't come for the sake of such a sight?"

"Now I understand the man's life," I exclaimed. "He has made a world of marvels for himself!"

"But I don't see any fish," said the Canadian.

"What does it matter to you, friend Ned," answered Conseil, "since you know nothing about them?"

"I! A fisherman!" cried Ned Land.

And thereupon a dispute arose between the two friends, for each had some knowledge of fish, though in a very different way.

Everyone knows that fish form the fourth and last class in the embranchment of vertebrates. They have been rightly defined as "vertebrates with double circulation and cold blood, breathing through gills, and made to live in water." They are composed of two distinct series: the series of bony fish—that is to say, those whose spines are made of cartilaginous vertebrate.

Perhaps the Canadian knew this distinction, but Conseil knew much more, and now that he had made friends with Ned, he could not allow himself to seem less learned than he. He accordingly said to him—

"Friend Ned, you are a killer of fish—a very skilful fisher. You have taken a great number of these interesting animals. But I wager that you do not know how they are classified."

"Yes, I do," answered the harpooner seriously. "They are classified into fish that are good for food and fish that are not."

"That is a greedy distinction," answered Conseil. "But do you know the difference between bony and cartilaginous fish?"

"Perhaps I do, Conseil."

"And the subdivision of these two grand classes?"

"I daresay I do," answered the Canadian.

"Well, friend Ned, listen and remember! The bony fish are subdivided into six orders. Primo, the acanthopterygii, of which the upper jaw is complete, mobile with gills in the form of a comb. This order comprises fifteen families—that is to say, the three-fourths of known fish. Type: the common perch."

"Pretty good eating," answered Ned Land.

"Secundo," continued Conseil, "the abdominals, an order of fish whose ventral fins are placed behind the pectoral, without being attached to the shoulder-bones—an order which is divided into five families, and comprises most fresh-water fish. Type the carp, roach, salmon, pike, &c."

"Perch!" said the Canadian disdainfully; "fresh-water fish!"

"Tertio," said Conseil, "the subrachians, with ventral fins under the pectoral, and fastened to the shoulder-bones. This order contains four families. Type: plaice, mud-fish, turbots, brills, soles, &c."

"Excellent!—excellent!" cried the harpooner, who would only think of them from their eatable point of view.

"Quarto," said Conseil, nowise confused, "the apodes with long bodies and no ventral fins, covered with a thick and often sticky skin—an order that only comprises one family. Type: the eel, wolf-fish, swordfish, lance, &c."

"Middling!—only middling!" answered Ned Land.

"Quinto," said Conseil, "the lophiadæ, distinguished by the bones of the carpus being elongated, and forming a kind of arm, which supports the pectoral fins. Type: the angler, or fishing frog."

"Bad!—bad!" replied the harpooner.

"Sexto and lastly," said Conseil, "the plectognathes, which include those which have the maxillary bones anchylosed to the sides of the intermaxillaries, which alone form the jaws—an order which has no real ventral fins, and is composed of two families. Type: the sun-fish."

"Which any saucepan would be ashamed of!" cried the Canadian.

"Did you understand, friend Ned?" asked the learned Conseil.

"Not the least in the world, friend Conseil," answered the harpooner. "But go on, for you are very interesting."

"As to the cartilaginous fish," continued the imperturbable Conseil, "they only include three orders."

"So much the better," said Ned.

"Primo, the cyclostomes, with circular mouths and gills opening by numerous holes—an order including only one family. Type: the lamprey."

"You must get used to it to like it," answered Ned Land.

"Secundo, the selachii, with gills like the cyclostomes, but whose lower jaw is mobile. This order, which is the most important of the class, includes two families. Types: sharks and rays."

"What!" cried Ned; "rays and sharks in the same order? Well, friend Conseil, I should not advise you to put them in the same jar."

"Tertio," answered Conseil, "the sturiones, with gills opened as usual by a single slit, furnished with an operaculum—an order which includes four genera. Type: the sturgeon."

"Well, friend Conseil, you have kept the best for the last, in my opinion, at least. Is that all?"

"Yes, Ned," answered Conseil; "and remark that even when you know that you know nothing, for the families are subdivided into genera, sub-genera, species, varieties."

"Well, friend Conseil," said the harpooner, leaning against the glass of the panel, "there are some varieties passing now."

"Yes!—some fish," cried Conseil. "It is like being at an aquarium."

"No," I answered, "for an aquarium is only a cage, and those fish are as free as birds in the air."

"Well, now, Conseil, tell me their names!—tell me their names!" said Ned Land.

"I?" answered Conseil; "I could not do it; that is my master's business."

And, in fact, the worthy fellow, though an enthusiastic classifier, was not a naturalist, and I do not know if he could have distinguished a tunny-fish from a bonito. The Canadian, on the contrary, named them all without hesitation.

"A balister," said I.

"And a Chinese balister too!" answered Ned Land.

"Genus of the balisters, family of the scleroderms; order of the plectognaths," muttered Conseil.

Decidedly, between them, Ned Land and Conseil would have made a distinguished naturalist.

The Canadian was not mistaken. A shoal of balisters with fat bodies, grained skins, armed with a spur on their dorsal fin, were playing round the *Nautilus* and agitating the four rows of quills bristling on either side of their tails. Nothing could be more admirable than their grey backs, white stomachs, and gold spots that shone amidst the waves. Amongst them undulated skates like a sheet abandoned to the winds, and with them I perceived, to my great joy, the Chinese skate, yellow above, pale pink underneath, with three darts behind the eye—a rare species, and even doubtful in the time of Lacepède, who had never seen any except in a book of Japanese drawings.

For two hours a whole aquatic army escorted the *Nautilus*. Amidst their games and gambols, whilst they rivalled each other in brilliancy and speed, I recognised the green wrasse, the surmullet, marked with a double black stripe; the goby, with its round tail, white with violet spots; the Japanese mackerel, with blue body and silver head; brilliant, the azure fish, the name of which beggars all description, gilt heads with a black band down their tails; aulostones with flute-like noses, real sea-woodcocks, of which some specimens attain a yard in length; Japanese salamanders; sea-eels, serpents six feet long with bright little eyes and a huge mouth bristling with teeth, &c.

Our admiration was excited to the highest pitch. Ned named the fish, Conseil classified them, and I was delighted with their vivacity and the beauty of their forms. It had never been my lot to see these animals living and free in their natural element. I shall not cite all the varieties that passed before our dazzled eyes, all that collection from the Japanese and Chinese seas. More numerous than the birds of the air, these fish swam round us, doubtless attracted by the electric light.

Suddenly light again appeared in the saloon. The iron panels were again closed. The enchanting vision disappeared. But long after that I was dreaming still, until my eyes happened to fall on the instruments hung on the partition. The compass still indicated the direction of N.N.E., the manometer indicated a pressure of five atmospheres, corresponding to a depth of 100 fathoms, and the electric log gave a speed of 15 miles an hour.

I expected Captain Nemo, but he did not appear. The clock was on the stroke of five. Ned Land and Conseil returned to their cabin, and I regained my room. My dinner was laid there. It consisted of turtle soup made of the most delicate imbricated hawksbill turtle, of a delicate white surmullet, slightly crimped, of which the liver, cooked by itself, made a delicious dish, and fillets of the emperor-holocanthus, the flavour of which appeared to me superior even to salmon.

I passed the evening reading, writing, and thinking. Then sleep overpowered me, and I stretched myself on my zostera couch and slept profoundly, whilst the *Nautilus* glided rapidly along the current of the Black River.

CHAPTER XV

A Written Invitation

The next day, the 9th of November, I awoke after a long sleep that had lasted twelve hours. Conseil came, as was his custom, to ask "how monsieur had passed the night," and to offer his services. He had left his friend the Canadian sleeping like a man who had never done anything else in his life.

I let the brave fellow chatter on in his own fashion, without troubling to answer him much. I was anxious about the absence of Captain Nemo during our spectacle of the evening before, and hoped to see him again that day.

I was soon clothed in my byssus garments. Their nature provoked many reflections from Conseil. I told him they were manufactured with the lustrous and silky filaments which fasten a sort of shell, very abundant on the shores of the Mediterranean, to the rocks. Formerly beautiful materials—stockings and gloves—were made from it, and they were both very soft and very warm. The crew of the *Nautilus* could, therefore, be clothed at a cheap rate, without help of either cotton-trees, sheep, or silkworms of the earth.

When I was dressed I went into the saloon. It was deserted.

I plunged into the study of the conchological treasures piled up in the cases. I ransacked in great herbals filled with the rarest marine plants, which, though dried up, retained their lovely colours. Amongst these precious hydrophytes I remarked vorticellæ, pavoniæ, vine-leaved caulerps, calli-brichaceæ, delicate ceramies with scarlet tints, fan-shaped agari, acalephæ, like much-depressed mushrooms, which were for a long time classified amongst the zoophytes—in short, a perfect series of algæ.

The whole day passed without my being honoured with a visit from Captain Nemo. The panels of the saloon were not opened. Perhaps they did not wish us to get tired of such beautiful things.

The direction of the *Nautilus* kept N.N.E., its speed at twelve miles, its depth between twenty-five and thirty fathoms.

The next day, the 10th of November, the same desertion, the same solitude. I did not see one of the ship's crew. Ned and Conseil passed the greater part of the day with me. They were astonished at the inexplicable absence of the captain. Was the singular man ill? Did he mean to alter his plans about us?

After all, as Conseil said, we enjoyed complete liberty; we were delicately and abundantly fed. Our host kept to the terms of his treaty. We could not complain, and, besides, the singularity of our destiny reserved us such great compensations that we had no right to accuse it.

That day I began the account of these adventures, which allowed me to relate them with the most scrupulous exactness, and, curious detail, I wrote it on paper made with marine zostera.

Early in the morning of November 11th, the fresh air spread over the interior of the *Nautilus* told me that we were again on the surface of the ocean to renew our supply of oxygen. I went to the central staircase and ascended it to the platform. It was 6 a.m. The weather was cloudy, the sea grey, but calm. There was scarcely any swell. I hoped to meet Captain Nemo there. Would he come? I only saw the helmsman in his glass cage. Seated on the upper portion of the hull, I drank in the sea-breeze with delight.

Little by little the clouds disappeared under the action of the sun's rays. The clouds announced wind for all that day. But the wind was no concern to the *Nautilus*. I was admiring this joyful sunrise, so gay and reviving, when I heard someone coming up to the platform. I prepared to address Captain Nemo, but it was his mate—whom I had already seen during the captain's first visit—who appeared. He did not seem to perceive my presence, and with his powerful glass he swept the horizon, after which he approached the stair-head and called out some words which I reproduce exactly, for every morning they were uttered under the same conditions. They were the following:—

"Nautron respoc lorni virch."

What those words meant I know not.

After pronouncing them the mate went below again, and I supposed that the *Nautilus* was going to continue her submarine course. I therefore followed the mate and regained my room.

Five days passed thus and altered nothing in our position. Each morning I ascended to the platform. The same sentence was pronounced by the same individual. Captain Nemo did not appear.

I had made up my mind that I was not going to see him again, when on the 16th of November, on entering my room with Ned Land and Conseil, I found a note directed to me upon the table.

I opened it with impatient fingers. It was written in a bold, clear hand, of slightly Gothic character, something like the German types.

The note contained the following:—

"To Professor Aronnax, on board the *Nautilus*.

"*November 16th*, 1867.

"Captain Nemo invites Professor Aronnax to a hunt which will take place tomorrow morning in the forest of the island of Crespo. He hopes nothing will prevent the professor joining it, and he will have much pleasure in seeing his companions also.

"The Commander of the *Nautilus*,

"Captain Nemo."

"A hunt!" cried Ned.

"And in the forests of Crespo Island," added Conseil.

"Then that fellow does land sometimes," said Ned Land.

"It looks like it," said I, reading the letter again.

"Well, we must accept," replied the Canadian. "Once on land we can decide what to do. Besides, I shall not be sorry to eat some fresh meat."

I consulted the planisphere as to the whereabouts of the island of Crespo, and in 32° 40' north lat. and 167° 50' west long. I found a small island which was reconnoitred in 1801 by Captain Crespo, and which was marked in old Spanish maps as Rocca de la Plata, or "Silver Rock." We were then about 1,800 miles from our starting-point, and the course of the *Nautilus*, a little changed, was bringing it back towards the south-east. I pointed out to my companions the little rock lost in the midst of the North Pacific.

"If Captain Nemo does land sometimes," I said, "he at least chooses quite desert islands."

Ned Land shrugged his shoulders without speaking, and he and Conseil left me. After supper, which was served by the mute and impassible steward, I went to bed, not without some anxiety.

The next day, November 17th, when I awoke, I felt that the *Nautilus* was perfectly still. I dressed quickly and went to the saloon.

Captain Nemo was there waiting for me. He rose, bowed, and asked me if it was convenient for me to accompany him.

As he made no allusion to his eight days' absence I abstained from speaking of it, and answered simply that my companions and I were ready to follow him.

"May I ask you, captain," I said, "how it is that, having broken all ties with earth, you possess forests in Crespo Island?"

"Professor," answered the captain, "my forests are not terrestrial forests but submarine forests."

"Submarine forests!" I exclaimed.

"Yes, professor."

"And you offer to take me to them?"

"Precisely."

"On foot?"

"Yes, and dryfooted too."

"But how shall we hunt?—with a gun?"

"Yes, with a gun."

I thought the captain was gone mad, and the idea was expressed on my face, but he only invited me to follow him like a man resigned to anything. We entered the dining-room, where breakfast was laid.

"M. Aronnax," said the captain, "will you share my breakfast without ceremony? We will talk as we eat. You will not find a restaurant in our walk though you will a forest. Breakfast like a man who will probably dine very late."

I did honour to the meal. It was composed of different fish and slices of holithuria, excellent zoophytes, cooked with different sea-weeds, such as the *Porphyria laciniata* and the *Laurentia primafetida*. We drank clear water, and, following the captain's example, I added a few drops of some fermented liquor, extracted by the Kamschatchan method from a sea-weed known under the name of *Rhodomenia palmata*. Captain Nemo went on eating at first without saying a word. Then he said to me—

"When I invited you to hunt in my submarine forests, professor, you thought I was mad. You judged me too lightly. You know as well as I do that man can live under water, providing he takes with him a provision of air to breathe. When submarine work has to be done, the workman, clad in an impervious dress, with his head in a metal helmet, receives air from above by means of pumps and regulators."

"Then it is a diving apparatus?"

"Yes, but in one that enables him to get rid of the indiarubber tube attached to the pump. It is the Rouquayrol-Denayrouze apparatus, invented by two of your own countrymen, but which I have brought to perfection for my own use, and which will allow you to risk yourself in the water without suffering. It is composed of a reservoir of thick iron plates, in which I store the air under a pressure of fifty atmospheres. This reservoir is fastened on to the back by means of braces, like a soldier's knapsack; its upper part forms a box, in which the air is kept by means of bellows, and which cannot escape except at its normal tension. Two indiarubber pipes leave this box and join a sort of tent, which imprisons the nose and mouth; one introduces fresh air, the other lets out foul, and the tongue closes either according to the needs of respiration. But I, who encounter great pressure at the bottom of the sea, am obliged to shut my head in a globe of copper, into which the two pipes open."

"Perfectly, Captain Nemo; but the air that you carry with you must soon be used up, for as soon as it only contains fifteen per cent. of oxygen, it is no longer fit to breathe."

"I have already told you, M. Aronnax, that the pumps of the *Nautilus* allow me to store up air under considerable pressure, and under these conditions the reservoir of the apparatus can furnish breathable air for nine or ten hours."

"I have no other objection to make," I answered. "I will only ask you one thing, captain. How do you light your road at the bottom of the ocean?"

"With the Ruhmkorff apparatus, M. Aronnax. It is composed of a Bunsen pile, which I do not work with bichromate of potassium, but with sodium. A wire is introduced, which collects the electricity produced, and directs it towards a particularly-made lantern. In this lantern is a spiral glass which contains a small quantity of carbonic gas. When the apparatus is at work the gas becomes luminous, and gives out a white and continuous light. Thus provided, I breathe and see."

"But, Captain Nemo, what sort of a gun do you use?"

"It is not a gun for powder, but an air-gun. How could I manufacture gunpowder on board without either saltpetre, sulphur, or charcoal?"

"Besides," I added, "to fire under water in a medium 855 times denser than air, very considerable resistance would have to be conquered."

"That would be no difficulty. There exist certain Felton guns, perfected in England by Philip Coles and Burley, by the Frenchman Furcy and the Italian Landi, furnished with a peculiar system of closing, which can be fired under these conditions. But, I repeat, having no powder, I use air under great pressure, which the pumps of the *Nautilus* furnish abundantly."

"But this air must be rapidly consumed."

"Well, have I not my Rouquayrol reservoir, which can furnish me with what I need? All I want for that is a tap *ad hoc*. Besides, you will see for yourself, M. Aronnax, that during these submarine shooting excursions you do not use either much air or bullets."

"But it seems to me that in the half-light, and amidst a liquid so much more dense than the atmosphere, bodies cannot be projected far, and are not easily mortal."

"Sir, with these guns every shot is mortal, and as soon as the animal is touched, however slightly, it falls crushed."

"Why?"

"Because they are not ordinary bullets. We use little glass percussion-caps, invented by the Austrian chemist Leneibroek, and of which I have a considerable provision. These glass caps, covered with steel, and weighted with a leaden bottom, are really little Leyden bottles, in which electricity is forced to a very high tension. At the slightest shock they go off, and the animal, however powerful it may be, falls dead. I must add that these caps are not larger than the No. 4, and the charge of an ordinary gun could contain ten of them."

"I will argue no longer," I replied, rising from the table. "The only thing left me is to take my gun. Besides, where you go I will follow."

Captain Nemo then led me aft of the *Nautilus*, and whilst passing the cabin of Ned Conseil, I called my two companions, who followed me immediately. Then we came to a kind of cell, situated near the engine-room, in which we were to put on our walking dress.

CHAPTER XVI

At the Bottom of the Sea

This cell was, properly speaking, the arsenal and wardrobe of the *Nautilus*. A dozen diving apparatus, hung from the wall, awaited our use.

Ned Land, seeing them, manifested evident repugnance to put one on.

"But, my worthy Ned," I said, "the forests of Crespo Island are only submarine forests!"

The disappointed harpooner saw his dreams of fresh meat fade away.

"And you, M. Aronnax, are you going to put on one of those things?"

"I must, Master Ned."

"You can do as you please, sir," replied the harpooner shrugging his shoulders, "but as for me, unless I am forced, I will never get into one."

"No one will force you, Ned," said Captain Nemo.

"Does Conseil mean to risk it?" said Ned.

"I shall follow monsieur wherever he goes," answered Conseil.

Two of the ship's crew came to help us on the call of the captain and we donned the heavy and impervious clothes made of seamless indiarubber, and constructed expressly to resist considerable pressure. They looked like a suit of armour, both supple and resisting, and formed trousers and coat; the trousers were finished off with thick boots, furnished with heavy leaden soles. The texture of the coat was held together by bands of copper, which crossed the chest, protecting it from the pressure of the water, and leaving the lungs free to act; the sleeves ended in the form of supple gloves, which in no way restrained the movements of the hands.

There was much difference noticeable between these perfected diving apparatus and the old, shapeless cork breastplates, sea-jackets, boxes, &c., in vogue during the eighteenth century.

Captain Nemo and one of his companions—a sort of Hercules, who must have been of prodigious strength— Conseil, and myself, were soon enveloped in these dresses. There was nothing left but to put our heads into the metallic globes. But before proceeding with this operation I asked the captain's permission to examine the guns we were to take.

One of the crew gave me a simple gun, the butt-end of which, made of steel and hollowed in the interior, was rather large; it served as a reservoir for compressed air, which a valve, worked by a spring, allowed to escape into a metal tube. A box of projectiles, fixed in a groove in the thickness of the butt-end, contained about twenty electric bullets, which, by means of a spring, were forced into the barrel of the gun. As soon as one shot was fired another was ready.

"Captain Nemo," said I, "this arm is perfect and easily managed; all I ask now is to try it. But how shall we gain the bottom of the sea?"

"At this moment, professor, the *Nautilus* is stranded in five fathoms of water, and we have only to start."

"But how shall we get out?"

"You will soon see."

Captain Nemo put on his helmet. Conseil and I did the same, not without hearing an ironical "Good sport" from the Canadian. The upper part of our coat was terminated by a copper collar, upon which the metal helmet was screwed. As soon as it was in position the apparatus on our backs began to act, and, for my part, I could breathe with ease.

I found when I was ready, lamp and all, that I could not move a step. But this was foreseen. I felt myself pushed along a little room contiguous to the wardrobe-room. My companions, tugged along in the same way, followed me. I heard a door, furnished with obturators, close behind us, and we were wrapped in profound darkness.

114

After some minutes I heard a loud whistling, and felt the cold mount from my feet to my chest. It was evident that they had filled the room in which we were with sea-water by means of a tap. A second door in the side of the *Nautilus* opened then. A faint light appeared. A moment after, our feet were treading the bottom of the sea.

And now, how could I retrace the impression made upon me by that walk under the sea? Words are powerless to describe such marvels. When the brush itself is powerless to depict the particular effects of the liquid element, how can the pen reproduce them?

Captain Nemo walked on in front, and his companion followed us some steps behind. Conseil and I remained near one another, as if any exchange of words had been possible through our metallic covering. I no longer felt the weight of my clothes, shoes, air-reservoir, nor of that thick globe in the midst of which my head shook like an almond in its shell.

The light which lighted up the ground at thirty feet below the surface of the ocean astonished me by its power. The solar rays easily pierced this watery mass and dissipated its colour. One easily distinguished objects 120 yards off. Beyond that the tints faded into fine gradations of ultramarine, and became effaced in a vague obscurity. The water around me only appeared a sort of air, denser than the terrestrial atmosphere, but nearly as transparent. Above me I perceived the calm surface of the sea.

We were walking on fine even sand, not wrinkled, as it is on a flat shore which keeps the imprint of the billows. This dazzling carpet reflected the rays of the sun with surprising intensity. Shall I be believed when I affirm that at that depth of thirty feet I saw as well as in open daylight?

For a quarter of an hour I trod on this shining sand, sown with the impalpable dust of tinted shells. The hull of the *Nautilus*, looking like a long rock, disappeared by degrees; but its lantern, when night came, would facilitate our return on board. I put back with my hands the liquid curtains which

115

closed again behind me, and the print of my steps was soon effaced by the pressure of the water.

I soon came to some magnificent rocks, carpeted with splendid zoophytes, and I was at first struck by a special effect of this medium.

It was then 10 a.m. The rays of the sun struck the surface of the waves at an oblique angle, and at their contact with the light, composed by a refraction as through a prism, flowers, rocks, plants, and polypi were shaded at their edges by the seven solar colours; it was a grand feast for the eyes this complication of tints, a veritable kaleidoscope of green, yellow, orange, violet, indigo, and blue—in a word, all the palette of an enthusiastic colourist.

Before this splendid spectacle Conseil and I both stopped. Varegated isis, clusters of pure tuffed coral, prickly fungi and anemones adhering by their muscular disc, made perfect flowerbeds, enamelled with porphitæ, decked with their azure tentacles, sea-stars studding the sand, and warted asterophytons, like fine lace embroidered by the hands of Naïads, whose festoons waved in the gentle undulations caused by our walk. It was quite a grief to me to crush under my feet the brilliant specimens of molluscs which lay on the ground by thousands, the concentric combs, the hammer-heads, the donaces, real bounding shells, the broques, the red helmits, the angel-winged strombes, the aphysies, and many other products of the inexhaustible ocean. But we were obliged to keep on walking, whilst above our heads shoals of physalia, letting their ultramarine tentacles float after them, medusæ, with their rose-pink opaline parasols festooned with an azure border, sheltered us from the solar rays, and panophyrian pelagies, which, had it been dark, would have showered their phosphorescent gleams over our path.

All these wonders I saw in the space of a quarter of a mile. Soon the nature of the soil changed; to the sandy plains succeeded an extent of slimy mud composed of equal parts of siliceous and calcareous shells. Then we travelled over meadows of seaweed so soft to the foot that they would rival the softest carpet made by man. And at the same time that verdure was spread under our feet, marine plants, of which more than two thousand species are known, were growing on the surface of the ocean. I saw long ribands of fucus floating, some globular and others tubulous; laurenciæ and cladostephi, of most delicate foliage, and some rhodomeniæ and palmatæ resembling the fan of a cactus. I noticed that the green plants kept near the surface, whilst the red occupied a middle depth, leaving to the black or brown hydrophytes the care of forming gardens and flower-beds in the remote depths of the ocean. The family of seaweeds produces the largest and smallest vegetables of the globe.

We had left the *Nautilus* about an hour and a half. It was nearly twelve o'clock; I knew that by the perpendicularity of the sun's rays, which were no longer refracted. The magical colours disappeared by degrees, and the emerald and sapphire tints died out. We marched along with a regular step which rang upon the ground with astonishing intensity; the slightest sound is transmitted with a speed to which the ear is not accustomed on the earth—in fact, water is a better conductor of sound than air in the ratio of four to one.

The ground gradually sloped downwards, and the light took a uniform tint. We were at a depth of more than a hundred yards, and bearing a pressure of ten atmospheres. But my diving apparatus was so small that I suffered nothing from this pressure. I merely felt a slight discomfort in my finger-joints, and even that soon disappeared. As to the fatigue that this walk in such unusual harness might be expected to produce, it was nothing. My movements, helped by the water, were made with surprising facility.

At this depth of three hundred feet I could still see the rays of the sun, but feebly. To their intense brilliancy had succeeded a reddish twilight, middle term between day and night. Still we saw sufficiently to guide ourselves, and it was not yet necessary to light our Ruhmkorff lamps.

117

At that moment Captain Nemo stopped. He waited for me to come up to him, and with his finger pointed to some obscure masses which stood out of the shade at some little distance.

"It is the forest of Crespo Island," I thought, and I was not mistaken.

CHAPTER XVII

A Submarine Forest

We had at last arrived on the borders of this forest, doubtless one of the most beautiful in the immense domain of Captain Nemo. He looked upon it as his own, and who was there to dispute his right? This forest was composed of arborescent plants, and as soon as we had penetrated under its vast arcades, I was struck at first by the singular disposition of their branches, which I had not observed before.

None of those herbs which carpeted the ground—none of the branches of the larger plants, were either bent, drooped, or extended horizontally. There was not a single filament, however thin, that did not keep as upright as a rod of iron. The fusci and lianas grew in rigid perpendicular lines, commanded by the density of the element which had produced them. When I bent them with my hand these plants immediately resumed their first position. It was the reign of perpendicularity.

I soon accustomed myself to this fantastic disposition of things, as well as to the relative obscurity which enveloped us. The soil of the forest seemed covered with sharp blocks difficult to avoid. The submarine flora appeared to me very perfect, and richer than it would have been in the Arctic or tropical zones, where these productions are less numerous. But for some minutes I involuntarily confounded the genera, taking zoophytes for hydrophytes, animals for plants. And who would not have been mistaken? The fauna and flora are so nearly allied in this submarine world.

I noticed that all these productions of the vegetable kingdom had no roots, and only held on to either sand, shell, or rock. These plants drew no vitality from anything but the water. The greater number, instead of leaves, shot forth blades of capricious shapes, comprised within a scale of colours—pink, carmine, red, olive, fawn, and brown.

"Curious anomaly, fantastic element," said an ingenious naturalist. "Where the animal kingdom blossoms the vegetable does not."

Amongst these different shrubs, as large as the trees of temperate zones, and under their humid shade, were massed veritable bushes of living flowers, hedges of zoophytes, on which blossomed meandrina with tortuous stripes, yellow cariophylles with transparent tentacles, grassy tufts of zoantharia, and, to complete the illusion, the fish-flies flew from branch to branch like a swarm of humming-birds, whilst yellow lepisacomthi, with bristling jaws, dactylopteri, and monocentrides rose at our feet like a flight of snipes.

About one o'clock Captain Nemo gave the signal to halt. I, for my part, was not sorry, and we stretched ourselves under a thicket of alariæ, the long thin blades of which shot up like arrows.

This short rest seemed delicious to me. Nothing was wanting but the charm of conversation, but it was impossible to speak— I could only approach my large copper head to that of Conseil. I saw the eyes of the worthy fellow shine with contentment, and he moved about in his covering in the most comical way in the world.

After this four hours' walk I was much astonished not to find myself violently hungry, and I cannot tell why, but instead I was intolerably sleepy, as all divers are. My eyes closed behind their thick glass, and I fell into an unavoidable slumber, which the movement of walking had alone prevented up till then. Captain Nemo and his robust companion, lying down in the clear crystal, set us the example.

How long I remained asleep I cannot tell, but when I awoke the sun seemed sinking towards the horizon. Captain Nemo was already on his feet, and I was stretching myself when an unexpected apparition brought me quickly to my feet.

A few steps off an enormous sea-spider, more than a yard high, was looking at me with his squinting eyes ready to spring upon me. Although my dress was thick enough to defend me against the bite of this animal, I could not restrain a movement of horror. Conseil and the sailor of the *Nautilus* awoke at that moment. Captain Nemo showed his companions the hideous crustacean, and a blow from the butt-end of a gun killed it, and I saw its horrible claws writhe in horrible convulsions.

This accident reminded me that other animals, more to be feared, might haunt these obscure depths, and that my diver's dress would not protect me against their attacks. I had not thought of that before, and resolved to be on my guard. I supposed that this halt marked the limit of our excursion, but I was mistaken, and instead of returning to the *Nautilus*, Captain Nemo went on.

The ground still inclined and took us to greater depths. It must have been about three o'clock when we reached a narrow valley between two high cliffs, situated about seventy-five fathoms deep. Thanks to the perfection of our apparatus, we were forty-five fathoms below the limit which Nature seems to have imposed on the submarine excursions of man.

I knew how deep we were because the obscurity became so profound—not an object was visible at ten paces. I walked along groping when I suddenly saw a white light shine out. Captain Nemo had just lighted his electric lamp. His companion imitated him. Conseil and I followed their example. By turning a screw I established the communication between the spool and the glass serpentine, and the sea, lighted up by our four lanterns, was illuminated in a radius of twenty-five yards.

Captain Nemo still kept on plunging into the dark depths of the forest, the trees of which were getting rarer and rarer. I remarked that the vegetable life disappeared sooner than the animal. The medusæ had already left the soil, which had become arid, whilst a prodigious number of animals, zoophytes, articulata, molluscs, and fish swarmed there still.

As we walked I thought that the light of our Ruhmkorff apparatus could not fail to draw some inhabitants from these sombre depths. But if they did approach us they at least kept a respectful distance from the hunters. Several times I saw Captain Nemo stop and take aim; then, after some minutes' observation, he rose and went on walking.

At last, about four o'clock, this wonderful excursion was ended. A wall of superb rocks rose up before us, enormous granite cliffs impossible to climb. It was the island of Crespo. Captain Nemo stopped suddenly. We stopped at a sign from him. Here ended the domains of the captain.

The return began. Captain Nemo again kept at the head of his little band, and directed his steps without hesitation. I thought I perceived that we were not returning to the *Nautilus* by the road we had come. This new one was very steep, and consequently very painful. We approached the surface of the sea rapidly. But this return to the upper beds was not so sudden as to produce the internal lesions so fatal to divers. Very soon light reappeared and increased, and as the sun was already low on the horizon refraction edged the different objects with a spectral ring.

At a depth of ten yards we were walking in a swarm of little fish of every sort, more numerous than birds in the air, and more agile too. But no aquatic game worthy of a shot had as yet met our gaze.

At that moment I saw the captain put his gun to his shoulder and follow a moving object into the shrubs. He fired, I heard a feeble hissing, and an animal fell a few steps from us.

It was a magnificent sea-otter, a veritable enhydrus, the only quadruped which is exclusively marine. This otter was five feet long, and must have been very valuable. Its skin, chestnut brown above and silvery underneath, would have made one of those beautiful furs so sought after in the Russian and Chinese markets; the fineness and lustre of its coat was certainly worth at least eighty pounds. I admired this curious mammal—its rounded head and short ears, round eyes and white whiskers, like those of a cat, with webbed feet and claws and tufted tail. This precious animal, hunted and tracked by fishermen, is becoming very rare, and it takes refuge principally in the northern parts of the Pacific, where it is likely that its race will soon become extinct. Captain Nemo's companion took up the animal and threw it over his shoulders, and we continued our route.

During the next hour a plain of sand lay stretched before us. Sometimes it rose within two yards and some inches of the surface of the water. I then saw the reflection of our images above us, like us in every point, except that they walked with their heads downwards and their feet in the air.

The thick waves above us looked like clouds above our heads—clouds which were no sooner formed than they vanished rapidly. I even perceived the shadows of the large birds as they floated on the surface of the water.

On this occasion I was witness to one of the finest gun-shots which ever made a hunter's nerve thrill. A large bird, with great breadth of wing, hovered over us. Captain Nemo's companion shouldered his gun and fired when it was only a few yards above the waves. The bird fell dead, and the fall brought it in reach of the skilful hunter's grasp. It was an albatross of the finest kind.

Our march was not interrupted by this incident. I was worn out by fatigue when we at last perceived a faint light half a mile off. Before twenty minutes were over we should be on board and able to breathe with ease, for it seemed to me that my reservoir of air was getting very deficient in oxygen, but I did not reckon upon a meeting which delayed our arrival.

I was about twenty steps behind Captain Nemo when he suddenly turned towards me. With his vigorous hand he threw me to the ground, whilst his companion did the same to Conseil. At first I did not know what to think of this sudden attack, but I was reassured when I saw that the captain lay down beside me and remained perfectly motionless.

I was stretched on the ground just under the shelter of a bush of algæ, when, on raising my head, I perceived enormous masses throwing phosphorescent gleams pass blusteringly by.

My blood froze in my veins. I saw two formidable sharks

threatening us; they were terrible creatures, with enormous tails and a dull and glassy stare, who threw out phosphorescent beams from holes pierced round their muzzles. Monstrous brutes which would crush a whole man in their jaws! I do not know if Conseil stayed to classify them. For my part, I noticed their silver stomachs and their formidable mouths bristling with teeth from a very unscientific point of view—more as a possible victim than as a naturalist.

Happily, these voracious animals see badly. They passed without perceiving us, brushing us with their brownish fins, and we escaped, as if by a miracle, this danger, certainly greater than the meeting of a tiger in a forest.

Half an hour after, guided by the electric light, we reached the *Nautilus*. The outside door had remained open, and Captain Nemo closed it as soon as we had entered the first cell. Then he pressed a knob. I heard the pumps worked inside the vessel. I felt the water lower around me, and in a few moments the cell was entirely empty. The inner door then opened, and we entered the wardrobe-room.

There our diving dresses were taken off, and, quite worn out from want of food and sleep, I returned to my room, lost in wonder at this surprising excursion under the sea.

CHAPTER XVIII

Four Thousand Leagues Under the Pacific

The next morning, the 18th of November, I was perfectly recovered from my fatigue of the day before, and I went up on to the platform at the very moment that the mate was pronouncing his daily sentence. It then came into my mind that it had to do with the state of the sea, and that it signified "There is nothing in sight."

And, in fact, the ocean was quite clear. There was not a sail on the horizon. The heights of Crespo Island had disappeared during the night. The sea, absorbing the colours of the solar prism, with the exception of the blue rays, reflected them in every direction, and was of an admirable indigo shade. A large wave was regularly undulating its surface.

I was admiring this magnificent aspect of the sea when Captain Nemo appeared. He did not seem to perceive my presence, and began a series of astronomical observations. Then, when he had ended his operation, he went and leaned against the cage of the watch-light and watched the surface of the ocean.

In the meantime about twenty sailors from the *Nautilus*, strong and well-built men, ascended upon the platform. They came to draw in the nets which had been out all night. These sailors evidently belonged to different nations, although they were all of the European type. I recognised, to a certainty, Irishmen, Frenchmen, some Slavs, one Greek, or a Candiote. These men spoke very little, and only used the strange idiom of which I could not even guess the origin, so that I could not question them.

The nets were hauled in. They were a species of "chaluts," like those used on the Normandy coast, vast pockets which a floating yard and a chain marled into the lower stitches keep half open. These pockets, thus dragged along in their iron gauntlets, swept the bottom of the ocean, and took in all its products on their way. That day they brought in curious specimens from these fish-fields—lophiadæ, that from their comical movements have acquired the name of buffoons; black commersons, furnished with antennæ, undulating balisters, encircled with red bands, orthragorisci, with very subtle venom; olive-coloured lampreys, macrorhynci, covered with silver scales; trichiuri, with an electric power equal to that of the gymnotus and cramp-fish; scaly notopleri, with transverse brown bands; greenish cod, several varieties of gobies, &c.; and, lastly, several fish of larger size, a caranx with a prominent head more than a yard long, several fine bonitos, bedizened with blue and silver colours, and three magnificent tunnies, which, in spite of their speed, had not escaped the net.

I reckoned that the haul had brought in more than nine hundredweight of fish. It was a fine haul, but not to be wondered at. We should not want for food.

These different products of the sea were immediately lowered down by the panel leading to the storerooms, some to be eaten fresh, others to be preserved.

The fishing ended and the provision of air renewed, I thought that the *Nautilus* was going to continue its submarine excursion, and I was preparing to return to my room, when, without further preamble, the captain turned to me and said—

"Is not the ocean gifted with real life, professor? It is sometimes gentle, at other times tempestuous. Yesterday it slept as we did, and now it has awaked after a peaceful night."

Neither "Good morning" nor "Good evening!" It was as though this strange personage was continuing a conversation already commenced with me.

"See now," he said, "it wakes under the sun's influence. It will now renew its diurnal existence. It is deeply interesting to watch the play of its organisation. It possesses a pulse and arteries, it has its spasms, and I agree with the learned Maury, who discovered in it a circulation as real as the circulation of blood in animals."

It was certain that Captain Nemo expected no answer from me, and it appeared to me useless to keep saying "Evidently," or "You are right," or "It must be so." He spoke rather to himself, taking some time between each sentence. It was a meditation aloud.

"Yes," said he, "the ocean possesses a veritable circulation, and in order to cause it, it sufficed the Creator of all things to multiply in it caloric, salt, and animalculæ. Caloric creates the different densities, the cause of currents and under-currents. Evaporation, which does not go on at all in hyperborean regions, and is very active in the equatorial zones, constitutes a permanent exchange between tropical and polar water. Besides, I have felt the perpendicular currents which form the real respiration of the ocean. I have seen the molecule of sea-water warmed on the surface, re-descend to the depths, reach its maximum of density at 2° below zero, then, cooling again, become lighter, and ascend again. You will see at the poles the consequences of this phenomenon, and you will understand why, according to the law of provident Nature, freezing can never take place except on the surface of the water!"

Whilst Captain Nemo was finishing his sentence I said to myself, "The Pole! Does the daring man intend to take us as far as there?"

In the meantime the captain had stopped talking, and was contemplating the element he so incessantly studied. Then he resumed.

"The salts," said he, "exist in a considerable quantity in the sea, professor, and if you were to take out all it contains in solution, you would make a mass of four million and a half square miles, which, spread over the globe, would form a layer more than ten yards deep. And do not think that the presence of this salt is due to a caprice of Nature. No. It makes sea-water less capable of evaporation, and prevents the wind taking off too great a quantity of vapour, which, when it condenses, would submerge the temperate zones. It has a great balancing part to play in the general economy of the globe!"

Captain Nemo stopped, rose, took several steps on the platform, and came back towards me.

"As to the infusoria, as to the hundreds of millions of animalculæ which exist by millions in a drop of water, and of which it takes 800,000 to weigh a milligramme, their part is not less important. They absorb the marine salts, they assimilate the solid elements of water, and, veritable manufacturers of calcareous continents, they make coral and madrepores, and then the drop of water deprived of its mineral element is lightened, mounts to the surface, absorbs there the salt left by evaporation, is weighted, sinks again, and takes back to the animalculæ new elements to absorb. Hence a double current, ascending and descending, always movement and life—life more intense than that of continents, more exuberant, more infinite, flourishing in every part of this ocean, element of death to man, they say, element of life to myriads of animals, and to me!"

When Captain Nemo spoke thus he was transfigured, and evoked in me extraordinary emotion.

"True existence is there," added he, "and I could conceive the foundation of nautical towns, agglomeration of submarine houses, which, like the *Nautilus*, would go up every morning to breathe on the surface of the water—free towns, if ever there were any, independent cities! And yet who knows if some despot—"

Captain Nemo finished his sentence by a violent gesture. Then, addressing himself directly to me as if to drive away some gloomy thought, he said—

"M. Aronnax, do you know how deep the ocean is?"

"I know at least, captain, what the principal soundings have taught us."

"Could you repeat them to me, so that I might counter-register them if necessary?"

"Here are some that occur to me," I answered. "If I am not mistaken they have found an average depth of 8,200 metres in the North Atlantic, and 2,500 metres in the Mediterranean. The most remarkable soundings have been taken in the South Atlantic, near the 35th degree; and they have given 1,200 metres, 14,081 metres, and 15,149 metres—in short, it is estimated that if the bottom of the sea was levelled its average depth would be about five miles."

"Well, professor," answered Captain Nemo, "we shall show you better than that, I hope. As to the average depth of this part of the Pacific, I can tell you that it is only 4,000 metres."

That said, Captain Nemo went towards the panel and disappeared down the ladder. I followed him, and went into the saloon. The screw then began to work, and the log gave twenty miles an hour.

For days and weeks Captain Nemo was very sparing of his visits. I only saw him at rare intervals. His mate pricked the ship's course regularly on the chart, and I could always tell the exact route of the *Nautilus*.

Conseil and Land passed long hours with me. Conseil had related to his friend the marvels of our excursion, and the Canadian regretted not having accompanied us.

Almost every day, during some hours, the panels of the saloon were opened, and our eyes were never tired of penetrating the mysteries of the submarine world.

The general direction of the *Nautilus* was S.E., and it kept between 100 and 150 yards depth. One day, however—I do not know by what caprice—it reached the beds of water situated at 2,000 yards. On the 26th of November, at 3 a.m., the *Nautilus* crossed the tropic of Cancer by long. 172°. On the 27th it sighted the Sandwich Islands, where the illustrious Cook met his death on the 14th of February, 1779. We had then made 4,860 leagues from our starting-point. In the morning, when I arrived on the platform, I saw, two miles to the windward, Hawaii, the largest of the seven islands which form this archipelago. I clearly distinguished its cultivated border, the different chains of mountains which run parallel to the coast, and its volcanoes, the highest of which is the Mouna-Rea. Amongst other specimens brought up by the nets in this part of the ocean were several polypi of graceful form, which are peculiar to that region.

The *Nautilus* still kept a north-easterly direction. It crossed the equator on December 1st by 142°, and the 4th of the same month, after a rapid passage during which no particular incident happened, we sighted the group of the Marquesas. I perceived, at a distance of three miles, by 8° 57' south and 139° 32' west the point Martin de Nouka-Hiva, the principal of this group, which belongs to France. I only saw the wooded mountains outlined on the horizon, for Captain Nemo did not like to draw near any land. There the nets brought in some fine specimens of fish—choryphenes with azure fins and golden tails, the flesh of which is without a rival in the world; hologymnoses, nearly destitute of scales, but of exquisite flavour; ostorhyncs with bony jaws and yellowish thasards, as good as bonitoes—all fish worthy of being classified in the pantries on board.

After leaving these charming islands protected by the French flag, from the 4th to the 11th of December the *Nautilus* sailed over 2,000 miles. This navigation was marked by the meeting of an immense shoal of calmars, curious molluscs, near neighbours to the cuttle. The French fishermen call them *encornets;* they belong to the class of cephalopods and the family of the dibranches, that comprehends the cuttles and argonauts. These animals were particularly studied by the naturalists of antiquity, and they furnished numerous metaphors to the orators of the Agora, as well as excellent dishes for the tables of the rich citizens, if we can believe Athenæus, a Greek doctor who lived before Galen.

It was during the night between the 9th and 10th of December that the *Nautilus* met with the shoal of molluscs that are particularly nocturnal. They could be counted by millions. They were emigrating from the temperate to the warmer zones, following the track of herrings and sardines. We watched them through the crystal panes, swimming backwards with extreme rapidity, moving by means of their locomotive tube, pursuing fish and molluscs, eating the little ones, eaten by the big ones, and agitating, in indescribable confusion, the ten arms that Nature has placed on their heads, like a crest of pneumatic serpents. The *Nautilus*, notwithstanding its speed, sailed for several hours in the midst of these animals, and its nets drew in an innumerable quantity, amongst which I recognised the nine species that Orbigny has classified as belonging to the Pacific Ocean.

It will be seen that during this voyage the sea was prodigal of its most marvellous spectacles. It varied them infinitely. It changed its scenes and grouping for the pleasure of our eyes, and we were called upon, not only to contemplate the works of the Creator amidst the liquid element, but to penetrate as well into the most fearful mysteries of the ocean.

During the day of the 11th of December I was reading in the saloon. Ned Land and Conseil were looking at the luminous water through the half-open panels. The *Nautilus* was stationary; it was keeping at a depth of 1,000 yards, a region not much inhabited, in which large fish alone make rare appearances.

I was reading at that moment a charming book by Jean Macé, *Les Serviteurs de l'Estomac*, and I was learning the ingenious lessons it gives, when Conseil interrupted me.

"Will monsieur come here for a moment?" said he in a singular voice.

I rose, went to the window, and looked out. Full in the electric light an enormous black mass, immovable, was suspended in the midst of the waters. I looked at it attentively, trying to make out the nature of this gigantic cetacean. But an idea suddenly came into my mind.

"A vessel!" I cried.

"Yes," replied the Canadian, "a disabled ship sunk perpendicularly."

Ned Land was right. We were close to a vessel of which the tattered shrouds still hung from their chains. The hull seemed to be in good order, and it could not have been wrecked more

131

than a few hours; the vessel had had to sacrifice its mast. It lay on its side, had filled, and was heeling over to port. This skeleton of what it had once been was a sad spectacle under the waves, but sadder still was the sight of the deck, where corpses, bound with rope, were still lying. I counted five; one man was at the helm, and a woman stood by the poop holding an infant in her arms; she was quite young. I could clearly see her features by the light of the *Nautilus*—features which the water had not yet decomposed. In a last effort she had raised the child above her head, and the arms of the little one were round its mother's neck. The sailors looked frightful, and seemed to be making a last effort to free themselves from the cords that bound them to the vessel. The helmsman alone, calm, with a clear, grave face and iron-grey hair glued to his forehead, was clutching the wheel of the helm, and seemed, even then, to be guiding the vessel through the depths of the ocean!

What a scene! It struck us dumb, and our hearts beat faster at the sight of this wreck, photographed at the last moment, and I already saw, advancing towards it with hungry eyes, enormous sharks attracted by the human flesh!

The *Nautilus* just then turned round the submerged vessel, and I read on the stern "Florida, Sunderland."

CHAPTER XIX

Vanikoro

This terrible spectacle inaugurated the series of maritime catastrophes which the *Nautilus* was to meet with on her route. Since it had been in more frequented seas we had often perceived the hulls of ships—wrecked vessels which were rotting in the midst of the waters, and, deeper down, cannons, bullets, anchors, chains, and other iron objects which were being eaten up by the rust.

We lived in the *Nautilus* our usual isolated lives, and on the 11th of December we sighted the archipelago of Pomotou, the ancient "dangerous group" of Bougainville, which extends over a space of 500 leagues from the E.S.E. to W.N.W., between 13° 30' and 23° 50' south and 125° 30' and 151° 30' west, from Ducie Island to that of Lazareffe.

This archipelago covers an area of 370 square leagues, and is formed of sixty groups of islands, amongst which is the Gambier group, over which France rules. These islands are of coral formation. They slowly but continuously rise by the work of the polypi, which will one day join them together. Then this new island will be joined to the neighbouring archipelagoes, and a fifth continent will stretch from New Zealand and New Caledonia to the Marquesas.

The day that I developed this theory before Captain Nemo he answered me coldly—

"The earth does not want new continents, but new men!"

The hazards of its navigation had precisely conducted the *Nautilus* towards the island of Clermont-Tonnerre, one of the most curious of the group, which was discovered in 1822 by Captain Bell, of the *Minerva*. I could now study the madreporal system to which the islands of this ocean are due.

Madrepores, which must not be mistaken for corals, have a tissue covered with a calcareous crust, and the modifications of its structure have made Mr. Milne-Edwards, my illustrious master, classify them into five sections. The little animalculæ which these polypi secrete live by millions at the bottom of their cells. It is their calcareous deposit which becomes rocks, reefs, and large and small islands. Here they form a ring surrounding a lagoon or small interior lake, which gaps put into communication with the sea. There they make barriers of reefs like those which exist on the coasts of New Caledonia and the different Pomotou Islands. In other places, such as Réunion and Maurice, they raise fringed reefs, high straight walls, near which the depths of the ocean are considerable.

As we were coasting at some cable-lengths only off the shore of the island of Clermont-Tonnerre I admired the gigantic work accomplished by these microscopical workmen. These walls are specially the work of madrepores, known as milleporas, porites, astræas, and meandrines. These polypi breed particularly in the rough beds on the surface of the sea, and consequently it is from their upper part that they begin their substructure, which sinks gradually with the *débris* of secretions which support them. Such is at least Mr. Darwin's theory, who thus explains the formation of the *atolls*, which I think a superior theory to that which gives for basis of madreporical works the summits of mountains or volcanoes that are submerged some feet below the level of the sea.

I could closely observe these curious walls, for the fathom-line gave them perpendicularly more than 300 yards in depth, and our electric light made the calcareous matter shine brilliantly.

Replying to a question Conseil asked me as to how long it took these colossal barriers to grow, I astonished him much by telling him that learned men reckoned the growth to be one eighth of an inch in a century.

"Then how long has it taken to raise these walls?" he said.

"Four hundred and ninety-two thousand years, Conseil. Besides, the formation of coal and the mineralising of the forests buried by the deluge has taken a much longer time still."

When the *Nautilus* returned to the surface of the ocean I could take in all the development of this low and wooded island of Clermont-Tonnerre. Its madreporal rocks were evidently fertilised by water-spouts and tempests. One day some grain, carried away from neighbouring land by a tempest of wind, fell on these calcareous layers, mixed with the decomposed detritus of fish and marine plants which formed vegetable soil. A coconut, pushed along by the waves, arrived on this new coast. The germ took root. The tree grew and stopped the vapour of the water. Streams were born, vegetation spread little by little. Animalculæ, worms, insects landed upon trunks of trees, torn away from other islands by the wind. Turtles came to lay their eggs. Birds built their nests in the young trees. In that manner animal life was developed, and, attracted by verdure and fertility, man appeared. Thus these islands, the immense works of microscopical animals, were formed.

Towards evening Clermont-Tonnerre was lost in the distance, and the route of the *Nautilus* was changed perceptibly. After having touched the tropic of Capricorn, in long. 135°, it directed its course W.N.W., sailing up the whole tropical zone again. Although the sum her sun was prodigal of its rays, we did not suffer at all from the heat, for at thirty or forty yards below the water the temperature did not rise above ten to twelve degrees.

On the 15th of December we left to the east the bewitching archipelago of the Society Islands and the graceful Tahiti, the queen of the Pacific. I perceived in the morning the elevated summits of this island. Its waters furnished our tables with excellent fish, mackerel, bonitoes, and albicores, and some varieties of a sea-serpent called munirophis.

The *Nautilus* had come 8,100 miles; 9,720 miles were registered by the log as we passed between the archipelago of Tonga-Tabou, where perished the crews of the *Argo*, the *Port-au-Prince*, and the *Duke of Portland*, and the Navigator archipelago, where Captain Langle, the friend of La Pérouse, was killed. Then we sighted the archipelago Viti, where the natives massacred the crews of *L'Union*, and Captain Bureau, of Nantes, commander of *L'Aimable Josephine*.

This archipelago, which stretches over one hundred leagues from north to south, and ninety leagues from east to west, is comprised between 6° and 2° of S. and 179° of west. It is composed of a number of large and small islands and reefs, amongst which are the islands of Viti-Levou, of Vanona-Levou and Kandubon.

It was Tasman who discovered this group in 1643, the same year that Torricelli invented the barometer and Louis XIV. ascended the throne. I leave it to be imagined which of these facts was the more useful to humanity. Afterwards came Cook in 1714, D'Entrecasteaux in 1793, and, lastly, Dumont d'Urville in 1827 unravelled all the geographical chaos of this archipelago.

The *Nautilus* approached Wailia Bay, the scene of the terrible adventures of Captain Dillon, who was the first to clear up the mystery of the shipwreck of La Pérouse.

This bay, after several draggings, furnished us with abundance of excellent oysters. We ate them immoderately, opening them on our own table, according to the precept of Seneca. These molluscs belong to the species known under the name of *"ostrea lamellosa,"* which is very common in Corsica. This Wailia bank must be considerable, and certainly without multiplied causes of destruction, the oysters would end by filling up the bays, as each contains two millions of eggs.

If Ned Land had not to repent of his greediness in this case, it was because the oyster is the only dish which never provokes indigestion. In fact, it takes at least sixteen dozen of these acephalous molluscs to furnish the quantity of azote necessary to the daily food of one man.

On the 25th of December the *Nautilus* sailed into the midst of the New Hebrides, which Quiros discovered in 1606, which Bougainville explored in 1768, and to which Cook gave its present name in 1773. This group is composed principally of nine large islands, that form a band of 120 leagues from the N.N.W. to the S.S.E. between 15° and 2° south, and 164° and 168°. We passed rather near to the island of Aurou, that at noon looked to me like a mass of green woods, surmounted by a peak of great height.

That day being Christmas Day, Ned Land seemed to me to regret that it could not be celebrated as the family *fête* dear to Protestant hearts.

I had not seen Captain Nemo for a week, when, on the 27th, in the morning, he entered the saloon, looking like a man who had seen you five minutes before. I was occupied in tracing the route of the *Nautilus* on the planisphere. The captain approached, put his finger on a spot in the map, and pronounced this one word:—

"Vanikoro."

This name was magical. It was the name of the islands upon which the vessels of La Pérouse had been lost. I rosed immediately.

"Is the *Nautilus* taking us to Vanikoro?" I asked.

"Yes, professor," answered the captain.

"And can I visit these celebrated islands where the *Boussole* and *Astrolabe* were lost?"

"If you please, professor."

"When shall we reach Vanikoro?"

"We are there now, professor."

Followed by Captain Nemo I went up to the platform, and from there I looked with avidity round the horizon.

To the N.E. emerged two volcanic islands of unequal size, surrounded by coral reefs measuring forty miles in circumference. We were in presence of Vanikoro Island, properly so called, to which Dumont d'Urville gave the name of Ile de la Recherche; we were just in front of the little harbour of Vanou, situated in 16° 4' south lat. and 164° 32' east long. The land seemed covered with verdure from the shore to the summits of the interior, crowned by Mount Kapogo, 3,000 feet high.

The *Nautilus*, after having crossed the exterior ring of rocks through a narrow passage, was inside the reefs where the sea is from thirty to forty fathoms deep. Under the verdant shade of some mangroves I perceived several savages, who looked extremely astonished at our approach. Perhaps they took the long body advancing along the surface of the water for some formidable cetacean that they ought to guard themselves against. At that moment Captain Nemo asked me what I knew about the shipwreck of La Pérouse.

"What everyone knows, captain," I answered.

"And can you tell me what everyone knows?" he asked in a slightly ironical tone.

"Easily."

I then related what the last works of Dumont d'Urville had made known, of which the following is an abridgment:—La Pérouse and his second in command, Captain Langle, were sent by Louis XVI., in 1785, to make a voyage round the world. They equipped the corvettes, the *Boussole* and the *Astrolabe*, neither of which was again heard of.

In 1791 the French Government, rightly uneasy about the fate of the two corvettes, equipped two large merchantmen, the *Recherche* and the *Espérance*, which left Brest on the 28th of September, under the orders of Bruni d'Entrecasteaux. Two months afterwards it was learnt, through the testimony of Bowen, captain of the *Albermarle*, that the *débris* of ship-wrecked vessels had been seen on the coasts of New Georgia. But D'Entrecasteaux, ignoring this communication, which was rather uncertain, made for the Admiralty Islands, designated in a report of Captain Hunter's as the scene of La Pérouse's shipwreck.

His search was fruitless. The *Espérance* and *Recherche* even passed before Vanikoro without stopping there, and, on the whole, this voyage was very unfortunate, for it cost the life of D'Entrecasteaux, of two of his mates, and several sailors of his crew.

It was an old Pacific seaman, Captain Dillon, who first found indisputable traces of the shipwreck. On May 15th, 1824, his ship, the *Saint Patrick,* passed near the Island of Tikopia, one of the New Hebrides. There a Lascar, having hailed him in a pirogue, sold him the silver handle of a sword that had something engraved on it. The Lascar said that six years before, while he was staying at Vanikoro, he had seen two Europeans who belonged to ships wrecked many years before upon the reefs of the island.

Dillon guessed that he referred to the ships of La Pérouse, the disappearance of which had troubled the entire world. He wished to reach Vanikoro, where, according to the Lascar, numerous *débris* of the wrecks were to be found; but contrary winds and currents prevented him. Dillon returned to Calcutta. There he interested the Asiatic Society and the East India Company in his search. A ship, to which they gave the name of the *Recherche,* was placed at his disposal, and he set out on the 23rd of January, 1827, accompanied by a French agent.

The *Recherche,* after touching at several points in the Pacific, anchored before Vanikoro the 7th of July, 1827, in this same harbour of Vanou where the *Nautilus* is now floating. There he gathered together numerous remains of the wrecks—iron utensils, anchors, pulley-strops, swivel-guns, an 18lb. shot, *débris* of astronomical instruments, a piece of taffrail, and a bronze bell, bearing the inscription, *Bazin m'a fait,* the mark of the foundry of Brest Arsenal, about 1785. Doubt was no longer possible.

Dillon, to complete his information, remained upon the scene of the disaster till the month of October. Then he left Vanikoro, made for New Zealand, anchored at Calcutta on the 7th of April, 1828, and returned to France, where he was received very warmly by Charles X.

Dumont d'Urville, commander of the *Astrolabe,* had set sail, and two months after Dillon had left Vanikoro he anchored before Hobart Town. There he heard of the results obtained by Dillon, and, moreover, he learnt that a certain James Hobbs, mate on board the *Union,* of Calcutta, having landed on an island situated by 80° 18' south lat. and 156° 30' east long., had noticed bars of iron and red stuffs being used by the natives of the place. Durmont d'Urville was perplexed, and did not know if he ought to credit these reports, made by newspapers little worthy of confidence. However, he decided to go on Dillon's track.

On the 10th of February, 1828, the *Astrolabe* anchored before Tikopia, and took for guide and interpreter a deserter who had taken refuge on that island, set sail for Vanikoro, and sighted it on the 12th of February, coasted its reefs until the 14th, and on the 20th only anchored inside the barrier, in the harbour of Vanou.

On the 23rd several officers went round the island and brought back some unimportant *débris*. The natives, adopting a system of denials and evasions, refused to take them to the scene of the disaster. This suspicious conduct led to the belief that they had ill-treated the shipwrecked men, and, in fact, they seemed to fear that Dumont d'Urville and his companions were come to revenge La Pérouse and his unfortunate companions.

However, on the 26th, decided by presents, and understanding that they had nothing to fear, they conducted the mate, M. Jacquinot, to the place of shipwreck.

There, in three to four fathoms of water, between the reefs of Pacou and Vanou, lay anchors, cannons, pigs of iron and lead, encrusted in the calcareous concretion. The longboat and the whaler from the *Astrolabe* were sent to this place, and, not without much fatigue, their crews succeeded in raising an anchor weighing 800 pounds, an 800-pound brass cannon, some pigs of lead, and two copper swivel guns.

Dumont d'Urville, by questioning the natives, learnt also that La Pérouse, after having lost his two ships on the reefs of the island, had built a smaller vessel, only to be lost a second time—no one knew where. The commander of the *Astrolabe* then, under a thicket of mangroves, caused a cenotaph to be raised to the memory of the celebrated navigator and his companions. It was a simple quadrangular pyramid on a coral foundation, in which there was no iron to tempt the cupidity of the natives. Then Dumont d'Urville wished to depart, but his crew were worn out by the fevers of these unhealthy shores, and he was so ill himself that he could not get under sail before the 17th of March.

In the meantime the French Government, fearing that Dumont d'Urville was not acquainted with Dillon's movements, had sent the sloop *Bayonnaise*, commanded by Legoarant de Tromelin, who was stationed on the West Coast of America. He anchored before Vanikoro some months after the departure of the Astrolabe, found no new document, but saw that the savages had respected La Pérouse's mausoleum. Such is the substance of what I told Captain Nemo.

"Then," he said, "they do not know where the third vessel, built by the shipwrecked men on the island of Vanikore, perished?"

"No one knows."

Captain Nemo answered nothing, and made me a sign to follow him to the saloon. The *Nautilus* sank some yards below the surface of the waves, and then the panels were drawn back. I rushed towards the window, and under the crustations of coral covered with fungi, syphonules, alcyons, madrepores, through myriads of charming fish—jirells, glyphisidons, pomphérides, diacopes, holocentres—I recognised certain objects which the drags could not bring up—iron stirrups, anchors, cannons, bullets, capstan fittings, the stem of a ship— all objects from shipwrecked vessels, now carpeted with living flowers. While I was looking upon these sad remnants Captain Nemo said to me in a grave voice—

"Commander La Pérouse started the 7th of December, 1785, with his ships the *Boussole* and the *Astrolabe*. He anchored first in Botany Bay, visited the Friendly Isles, New Caledonia, made for Santa Cruz, and touched at Namouka, one of the Hapai group. Then his ships arrived on the unknown reefs of Vanikoro. The *Boussole*, which went first, struck on the south coast. The

141

Astrolabe went to help, and met with the same fate. The former ship was almost immediately destroyed; but the Astrolabe, sheltered by the wind, lasted some days. The natives received the shipwrecked men very well. They installed themselves on the island, and built a smaller vessel with the remains of the two large ones. Some of the sailors chose to remain at Vanikoro. The others, weakened by illness, started with La Pérouse. They directed their course towards the Solomon Islands. They all perished on the western coast of the principal island of the group, between Capes Deception and Satisfaction."

"And how do you know that?" I exclaimed.

"This is what I found on the very spot of the last shipwreck."

Captain Nemo showed me a tin box, stamped with the French arms, and corroded by the salt water. He opened it, and I saw a mass of papers, yellow but still readable. They were the instructions of the *Ministre de la Marine* to the Commander La Pérouse, annotated on the margin in the handwriting of Louis XVI.

"Ah, that is a fine death for a sailor!" then said Captain Nemo; "a coral tomb is a tranquil one, and may Heaven grant that my companions and I may never have another!"

CHAPTER XX

Torres Straits

During the night between the 27th and 28th of December the *Nautilus* left the neighbourhood of Vanikoro with excessive speed. Its direction was south-west, and in three days it cleared the 750 leagues that separate the group of La Pérouse from the south-east point of Papua. Early on the morning of the 1st of January, 1863, Conseil joined me on the platform.

"Monsieur," said the brave fellow, "will monsieur allow me to wish him a happy New Year?"

"Why, anyone would think, Conseil, that I was in Paris in my Jardin des Plantes study. Thank you for your good wishes, only I should like to ask you what you mean by a 'happy year' in our present circumstances? Will this year bring the end of our imprisonment, or will it see us continue this strange voyage?"

"I do not know quite what to say to monsieur," answered Conseil. "It is certain that we see curious things, and the last two months we have not had time to be dull. The last marvel is always the most astonishing, and if this rate of progress is maintained I do not know how it will end. My opinion is that we shall never find such another occasion."

"Never, Conseil."

"Besides, M. Nemo, who well justifies his Latin name, is not more troublesome than if he did not exist. I therefore think a happy year would be a year which would allow us to see everything."

"To see everything, Conseil? That would perhaps take too long. But what does Ned Land think about it?"

"Ned thinks exactly the contrary to what I do," answered Conseil. "He has a positive mind and an imperious stomach. To look at fish and always eat it does not suffice him. The want of wine, bread, and meat scarcely agrees with the worthy Saxon, to whom beefsteaks are familiar, and who is not frightened at brandy or gin taken in moderation."

"For my own part, Conseil, it is not that which torments me, and I accommodate myself very well to the food on board."

"And so do I," answered Conseil, "and I think as much of remaining as Land does of taking flight. Therefore, if the year that is beginning is not a happy one for me it will be for him; or *vice versa*. By that means someone will be satisfied. In short, to conclude, I wish monsieur anything that would please him."

"Thank you, Conseil; only I must ask you to put off the question of a New Year's present, and to accept provisionally a shake of the hand. That is all I have upon me."

"Monsieur has never been so generous."

And thereupon the worthy fellow went away.

On the 22nd of January we had made 11,340 miles, or 5,250 French leagues, from our point of departure in the Japanese seas. Before the prow of the *Nautilus* extended the dangerous regions of the coral sea on the N.E. coast of Australia. Our boat coasted at a distance of some miles the dangerous bank on which Captain Cook's ships were lost on June 10th, 1770. The vessel Cook was on struck on a rock, and if it did not go down it was, thanks to this circumstance, that a piece of coral, struck off by the shock, remained fixed in the half-open hull.

I should have much liked to visit this reef 360 leagues long, against which the sea, always rough there, broke with a formidable intensity and a noise like the rolling of thunder. But at that moment the inclined planes of the *Nautilus* dragged us down to a great depth. I could see nothing of these high coral walls. I was obliged to content myself with different specimens of fish brought in by our nets. I remarked, amongst others, germons, a species of mackerel as large as tunny-fish, with bluish sides, striped with transverse bands, which disappear with the life of the animal. These fish accompanied us in shoals, and furnished our table with excessively delicate dishes. They also took a great number of greenish giltheads, about five inches long, tasting like the dorado fish, and flying pyrapeds, real submarine swallows, which in dark nights alternately strike the air and water with their phosphorescent gleams. Amongst the molluscs and the zoophytes I found in the meshes of the net several species of alcyonarians, echini, hammers, spurs, dials, cerites, and hyalleæ. The flora was represented by beautiful sea-weeds, laminariæ, and macrocystes, impregnated with the mucilage that transudes through their pores, and amongst which I found an admirable *nemastoma geliniarois* that was classed amongst the natural curiosities of the museum.

Two days after crossing the coral sea, on the 4th of January, we sighted the Papuan coasts. On this occasion Captain Nemo informed me that it was his intention to get into the Indian Ocean by Torres Straits. His communication ended there. Ned Land saw with pleasure that this route would take him nearer to the European seas.

The Torres Straits are considered no less dangerous on account of the reefs with which they bristle than because of the savage inhabitants who frequent their shores. They separate New Holland from the large island of Papua, named also New Guinea.

Papua is 400 leagues long and 130 leagues wide, and has a surface of 40,000 geographical miles. It is situated between 0° 19' and 10° 2' south latitude, and between 128° 23' and 146° 15' longitude. At noon, whilst the mate was taking the sun's altitude, I perceived the summits of the Arfalxs mountains, rising by plains, and terminating in sharp peaks. This land, discovered in 1511 by the Portuguese Francisco Serrano, was successively visited by Don José de Meneses in 1526, by Grijalva in 1527, by the Spanish General Alvar de Saavedra in 1528, by Juigo Ortez in 1545, by the Dutchman Shouten in 1616, by Nicolas Sruick in 1753, by Tasman, Dampier, Fumel, Carteret, Edwards, Bougainville, Cook, Forrest, MacClure, by D'Entrecasteaux in 1792, by Duperrey in 1823, and by Dumont d'Urville in 1827. "It is the focus of the blacks who occupy all Malaysia," says M. de Rienzi, and I little thought that the chances of this navigation were going to bring me in presence of the formidable Andamenes.

145

The *Nautilus* then entered the most dangerous straits on the globe, those that the boldest seamen dare scarcely cross, the straits that Luis Vaez de Torres affronted when returning from the South Seas, and in which, in 1840, the stranded corvettes of Dumont d'Urville were on the point of being totally wrecked. The *Nautilus* itself, superior to all dangers of the sea, was going, however, to make the acquaintance of its coral reefs.

The Torres Straits are about thirty-four leagues wide, but it is obstructed by an innumerable quantity of islands, reefs, and rocks, which make its navigation almost impracticable. Captain Nemo consequently took every precaution to cross it. The *Nautilus*, on a level with the surface of the water, moved slowly along. Its screw, like the tail of a cetacean, slowly beat the billows.

Profiting by this situation, my two companions and I took our places on the constantly-deserted platform. Before us rose the helmsman's cage, and I am very much mistaken if Captain Nemo was not there directing his *Nautilus* himself.

I had spread out before me the excellent charts of the Torres Straits, taken by the hydrographical engineer, Vincendon Dumoulin, and the midshipman Coupvent-Desbois—now an admiral—who made part of Dumont d'Urville's état-major during his last voyage round the world. They are, along with those of Captain King, the best charts for threading the maze at this narrow passage, and I consulted them with scrupulous attention.

Around the *Nautilus* the sea was furiously rough. The current of the waves, which was bearing from S.E. to N.W. with a speed of two and a half miles, broke over the coral reefs that emerged here and there.

"An ugly sea!" said Ned Land to me.

"Detestable indeed," I answered, "and one that is not suitable to such a vessel as the *Nautilus*."

"That confounded captain must be very certain of his route," answered the Canadian, "for I see coral reefs which would break its keel in a thousand pieces if it only just touched them!"

The situation was indeed dangerous, but the *Nautilus* seemed to glide off the dangerous reefs as if by enchantment. It did not exactly follow the routes of the *Astrolabe* and *Zélée*, for they proved fatal to Dumont d'Urville. It bore more northwards, coasted the Island of Murray, and came back south-west towards Cumberland Passage. I thought it was going to enter it, when going back N.W. it went amongst a large quantity of little-known islands and islets towards Sound Island and Mauvais Canal.

I was wondering if Captain Nemo, foolishly imprudent, was going to take his vessel into that pass where Dumont d'Urville's two corvettes were stranded, when he again changed his direction, and cutting straight through to the west, he steered for the Island of Bilboa. It was then three o'clock in the afternoon. The ebb tide was just beginning. The *Nautilus* approached this island, which I still think I see with its remarkable border of screw-pines. We were coasting at a distance of two miles.

Suddenly a shock overthrew me. The *Nautilus* had just touched on a reef, and was quite still, laying lightly to port side.

When I rose I saw Captain Nemo and his second on the platform. They were examining the situation of the vessel, and talking in their incomprehensible dialect.

The situation was the following:—Two miles on the starboard appeared the Island of Gilboa, the coast of which was rounded from N. to W.; like an immense arm towards the S. and E. some heads of coral rocks were jutting, which the ebb tide left uncovered. We had run aground, and in one of the seas where the tides are very slight, an unfortunate circumstance in the floating of the *Nautilus*; however, the vessel had in no wise suffered, its keel was so solidly joined; but although it could neither sink nor split, it ran the risk of being for ever fastened on to these reefs, and then Captain Nemo's submarine apparatus would be done for.

I was reflecting thus, when the captain, cool and calm, always master of himself, appearing neither vexed nor moved, came up.

147

"An accident?" I asked.

"No, an incident," he answered.

"But an incident," I replied, "which will perhaps again force you to become an inhabitant of the land from which you flee."

Captain Nemo looked at me in a curious manner, and made a negative gesture. It was as much as to say to me that nothing would ever force him to set foot on land again. Then he said—

"Besides, M. Aronnax, the *Nautilus* is not lost. It will yet carry you amid the marvels of the ocean. Our voyage is only just begun, and I do not wish to deprive myself so soon of the honour of your company."

"But, Captain Nemo," I replied, without noticing the irony of his sentence, "the *Nautilus* ran aground at high tide. Now tides are not strong in the Pacific, and if you cannot lighten the *Nautilus* I do not see how it can be floated again."

"Tides are not strong in the Pacific—you are right, professor," answered Captain Nemo; "but in Torres Straits there is a difference of five feet between the level of high and low tide. Today is the fourth of January, and in five days the moon will be at the full. Now I shall be very much astonished if this complaisant satellite does not sufficiently raise these masses of water, and render me a service which I wish to owe to her alone."

This said, Captain Nemo, followed by his second, went down again into the interior of the *Nautilus*. The vessel remained as immovable as if the coral polypi had already walled it up in their indestructible cement.

"Well, sir?" said Ned Land, who came to me after the departure of the captain.

"Well, friend Ned, we must wait patiently for high tide on the ninth. It appears that the moon will be kind enough to set us afloat again."

"Really?"

"Really."

"And this captain is not going to weigh anchor, to set his machine to work, or to do anything to get the vessel off?"

"Since the tide will suffice," answered Conseil simply.

The Canadian looked at Conseil, then shrugged his shoulders. It was the seaman who spoke in him.

"Sir," he replied, "you may believe me when I tell you that this piece of iron will never be navigated again, either on or under the seas. It is only fit to be sold by weight. I think, then, that the moment is come to part company with Captain Nemo."

"Friend Ned," I answered, "I do not despair, like you, of this valiant *Nautilus*, and in four days we shall know what to think of these tides on the Pacific. Besides, the advice to fly might be opportune if we were in sight of the coasts of England or Provence, but in the Papuan regions it is another thing, and it will be quite time to resort to that extremity if the *Nautilus* does not succeed in getting off, which I should look upon as a grave event."

"But still we might have a taste of land," replied Ned Land. "There is an island; on that island there are trees; under those trees are terrestrial animals, bearers of cutlets and roast beef, which I should like to be able to taste."

"There friend Ned is right," said Conseil, "and I am of his opinion. Could not monsieur obtain from his friend Captain Nemo the permission to be transported to land, if it was only not to lose the habit of treading the solid parts of our planet?"

"I can ask him," I answered, "but he will refuse."

"Let monsieur risk it," said Conseil, "and then we shall know what to think about the captain's amiability."

To my great surprise Captain Nemo gave the permission I asked for, and he gave it me very courteously, without even exacting from me a promise to come back on board. But a flight across the lands of New Guinea would have been very perilous, and I should not have advised Ned Land to attempt it. It was better to be a prisoner on board the *Nautilus* than to fall into the hands of the natives of Papua.

The longboat was put at our disposal the next morning. I did not seek to know if Captain Nemo would accompany us. I thought even that no man of the crew would be given to us, and that Ned Land alone would have the care of directing the vessel. Besides, land was not more than two miles distant, and it was only play to the Canadian to conduct this light boat amongst the lines of reefs so fatal to large ships.

The next day, January 5th, the boat, its deck taken off, was lifted from its niche, and launched from the top of the platform. Two men sufficed for this operation. The oars were in the boat, and we had only to take our place.

At eight o'clock, armed with guns and hatchets, we descended the sides of the *Nautilus*. The sea was pretty calm. A slight breeze was blowing from land. Conseil and I rowed vigorously, and Ned steered in the narrow passages between the breakers. The boat was easily managed, and fled along rapidly.

Ned Land could not contain his joy. He was a prisoner escaped from prison, and did not think of the necessity of going back to it again.

"Meat!" he repeated. "We are going to eat meat, and what meat! Real game!—no bread, though! I don't say that fish is not a good thing, but you can have too much of it, and a piece of fresh venison, grilled over burning coals, would be an agreeable variation to our ordinary fare."

"Gourmand!" said Conseil. "He makes the water come into my mouth!"

"You do not know yet," I said, "if there is any game in these forests, or if the game will not hunt the hunter himself."

"Well, M. Aronnax," replied the Canadian, whose teeth seemed sharpened like the edge of a hatchet, "but I will eat tiger—a loin of tiger—if there is no other quadruped on this island."

"Friend Ned is alarming," answered Conseil.

"Whatever animal it is," replied Ned Land, "whether it is one with four paws and no feathers or two paws and feathers, it will be saluted by my first shot."

"Good," I replied; "you are already beginning to be imprudent."

"Never fear, M. Aronnax," answered the Canadian; "row along; I only ask twenty-five minutes to offer you a dish of my sort."

At half-past eight the boat of the *Nautilus* ran softly aground on a strand of sand, after having happily cleared the coral reef which surrounds the Island of Gilboa.

CHAPTER XXI

Some Days on Land

Touching land again made a great impression on me. Ned Land struck the ground with his foot as if to take possession of it. Yet we had only been, according to Captain Nemo's expression, the "passengers of the *Nautilus*" for two months—that is to say, in reality, we had only been the captain's prisoners for two months.

In a very short time we were within a gunshot of the coast. The soil was almost entirely madreporic, but certain dried-up beds of streams, strewed with granitic *débris*, demonstrated that this island was owing to a primordial formation. All the horizon was hidden by a curtain of admirable forests. Enormous trees, some 200 feet high, with garlands, of creepers joining their branches, were real natural hammocks, which were rocked in the slight breeze. They were mimosas, ficus, casuarinas, teak-trees, hibiscus, pendanus, palm-trees, mixed in profusion; and under the shelter of their verdant vault, at the foot of their gigantic stype, grew orchids, leguminous plants, and ferns.

But without noticing all these fine specimens of Papuan flora, the Canadian abandoned the agreeable for the useful. He perceived a coconut tree, brought down some nuts, broke them, and we drank their milk and ate their kernel with a relish that protested against the ordinary fare of the *Nautilus*.

"Excellent!" said Ned Land.

"Exquisite!" answered Conseil.

"I do not think," said the Canadian, "that your Nemo would object to our taking back a cargo of coconuts on board."

"I do not think so," I answered, "but he would not taste them himself."

"So much the worse for him," said Conseil.

"And so much the better for us," replied Ned Land; "there will be more left."

"One word only, Land," I said to the harpooner, who was beginning to ravage another coconut tree. "Coconuts are good things, but before filling the boat with them I think it would be wise to see if the island does not produce some substance no less useful. Fresh vegetables would be well received in the kitchen of the *Nautilus*."

"Monsieur is right," answered Conseil, "and I propose to reserve three places in our boat—one for fruit, another for vegetables, and the third for venison, of which I have not seen the slightest sample yet."

"We should not despair of anything, Conseil," answered the Canadian.

"Let us go on with our excursion," I replied, "and keep a sharp look-out. Although the island appears to be inhabited, it might contain individuals who would be easier to please than we on the nature of the game."

"Ha! ha!" said Ned Land, with a very significant movement of the jaw.

"What is it, Ned?" cried Conseil.

"I am beginning to understand the charms of cannibalism," answered the Canadian.

"What are you talking about, Ned?" replied Conseil. "If you are a cannibal, I shall no longer feel safe with you in the same cabin! Shall I wake one day and find myself half devoured?"

"Friend Conseil, I like you very much, but not enough to eat you, unless I am obliged."

"I do not trust to it," answered Conseil. "Well, let us start; we must really bring down some game to satisfy this cannibal, or one of these fine mornings monsieur will only find pieces of a servant to serve him."

In such-like conversation we penetrated the sombre vaults of the forest, and for two hours walked about it in every direction.

Fortune favoured us in this search after edibles, and one of the most useful products of tropical zones furnished us with a valuable article of food which was wanting on board—I mean the bread-tree, which is very abundant in the Island of

Gilboa, and I remarked there principally that variety destitute of seeds which bears in Malaysian the name of "Rima." This tree was distinguished from others by its straight trunk forty feet high; its summit, gracefully rounded and formed of large multi-lobe leaves, designated sufficiently to the eyes of a naturalist the artocarpus, which has been very happily naturalised in the Mascareigne Islands. From its mass of verdure stood out large globular fruit two and a-half inches wide, with a rough skin in an hexagonal pattern—a useful vegetable, with which Nature has gratified the regions in which wheat is wanting, and which, without exacting any culture, gives fruit for eight months in the year. Ned Land knew this fruit well; he had eaten it before in his numerous voyages, and he knew how to prepare its edible substance. The sight of it excited his appetite, and he could contain himself no longer.

"Sir," he said to me, "may I die if I don't taste a little of that bread-fruit!"

"Taste, friend Ned—taste as much as you like. We are here to make experiments; let us make them."

"It will not take long," answered the Canadian; and with a burning-glass he lighted a fire of dead wood which crackled joyously.

During this time Conseil and I chose the best fruits of the artocarpus. Some were not ripe enough, and their thick skin covered a white but slightly fibrous pulp. There were a great number of others, yellow and gelatinous, ready for gathering.

There was no kernel in this fruit. Conseil took a dozen to Ned Land, who placed them on a fire of cinders, after having cut them into thin slices, during which he kept saying—

"You will see, sir, how good this bread is!"

"Especially when one has been deprived of it for so long, Conseil."

"It is better than bread," added the Canadian; "it is like delicate pastry. Have you never eaten any, sir?"

"No, Ned."

"Well, then, prepare for something very good. If you don't return to the charge I am no longer the king of harpooners."

In a short time the side exposed to the fire was quite black. In the interior appeared a white paste and a sort of tender crumb, with a taste something like that of an artichoke.

It must be acknowledged this bread was excellent, and I ate it with great pleasure.

"Unfortunately," I said, "such paste will not keep fresh; and it appears useless to me to make any provision for the vessel."

"Why, sir," cried Ned Land, "you speak like a naturalist, but I am going to act like a baker. Gather some of the fruit, Conseil; we will take it on our return."

"And how do you prepare it?" I asked.

"By making a fermented paste with its pulp, which will keep any length of time. When I wish to use it I will have it cooked in the kitchen on board; and, notwithstanding its slightly acid taste, you will find it excellent."

"Then, Ned, I see that nothing is wanting to this bread."

"Yes, professor," answered the Canadian; "we want fruit, or at least vegetables."

"Let us seek the fruit and vegetables."

When our gathering was over we set out to complete this terrestrial dinner. Our search was not a vain one, and towards noon we had made an ample provision of bananas. These delicious productions of the torrid zone ripen all through the year, and the Malaysians, who have given them the name of "pisang," eat them raw. With these bananas we gathered enormous "jaks" with a very decided taste, savoury mangoes, and pineapples of an incredible size. But this gathering took up a great deal of our time, which there was no cause to regret.

Conseil watched Ned continually. The harpooner marched on in front, and during his walk across the forest he gathered with a sure hand the excellent fruit with which to complete his provisions.

"You do not want anything more, Ned, do you?"

"Hum," said the Canadian.

"Why, what have you to complain of?"

"All these vegetables cannot constitute a meal," answered Ned; "they are only good for dessert. There is the soup and the roast."

"Yes," said I. "Ned had promised us cutlets, which seemed to me very problematic."

"Sir," answered the Canadian, "our sport is not only not ended, but is not even begun. Patience! We shall end by meeting with some animal or bird, and if it is not in this place it will be in another."

"And if it is not today it will be tomorrow," added Conseil, "for we must not go too far away. I vote to go back to the boat now."

"What, already?" cried Ned.

"We must come back before night," I said.

"What time is it?" asked the Canadian.

"Two o'clock at least," answered Conseil.

"How the time does go on dry land!" cried Ned Land with a sigh of regret.

We came back across the forest, and completed our provision by making a razzia of palm cabbages, which we were obliged to gather at the summit of the trees, and little beans which I recognised as being the "abrou" of the Malaysians, and yams of a superior quality.

We were overburdened when we arrived at the boat, yet Ned Land did not think his provisions sufficient. But fortune favoured him. At the moment of embarking he perceived several trees from twenty-five to thirty feet high, belonging to the palm species. These trees, as precious as the artocarpus, are justly counted amongst the most useful products of Malaysia. There were sago-trees, vegetables which grow without culture, and reproduce themselves like blackberries by their shoots and seeds. Ned Land knew how to treat these trees. He took his hatchet, and, using it vigorously, he soon brought two or three sago-trees level with the ground, their ripeness being recognised by the white powder dusted over their branches.

I watched him more with the eyes of a naturalist than those of a famished man. He began by stripping the bark from each trunk, an inch thick, which covered a network of long fibres, forming inextricable knots, that a sort of gummy flour cemented. This flour was sago, an edible substance which forms the principal article of food of the Melanesian population. Ned Land was content for the time being to cut these trunks in pieces, as he would have done wood to burn, meaning to extract the flour later on, and to pass it through a cloth in order to separate it from its fibrous ligaments, to leave it to dry in the sun, and let it harden in moulds.

At last, at five o'clock in the evening, loaded with our riches, we left the shores of the island, and half an hour later reached the *Nautilus*. No one appeared on our arrival. The enormous iron cylinders seemed deserted. When the provisions were embarked I went down to my room. There I found my supper ready. I ate it, and then went to sleep.

The next day, January 6th, there was nothing new on board. No noise in the interior, not a sign of life. The canoe had remained alongside, in the very place where we had left it. We resolved to return to the Island of Gilboa. Ned Land hoped to be more fortunate than before from a hunting point of view, and wished to visit another part of the forest.

We set out at sunrise. The boat, carried away by the waves, which were flowing inland, reached the island in a few minutes. We landed, and thinking it was better to trust to the instinct of the Canadian, we followed Ned Land, whose long legs threatened to outdistance us. Ned Land went up the coast westward, and fording some beds of streams, he reached the high plain, bordered by the admirable forests. Some kingfishers were on the banks of the stream, but they would not let themselves be approached; their circumspection proved to me that these fowl knew what to think of bipeds of our sort, and I therefore concluded that, if the Island were not inhabited, it was at least frequented by human beings. After having crossed some rich meadow land we reached the borders of a little wood, animated by the song and flight of a great number of birds.

"There are only birds yet," said Conseil.

"But some of them are good to eat," answered the harpooner.

"No, friend Ned," replied Conseil, "for I see nothing but simple parrots."

"Friend Conseil," answered Ned gravely, "a parrot is the friend of those who have nothing else to eat."

"And I may add," I said, "that this bird, well prepared, is quite worth eating."

Under the thick foliage of this wood, a whole world of parrots were flying from branch to branch, only waiting for a better education to speak the human language. At present they were screeching in company with paroquets of all colours, grave cockatoos who seemed to be meditating upon some philosophical problem, whilst the loris, of a bright red colour, passed like a morsel of stamen carried off by the breeze, amidst kalaos of noisy flight, papouas, painted with the finest shades of azure, and a whole variety of charming, but generally not edible, birds.

However, a bird peculiar to these lands, and which has never passed the islands of Arrow and the Papua Islands, was wanting to this collection. But fortune reserved me the favour of admiring it before long.

After having crossed a thicket of moderate thickness we found a plain again obstructed with bushes. I then saw a magnificent bird rise, the disposition of whose long tails forces them to fly against the wind. The undulating flight, the grace of their aërial curves, the play of their colours, attracted and charmed the eye. I had no trouble to recognise them.

"Birds of Paradise!" I cried.

"Order of sparrows, section of clystornores," answered Conseil.

"Family of partridges?" asked Ned Land.

"I do not think so, Land. Nevertheless, I count on your skill to catch one of these charming productions of tropical nature."

"I will try, professor, although I am more accustomed to handle the harpoon than the gun."

The Malays, who carry on a great trade with these birds with the Chinese, have several means of taking them which we cannot employ. Sometimes they place nets on the summits of high trees that the birds of Paradise prefer to inhabit. Sometimes they catch them with a viscous birdlime, that paralyses their movements; they even poison the fountains that the birds generally drink from. We were obliged to fire at them while flying, which gave us few chances of hitting them, and, in fact, we exhausted in vain a part of our ammunition.

About 11 a.m. we had traversed the first range of mountains that form the centre of the island, and we had killed nothing. Hunger drove us on. The hunters had relied on the products of the chase, and they had done wrong. Fortunately, Conseil, to his great surprise, made a double shot, and secured breakfast. He brought down a white and a wood pigeon, which, quickly plucked and suspended to a skewer, were roasted before a flaming fire of dead wood. Whilst these interesting animals were cooking, Ned had prepared the fruit of the "artocarpus," then the pigeons were devoured to the bones, and pronounced excellent. Nutmegs, with which they are in the habit of stuffing their crops, flavours their flesh, and makes it delicious.

"It is like the fowls that eat truffles," said Conseil.

"And now, Ned, what is there wanting?" I asked the Canadian.

"Some four-footed game, M. Aronnax," answered Ned Land. "All these pigeons are only side-dishes and mouthfuls, and until I have killed an animal with cutlets I shall not be content."

"Nor I, Ned, until I have caught a bird of Paradise."

"Let us go on with our hunting," answered Conseil, "but towards the sea. We have reached the first declivities of the mountains, and I think we had better regain the forest regions."

It was sensible advice, and was followed. After an hour's walk we reached a veritable forest of sago-trees. Some inoffensive serpents fled at the sound of our footsteps. The birds of Paradise fled at our approach, and I really despaired of getting near them, when Conseil, who was walking on in front, suddenly stooped, uttered a cry of triumph, and came back to me, carrying a magnificent bird of Paradise.

"Ah, bravo! Conseil," I exclaimed.

"Monsieur is very kind," answered Conseil.

"No, my boy, that was a master stroke, not only to take one of these birds living, but to catch it simply by hand."

"If master will examine it closely, he will see that my merit has not been great."

"Why, Conseil?"

"Because this bird is as intoxicated as a quail."

"Intoxicated?"

"Yes, intoxicated with the nutmegs he was devouring under the nutmeg-tree where I found him. See, friend Ned, see the monstrous effects of intemperance."

"You need not grudge me the gin I've drunk the last two months!" answered the Canadian.

In the meantime I examined the curious bird. Conseil was not mistaken. The bird of Paradise, intoxicated by the spirituous juice, was powerless. It could not fly, and could hardly walk. But that did not make me uneasy. I left it time to get over the effect of its nutmegs.

This bird belonged to the finest of the eight species which are counted in Papua and the neighbouring islands. It was "the large emerald," one of the rarest. It measured nine inches in length, its head was relatively small, and its eyes, placed near the opening of the beak, were small too. But its colours were admirable; it had a yellow beak, brown legs and claws, nut-coloured wings with purple borders, a pale yellow head and back of neck, emerald throat, and maroon breast. Two horned downy nets rose above the tail, that was prolonged by two very light feathers of admirable fineness, completing the effect of this marvellous bird, that the natives have poetically named "bird of the sun."

I much wished to be able to take this superb specimen back to Paris, in order that I might make a present of it to the Jardin des Plantes, which does not possess a single living one.

"Is it so rare, then?" asked the Canadian, in the tone of a hunter who does not care much for it as game.

"Very rare, my brave companion, and, above all, very difficult to take alive, and even dead these birds are the object of an important traffic. Hence the natives fabricate them as pearls and diamonds are fabricated."

"What!" cried Conseil, "they make false birds of Paradise?"

"Yes, Conseil."

"Does monsieur know how the natives set about it?"

"Perfectly. These birds, during the eastern monsoon, lose the magnificent feathers which surround their tails, and which naturalists call subulate feathers. The false coiners gather up these feathers, which they skilfully fasten on to some poor parrot previously mutilated. Then they die the suture, varnish the bird, and send to the museums and amateurs of Europe the product of their singular industry."

"Good!" said Ned Land; "if they have not the bird they at least have its feathers, and as they don't want to eat it, I see no harm!"

But if my desires were satisfied by the possession of the bird of Paradise, the Canadian's were not yet. Happily, about two o'clock Ned Land killed a magnificent hog, one of those the natives call "bari-outang." The animal came in time to give us real quadruped meat, and it was well received. Ned Land was very proud of his shot. The hog, struck by the electric bullet, had fallen stone dead.

The Canadian soon skinned and prepared it after having cut out half-a-dozen cutlets to furnish us with grilled meat for our evening meal. Then we went on with the chase that was again to be marked by Ned and Conseil's exploits.

The two friends, by beating the bushes, roused a herd of kangaroos that fled away bounding on their elastic paws. But these animals did not take flight too rapidly for the electric capsule to stop them in their course.

"Ah, professor," cried Ned Land, excited by the pleasure of hunting, "what excellent game, especially stewed! What provisions for the *Nautilus*! Two, three, five down! And when I think that we shall eat all that meat, and that those imbeciles on board will not have a mouthful!"

I think that in his delight the Canadian, if he had not talked so much, would have slaughtered the whole herd! But he contented himself with a dozen of these interesting marsupians, which, as Conseil informed us, form the first order of agreacentiary mammals.

These animals were small. They belong to a species of kangaroo "rabbits" that live habitually in the hollow of trees, and that are of extraordinary speed; but although they are of middling size, they, at least, furnish excellent meat.

We were very much satisfied with the result of our hunt. The delighted Ned proposed to return the next day to this enchanted island, which he wanted to clear of all its edible quadrupeds. But he reckoned without circumstances.

At 6 p.m. we returned to the shore. Our boat was stranded in its place. The *Nautilus*, like a long rock, emerged from the waves two miles from the island. Ned Land, without more delay, began to prepare the dinner. He understood all about cooking well. The cutlets of "bari-outang," grilled on the cinders, soon scented the air with a delicious odour.

But here I perceive that I am walking in the footsteps of the Canadian in delight before grilled pork. May I be pardoned as I have pardoned Ned Land, and from the same motives? In short, the dinner was excellent. Two wood-pigeons completed this extraordinary bill of fare. The sago paste, the artocarpus bread, mangoes, half-a-dozen pineapples, and the fermented liquor of some coconuts delighted us. I even think that the ideas of my worthy companions were not so clear as they might be.

"Suppose we do not return to the *Nautilus* this evening," said Conseil.

"Suppose we never return," added Ned Land.

Just then a stone fell at our feet and cut short the harpooner's proposition.

CHAPTER XXII

Captain Nemo's Thunderbolt

We looked towards the forest without rising, my hand stopping in its movement towards my mouth, Ned Land's completing its office.

"A stone does not fall from the sky," said Conseil, "without deserving the name of aërolite."

A second stone, carefully rounded, which struck out of Conseil's hand a savoury pigeon's leg, gave still more weight to his observations.

We all three rose and shouldered our guns, ready to reply to any attack.

"Can they be monkeys?" asked Ned Land.

"Something like them," answered Conseil; "they are savages."

"The boat," said I, making for the sea. In fact, we were obliged to beat a retreat, for about twenty natives, armed with bows and slings, appeared on the skirts of the thicket that hid the horizon one hundred steps off.

Our boat was anchored at about sixty feet from us.

The savages approached us, not running, making most hostile demonstrations. It rained stones and arrows.

Ned Land did not wish to leave his provisions, notwithstanding the imminence of the danger. He went on tolerably fast with his pig on one side and his kangaroos on the other.

In two minutes we were on shore. It was the affair of an instant to land the boat with the provisions and arms, to push it into the sea, and to take the two oars. We had not gone two cables' length when a hundred savages, howling and gesticulating, entered the water up to their waists. I watched to see if their appearance would not attract some men from the *Nautilus* on to the platform.

But no. The enormous machine, lying off, seemed absolutely deserted. Twenty minutes after we ascended the sides; the panels were open. After we had made the boat fast we re-entered the interior of the *Nautilus*.

I went to the saloon, from whence I heard some chords. Captain Nemo was there, bending over his organ, and plunged into a musical ecstasy.

"Captain," I said to him.

He did not hear me.

"Captain," I repeated, touching his hand.

He shuddered and turned.

"Ha, it is you, professor?" he said to me. "Well, have you had good sport? Have you botanised successfully?"

"Yes, captain," answered I, "but we have, unfortunately, brought back a troop of bipeds, whose neighbourhood appears to me dangerous."

"What bipeds?"

"Savages."

"Savages?" answered Captain Nemo in an ironical tone. "And you are astonished, professor, that having set foot on one of the lands of this globe, you find savages there? Where are there no savages? Besides, those you call savages, are they worse than others?"

"But, captain——"

"For my part, sir, I have met with some everywhere."

"Well," I answered, "if you do not wish to receive any on board the *Nautilus*, you will do well to take some precautions."

"Make yourself easy, professor; there is nothing worth troubling about."

"But these natives are numerous."

"How many did you count?"

"A hundred at least."

"M. Aronnax," answered Captain Nemo, who had again placed his fingers on the organ keys, "if all the natives of Papua were gathered together on that shore, the *Nautilus* would have nothing to fear from their attacks."

The captain's fingers were then running over the keys of the instrument, and I noticed that he only struck the black keys, which gave to his melodies an essentially Scotch character. He had soon forgotten my presence, and was plunged into a reverie that I did not seek to dissipate.

I went up again on to the platform. Night had already come, for in this low latitude the sun sets rapidly, and there is no twilight. I could only see the island indistinctly. But the numerous fires lighted on the beach showed that the natives did not dream of leaving it.

I remained thus alone for several hours, sometimes thinking about the natives, but not otherwise anxious about them, for the imperturbable confidence of the captain gained upon me, sometimes forgetting them to admire the splendours of the tropical night. My thoughts fled to France in the wake of the zodiacal stars which in a few hours would shine there. The moon shone brilliantly amidst the constellations of the zenith. I then thought that this faithful and complaisant satellite would come back tomorrow to the same place to draw the waves and tear away the *Nautilus* from its coral bed. About midnight, seeing that all was tranquil on the dark waves, as well as under the trees on the shore, I went down to my cabin and went peacefully to sleep.

The night passed without misadventure. The Papuans were, doubtless, frightened by the very sight of the monster stranded in the bay, for the open panels would have given them easy access to the interior of the *Nautilus*.

At 6 a.m., on January 8th, I went up on the platform. The morning was breaking. The island soon appeared through the rising mists, its shores first, then its summits.

The natives were still there, more numerous than the day before, perhaps five or six hundred strong. Some of them, taking advantage of the low tide, had come on to the coral heads at less than two cables' length from the *Nautilus*. I easily recognised them. They were real Papuans of athletic stature, men of fine breed, with wide high foreheads, large, but not broad, and flat noses, and white teeth. Their woolly hair, dyed red, showed off their bodies, black and shining like those of the

Nubians. From the cut and distended lobes of their ears hung bone chaplets. These savages were generally naked. Amongst them I remarked some women, dressed from the hips to the knees in a veritable crinoline of herbs, which hung to a vegetable waistband. Some of the chiefs had ornamented their necks with a crescent and collar of red and white glass beads. Nearly all were armed with bows, arrows, and shields, carrying on their shoulders a sort of net, containing the rounded stones which they threw with great skill from their slings.

One of these chiefs, rather near the *Nautilus*, was examining it attentively. He must have been a "mado" of high rank, for he was draped in a plaited garment of banana-leaves, scalloped at the edges, and set off with brilliant colours. I could easily have shot this native, who was within short range, but I thought it better to wait for really hostile demonstrations. Between Europeans and savages it is better that the savages should make the attack.

During the whole time of low water these natives roamed about near the *Nautilus*, but they were not noisy. I heard them frequently repeat the word "Assai," and from their gestures I understood that they invited me to land, an invitation that I thought it better to decline.

So on that day the boat did not leave the vessel, to the great displeasure of Ned Land, who could not complete his provisions. This skilful Canadian employed his time in preparing the meat and farinaceous substances he had brought from the Island of Gilboa. As to the savages, they returned to land about 11 a.m., as soon as the heads of coral began to disappear under the waves of the rising tide. But I saw their number considerably increase on the shore. It was probable that they came from the neighbouring islands, or from Papua proper. However, I had not seen a single native pirogue.

Having nothing better to do, I thought of dragging these limpid waters, under which was a profusion of shells, zoophytes, and marine plants. It was, moreover, the last day the

Nautilus was to pass in these seas if it was set afloat the next day, according to Captain Nemo's promise.

I therefore called Conseil, who brought me a small light drag, something like those used in the oyster-fisheries.

"What about these savages?" Conseil asked me. "They do not seem to me to be very cruel."

"They are cannibals, however, my boy."

"It is possible to be a cannibal and an honest man," answered Conseil, "as it is possible to be a gourmand and honest. One does not exclude the other."

"Good, Conseil! I grant you there are honest cannibals, and that they honestly devour their prisoners. But as I do not care about being eaten, even honestly, I shall take care what I am about, for the commander of the *Nautilus* does not appear to be taking any precaution. And now to work."

For two hours our dragging went on actively, but without bringing up any rarity. The drag was filled with Midas-ears, harps, melames, and, particularly, the finest hammers I ever saw. We also took some holothurias, pearl oysters, and a dozen small turtles, which were kept for the pantry on board.

But at the very moment when I expected it least I put my hand on a marvel—I ought to say on a natural deformity—very rarely met with. Conseil had just brought up the drag full of ordinary shells when all at once he saw me thrust my hand into the net, draw out a shell, and utter a conchological cry—that is to say, the most piercing cry that human throat can utter.

"Eh? what is the matter with monsieur?" asked Conseil, much surprised. "Has monsieur been bitten?"

"No, my boy; and yet I would willingly have paid for my discovery with the loss of a finger."

"What discovery?"

"This shell," I said, showing the object of my triumph.

"It is simply an olive porphyry, genus olive, order of the pectini-branchidæ, class of gasteropods, sub-class of molluscs——"

"Yes, Conseil, but instead of this spiral being from right to left this olive turns from left to right!"

"Is it possible?" cried Conseil.

"Yes, my boy; it is a sinister shell."

"A sinister shell!" repeated Conseil with a palpitating heart.

"Look at its spiral."

"Ah, monsieur may believe me," said Conseil, taking the precious shell with a trembling hand, "I have never felt a like emotion!"

And there was cause for emotion! It is well known, as the naturalists have caused to be remarked, that dextrality is a law of Nature. The stars and their satellites in their rotatory movements go from right to left. Man oftener uses his right than his left hand, and consequently his instruments, apparatus, staircases, locks, watchsprings, &c., are put together so as to be used from right to left. Nature has generally followed the same law in the spiral of its shells; they are all dexter, with rare exceptions, and when it happens that their spiral is sinister amateurs pay their weight in gold.

Conseil and I were plunged in the contemplation of our treasure, and I was promising myself to enrich the museum with it, when a stone, untowardly hurled by a native, broke the precious object in Conseil's hand.

I uttered a cry of despair! Conseil seized my gun, and aimed at a savage who was swinging his sling in the air about ten yards from him. I wished to stop him, but he had fired and broken the bracelet of amulets which hung upon the arm of the native.

"Conseil!" I cried—"Conseil!"

"What, does not monsieur see that this cannibal began the attack?"

"A shell is not worth a man's life," I said.

"Ah, the rascal!" cried Conseil; "I would rather he had broken my arm!"

Conseil was sincere, but I was not of his opinion. However, the situation had changed during the last few minutes, and we had not perceived it. About twenty pirogues then surrounded the *Nautilus*. These pirogues, hollowed in the trunks of trees, long, narrow, and well calculated for speed, were kept in equilibrium by means of double balances of bamboo, which floated on the surface of the water. They were worked by skilful paddlers, half-naked, and their approach made me uneasy. It was evident that these Papuans had already had some relations with Europeans, and knew their ships. But what must they have thought of this long iron cylinder, without either masts or funnel? Nothing good, but they kept first at a respectful distance. However, seeing it did not move, they regained confidence by degrees and tried to familiarise themselves with it. Now it was precisely this familiarity which it was necessary to prevent. Our arms, which made no noise, could only produce an indifferent effect on these natives, who only respect noisy weapons. A thunderbolt without the rolling of thunder would not much frighten men, although the danger exists in the lightning and not in the noise.

At that moment the pirogues approached nearer the *Nautilus*, and a shower of arrows fell upon it.

"Why, it hails," said Conseil, "and perhaps poisoned hail."

"I must tell Captain Nemo," said I, going through the panel.

I went down to the saloon. I found no one there. I ventured to knock at the door of the captain's room.

A "Come in!" answered me.

I entered, and found Captain Nemo occupied with a calculation where x and other algebraical signs were plentiful.

"I fear I am disturbing you," said I.

"Yes, M. Aronnax," answered the captain, "but I think you must have serious reasons for seeing me."

"Very serious; we are surrounded by the pirogues of the natives, and in a few minutes we shall certainly be assailed by several hundreds of savages."

"Ah," said Captain Nemo, tranquilly, "so they are here with their pirogues?"

"Yes."

"Well, all we have to do is to shut the panels."

"Precisely, and I came to tell you."

"Nothing is easier," said Captain Nemo.

Pressing an electric bell he transmitted an order to the crew's quarters.

"That's done, sir," said he after a few minutes; "the boat is in its place, and the panels are shut. You do not fear, I imagine, that these gentlemen can break in walls which the balls from your frigate could not touch?"

"No, captain, but there exists another danger."

"What is that, sir?"

"It is that tomorrow, at the same time, you will be obliged to open the panels to renew the air of the *Nautilus*."

"Certainly, sir, as our vessel breathes like the cetaceans do."

"Now, if at that moment the Papuans occupied the platform, I do not know how you could prevent them entering."

"Then you believe they will get up on the vessel?"

"I am certain of it."

"Well, let them. I see no reason for preventing them. These Papuans are poor devils, and I will not let my visit to Gilboa cost the life of one poor wretch."

That said, I was going to withdraw, but Captain Nemo retained me, and invited me to take a seat near him. He questioned me with interest about our excursions on land and our sport, and he did not seem to understand the need for meat that impassioned the Canadian. Then the conversation touched upon divers subjects, and without being more communicative, Captain Nemo showed himself more amiable.

Amongst other things we spoke of the present position of the *Nautilus*, abandoned precisely in this strait, where Dumont d'Urville was nearly lost.

"He was one of your great seamen," said the captain, "one of your intelligent navigators, this D'Urville! He was the French Captain Cook. Unfortunate *savant!* after having braved the southern ice-banks, the coral reefs of Oceania, and the cannibals of the Pacific, to perish miserably in a railway train! If that energetic man could think during the last seconds of his existence, you imagine what must have been his last thoughts!"

Whilst speaking thus Captain Nemo seemed moved, and I

put this emotion to his credit.

Then, map in hand, we looked over again the works of the French navigator, his voyages of circumnavigation, his double attempt to reach the South Pole that led to the discovery of Adélie and Louis Philippe Lands; lastly, his hydrographical surveys of the principal Oceanian islands.

"What your D'Urville did on the surface I have done in the interior of the ocean,"said Capain Nemo, "and more easily and completely than he. The *Astrolabe* and the *Zélée*, continually tossed about by the waves, could not be so good as the *Nautilus*, for it is a quiet study and really sedentary in the midst of the waters!"

"However, captain." I said, "there is one point of resemblance between the corvettes of Dumont d'Urville and the *Nautilus*."

"What is that, sir?"

"The *Nautilus* is stranded like them."

"The *Nautilus* is not stranded," replied Captain Nemo coldly. "The *Nautilus* is made to repose on the bed of the waters, and the difficult work, the manœuvres that D'Urville was obliged to have recourse to, to get his corvettes afloat again, I shall not undertake. The *Astrolabe* and *Zélée* nearly perished, but the *Nautilus* runs no risk. Tomorrow, at the said day and hour, the tide will quietly raise it, and it will recommence its navigation through the seas."

"Captain," I said, "I do not doubt."

"Tomorrow," added the captain, rising—"tomorrow at 2.40 p.m. the *Nautilus* will be afloat again, and I will leave without damage Torres Straits."

These words pronounced in a very curt tone, Captain Nemo bowed slightly. It was my dismissal, and I went back to my room.

There I found Conseil, who desired to know the result of my interview with the captain.

"My boy," I replied, "when I seemed to think that his *Nautilus* was threatened by the natives of Papua, the captain answered me very ironically. I have, therefore, only one thing to say to you—have confidence in him, and go to sleep in peace."

"Does monsieur require my services?"

"No, my friend. What is Ned Land doing?"

"He is making a kangaroo pasty that will be a marvel!"

I was left alone. I went to bed, but slept badly. I heard the savages stamping about on the platform making a deafening noise. The night passed thus without the crew seeming to come out of their habitual inertia. They were not more anxious about the presence of these cannibals than the soldiers of an ironclad fortress would be about the ants that crawl over the iron.

I rose at 6 a.m. The panels had not been opened. The air, therefore, had not been renewed in the interior, but the reservoirs, filled ready for any event, sent some cubic yards of oxygen into the impoverished atmosphere of the *Nautilus*.

I worked in my room till noon without seeing Captain Nemo, even for an instant. There seemed to be no preparation for departure made on board.

I waited for some time longer, and then went into the saloon. The clock was at half-past two. In ten minutes the tide would be at its maximum, and if Captain Nemo had not made a boasting promise the *Nautilus* would be immediately set free. If not, many months would pass before it would leave its coral bed.

In the meantime several shocks were felt in the hull of the vessel. I heard its sides grate against the calcareous asperities of the coral.

At 2.35 p.m. Captain Nemo appeared in the saloon.

"We are going to start," said he.

"Ah!" I said.

"I have given orders to have the panels opened."

"What about the Papuans?"

"The Papuans?" answered Captain Nemo, slightly raising his shoulders.

"Will they not penetrate into the interior of the *Nautilus*?"

"How can they?"

"Through the panels you have had opened."

"M. Aronnax," answered Captain Nemo tranquilly, "it is not so easy to enter the *Nautilus* through its panels, even when they are opened."

I looked at the captain.

"You do not understand?" he asked.

"Not at all."

"Well, come, and you will see."

I went towards the central staircase. There Ned Land and Conseil, much puzzled, were looking at some of the crew, who were opening the panels, whilst cries of rage and fearful vociferations resounded outside.

The lids were opened on the outside. Seventy horrible faces appeared. But the first of the natives who put his hand on the balustrade, thrown backwards by some invisible force, fled, howling and making extraordinary gambols.

Ten of his companions succeeded him. Ten had the same fate.

Conseil was in ecstasies. Ned Land, carried away by his violent instincts, sprang up the staircase. But as soon as he had seized the hand-rail with both hands he was overthrown in his turn.

"Malediction!" he cried. "I am thunderstruck."

That word explained it all to me. It was no longer a hand-rail but a metal cable, charged with electricity. Whoever touched it felt a formidable shock, and that shock would have been mortal if Captain Nemo had thrown all the current of his apparatus into this conductor. It may be truly said that between his assailants and himself he had hung an electric barrier that no one could cross with impunity.

In the meantime the frightened Papuans had beaten a retreat, maddened with terror. We, half-laughing, consoled and frictioned the unfortunate Ned Land, who was swearing like one possessed.

But at that moment the *Nautilus*, raised by the last tidal waves, left its coral bed at that fortieth minute exactly fixed by the captain. Its screw beat the waves with majestic slowness. Its speed increased by degrees, and navigating on the surface of the ocean, it left safe and sound the dangerous passages of Torres Straits.

CHAPTER XXIII

Ægri Somnia

The following day, the 10th of January, the *Nautilus* resumed its course under the water, but at a remarkable speed, which I could not estimate at less than thirty-five miles an hour. The rapidity of its screw was such that I could neither follow its turns nor count them.

When I thought that this marvellous electric agent, after having given movement, warmth, and light to the *Nautilus*, protected it likewise from exterior attacks, and transformed it into a holy ark, which no profane person could touch without being thunderstruck, my admiration was unbounded, and from the apparatus it ascended to the engineer who had created it.

We were speeding directly westward, and on January 11th we doubled Cape Wessel, situated in 135° long. and 10° north lat., which forms the eastern point of the Gulf of Carpentaria. The reefs were still numerous, but farther apart, and marked on the chart with extreme precision. The *Nautilus* easily avoided the Money Reefs on the larboard, and the Victoria Reefs on the starboard, situated in 130° long., and in the 10th parallel we were rigorously following.

The 13th of January Captain Nemo arrived in the sea of Timor and sighted the island of that name in longitude 122°. This island, the surface of which measures 16,255 square leagues, is governed by radjahs. These princes call themselves sons of crocodiles—that is to say, issues of the highest origin to which a human being can pretend. Their scaly ancestors swarm in the rivers of the island, and are the objects of particular veneration. They are protected, spoiled, worshipped, fed, young girls are offered to them for pasture, and woe to the stranger who lays hands on one of these sacred lizards.

But the *Nautilus* had nothing to do with these ugly animals. Timor was only visible for an instant at noon, whilst the first officer took our bearings. I likewise only caught a glimpse of

Kitti Island that forms a part of the group, and of which the women have a well-established reputation for beauty in Malaysian markets.

From this point the direction of the *Nautilus* in latitude was bent south-west. The prow was set for the Indian Ocean. Where was Captain Nemo's caprice going to take us to? Would he go up towards the coasts of Asia, or approach the shores of Europe? Both hardly probable resolutions for a man to take who was flying from inhabited continents. Would he then go down south? Would he double the Cape of Good Hope, then Cape Horn, and push on to the Antarctic Pole? Would he afterwards return to the seas of the Pacific, where his *Nautilus* would find easy and independent navigation? The future would show us.

After coasting the reefs of Cartier, Hibernia, Seringapatam, and Scott, the last efforts of the solid element against the liquid element, on the 14th of January we were beyond all land. The speed of the *Nautilus* was singularly slackened, and very capricious in its movements; sometimes it swam amidst the waters, sometimes floated on their surface.

During this period of the voyage Captain Nemo made interesting experiments on the different temperatures of the sea at different depths. In ordinary conditions these experiments are only made by means of complicated instruments, and are often doubtful, whether made by thermometric sounding lines, the glasses of which often break under the pressure of the water, or by apparatus based on the variation of resistance in metals to electric currents. The results thus obtained cannot be sufficiently controlled. On the contrary, Captain Nemo went himself to seek the temperature in the different depths, and his thermometer put into communication with the different liquid sheets gave him immediately and surely the degree he sought.

It was thus that, either by filling its reservoirs or descending obliquely by its inclined planes, the *Nautilus* successfully reached depths of three, four, five, seven, nine, and ten thousand metres, and the definitive result of these experiments was that the sea presented a permanent temperature of four and a half degrees at a depth of one thousand metres under all latitudes.

I followed these experiments with the most lively interest. Captain Nemo studied them with passion. I often asked myself to what end he made these observations. Was it for the good of his fellow-creatures? It was not probable, for one day his work must perish with him in some unknown sea unless he destined the results of his experiments for me. But that was to admit that my strange voyage would have a term, and this term I did not yet perceive.

However that may be, Captain Nemo told me of different calculations obtained by him which established the different evidence about the density of water in the principal seas of the globe. From that communication I drew some personal information which was not at all scientific.

It was during the morning of the 15th of January. The captain, with whom I was walking on the platform, asked me if I knew the different densities of sea-water. I answered in the negative, and added that rigorous observations were wanting to science on this subject.

"I have made those observations," he said to me, "and I can affirm that they are correct."

"That may be," I answered, "but the *Nautilus* is a world in itself, and the secrets of its *savants* do not reach the earth."

"You are right, professor," he answered after a short silence; "it is a world in itself. It is as much a stranger to the world as those planets that accompany this globe round the sun, and the world will never know the work of the *savants* in Jupiter and Saturn. Still, as chance has united our two lives, I give you the result of my observations."

"I shall be glad to hear it, captain."

"You know, professor, that sea-water is denser than fresh water, but that its density is not uniform. In fact, if I represent by one the density of fresh water, I find a twenty-eight-thousandth for the waters of the Atlantic, a twenty-six-thousandth for those of the Pacific, a thirty-thousandth for those of the Mediterranean——"

"Ah," thought I, "he adventures into the Mediterranean."

"An eighteen-thousandth for the waters of the Ionian Sea, and a twenty-thousandth for those of the Adriatic."

Decidedly the *Nautilus* did not avoid the frequented seas of Europe, and I hence concluded that it would take us—perhaps before long—towards more civilised lands. I thought that Ned Land would learn this detail with very natural satisfaction.

We passed several days in making all sorts of experiments on the saltness of the sea at different depths, on its electrification, coloration, transparency, and in all of them Captain Nemo displayed an ingenuity which was only equalled by his kindness towards me. Then, for some days, I saw him no longer, and again remained isolated on board.

On the 16th of January the *Nautilus* seemed to be sleeping at some yards only below the surface of the waves. Its electric apparatus was idle, and its immovable screw let it be rocked at the will of the currents. I supposed that the crew was occupied with interior reparations necessitated by the violence of the mechanical movements of the machine.

My companions and I were then witnesses of a curious spectacle. The panels of the saloon were open, and as the electric lantern of the *Nautilus* was not lighted, a vague obscurity reigned in the midst of the waters. The sky, which was stormy, and covered with thick clouds, only gave an insufficient light to the first depths of the ocean.

I was looking at the state of the sea under these conditions, and the largest fish only looked to me like half-formed shadows, when all at once the *Nautilus* was in broad light. I thought at first that the lantern had been relighted, and was projecting its electric brilliancy upon the liquid mass. I was mistaken, and after a rapid observation saw my error.

The *Nautilus* was floating amidst a phosphorescent layer, which in such obscurity became dazzling. It was produced by myriads of luminous animalculæ, the light of which was increased by being reflected against the metallic hull of the vessel. I then saw sheets of lightning amidst these luminous layers, like molten lead melted in a furnace, or metallic masses heated red hot, in such a manner that by opposition certain luminous portions made a shadow in this ignited medium, from which all shadow seemed as though it ought to be banished. No! it was not the calm irradiation of our habitual light. There was an unwonted vigour and movement in it. We felt that the light was living.

In fact, it was an infinite agglomeration of infusoria, of miliary "noctiluques," globules of diaphanous jelly, furnished with a filiform tentacle, of which 25,000 have been counted in 30 cubic centimetres of water. And their light was doubled by gleams peculiar to medusæ, asteriæ, and aureliæ, pholodestalles, and other phosphorescent zoophytes, impregnated with the greasy quality of organic matters decomposed by the sea, and perhaps by the mucus secreted by the fish.

During several hours the *Nautilus* floated among those brilliant sheets of water, and our admiration increased at seeing the large marine animals play among them like salamanders. I saw there amidst their fire that does not burn, elegant and rapid porpoises, indefatigable clowns of the sea, and istiophores three yards long, intelligent precursor of storms, the formidable sword of which struck against the glass of the saloon; and then appeared smaller fish, scembers, and others, which streaked the luminous atmosphere in their course.

This dazzling spectacle was enchanting! Perhaps some atmospheric condition augmented the intensity of the phenomenon. Perhaps some storm was going on above the waves, but at that depth of a few yards the *Nautilus* did not feel its fury, and was peacefully balancing itself amidst the tranquil waters.

Thus we went on our way, incessantly charmed by some new marvel. Conseil observed and classified his zoophytes, his articulates, his molluscs, and his fish. The days fled rapidly away, and I counted them no longer. Ned, according to his custom, tried to vary the fare on board. Veritable snails, we had become accustomed to our shell, and I affirmed that it is easy to become a perfect snail. This existence, then, appeared to us easy and natural, and we no longer thought of the different life that existed on the surface of the terrestrial globe, when an event happened to recall to us the strangeness of our situation.

On the 18th of January the *Nautilus* was in longitude 105°, in S. lat. 15°. The weather was threatening, the sea rough. The wind was blowing a strong gale from the east. The barometer, which had been going down for some days, announced an approaching war of the elements.

I had gone up on to the platform at the moment the first officer was taking his bearings. I expected as usual to hear the daily sentence pronounced. But that day it was replaced by another phrase not less incomprehensible. Almost immediately I saw Captain Nemo appear and sweep the horizon with a telescope.

For some minutes the captain remained immovable, without leaving the point inclosed in the field of his object-glass. Then he lowered his telescope and exchanged about ten words with his officer, who seemed to be a prey to an emotion that he tried in vain to suppress.

Captain Nemo, more master of himself, remained calm. He appeared, besides, to make certain objections, to which the officer answered by formal assurances—at least, I understood them thus by the difference of their tone and gestures.

I looked carefully in the direction they were observing without perceiving anything. Sky and water mixed in a perfectly clear horizon.

In the meantime Captain Nemo walked up and down the platform without looking at me, perhaps without seeing me. His step was assured, but less regular than usual. Sometimes he stopped, folded his arms, and looked at the sea. What was he seeking in that immense space? The *Nautilus* was then some hundreds of miles from the nearest coast.

The first officer had taken up his telescope again, and was obstinately interrogating the horizon, going and coming, stamping, and contrasting with his chief by his nervous excitement.

This mystery must necessarily be soon cleared up, for, obeying an order of Captain Nemo's, the machine, increasing its propelling power, gave a more rapid rotatory movement to the screw.

At that moment the officer again attracted the captain's attention, who stopped his walk and directed his telescope towards the point indicated. He observed it for a long time. I, feeling very curious about it, went down to the saloon and brought up an excellent telescope that I generally used. Then leaning it against the lantern cage that jutted in front of the platform, I prepared to sweep all the line of sky and sea. But I had not placed my eye to it when the instrument was quickly snatched out of my hands.

I turned. Captain Nemo was before me, but I hardly knew him. His physiognomy was transfigured. His eyes shone with sombre fire under his frowning eyebrows. His teeth glittered between his firm-set lips. His stiffened body, closed fists, and head set hard on his shoulders, showed the violent hatred breathed by his whole appearance. He did not move. My telescope, fallen from his hand, had rolled to his feet.

Had I, then, unintentionally provoked this angry attitude? Did the incomprehensible personage imagine that I had surprised some secret interdicted to the guests of the *Nautilus*?

No! I was not the object of this hatred, for he was not looking at me; his eyes remained fixed on the impenetrable point of the horizon.

At last Captain Nemo recovered his self-possession. His face, so profoundly excited, resumed its habitual calmness. He addressed some words in a foreign tongue to his officer, and then turned towards me again.

"M. Aronnax," said he in a rather imperious tone, "I require from you the fulfilment of one of the engagements that bind me to you."

"What is that, captain?"

"To let yourself be shut up—you and your companions—until I shall think proper to set you at liberty again."

"You are master here," I answered, looking at him fixedly. "But may I ask you one question?"

"No, sir, not one!"

After that I had nothing to do but obey, as all resistance would have been impossible.

I went down to the cabin occupied by Ned Land and Conseil, and I told them of the captain's determination. I leave it to be imagined how that communication was received by the Canadian. Besides, there was no time for any explanation. Four of the crew were waiting at the door, and they conducted us to the cell where we had passed our first night on board the *Nautilus*.

Ned Land wanted to expostulate, but for all answer the door was shut upon him.

"Will monsieur tell me what this means?" asked Conseil.

I related what had happened to my companions. They were as astonished as I, and not more enlightened.

I was overwhelmed with reflections, and the strange look on Captain Nemo's face would not go out of my head. I was incapable of putting two logical ideas together, and was losing myself in the most absurd hypotheses, when I was aroused by these words of Ned Land:—

"Why, they have laid dinner for us!"

In fact, the table was laid. It was evident that Captain Nemo had given this order at the same time that he caused the speed of the *Nautilus* to be hastened.

"Will monsieur allow me to recommend something to him?" asked Conseil.

"Yes, my boy," I replied.

"It is that monsieur should breakfast. It would be prudent, for we do not know what may happen."

"You are right, Conseil."

"Unfortunately," said Ned Land, "they have only given us the usual fare on board."

"Friend Ned," replied Conseil, "what should you say if you had had no dinner at all?"

That observation cut short the harpooner's grumbling.

We sat down to dinner. The meal was eaten in silence. I ate little. Conseil forced himself to eat for prudence sake, and Ned Land ate as usual. Then, breakfast over, we each made ourselves comfortable in a corner.

At that moment the luminous globe that had been lighting us went out and left us in profound darkness. Ned Land soon went to sleep, and, what astonished me, Conseil went off into a heavy slumber. I was asking myself what could have provoked in him so imperious a need of sleep, when I felt heaviness creep over my own brain. My eyes, which I wished to keep open, closed in spite of my efforts. I became a prey to painful hallucinations. It was evident that soporific substances had been mixed with the food we had just eaten. Imprisonment, then, was not enough to conceal Captain Nemo's projects from us; we must have sleep as well.

I heard the panels closed. The undulations of the sea, that of a slight rolling motion, ceased. Had the *Nautilus*, then, left the surface of the ocean? Had it again sunk to the motionless depth?

I wished to resist sleep. It was impossible. My breathing became weaker. I felt a deathlike coldness freeze and paralyse my limbs. My eyelids fell like leaden coverings over my eyes. I could not raise them. A morbid slumber, full of hallucinations, took possession of my whole being. Then the visions disappeared and left me in complete insensibility.

CHAPTER XXIV

The Coral Kingdom

The next day I awoke with my faculties singularly clear. To my great surprise I was in my own room. My companions had doubtless been carried to their cabin without being more aware of it than I. They knew no more what had happened during the night than I, and to unveil the mystery I only depended on the hazards of the future.

I then thought of leaving my room. Was I once more free or a prisoner? Entirely free. I opened the door, went through the waist, and climbed the central staircase. The panels, closed the night before, were opened. I stepped on to the platform.

Ned Land and Conseil were awaiting me there. I questioned them; they knew nothing. They had slept a dreamless sleep, and had been much surprised to find themselves in their cabin on awaking.

As to the *Nautilus*, it appeared to us tranquil and mysterious as usual. It was floating on the surface of the waves at a moderate speed. Nothing on board seemed changed.

Ned Land watched the sea with his penetrating eyes. It was deserted. The Canadian signalled nothing fresh on the horizon—neither sail nor land. There was a stiff west breeze blowing, and the vessel was rolling under the influence of long waves raised by the wind.

The *Nautilus*, after its air had been renewed, was kept at an average depth of fifteen yards, so as to rise promptly, if necessary, to the surface of the waves, an operation which, contrary to custom, was performed several times during that day of January 19th. The second then went up on the platform, and the accustomed sentence was heard in the interior of the vessel.

Captain Nemo did not appear. Of the men on board I only saw the impassible steward, who served me with his usual exactitude and speechlessness.

About 2 p.m. I was in the saloon, occupied in classifying my notes, when the captain opened the door and appeared. I bowed to him. He returned it almost imperceptibly, without uttering a word. I went on with my work, hoping he would perhaps give me some explanation of the events that had occurred the previous night. He did nothing of the kind. I looked at him. His face appeared to me fatigued; his reddened eyelids showed they had not been refreshed by sleep; his physiognomy expressed profound and real grief. He walked about, sat down, rose up, took a book at random, abandoned it immediately, consulted his instruments without making his usual notes, and did not seem able to keep an instant in peace.

At last he came towards me and said—

"Are you a doctor, M. Aronnax?"

I so little expected such a question that I looked at him for some time without answering.

"Are you a doctor?" he repeated. "Several of your colleagues have studied medicine—Gratiolet, Moquin-Tandon, and others."

"Yes," I said; "I am doctor and surgeon. I was in practice for several years before entering the museum."

"That is well."

My answer had evidently satisfied Captain Nemo, but not knowing what he wanted, I awaited fresh questions, meaning to answer according to circumstances.

"M. Aronnax," said the captain, "will you consent to care for a sick man?"

"There is someone ill on board?"

"Yes."

"I am ready to follow you."

"Come."

I must acknowledge that my heart beat faster. I do not know why I say some connection between the illness of this man of the crew and the events of the night before, and this mystery preoccupied me at least as much as the sick man.

Captain Nemo conducted me aft of the *Nautilus*, and made me enter a cabin situated in the crew's quarters.

There, upon a bed, a man of some forty years, with an energetic face and true Anglo-Saxon type, was reposing.

I bent over him. He was not only a sick man but a wounded one too. His head, wrapped in bandages, was resting on a double pillow. I undid the bandages, and the wounded man, looking with his large fixed eyes, let me do it without uttering a single complaint.

The wound was horrible. The skull, crushed by some blunt instrument, showed the brain, and the cerebral substance had sustained profound attrition. Clots of blood had formed in the wound the colour of wine-dregs. There had been both contusion and effusion of the brain. The breathing of the sick man was slow, and spasmodic movements of the muscles agitated his face. The cerebral phlegmasia was complete, and caused paralysis of movement and feeling.

I felt the pulse; it was intermittent. The extremities were already growing cold, and I saw that death was approaching without any possibility of my preventing it. After dressing the wound I bandaged it again, and turned towards Captain Nemo.

"How was this wound caused?" I asked.

"What does it matter?" answered the captain evasively. "A shock of the *Nautilus* broke one of the levers of the machine, which struck this man. But what do you think of his condition?"

I hesitated to reply.

"You may speak," said the captain; "this man does not understand French."

I looked a last time at the wounded man, then I answered—

"He will be dead in two hours."

"Can nothing save him?"

"Nothing."

Captain Nemo clenched his hand, and his eyes, which I did not think made for weeping, filled with tears.

For some time I still watched the dying man, whose life seemed gradually ebbing. He looked still paler under the electric light that bathed his deathbed. I looked at his intelligent head, furrowed with premature lines which misfortune, misery perhaps, had long ago placed there. I tried to learn the secret of his life in the last words that escaped from his mouth.

"You can go now, M. Aronnax," said Captain Nemo.

I left the captain in the room of the dying man, and went back to my room much moved by this scene. During the whole day I was agitated by sinister presentiments. I slept badly that night, and, amidst my frequently-interrupted dreams, I thought I heard distant sighs and a sound like funeral chants. Was it the prayer for the dead murmured in that language which I could not understand?

The next morning I went up on deck. Captain Nemo had preceded me there. As soon as he perceived me he came to me.

"Professor," said he, "would it suit you to make a submarine excursion today?"

"With my companions?" I asked.

"If they like."

"We are at your disposition, captain."

"Then please put on your diving-dresses."

Of the dying or dead there was no question. I went to Ned Land and Conseil and told them of Captain Nemo's proposal. Conseil accepted it immediately, and this time the Canadian seemed quite ready to go with us.

It was 8 a.m. At half-past we were clothed for our walk, and furnished with our breathing and lighting apparatus. The double door was opened, and accompanied by Captain Nemo, who was followed by a dozen men of the crew, we set foot at a depth of ten yards on the firm ground where the *Nautilus* was stationed.

A slight incline brought us to an undulated stretch of ground at about fifteen fathoms depth. This ground differed completely from any I saw during my first excursion under the waters of the Pacific Ocean. Here there was no fine sand, no submarine meadows, no seaweed forests. I immediately recognised this region of which Captain Nemo was doing the honours. It was the kingdom of coral.

In the embranchment of the zoophytes and the alcyon class, the order of gorgoneæ, isidiæ, and corollariæ are noticed. It is to the last that coral belongs—that curious substance that was by turns classified in the mineral, vegetable, and animal kingdoms. A remedy of the ancients, a jewel of modern times, it was not until 1694 that the Marseillais Peysonnel definitively placed it in the animal kingdom.

Coral is an assemblage of animalculæ, united on a polypier of a stony and breakable nature. These polypiers have a unique generator which produces them by gemmation, and they possess an existence of their own at the same time that they participate in the common life. It is, therefore, a sort of natural socialism. I knew the result of the last works made on this strange zoophyte, which mineralises at the same time that it arborises, according to the very just observation of naturalists; and nothing could be more interesting to me than to visit one of the petrified forests that Nature has planted at the bottom of the sea.

The Ruhmkorff apparatus were set going, and we followed a coral bank in process of formation, which, helped by time, would one day close in that portion of the Indian Ocean. The route was bordered by inextricable bushes formed by the entanglement of shrubs that the little white-starred flowers covered. Sometimes, contrary to the land plants, these arborisations, rooted to the rocks, grew from top to bottom.

The light produced a thousand charming effects, playing amidst the branches that were so vividly coloured. It seemed to me as if the membraneous and cylindrical tubes trembled under the undulation of the waves. I was tempted to gather their fresh petals, ornamented with delicate tentacles, some freshly opened, others scarcely out, whilst light and rapid-swimming fish touched them slightly in passing like a flock of birds. But when my hand approached these living flowers, these animated sensitive plants, the whole colony was put on the alert. The white petals re-entered their red cases, the flowers vanished from my gaze, and the bushes changed into blocks of stony knobs.

Chance had brought me in presence of the most precious specimens of this zoophyte. This coral was as valuable as that found in the Mediterranean, on the coasts of France, Italy, and Barbary. It justified by its brilliant tints the poetic names of "Flower of Blood" and "Froth of Blood" which commerce gives to its most beautiful productions. Coral is sold as high as £10 a pound, and in this place the liquid masses covered the fortune of a world of coral-dealers. This precious matter often mixed with other polypiers, then formed the compact and inextricable compound called "macciota," on which I noticed several beautiful specimens of pink coral.

But soon the bushes contracted, and the arborisations increased. Real petrified thickets and long triforiums of fantastic architecture opened before our steps. Capain Nemo entered a dark gallery, the inclined plane of which led us down to a depth of 100 yards. The light of our serpentines sometimes produced magical effects by following the rough outlines of the natural arches and pendants, like bushes, which it pricked with points of fire. Amongst the coralline shrubs I noticed other polypiers no less curious, melites and irises with articulated ramifications, also reefs of coral, some green, some red, like seaweed incrusted in their calcareous salts, which naturalists, after long discussion, have definitely classified in the vegetable kingdom. But, according to the remark of a thinker, "This is perhaps the real point where life obscurely rises from its stony sleep, without altogether leaving its rude starting-point."

At last, after two hours' walking, we reached a depth of about 150 fathoms—that is to say, the extreme limit that coral begins to form itself. But there it was no longer the isolated shrub nor the modest thicket of low brushwood. It was the immense forest, the great mineral vegetations, the enormous petrified trees, united by garlands of elegant plumarias, sea-bindweed, all decked off with colours and shades. We passed freely under their high branches lost in the depths of the water above, whilst, at our feet the tubipores, meandrines, stars, fungi, and caryopbyllidæ formed a carpet of flowers strewed with dazzling gems.

It was an indescribable spectacle! Ah, why could we not communicate our sensations? Why were we imprisoned under these masks of metal and glass? Why were words between us forbidden? Why did we not at least live the life of the fish that people the liquid element, or rather that of the amphibians who, during long hours, can traverse as they like the double domain of land and water?

In the meantime Captain Nemo had stopped. My companions and I imitated him, and, turning round, I saw that his men had formed a semicircle round their chief. Looking with more attention, I noticed that four of them were carrying an object of oblong form on their shoulders.

We were then in the centre of a vast open space surrounded by high arborisations of the submarine forest. Our lamps lighted up the space with a sort of twilight which immoderately lengthened the shadows on the ground. At the limit of the open space darkness again became profound, and was only "made visible" by little sparks reflected in the projections of the coral.

Ned Land and Conseil were near me. We looked on, and the thought that I was going to assist at a strange scene came into my mind. As I looked at the ground I saw that it was raised in certain places by slight excrescences incrusted with calcareous deposits, and laid out with a regularity that betrayed the hand of man.

In the centre of the open space, on a pedestal of rocks roughly piled together, rose a coral cross, which extended its long arms, that one might have said were made of petrified blood.

Upon a sign from Captain Nemo one of his men came forward, and at some feet distance from the cross began to dig a hole with a pickaxe that he took from his belt.

I then understood it all! This space was a cemetery; this hole a grave; this oblong object the body of the man who had died during the night! Captain Nemo and his men came to inter their companion in this common resting-place in the depths of the inaccessible ocean!

My mind was never so much excited before. More impressionable ideas had never invaded my brain! I would not see what my eyes were looking at!

In the meantime the tomb was being slowly dug. Fish fled hither and thither as their retreat was troubled. I heard on the calcareous soil the ring of the iron pickaxe that sparkled when it struck some flint lost at the bottom of the sea. The hole grew larger and wider, and was soon deep enough to receive the body.

Then the bearers approached. The body, wrapped in a tissue of white byssus, was lowered into its watery tomb. Captain Nemo, with his arms crossed on his chest, and all the friends of the man who had loved them, knelt in the attitude of prayer. My two companions and I bent religiously.

The tomb was then filled with the matter dug from the soil, and formed a slight excrescence.

When this was done Captain Nemo and his men rose; then, collecting round the tomb, all knelt again, and extended their hands in sign of supreme adieu.

Then the funeral procession set out for the *Nautilus* again, repassing under the arcades of the forest, amidst the thickets by the side of the coral-bushes, going uphill all the way.

At last the lights on board appeared. Their luminous track guided us to the *Nautilus*. We were back at one o'clock.

At soon as I had changed my clothes I went up on to the platform, and, a prey to a terrible conflict of emotions, I went and seated myself near the lantern-cage.

Captain Nemo joined me there. I rose and said—

"Then, as I foresaw, that man died in the night?"

"Yes, M. Aronnax," answered Captain Nemo.

"And now he is resting by the side of his companions in the coral cemetery?"

"Yes, forgotten by everyone but us! We dig the grave, and the polypi take the trouble of sealing our dead therein for eternity!"

And hiding his face in his hands with a brusque gesture, the captain tried in vain so suppress a sob. Then he added—

"That is our peaceful cemetery, at some hundreds of feet below the surface of the waves!"

"Your dead sleep, at least, tranquil, captain, out of reach of the sharks!"

"Yes, sir," answered Captain Nemo gravely, "of sharks and men!"

PART II

CHAPTER I

The Indian Ocean

Here begins the second part of this voyage under the sea. The first ended with the painful scene at the coral cemetery, which has left a profound impression on my mind. Thus, then, in the bosom of the immense ocean Captain Nemo's entire life was passed, and he had even prepared his grave in the most impenetrable of its depths. There not one of the ocean monsters would trouble the last slumber of the inhabitants of the Nautilus—of these men, riveted to each other in death as in life! "Nor man either!" Captain Nemo had added. There was always in him the same implacable and ferocious defiance towards all human society.

I no longer contented myself with the hypotheses that satisfied Conseil. The worthy fellow persisted in only seeing in the commander of the *Nautilus* one of the unappreciated *savants* who give back to humanity disdain for indifference. He was still for him a misunderstood genius, who, tired of the deceptions of the world, had sought refuge in the inaccessible medium where he could freely exercise his instincts. But, in my opinion, that hypothesis only explained one of Captain Nemo's aspects.

In fact, the mystery of that last night during which we had been enchained in prison and sleep, the precaution so violently taken by the captain of snatching from my eyes the telescope ready to sweep the horizon, the mortal wound of that man due to an inexplicable shock of the *Nautilus*—all that inclined me in a fresh direction. No! Captain Nemo did not content himself with flying from mankind! His formidable apparatus not only served his instincts of liberty, but was perhaps also the instrument of terrible revenge.

At this moment I recollect nothing clearly, I only see glimmers in the dark, and I must confine myself to writing thus, to speak under the direction of events.

Nothing really binds us to Captain Nemo. He knows that to escape from the *Nautilus* is impossible. We are not even prisoners of honour. We are only captives, prisoners disguised under the name of guests by an appearance of courtesy. Nevertheless, Ned Land has not renounced the hope of recovering his liberty. It is certain that he will profit by the first occasion chance offers him. I shall, doubtless, do the same, and yet it will not be without a sort of regret that I shall take away what the captain's generosity has allowed us to penetrate of the mysteries of the *Nautilus*. For, after all, is the man to be hated or admired? Is he a victim or an executioner? And, to speak frankly, I should like before leaving him for ever to have accomplished the submarine tour round the world of which the beginning has been so magnificent. I should like to have observed the complete series of marvels piled under the seas of the globe. I should like to have seen what no man has seen before, even if I should pay with my life for this insatiable desire to learn! What have I yet discovered? Nothing, or nearly nothing, since we have only yet been over 6,000 leagues of the Pacific.

However I know that the *Nautilus* is approaching inhabited lands, and that, if some chance of salvation was offered to us, it would be cruel to sacrifice my companions to my passion for the unknown. I must follow them, perhaps guide them. But will this occasion ever present itself? The man deprived by force of his freedom desires it may, but the *savant*, the learner, dreads it.

That day, the 21st of January, 1868, at noon, the first officer came to take the height of the sun. I went up on to the platform, lighted a cigar, and followed the operation. It appeared evident to me that this man did not understand French, for I made several reflections aloud which must have drawn from him some involuntary sign of attention if he had understood them, but he remained impassible and mute.

Whilst he was making his observation with his sextant, one of the sailors of the *Nautilus*—the vigorous man who had accompanied us in our first excursion to Crespo Island—came to clean the glass of the lantern. I then examined the installation of this apparatus, the power of which was increased a hundredfold by the lenticular rings that were placed like those of lighthouses, and which kept its light on a convenient level. The electric lamp was put together so as to give all its lighting power. Its light, in fact, was produced in a vacuum which assured its regularity and intensity at the same time. This vacuum also economised the graphite points between which the luminous arc is developed—a prudent economy for Captain Nemo, who might not have been able to renew them easily. But in these conditions wear was almost insensible.

When the *Nautilus* was prepared to continue her submarine journey, I went down to the saloon. The panels were closed, and our course was directly west.

We were ploughing through the waves of the Indian Ocean, a vast liquid plain of 1,200,000,000 acres' extent, the waters of which are so transparent that they make anyone looking into their depths quite giddy. The *Nautilus* generally floated in a depth of between a hundred and two hundred fathoms. We went on thus for several days. To any other than myself, who had a great love for the sea, the hours would have seemed long and monotonous; but my daily walks upon the platform, when I acquired new strength in the reviving air of the ocean, the sight of these rich waters through the windows of the saloon, reading, and the compiling of my memoirs, took up all my time, and did not leave me an idle or weary moment.

The health of all on board kept in a very satisfactory state. The fare on board suited us perfectly, and, for my own part, I could have dispensed with the variations which Ned Land, through spirit of protestation, was ingenious in making to it. More, in so constant a temperature there were no colds to fear; besides, the madrepore *Dendrophyllæ*, known in Provence as "sea-samphire," and of which there existed a reserve on board, would have furnished with the dissolving flesh of its polypi an excellent remedy for coughs.

During several days we saw a great quantity of aquatic birds, sea-mews, or gulls and palmipeds. Some were skilfully killed and prepared in a certain way; they furnished a very acceptable kind of game. Amongst the larger varieties, those who fly a long distance from land, and rest occasionally upon the surface of the water, I noticed some magnificent albatrosses, whose cry is as discordant as the bray of an ass. The family of the totipalmates was represented by the sea-swallows, who quickly caught up the fish that appeared on the surface of the water; and by numerous phaetons, or lepturi, amongst others the phaeton with red stripes, as large as a pigeon, and whose white plumage, tinted with red, sets off the black of the wings.

The nets of the *Nautilus* brought in several kinds of marine tortoise, with a convex back, the shell of which is greatly esteemed. These reptiles, who dive easily, can keep a long time under the water by closing the fleshy safety valve situated at the external orifice of their nasal canal. Some of these fish, when taken, were still sleeping in their carapace, sheltered from marine animals. The flesh of these tortoises was not particularly good, but their eggs made an excellent dish.

I remarked many kinds of fish which I had not before observed. I shall notice chiefly the ostracions of the Red Sea, the Indian Ocean, and that part of the ocean which washes the shores of tropical America. These fish, like the tortoise, the sea-hedgehog, and the crustacea, are protected by a breastplate which is neither crustaceous nor stony, but real bone. Sometimes it takes the form of a solid triangle, sometimes of a solid quadrangle. Amongst the triangular ones I noticed some of an inch and a half in length, having wholesome flesh of a delicious flavour, a brown tail, and yellow fins, and I recommend their introduction into fresh water, to which a certain number of sea-fish easily accustom themselves. There were some quadrangular ostracions that had four large tubercles on their backs; some that were dotted over with white spots on the under side of their bodies, and that could be tamed like birds; trigons, provided with spikes formed by the lengthening of their bony covering, and to which, owing to their singular grunting, has been given the name of "sea-hogs;" dromedaries with great humps in the form of a cone, the flesh of which is hard and leathery.

I borrow from the daily notes kept by Conseil the notice of several fish of the petrodon genus peculiar to these seas, with red backs and white chests, distinguished by three rows of longitudinal filaments, and electrical ones, seven inches long, decked in the liveliest colours. Then, as specimens of other kinds, ovoids resembling dark brown eggs, marked with white bands, and no tails; cliodons, real sea-porcupines, furnished with spikes, and able to swell in such a way as to look like cushions bristling with darts; hippocampi, common to every ocean; pegasi with long snouts, much-elongated pectoral fins, formed in the shape of wings, which allow them, if not to fly, at least to spring into the air; pigeon spatulæ, with tails covered with many scaly rings; macrognathi with long jaws, an excellent fish, nine inches long, and bright with most agreeable colours; pale calliomores, with rugged heads; myriads of flying-blennies, striped with black, with long pectoral fins, gliding with prodigious velocity on the surface of the water; delicious veliferous fish that can hoist their fins like so many sails spread to favourable currents; splendid kurtes, to which Nature has been prodigal of yellow, sky-blue, gold, and silver; tricoptera, the wings of which are formed of filaments; bullheads always slimy, which make a sort of buzzing; trygles, the liver of which is regarded as poison; bodians that wear movable blinkers on their eyes; lastly, chælodans, with long tubular muzzles, that kill insects by shooting them as from an air-gun, with a single drop of water, a gun that neither the Chassepot nor Remington foresaw—real gnat-snappers of the ocean.

In the eighty-ninth genus of fish, classified by Lacépède, belonging to the second sub-class of ossified fish, characterised by an opercule and a bronchial membrane, I remarked the scorpæna, the head of which is furnished with spikes, and that has but one dorsal fin; these animals are clothed or not, according to the sub-class they belong to, with small scales. The second sub-class gave us specimens of didactyles, fourteen or fifteen inches long, striped with yellow, but with fantastically-shaped heads. The first sub-class furnished several specimens of the bizarre fish justly-named "sea-toad," with a large head, sometimes pierced with deep sinuses, sometimes swollen over with protuberances; it carries irregular and hideous horns; its body and tail are covered with callosities; its quills make dangerous wounds; it is repulsive and horrible.

From the 21st to the 23rd of January the *Nautilus* went at the rate of 250 leagues in 24 hours, or 22 miles an hour. The cause of our seeing so many different varieties of fish was that, being attracted by the electric light, they tried to accompany us; the greater number, distanced by our speed, remained behind. Some of them, however, kept their place for a certain time in the waters of the *Nautilus*.

On the morning of the 24th, in south latitude 12°5' and longitude 94°33', we sighted Keeling Island, a madrepore formation, planted with magnificent cocoas, and which has been visited by Mr. Darwin and Captain Fitz-Roy. The *Nautilus* kept along the shores of this desert island for some little distance. The nets brought up numerous specimens of polypi and curious shells of mollusca. Some valuable specimens of delphinula enriched Captain Nemo's treasures, to which I added an astræa punctifera, a kind of parasite polypus, often fixed upon a shell.

Soon Keeling Island disappeared from the horizon, and we directed our course to the north-west, towards the Indian peninsula.

"Civilised land," said Ned Land to me that day. "That is better than the islands of Papua, where you meet with more savages than venison! On that Indian ground, professor, there are roads, railways, English, French, or Hindoo towns. One would not go five miles without meeting with a countryman. Well, is it not the moment to take French leave of Captain Nemo?"

"No, Ned, no," I answered in a very determined tone. "Let us see what comes of it. The *Nautilus* is getting nearer the inhabited continents. It is going back towards Europe; let it take us there. Once in our own seas, we shall see what prudence advises us to attempt. Besides, I do not suppose that Captain Nemo would allow us to go and shoot on the coasts of Malabar or Coromandel, as he did in the forests of New Guinea."

"Well, sir, can't we do without his permission?"

I did not answer the Canadian, for I did not wish to argue. At the bottom of my heart I wished to exhaust to the end the chances of destiny that had thrown me on board the *Nautilus*.

From Keeling Island our progress became slower, our route more varied, and we often went to great depths. Inclined planes, which were placed by levers obliquely to the water-line, were made use of several times. We went thus about two miles, but without ever ascertaining the greatest depths of the Indian Ocean, the bottom of which has never been reached even by soundings of seven thousand fathoms. As to the temperature in the deepest waters, the thermometer invariably indicated 4° above zero. I observed that the water is always colder on the higher than on the lower levels of the sea.

On the 25th of January, the ocean being entirely deserted, the *Nautilus* passed the day on the surface, beating the waves with her powerful screw and making them rebound to a great height. In these conditions how much the *Nautilus* must have looked like a gigantic cetacean! I passed three-quarters of this day upon the platform. I looked at the sea. Nothing to be seen on the horizon till, about four o'clock, a steamer appeared, going westward. Her masts were visible for an instant, but she could not see the *Nautilus*, as she was too low in the water. I thought that this steamboat probably belonged to the P. and O. Company, which runs between Ceylon and Sydney, touching at King George's Point and Melbourne.

At 5 p.m., before that short twilight which unites the day to the night in tropical zones, Conseil and I were astonished by a curious sight. There is a charming animal which to meet, according to the ancients, was a good omen. Aristotle, Athenæus, Pliny, Oppian, studied its habits and exhausted on its account all the poesy of the *savants* of Greece and Italy. They called it *Nautilus* and *pompylius;* but modern science has not ratified their appellation, and this mollusc is now known under the name of "argonaut."

Had anyone consulted Conseil he would have learnt from the brave fellow that the branch of molluscs is divided into five classes, that the first class, that of the cephalods, of which the subjects are sometimes bare, sometimes testaceous, comprehends two families—those of the dibranches and the tetrabranches, distinguished by the number of their branches; that the family of the dibranches includes three classes—the argonaut, calamary, and cuttle-fish; and that the family of the tetrabranches only contains a single one—the *Nautilus*. If after that nomenclature a rebellious mind could confuse the argonaut, which is acetabuliferous—that is to say, "bearer of ventilators"—with the *Nautilus*, which is tentaculiferous—that is to say, "bearer of tentacles"—he would have been in-excusable.

There was a shoal of argonauts then travelling along the surface of the ocean. We could count several hundreds. They belonged to the species of argonauts which are peculiar to the Indian Ocean.

These graceful molluscs moved themselves backwards along the water by means of a tube through which they propelled the water which they had already drawn in. Of their eight tentacles six were long and thin, and were floating on the water, while the two others were rolled up flat and spread out to the wind like light sails. I could distinctly see their spiral-shaped and fluted shells that Cuvier justly compares to an elegant skiff, for these shells carry the animal which has formed them without its adhering to them.

"The argonaut is at liberty to leave its shell," said I to Conseil, "but it never makes use of its liberty."

"That is like Captain Nemo," replied Conseil. "He would have done better to call his ship the *Argonaut*."

The *Nautilus* floated in the midst of this shoal of molluscs for about an hour. Then I know not what sudden fright seized them. As if at a signal, every sail was suddenly furled, the tentacles folded, the bodies rolled up, the shells being turned over changed their centre of gravity, and the whole fleet disappeared under the waves. This was all instantaneous, and never did the ships of a squadron manœuvre with more uniformity.

At this moment night came on suddenly, and the waves, hardly raised by the breeze, lay peacefully about the *Nautilus*.

The next day, the 26th of January, we cut the equator at the eighty-second meridian and entered into the northern hemisphere.

During this day a formidable shoal of sharks accompanied us—terrible creatures which swarm in these seas and make them very dangerous.

These were "castracio phillippi"—sharks with brown backs and whitish bellies, armed with eleven rows of teeth, and having their necks marked with a great black spot surrounded with white, which looked like an eye. There were some sharks with rounded muzzles and marked with dark spots. These powerful animals often dashed themselves against the windows of the saloon with an amount of violence that made us tremble. At such times Ned Land was no longer master of himself. He was impatient to go to the surface of the water and harpoon these monsters, especially some that had their jaws studded with teeth like a mosaic; and large tiger-sharks, about six yards long, which provoked him particularly. But soon the *Nautilus* increased her speed, and quickly left behind the most rapid of these monsters.

On the 27th of January, at the entrance of the vast Bay of Bengal, we frequently met with a horrible spectacle—dead bodies which floated on the surface of the water! These were the dead of the Indian villages, drifted by the Ganges to the open sea, and which the vultures, the only undertakers of the country, had not yet been able to devour. But the sharks did not fail to help them in their horrible task.

About 7 p.m. the *Nautilus*, half immersed, was sailing in the midst of a sea of milk. As far as the eye could see the ocean appeared turned to milk. Was this the effect of the lunar rays? No, for the moon being scarcely two days old was still hidden below the horizon by the rays of the sun. The whole sky, although illuminated by the sidereal rays, appeared black by contrast with the whiteness of the waters.

Conseil could not believe his eyes, and questioned me as to the causes of this singular phenomenon. Happily I was able to answer him.

"This vast extent of white waves," said I, "which is frequently to be seen upon the coast of Amboyna as well as in these parts, is called a milk sea."

"But," said Conseil, "what is the cause of such an effect, for this water is not really changed into milk, I suppose?"

"No, certainly not. This whiteness which astonishes you so much is owing to the presence of myriads of infusoria, a kind of luminous little worm, colourless and gelatinous, no thicker than a hair, and no longer than the .007 of an inch. Some of these little animals adhere to one another for the space of several leagues."

"Several leagues?" cried Conseil.

"Yes, my boy, and do not try to compute the number of these infusoria. You would not succeed, for, if I am not mistaken, certain navigators have floated on these seas of milk for more than forty miles."

I do not know if Conseil paid any attention to my recommendation, but he appeared lost in profound thought, seeking, perhaps, to estimate how many .007 of an inch there are in forty miles. For my own part, I continued to watch the phenomenon. During several hours the *Nautilus* furrowed the milky waves with its prow, and I remarked that it glided noiselessly upon the soapy water as if it was floating in the eddies of foam that the currents and counter-currents of bays sometimes leave between them.

Towards midnight the sea suddenly resumed its ordinary colour, but behind us, as far as the limits of the horizon, the sky, reflecting the whiteness of the waves, for a long time seemed impregnated with the uncertain light of the aurora borealis.

CHAPTER II

A Fresh Proposition of Captain Nemo's

When the *Nautilus* returned at noon on the 28th or February to the surface of the sea in 9°4' north latitude, we could see land about eight miles to westward. The first thing I saw was a group of mountains about 2,000 feet high, the forms of which were very peculiar. I found when the bearings had been taken that we were near the Island of Ceylon, that pearl which hangs from the ear of the Indian peninsula.

I went to look in the library for a book giving an account of this island, one of the most fertile on the globe. At this moment Captain Nemo and the mate appeared. The captain glanced at the map, then turned towards me.

"The Island of Ceylon," said he, "is very celebrated for its pearl fisheries. Would you like to see one of them, M. Aronnax?"

"I should indeed, captain."

"Well, that will be easy enough. Only if we see the fisheries we shall not see the fishermen. The annual working of the pearl fisheries has not yet begun. But that does not matter. I will give orders to make for the Gulf of Manaar, where we shall arrive during the night."

The captain said a few words to his first officer, who went out immediately. The *Nautilus* soon returned to her liquid element, and the manometer indicated that we were at a depth of thirty feet.

I looked on the map for the Gulf of Manaar; I found it by the ninth parallel on the N.W. coast of Ceylon. It was formed by the little Island of Manaar. In order to reach it we should have to go up all the western coast of Ceylon.

"Professor," then said Captain Nemo, "there are pearl fisheries in the Bay of Bengal, in the Indian Ocean, in the seas of China and Japan, in the Bay of Panama and the Gulf of California, but nowhere are such results obtained as at Ceylon. We shall arrive a little too soon, no doubt. The divers do not assemble till March in the Gulf of Manaar, and there for thirty days they give themselves up to this lucrative employment. There are about three hundred boats, and each boat has ten rowers and ten divers. These divers, divided into two groups, plunge into the sea alternately, diving to a depth of about thirteen yards by means of a heavy stone, which they hold between their feet, and a cord fastened to the boat."

"Then," said I, "the primitive method is still in use?"

"Yes," answered Captain Nemo, "although these fisheries belong to the most industrious nation in the world, to England. They were ceded to her by the treaty of Amiens in 1802."

"It seems to me, however, that a diving dress, such as you use, would be of great service in such an operation."

"Yes, for the unfortunate divers cannot remain long under water. The Englishman Percival, in his voyage to Ceylon, does speak of a Caffre who remained five minutes without rising to the surface, but I can hardly believe it. I know there are some divers who can stay under for fifty-seven seconds, and some as long as eighty-seven, but these cases are rare, and when the poor creatures return to the boats they bleed from ears and nose. I believe the usual time that divers can stay under is thirty seconds, and during this time they hasten to fill a small bag with the pearl oysters. These divers do not live to be old; their sight becomes weakened, and their eyes ulcerated; sores break out on their bodies, and very frequently they are seized with apoplexy at the bottom of the sea."

"Ah," said I, "it is a miserable occupation, and only serves for the gratification of vanity and caprice. But tell me, captain, what quantity of oysters can one boat take in a day?"

"From about forty to fifty thousand. They even say that in 1814 the English Government, fishing on its own account, its divers in twenty days' work brought up seventy-six millions of oysters."

"But at least these divers are sufficiently remunerated?" I asked.

"Scarcely, professor. At Panama they only earn one dollar a

week. And they oftener only earn one sol for each oyster that contains a pearl, and how many they bring up that contain none!"

"One sol only to the poor fellows who enrich their masters! It is odious!"

"Thus, then, professor," added the captain, "you and your companions shall see the oyster-bank of Manaar, and if by chance some early diver should be found there, we shall see him at work."

"Agreed, captain."

"But, M. Aronnax, you are not afraid of sharks?"

"Sharks?" cried I.

This question appeared to me at least a very idle one.

"Well?" continued Captain Nemo.

"I confess, captain, that I am not yet quite at home with that kind of fish."

"We are used to them," answered Captain Nemo, "and in time you will be so also. However, we shall be armed, and on the road we may have a shark-hunt. So good-bye till tomorrow, sir, and early in the morning."

This said in a careless tone, Captain Nemo left the saloon.

Now if you were invited to hunt the bear in the Swiss mountains you would say, "Very well, we'll go and hunt the bear tomorrow." If you were invited to hunt the lion in the plains of the Atlas, or the tiger in the jungles of India, you would say, "Ah, ah! It seems we are going to hunt lions and tigers!" But if you were invited to hunt the shark in its native element, you would, perhaps, ask time for reflection before accepting the invitation.

As to me, I passed my hand over my forehead, where stood several drops of cold sweat.

"I must reflect and take time," I said to myself. "To hunt otters in submarine forests, as we did in the forests of Crespo Island, is one thing, but to walk along the bottom of the sea when you are pretty sure of meeting with sharks is another! I am aware that in certain countries, especially in the Andaman Islands, the negroes do not hesitate to attack them with a dagger in one hand and a noose in the other, but I know, too, that many who affront these creatures do not return alive. Besides, I am not a negro, and if I were a negro I think a slight hesitation on my part would not be out of place."

And I began to dream of sharks, thinking of their vast jaws armed with multiplied rows of teeth, capable of cutting a man in two. I already felt a sharp pain in my loins. And then I could not digest the cool way in which the captain had made this deplorable invitation. Anyone would have thought it was only to follow some inoffensive fox!

"Good!" thought I. "Conseil will never come, and that will dispense me from accompanying the captain."

As to Ned Land, I must acknowledge I did not feel so sure of his prudence—a peril, however great, had always some attraction for his warlike nature.

I went on reading my book on Ceylon, but I turned over the leaves mechanically. I saw formidably-opened jaws between the lines. At that moment Conseil and the Canadian entered, looking calm, and even gay. They did not know what was awaiting them.

"Faith, sir," said Ned Land, "your Captain Nemo—whom the devil take!—has just made us a very amiable offer."

"Ah!" I said. "So you know——"

"Yes," interrupted Conseil, "the commander of the *Nautilus* has invited us to visit tomorrow, in company with monsieur, the magificent fisheries of Ceylon. He did it handsomely, and like a real gentleman."

"Did he not tell you anything more?"

"No, sir," answered the Canadian, "except that he had mentioned the little excursion to you."

"So he did," I said. "And he gave you no detail about——"

"Nothing, Mr. Naturalist. You will go with us, won't you?"

"I?—oh, of course! I see it is to your taste, Ned."

"Yes, it will be very curious."

"Dangerous too, perhaps," I said in an insinuating tone.

"Dangerous!" answered Ned Land. "A simple excursion on an oyster-bank dangerous?"

It was evident that Captain Nemo had not thought proper to awake the idea of sharks in the mind of my companions. I looked at them with a troubled eye as if some limb were wanting to them already. Ought I to warn them? Yes, certainly, but I hardly knew how to set about it.

"Monsieur," said Conseil to me, "would monsieur be kind enough to give us some details about the pearl fisheries?"

"Upon the way of fishing or upon the incidents that——"

"Upon the fishing," answered the Canadian. "Before going on to the ground it is well to know what it's like."

"Very well! Sit down, my friends, and I will tell you what I have just been reading myself."

Ned and Conseil seated themselves on an ottoman, and the first thing that Ned asked was—

"Sir, what is a pearl?"

"My good Ned," I answered, "to the poet the pearl is a tear of the ocean; to the Orientals it is a drop of solidified dew; to the ladies it is a jewel of an oblong form, of a glass-like brilliancy, of a mother-of-pearl substance, which they wear on their fingers, their necks, or in their ears; to the chemist it is a mixture of phosphate and carbonate of lime, with a little gelatine; and, lastly, to naturalists it is simply an unhealthy secretion of the organ which produces mother-of-pearl in certain bivalves."

"Branch of mollusca," said Conseil, "class of acephali, order of testacea."

"Precisely so, learned Conseil. Now, amongst these testacea, the earshell, tridacnæ, iris, turbots—in a word, all those that secrete mother-of-pearl—that is, the blue, bluish, violet, or white substance that lines the interior of their shells—are capable of producing pearls."

"Mussels too?" asked the Canadian.

"Yes, the mussels of certain streams in Scotland, Wales, Ireland, Saxony, Bohemia, and France."

"Good; I'll pay attention to that in future," answered the Canadian.

"But," I resumed, "the special mollusc which distils the pearl is the pearl oyster, the *meleagrina margaritifera*, the precious pintadine. The pearl is only a concretion of mother-of-pearl deposited in a globular form. It either adheres to the shell of the oyster or lies in the folds of the animal. The pearl adheres to the shell; it is loose in the flesh, but it always has a small hard substance, a barren egg, or a grain of sand for a kernel, around which the pearly substance deposits itself, year by year, in thin concentric layers."

"Are many pearls found in the same oyster?" asked Conseil.

"Yes," I answered, "mention has been made of an oyster, but I cannot help doubting it, which contained no less than a hundred and fifty sharks."

"A hundred and fifty sharks!" cried Ned Land.

"Did I say sharks?" I cried quickly. "I mean a hundred and fifty pearls. Sharks would be nonsense."

"Yes," said Conseil. "Will monsieur now tell us how they extract the pearls?"

"They do it in several ways, and very often when the pearls adhere to the shell the divers pull them off with pincers. But more frequently the oysters are laid upon the mat-weed which grows on the shore. Thus they die in the open air, and at the end of ten days they are sufficiently decomposed. Then they plunge them into large reservoirs of sea-water, then open and wash them. Now begins the double work of the sorters. Firstly they separate the layers of pearl, known in commerce under the name of clear silver, bastard whites, and bastard blacks; then they take the parenchyma of the oyster, boil it, and sift it in order to extract the very smallest pearls."

"Does the price of these pearls vary according to their size?" asked Conseil.

"Not only according to their size," answered I, "but according to their shape, their *water*—that is, their colour;

their lustre—that is, that brilliant and variegated display of colours which makes them so charming to the eye. The finest pearls are called virgin pearls; they alone are formed in the tissue of the mollusc; they are white, often opaque, but sometimes have the transparency of an opal, and generally have a spherical or oval form. When they are round they are made into bracelets; when oval into pendants, and, being the most precious, are sold separately. The pearls that adhere to the shell of the oyster are more irregular, and are sold by weight. In the lowest order are classed the little pearls, known under the name of seed-pearls; they are sold by measure, and are used specially for embroideries on church ornaments."

"But," said Ned Land, "the separating of the pearls according to their size must be a long and difficult process."

"Not so; it is managed by means of eleven sieves, pierced with a number of holes. The pearls which remain in the sieve that has from twenty to eighty holes are of the first order; those which do not escape through the sieve pierced with a hundred to eight hundred holes are of the second order; and, lastly, the pearls for which they use sieves pierced with nine hundred to a thousand holes are those called seed-pearls."

"That is ingenious," said Conseil, "and I see that the division and classifying of pearls are done mechanically. And now can monsieur tell us what these banks of pearl oysters bring in?"

"If we are to believe the book I have just been reading, the fisheries of Ceylon are worth annually three millions of sharks."

"Of francs," said Conseil, correcting me.

"Yes, of francs! Three millions of francs," I resumed. "But I believe that these fisheries bring in less now than they used to do. It is the same with the American fisheries, which, under the reign of Charles V., were worth four millions of francs, but are now reduced two-thirds. On the whole, we may estimate at nine millions of francs the annual value of the pearl fisheries."

"But," asked Conseil, "is there not some talk of celebrated pearls that have been quoted at a very high price?"

"Yes, my boy. They say that Cæsar offered to Servilia a pearl worth £4,800 of our money."

"I have even heard tell," said the Canadian, "that a certain lady of ancient times drank pearls in her vinegar."

"Cleopatra," suggested Conseil.

"It must have been nasty," added Ned Land.

"Detestable, friend Ned," answered Conseil; "but a little glass of vinegar that costs £60,000; it is a nice price."

"I am sorry I did not marry that lady," said the Canadian, moving about his arms in no very reassuring manner.

"Ned Land the husband of Cleopatra!" exclaimed Conseil.

"But I was to have been married, Conseil," answered the Canadian seriously, "and it was not my fault that it did not succeed. I even bought a pearl necklace for my young woman, Kate Tender, who, after all, went and married someone else. Well, that necklace did not cost me more than a dollar and a half, and yet, believe me, professor, the pearls it was made of would not even have passed through a sieve with only twenty holes in it."

"Those were only artificial pearls, Ned," said I, laughing, "simple glass globules covered with Eastern essence in the interior."

"That Eastern essence must be very dear," answered the Canadian.

"Almost nothing. It is only the silvery substance from the scales of the whitebait, taken off in the water and preserved in ammonia. It is of no value."

"Perhaps that's the reason Kate Tender married someone else," answered Ned Land philosophically.

"But," said I, "to return to pearls of great value, I do not think any sovereign has ever possessed one better than that of Captain Nemo."

"This one you mean," said Conseil, pointing to the magnificent jewel under its glass case.

"Certainly I am not mistaken in assigning it a value of two millions of——"

"Francs!" said Conseil quickly.

"Yes," said I, "two millions of francs, and I daresay it only cost the captain the trouble of picking it up."

"Eh!" cried Ned Land, "who says that during our excursion tomorrow we shall not meet with its fellow?"

"Bah!" said Conseil.

"And why not?"

"What use would millions be to us on board the *Nautilus*?"

"On board, no," said Ned Land; "but—elsewhere."

"Oh! elsewhere!" said Conseil, shaking his head.

"In point of fact," said I, "Ned Land is right. And if we ever take back to Europe or America a pearl worth millions, that at least will give great authenticity, and at the same time a great value, to the account of our adventures."

"I should think so," said the Canadian.

"But," said Conseil, who always returned to the instructive side of things, "is this diving for pearls dangerous?"

"No," answered I, "especially if one takes certain precautions."

"What risk can there be," said Ned Land, "except that of swallowing a few mouthfuls of sea-water?"

"You are right, Ned," said I; then trying to assume Captain Nemo's careless tone, "are you afraid of sharks, Ned?"

"I!" answered the Canadian, "a harpooner by profession! It is my business to laugh at them."

"But," said I, "there is no question of fishing them with a merlin, drawing them up on to the deck of a ship, and cutting off their tails with hatchets, of cutting them open, taking out their hearts, and throwing them back into the sea!"

"Then it means——"

"Yes, precisely."

"In the water?"

"In the water."

"Faith, with a good harpoon! You know, sir, these sharks are awkward fellows and badly put together. They must turn on their stomachs to nab you, and during that time——"

Ned Land had a way of saying the word "nab" that made my blood run cold.

"Well, and you, Conseil, what do you think of sharks?"

"I?" said Conseil; "I will tell monsieur frankly."

"There is some hope," thought I.

"If monsieur means to face the sharks," said Conseil, "I do not see why his faithful servant should not face them with him!"

CHAPTER III

A Pearl Worth Ten Millions

Night came. I went to bed and slept badly. Sharks played an important part in my dreams, and I found the etymology both just and unjust that made *requin*, the French for shark, come from the word "requiem."

The next day, at 4 a.m., I was awakened by the steward, whom Captain Nemo had specially placed at my service. I rose rapidly, dressed, and went into the saloon. Captain Nemo was waiting for me there.

"Are you ready to start, M. Aronnax?"

"I am ready."

"Then follow me, please."

"And my companions, captain?"

"They are waiting for us."

"Are we to put on our diving dresses?"

"Not yet. I have not allowed the *Nautilus* to come too near this coast, and we are still some way off Manaar Bank; but I have ordered the boat to be got ready, and it will take us to the exact point for landing, which will save us a rather long journey. It will have on board our diving dresses, and we shall put them on as soon as our submarine exploration begins."

Captain Nemo accompanied me to the central staircase, which led to the platform. Ned and Conseil were there, delighted at the notion of the pleasure party which was being prepared. Five sailors from the *Nautilus*, oars in hand, awaited us in the boat, which had been made fast against the side.

The night was yet dark. Heavy clouds covered the sky, and scarcely allowed a star to be seen. I looked towards the land, but saw nothing but a faint line inclosing three-quarters of the horizon from south-west to north-west. The *Nautilus* having moved up the western coast of Ceylon during the night, was now on the west of the bay, or rather gulf, formed by the land and the Island of Manaar.

There under the dark waters stretched the oyster-bank, an inexhaustible field of pearls, the length of which is more than twenty miles.

Captain Nemo, Conseil, Ned Land, and I took our places in the stern of the boat, and we moved off.

Our course was in a southerly direction. The rowers did not hurry themselves. I noticed that their vigorous strokes only succeeded each other every ten seconds, according to the method in use by the navy. We were silent. What was Captain Nemo thinking of? Perhaps of the land that we were approaching, and which he found too near him, contrary to the opinion of the Canadian, who thought it too far off.

About half-past five the first streaks of daylight showed more clearly the upper line of the coast. Flat enough in the east, it rose a little towards the south. Five miles still separated us from it, and the shore was indistinct, owing to the mist on the water. There was not a boat or a diver to be seen. It was evident, as Captain Nemo had warned me, that we had come a nonth too soon.

At 6 a.m. it became daylight suddenly, with that rapidity peculiar to the tropical regions, which have neither dawn nor twilight. I saw the land distinctly, with a few trees scattered here and there. The boat neared Manaar Island; Captain Nemo rose from his seat and watched the sea.

At a sign from him the anchor was dropped, but it had but a little distance to fall, for it was scarcely more than a yard to the bottom, and this was one of the highest points of the oyster-bank.

"Now, M. Aronnax," said Captain Nemo, "here we are. In a month numerous boats will be assembled here, and these are the waters that the divers explore so boldly. This bay is well placed for the purpose; it is sheltered from the high winds, the sea is never very rough here, which is highly favourable for divers' work. We will now put on our diving dresses and begin our investigations."

Aided by the sailors, I began to put on my heavy dress. Captain Nemo and my two companions also dressed themselves. None of the sailors from the *Nautilus* were to accompany us.

We were soon imprisoned to the throat in our indiarubber dresses, and the air apparatus was fixed to our backs by means of braces. There was no need for the Ruhmkorff apparatus. Before putting on the copper cap I had asked Captain Nemo about it.

"We shall not require it," said he. "We shall not go to any great depth, and the solar rays will give us light enough. Besides, it would be very imprudent to use an electric lantern under these waters; its brilliancy might unexpectedly attract some of the dangerous inhabitants of these shores."

As Captain Nemo uttered these words I turned towards Conseil and Ned Land. But my two friends had already encased their heads in their metal caps, and could neither hear nor reply.

I had one more question to ask Captain Nemo.

"Our weapons?" I asked, "our guns?"

"Guns! what for? Do not the mountaineers attack the bear dagger in hand, and is not steel surer than lead? Here is a stout blade; put it in your belt, and we will start."

I looked at my companions. They were armed like us, and more than this, Ned Land brandished an enormous harpoon which he had put into the boat before leaving the *Nautilus*.

Then, following the example of the captain, I let them put on my heavy copper helmet, and the air reservoirs were at once put in activity. Directly afterwards we were landed in about five feet of water upon a firm sand. Captain Nemo gave us a sign with his hand. We followed him, and going down a gentle slope, we disappeared under the waves.

There the ideas which had previously disturbed me left me. I became astonishingly calm. The ease of my movements increased my confidence, and the strangeness of the sight captivated my imagination.

The sun already sent a sufficient light under the water. The least object could be distinctly seen. After ten minutes' walk we were about sixteen feet under water, and the ground became nearly level.

On our steps, like snipe in a marsh, rose flights of curious fish of the class of manoptera, the subjects of which have no other fins than their tails. I recognised the Javanese, a veritable serpent ten nails long, with pale stomach, which one could easily mistake for the conger-eel were it not for the gold stripes on its flanks. In the class of stromatæ, of which the body is very flat and oval, I noticed parus, with brilliant colour, wearing their dorsal fin like a scythe, an edible fish, which, salted and dried, forms an excellent dish, known under the name of karawade; then tranquebars, belonging to the class of apsiphoroids, the body of which is covered with a scaly cuirasse, with eight longitudinal flaps.

The progressive elevation of the sun lighted up the mass of waters more and more. The ground gradually changed. To the fine sand succeeded a veritable embankment of rounded rocks, clothed with a carpet of molluscs and zoophytes. Amongst the specimens of these branches I noticed some placenæ, with thin and unequal shells, a sort of ostracion peculiar to the Red Sea and the Indian Ocean; some orange lucinæ with rounded shells, tubulated terebra, some of the purple persics that furnish the *Nautilus* with an admirable dye, rock fish four inches long that rose up under the waves like hands ready to seize you, turbites bristling with spikes, lingual hyantes, anatines, edible shells that are sold in the markets of Hindoostan, panopyres, slightly luminous; and lastly, admirable flabelliform occulines, magnificent fans that form one of the richest arborisations of these seas.

Amongst these living plants, and under thickets of hydrophytes, ran legions of clumsy articulates, particularly dented raninæ, the carapace of which forms a slightly-rounded triangle, virgues peculiar to this region, horrible parthenopes, the aspect of which is repulsive. An animal no less hideous that I met with several times was the enormous crab observed by Mr. Darwin, to which Nature has given the instinct and strength necessary to feed on coconut milk; they climb the trees on the shores, knock down the nuts, which are cracked by the fall, and open them with their powerful pincers. Here, under this clear water, the crab ran with unparalleled agility, whilst the turtles that frequent the coasts of Malabar moved slowly amidst the shaking rocks.

About seven o'clock we were at last on the bank of pintadines, where the pearl oysters breed by millions. These precious molluscs adhered to the rocks, strongly fastened to them by brown-coloured byssus that prevents them moving. In that these oysters are inferior to mussels, to which Nature has not refused all faculty of locomotion.

The pintadine *meleagrina*, the mother pearl, the valves of which are about equal, is a rounded thick shell, very rough on the outside. Some of these shells were foliated and marked with green bands that radiated from their summit. They belonged to the young oysters. The others with black and rough surfaces, ten years old and more, measured as much as five inches across.

Captain Nemo pointed out this prodigious accumulation of pintadines, and I understood that this mine was really inexhaustible, for the creative force of Nature is greater than the destructive instinct of man. Ned Land, faithful to this instinct, hastened to fill a net, which he carried at his side, with the finest of the molluscs.

But we could not stop. We were obliged to follow the captain, who appeared to choose paths known only to himself. The ground rose sensibly, and sometimes, when I raised my arm, it was above the surface of the sea. Then the level of the bank sank capriciously. Sometimes we rounded high rocks in the form of pyramids. In their dark fractures immense crustacea, reared up on their high paws like some war-machine, looked at us with fixed eyes, and under our feet crawled annelides and other curious creatures.

At this moment there opened before us a vast grotto, hollowed in a picturesque cluster of rocks, and carpeted with seaweed. At first this grotto appeared very dark to me. The solar rays seemed to die out there in successive gradations. The clear light became drowned light.

Captain Nemo entered. We followed him. My eyes soon became accustomed to the relative darkness. I saw the springing of the vault so capriciously distorted, supported by natural pillars, widely seated on their granitic bases, like the heavy columns of Tuscan architecture. Why did our incomprehensible guide lead us into the depths of this submarine crypt? I should soon know.

After descending a rather steep incline we were at the bottom of a sort of circular well. There Captain Nemo stopped and pointed to an object we had not perceived before.

It was an oyster of extraordinary dimensions, a gigantic tridacne, a font that would have contained a lake of holy water, a vase more than two yards across, and consequently larger than the one in the saloon of the *Nautilus*.

I approached this unparalleled mollusc. It was adhering by its byssus to a granite slab, and there it was developing itself in isolation amidst the calm waters of the grotto. I estimated the weight of this tridacne at 600lbs. Now such an oyster contains 30lbs. of meat, and it would take the stomach of a Gargantua to absorb some dozens.

Captain Nemo evidently knew of the existence of this bivalve. It was not the first visit he had paid to it, and I thought that in conducting us to that place he merely wished to show us a natural curiosity. I was mistaken. Captain Nemo had an interest in seeing the actual condition of this tridacne.

The two valves of the mollusc were half-open. The captain went up to them and put his dagger between them to prevent them shutting, then with his hand he raised the membranous tunic, fringed at the border, that formed the animal's mantle.

There, amidst its foliated pleats, I saw a pearl as large as a coconut. Its globular form, perfect limpidity, and admirable water made it a jewel of inestimable price. Carried away by curiosity, I stretched out my hand to take it, weigh it, feel it. But the captain stopped me, made a sign in the negative, and

221

drawing back his dagger by a rapid movement, he let the two valves fall together.

I then understood the purpose of Captain Nemo. By leaving this pearl wrapped up in the mantle of the tridacne he allowed it to grow insensibly. With each year the secretion of the mollusc added fresh concentric layers to it. The captain alone knew of this grotto where this admirable fruit of Nature was ripening; he alone was raising it, thus to speak, in order one day to transport it to his precious museum. Perhaps even, following the example of the Chinese and Indians, he had determined the production of this pearl by introducing under the folds of the mollusc some piece of glass and metal which was gradually being covered with the pearly matter. In any case, comparing this pearl with those I already knew, and those that shone in the captain's collection, I estimated its value at ten millions of francs at least. It was a superb natural curiosity, and not a jewel *de luxe*, for I do not know what feminine ears could have supported it.

The visit to the opulent tridacne was over. Captain Nemo left the grotto, and we went up on to the bank of pintadines again, amidst the clear waters that were not yet troubled by the work of the divers.

We walked separately, stopping or going on according to our pleasure. For my own part I had forgotten the dangers that my imagination had so ridiculously exaggerated. The bottom of the sea sensibly approached its surface, and soon my head passed above the oceanic level. Conseil joined me, and placing his glass plate next to mine, gave me a friendly salutation with his eyes. But this elevated plateau was only some yards long, and we were soon back again in our own element. I think I have now the right of calling it thus.

Ten minutes afterwards Captain Nemo suddenly stopped. I thought he was making a halt before going back. But no; with a gesture he ordered us to squat down near him on a large confractuosity. He was pointing to a point of the liquid mass, and I looked attentively.

At five yards from me a shade appeared and bent to the ground. The uneasy idea of sharks came into my mind. But I was mistaken, and this time we had not to do with any oceanic monster. It was a man, a living man, a black Indian, a diver, a poor fellow, no doubt, come to glean before the harvest. I perceived the bottom of his canoe anchored at some feet above his head. He plunged and went up again successively. A stone cut in the form of a sugar-loaf which he had tied to his foot, whilst a cord fastened him to the boat, made him descend more rapidly to the bottom. That was all his stock-in-trade. Arrived on the ground by about three fathoms' depth he threw himself on his knees and filled his bag with pintadines picked up at random. Then he went up again, emptied his bag, put on his stone again, and recommenced the operation that only lasted thirty seconds.

The diver did not see us. The shadow of the rock hid us from him. And, besides, how could a poor Indian ever suppose that men, beings like him, were there under the water, watching his movements, and losing no detail of his work?

He went up and plunged again several times. He did not bring up more than ten pintadines at each plunge, for he was obliged to tear them from the bank to which they were fastened by their strong byssus. And how many of these oysters for which he risked his life were destitute of pearls!

I watched him with profound attention. His work was done regularly, and for half an hour no danger seemed to threaten him. I was, therefore, getting familiar with the spectacle of this interesting fishery, when, all at once, at the moment the Indian was kneeling on the ground, I saw him make a movement of terror, get up, and spring to remount to the surface of the waves.

I understood his fear. A gigantic shadow appeared above the unfortunate plunger. It was an enormous shark advancing diagonally, with eyes on fire and open jaws. I was mute with terror, incapable of making a movement.

The voracious animal, with a vigorous stroke of his fin, was springing towards the Indian, who threw himself on one side and avoided the bite of the shark, but not the stroke of his tail, for that tail, striking him on the chest, stretched him on the ground.

This scene had hardly lasted some seconds. The shark returned to the charge, and turning on his back, it was prepared to cut the Indian in two, when I felt Captain Nemo, who was near me, suddenly rise. Then, his dagger in hand, he walked straight up to the monster, ready for a hand-to-hand struggle with him.

The shark, at the moment he was going to nab the unfortunate diver, perceived his fresh adversary, and going over on to its stomach again, directed itself rapidly towards him.

I still see the attitude of Captain Nemo. Thrown backwards, he was waiting with admirable *sang-froid* the formidable shark; when it threw itself upon him he threw himself on one side with prodigious agility, avoided the shock, and thrust his dagger into its stomach. But that was not the end. A terrible combat took place.

The shark reddened, so to speak. The blood flowed in streams from its wounds. The sea was dyed red, and across this opaque liquid I saw no more until it cleared a little, and I perceived the audacious captain holding on to one of the animal's fins, struggling hand-to-hand with the monster, belabouring its body with dagger thrusts without being able to reach the heart, where blows are mortal. The shark in the struggle made such a commotion in the water that the eddies threatened to overthrow me.

I wanted to run to the captain's aid. But, nailed down by horror, I could not move.

I looked on with haggard eyes. I saw the phases of the struggle change. The captain fell on the ground, overthrown by the enormous mass that was bearing him down. Then the jaws of the shark opened inordinately, and all would have been over for the captain, if, prompt as thought, harpoon in hand, Ned Land, rushing towards the shark, had not struck it with its terrible point. The waves became impregnated with a mass of blood. They were agitated by the movements of the shark that beat them with indescribable fury. Ned Land had not missed his aim. It was the death-rattle of the monster. Struck in the heart, it struggled in fearful spasms, the rebound of which knocked over Conseil.

In the meantime Ned Land had set free the captain, who rose unhurt, went straight to the Indian, quickly cut the cord which fastened him to the stone, took him in his arms, and with a vigorous kick, he went up to the surface of the sea. We all three followed him, and in a short time, miraculously saved, we reached the diver's boat.

Captain Nemo's first care was to recall the unfortunate man to life. I did not know if he would succeed. I hoped so, for the immersion of the poor fellow had not been long. But the blow from the shark's tail might have killed him. Happily, under the vigorous friction of Conseil and the captain, I saw the drowned man gradually recover his senses. He opened his eyes. What must have been his surprise, terror even, at seeing four large brass heads leaning over him! And, above all, what must he have thought when Captain Nemo, drawing from a pocket in his garment a bag of pearls, put it into his hand! This magnificent gift from the man of the sea to the poor Indian of Ceylon was accepted by him with a trembling hand. His frightened eyes showed that he did not know to what superhuman beings he owed at the same time his fortune and his life.

At a sign from the captain we went back to the bank of pintadines, and following the road we had already come along, half-an-hour's walking brought us to the anchor that fastened the boat of the *Nautilus* to the ground.

Once embarked, we each, with the help of the sailors, took off our heavy brass carapaces.

Captain Nemo's first word was for the Canadian.

"Thank you, Land," he said.

"It was by way of retaliation, captain," answered Ned Land. "I owed it you."

A pale smile glided over the captain's lips, and that was all.

"To the *Nautilus*," he said.

The boat flew over the waves. Some minutes later we met with the floating body of the shark.

By the black colour that marked the extremity of its fins I recognised the terrible melanopter of the Indian seas, of the species of sharks properly so called. Its length was more than twenty-five feet; its enormous mouth took up a third of its body. It was an adult; that was seen by its six rows of teeth placed in an isosceles triangle on the upper jaw.

Conseil looked at it with quite a scientific interest, and I am sure that he put it in the cartilaginous class, order of chondropterygians with fixed gills, family of selacians, and genus of sharks.

While I was contemplating the inert mass, a dozen of these voracious melanoptera appeared all at once round the boat; but, without taking any notice of us, they threw themselves on the carcass and disputed the pieces.

At half-past eight we were back on board the *Nautilus*.

Then I began to reflect on the incidents of our excursion to the Manaar Bank. Two observations naturally resulted from it. One was upon the unparalleled audacity of Captain Nemo, the other was his devoting his own life to saving a human being, one of the representatives of that race he was flying from under the seas. Whatever he might say, that man had not succeeded in entirely killing his own heart.

When I said as much to him, he answered me in a slightly moved tone—

"That Indian, professor, is an inhabitant of an oppressed country, and I am, and until my last breath shall be, the same."

CHAPTER IV

The Red Sea

During the day of the 29th of January the Island of Ceylon disappeared upon the horizon, and the *Nautilus,* at a speed of twenty miles an hour, glided amongst that labyrinth of canals that separate the Maldives from the Laccadives. It even sailed close to Kiltan Island, a land of madreporic origin, discovered by Vasco de Gama in 1499, and one of the nineteen principal islands of that archipelago of the Laccadives, situated between 10° and 14° 30' north lat. and 50° 72' east long.

We had then made 16,220 miles since our starting-point in the seas of Japan.

The next day—the 30th of January—when the *Nautilus* went up to the surface of the ocean, there was no longer any land in sight. It was going N.N.W., and directing its course towards that Sea of Oman, situated between Arabia and the Indian peninsula, into which the Persian Gulf flows.

It was evidently without egress. Where was Captain Nemo taking us? I could not tell. That did not satisfy the Canadian. He asked me that day where we were going.

"We are going where the captain pleases, Ned."

"That can't be far," answered the Canadian. "The Persian Gulf has no outlet, and if we enter it we shall soon have to come back."

"Well, we must, Mr. Land; and if, after the Persian Gulf, the *Nautilus* wishes to visit the Red Sea, the straits of Bab-el-Mandeb are there for it to go through."

"I need not inform you, sir," answered Ned Land, "that the Red Sea is as much shut up as the gulf, seeing the Isthmus of Suez has not yet been pierced; and even if it were, a vessel as mysterious as ours would not venture into its canals cut up with locks. So the Red Sea is not yet the road to Europe."

"I did not say that we were going to Europe."

"What do you suppose, then?"

"I suppose that after visiting the curious shores of Egypt and Arabia, the *Nautilus* will go down the Indian Ocean again, perhaps through the Mozambique Channel, perhaps by the Comoro Islands, so as to reach the Cape of Good Hope."

"And once at the Cape of Good Hope, what then?" asked the Canadian, singularly persistent.

"Well, we shall then go into the Atlantic, which we don't know yet. Why, Ned, are you tired, then, of your voyage under the sea? Are you wearied of the incessantly varied spectacle of submarine marvels? For my own part I should be extremely sorry to see the end of this voyage it is given to so few men to make."

"But do you know, M. Aronnax, that we shall soon have been three months imprisoned on board this *Nautilus*?"

"No, Ned, I don't know, I don't want to know, and I neither count the days nor hours."

"But how is it to end?"

"The end will come in its own good time. Besides, we can't do anything, and we are arguing uselessly. If you came to me and said, 'There is now a chance of escape,' I would discuss it with you. But such is not the case, and to tell you the truth, I do not believe Captain Nemo ever ventures into European seas."

By this short dialogue it will be seen that I was so fond of the *Nautilus* that I rowed in the same boat as its commander.

As to Ned Land, he ended the conversation by these words in a sort of monologue:—

"All that is very well, but in my opinion where compulsion begins pleasure ends."

For four days, until the 3rd of February, the *Nautilus* was in the Gulf of Oman, at different depths and various speed. It seemed to move about at random, as if hesitating upon what route to follow, but it never crossed the tropic of Cancer.

Upon leaving this sea we saw for an instant Muscat, the most important town of the country of Oman. I admired its strange aspect in the midst of the black rocks that surround it, and that show up its white houses and fortresses. I perceived the round domes of its mosques, the elegant point of its minarets, its fresh and verdant terraces. But it was only a vision, and the *Nautilus* soon sank under the sombre waves of its shores.

Then it coasted, at a distance of six miles, the Arabic coasts of Mahrah and Hadramaut, and its undulating line of mountains, relieved by ancient runs. On the 5th of February we at last entered the Gulf of Aden, a veritable funnel put into the bottle neck of Bab-el-Mandeb, which pours the Indian waters into the Red Sea.

On the 6th of February the *Nautilus* was floating in sight of Aden, perched on a promontory which a narrow isthmus joins to the continent, a sort of inaccessible Gibraltar that the English fortified afresh after taking it in 1839. I caught sight of the rich octagon minarets of that town, which was formerly the richest and most commercial place on that coast, if we are to believe the historian Edrisi.

I thought that when once Captain Nemo had reached that point he would turn back again; but I was mistaken, and, to my great surprise, he did nothing of the kind.

The next day, the 7th of February, we entered the Straits of Bab-el-Mandeb, the name of which means "Gate of Tears" in Arabic. It is twenty miles wide, and only thirty long, and for the *Nautilus*, at full speed, it was hardly the business of an hour. But I saw nothing, not even the Island of Perim, with which the British Government has fortified the position of Aden. Too many English or French steamers of the lines between Suez and Bombay, Calcutta, Melbourne, Bourbon, Mauritius, ploughed the narrow passage for the *Nautilus* to venture to show itself. So it kept prudently at a good depth. At last, at noon, we were ploughing the waves of the Red Sea.

The Red Sea, the celebrated lake of Biblical traditions, that rains scarcely refresh, that no important river waters, that an excessive evaporation pumps incessantly, and that loses each year a slice of liquid a yard and a half deep; a singular gulf which, if inclosed like a lake, would perhaps be entirely dried up; inferior in that to its neighbours the Caspian or

Asphaltite, the level of which has only lowered to the point where their evaporation precisely equals the quantity of water received by them.

This Red Sea is only 600 kilometers long by 240 wide. In the time of the Ptolemies and the Roman Emperors it was the great commercial artery of the world, and the piercing of the isthmus will one day give back to it its ancient importance, which the railways of Suez have already restored in part.

I did not even seek to understand the caprice of Captain Nemo that took us into this gulf. But I unfeignedly approved of the *Nautilus* entering it. It went at an average speed, sometimes keeping on the surface, sometimes plunging to avoid some ship. I could thus observe the inside and outside of this curious sea.

On the 8th of February, at early dawn, Mocha appeared, a town now in ruins, the walls of which fall even at the noise of cannon, and which shelter here and there verdant date-trees. It was formerly an important city, inclosing 6 public markets, 26 mosques, and to which its walls, defended by 14 forts, made a belt of 3 kilometers.

Then the *Nautilus* went nearer the African shores, where the depth of the sea is greater. There, in water of crystal-like limpidity, through the open panels we were allowed to contemplate admirable bushes of brilliant coral, and vast rocks clothed with a splendid fur of seaweeds and fucus.

What an indescribable spectacle! and what a variety of sites and landscapes did the volcanic islets and reefs make on the Lybian coast! But it was on the eastern banks that the arborisations appeared in all their beauty. It was on the coasts of Tehama, for there not only did terraces of zoophytes flower below the surface of the waves, but they formed picturesque banks for ten fathoms above, more capricious, though less highly coloured, than those that the humid vitality of the water kept so fresh.

What charming hours I passed thus at the saloon windows! What new specimens of submarine flora and fauna I admired in the brilliant light of our electric lantern! Agariciform fungi, slate-coloured actinies, amongst others the *thalassianthus aster*, rubipores like flutes, only waiting for the breath of the god Pan, shells peculiar to that sea which establish themselves in madreporic excavations, the base of which is turned in a short spiral, and lastly, a thousand specimens of a polypier that I had not observed before, the common sponge.

The class of spongiaires, the first group of polypiers, is precisely created by this curious product, the utility of which is incontestable. Sponge is not a vegetable, as some naturalists still say, but an animal of the last order, a polypier inferior to coral. Its animality is not doubtful, and we may admit the opinion of the ancients, who looked upon it as an intermediary between plants and animals. I ought to say, however, that naturalists have not agreed about the organisation of the sponge. According to some it is a polypier, and to others, such as Milne-Edwards, it is a solitary and unique individual.

The class of spongiaires contains about three hundred species, which are met with in many seas, and even in certain rivers, where they have received the name of "fluviatiles." But the waters they prefer are those of the Mediterranean, the Grecian Archipelago, the coasts of Syria and the Red Sea. There are produced and grow the fine soft sponges that are sometimes worth £5, the blonde Syrian sponge, the hard Barbary sponge, &c. But as I could not hope to study these zoophytes in the Levant, from which we were separated by the impassable Isthmus of Suez, I contented myself with observing them in the Red Sea.

I therefore called Conseil, whilst the *Nautilus*, at an average depth of five fathoms, was slowly coasting the lovely rocks of the Eastern coast.

There grew sponges of all forms, pedicular, foliated, globular, digitated. They exactly justified the names of basket, chalice, spindle, elk-horn, lion's-foot, peacock's-tail, Neptune's-glove, which divers, more poetic than *savants*, have given them. From their fibrous tissue, coated with a half-fluid gelatinous substance, little streams of water incessantly escaped, which, after having carried life into each cell, were expulsed from them by a contractile movement. This substance disappears after the death of the polypus, and putrefies, whilst it gives off ammonia. All that then remains are the gelatinous fibres of which the domestic sponge is composed, that become reddish, and are used for different purposes, according to its degree of elasticity, permeability, or resistance of maceration.

These polypiers adhere to the rocks, to the shells of molluscs, and even to the stalks of hydrophytes. They grow on the smallest confractuosities, some spreading out, others standing up, or hanging like coralline excrescences. I taught Conseil that these sponges were taken in two ways, by drags and by the hand. This latter method, that necessitates the employment of divers, is preferable, because by respecting the tissue of the polypier it leaves it superior value.

The other zoophytes that swarmed near the sponges consisted principally of medusæ of a very elegant species; the molluscs were represented by varieties of calmars, which, according to d'Orbigny, are special to the Red Sea, and the reptiles by the tortoise *virgata*, belonging to the genus of the cheloniæ, which furnished wholesome and delicate food for our table.

As to fish, they were numerous and often remarkable. Those that the nets of the *Nautilus* more frequently brought up were rays of a red-brick colour and oval form, with unequal blue spots on their bodies, recognisable by their double-dented spikes; silver-backed carnaks, pastenacks with dotted tails, and bockats, vast mantles two yards long, that undulated in the water; aodons, quite destitute of teeth, a sort of cartilagine like a dog-fish, dromedary-ostracions, the hump of which is terminated by a bent dart a foot and a half long; ophids, veritable sea-eels with silver tails, blue backs, brown pectorals with grey borders; fratoles, a species of stromatæ, zebred with narrow golden stripes, and decorated with the three colours of France; superb caranx, decorated with seven blue-black transversal bands, blue and yellow fins, and gold and silver scales; centropods, auriflamme mullets with yellow heads, scares, labres, balisters, gobies, &c., and a thousand other fish common to the seas we had already come through.

On the 9th of February the *Nautilus* was floating in that wide part of the Red Sea that is comprised between Souakin on the West Coast and Guonfodah on the East Coast, on a diameter of one hundred and ninety miles.

That day, at noon, after the position was taken, Captain Nemo came up on to the platform where I happened to be. I promised myself not to let him go down again without having at least made an attempt to ascertain his ulterior projects. He came to me as soon as he saw me, gracefully offered me a cigar, and said—

"Well, professor, does this Red Sea please you? Have you sufficiently observed the marvels it covers, its fish, zoophytes, beds of sponge, and forests of coral? Have you caught sight of the towns on its shores?"

"Yes, captain," I answered, "and the *Nautilus* has helped much in the study. Ah, it is an intelligent vessel!"

"Yes, sir, intelligent, audacious, and invulnerable! It neither dreads the terrible tempests of the Red Sea, nor its currents, nor its reefs."

"In fact," said I, "this sea is considered one of the worst, and, if I am not mistaken, its renown in ancient history was detestable."

"Detestable, M. Aronnax? Greek and Latin historians do not speak in its praise, and Strabo says it is particularly difficult at the season of the Etesian winds and the rainy season. The Arab Edrisi, who depicts it under the name of the Colzoum Golf, relates that ships perished in great numbers on its sand-banks, and that no one dare venture to sail on it at night. He says it is a sea subject to frightful tempests, strewn with inhospitable islands, and that 'offers nothing good,' either in its depths or on its surface. Such also is the opinion of Arrian, Agath-archides, and Artemidorus."

"It is easy to see," I replied, "that these historians have not been on board the *Nautilus*."

"Yes," answered the captain, smiling, "and in that respect the moderns are not better off than the ancients. It took many centuries to find out the mechanical power of steam! Who knows if in a hundred years there will be a second *Nautilus*? Progress is slow, M. Aronnax!"

"That is true," I answered; "our vessel is a century, perhaps several, in advance of its epoch. What a misfortune it is that such a secret must die with its inventor!"

Captain Nemo did not answer. After a short silence—

"You were speaking," said he, "of the opinion of ancient historians on the dangers of navigating the Red Sea?"

"That is true," I answered, "but were not their fears exaggerated?"

"Yes and no, M. Aronnax," answered Captain Nemo, who seemed to know the Red Sea thoroughly. "What is no longer dangerous for a modern vessel, well rigged, solidly built, master of its direction, thanks to obedient steam, offered perils of all sorts to ancient boats. We must picture to ourselves those first navigators adventuring in their barks, made of planks tied together with palm cords calked with resin, and lubricated with the fat of dog-fish. They had not even the instruments necessary to take their bearings, and they went by currents which they knew very little of. In such conditions shipwrecks were necessarily numerous. But in our own time the steamers that run between Suez and the South Seas have nothing to fear from the dangers of this gulf, in spite of contrary monsoons. Their captains and passengers do not prepare for their departure by propitiatory sacrifices, and, on their return, they no longer go ornamented with garlands and gold bandelettes to thank the gods in a neighbouring temple."

"I acknowledge," said I, "that steam seems to have killed

gratitude in the heart of seamen. But, captain, as you seem to have specially studies this sea, can you tell me the origin of its name?"

"There exist numerous explanations of it, M. Aronnax. Should you like to know the opinion of a chronicler of the fourteenth century?"

"Yes, I should."

"This fantastic man pretends that its name was given after the passage of the Israelites, when Pharaoh perished in the waves that closed over again at the voice of Moses:

"En signe de cette merveille
Devint la mer rouge et vermeille,
Non puis ne surent la nommer,
Autrement que la rouge mer."

"That is a poet's explanation, Captain Nemo," I replied, "but I cannot be content with that. I must ask for your personal opinion."

"This is it. According to me, M. Aronnax, the Red Sea is a translation of the Hebrew word 'Edrom,' and the ancients called it so from the peculiar colouring of its waters."

"But at present I have only seen limpid waves of no particular shade."

"Doubtless; but as you go towards the bottom of the gulf you will remark that singular appearance. I remember seeing Tor Bay as red as blood."

"And you attribute that colour to the presence of micro-scopical alga?"

"Yes. It is a mucilaginous purple matter produced by a sorry plantlet known under the name of *trichodesmies*, forty thousand of which would only fill the .03937 of a square inch. Perhaps you will meet with some when we are at Tor."

"Then, Captain Nemo, it is not the first time you have been in the Red Sea on board the *Nautilus*?"

"No, sir."

"Then as you spoke just now of the passage of the Israelites and the catastrophe of the Egyptians, may I ask if you have found any traces of that great historical fact under its waters?"

"No, professor, and that for an excellent reason."

"What reason?"

"That the very spot where Moses and all his people passed over is now so choked up with sand that camels can hardly bathe their legs there. You understand that my *Nautilus* would not find enough water there."

"Where is the spot?" I asked.

"It is situated a little above Suez, in that arm that used to form a deep estuary when the Red Sea extended to the Dead Sea. Now, whether this passage was miraculous or no, the Israelites did pass over it to reach the Promised Land, and Pharaoh's army perished precisely in the same spot. I think that if excavations were made in the sand many arms and instruments of Egyptian origin would be discovered."

"It is evident," I answered, "and it is to be hoped for the sake of archæologists that these excavations will be made sooner or later, when new towns will be built on that isthmus, after the Suez Canal has been pierced—a canal very useless to such a vessel as the *Nautilus*!"

"Doubtless, but useful to the entire world," said Captain Nemo. "The ancients well understood the utility for their commerce of establishing a communication between the Red Sea and the Mediterranean, but they did not dream of making a direct canal, and they took the Nile as an intermediary. It is very probable that the canal which joined the Nile to the Red Sea was begun under Sesostris. It is certain that 615 B.C. Necos undertook the making of a canal, fed by the waters of the Nile, across the plain of Egypt opposite Arabia. This canal took four days to ascend, and its width was so great that two triremes could pass abreast. It was continued by Darius, son of Hystaspes, and probably finished by Ptolemy II. Strabo saw it used for navigation, but the weakness of its slope between the point it started from, near Bubaste and the Red Sea, only made it navigable for some

236

months of the year. This canal was used for commerce until the century of the Antonines; abandoned, choked up with sand, then re-established by the order of the Caliph Omar, it was definitely filled up in 761 or 762 by the Caliph Al-Mansor, who wished to prevent provisions reaching Mohammed-ben-Abdoallah, who had revolted against him. During the expedition of Egypt your General Bonaparte found traces of this work in the desert of Suez, and, overtaken by the tide, he nearly perished a few hours before regaining Hadjaroth, in the very place where Moses had encamped 3,300 years before him."

"Well, captain, that which the ancients did not dare to undertake, the junction between the two seas that will abridge by thousands of miles the route from Cadiz to the Indies, M. Lesseps has done, and, before long, he will have changed Africa into an immense island."

"Yes, M. Aronnax, and you have the right to be proud of your countryman. He is one of the men that honour a nation more than the greatest captains! He began like so many others, by rebuffs and vexations, but he has triumphed, for he has genius and strength of will. And it is sad to think that what ought to have been an international work that would have sufficed to make a reign illustrious only succeeded through the energy of one man. Then all honour to M. de Lesseps!"

"Yes, honour to the great citizen!" I replied, quite surprised at the accent with which Captain Nemo had just spoken.

"Unfortunately," he resumed, "I cannot take you through the Suez Canal, but you will be able to see the long piers of Port Saïd the day after tomorrow when we shall be in the Mediterranean."

"In the Mediterranean?" I cried.

"Yes, professor. Does that astonish you?"

"What astonishes me is that we shall be there they day after tomorrow."

"Really?"

"Yes, captain, although I ought to be accustomed to being astonished at nothing on board your vessel."

"But why are you surprised now?"

"At the frightful speed your *Nautilus* must reach to find itself tomorrow in full Mediterranean, having made the tour of Africa and doubled the Cape of Good Hope."

"And who told you it would make the tour of Africa, professor? Who spoke of doubling the Cape of Good Hope?"

"Unless the *Nautilus* can move along *terra firma* and passes over the isthmus——"

"Or underneath, M. Aronnax."

"Underneath?"

"Certainly," answered Captain Nemo tranquilly. "It is a long time since Nature has done under that tongue of land what men are now doing on its surface."

"What! there exists a passage!"

"Yes, a subterranean passage that I have named Abraham Tunnel. It begins above Suez and ends in the Gulf of Pelusium."

"But the isthmus is only formed of moving sand."

"To a certain depth. But at a depth of fifty yards only there is a stratum of rock."

"And did you discover that passage by accident?" I asked, more and more surprised.

"By accident and reasoning, professor, and by reasoning more than by accident."

"Captain, I hear you, but my ear resists what it hears."

"Ah, sir! *Aures habent et non audient* belongs to all time. Not only does this passage exist, but I have passed by it several times. But for that I should not have adventured today into the impassable Red Sea."

"Would it be indiscreet to ask you how you discovered this tunnel?"

"Sir," answered the captain, "there can be no secret between people who are never to leave each other again."

I paid no attention to the insinuation, and awaited Captain Nemo's communication.

"Professor," said he, "it was a naturalist's reasoning that led me to discover this passage, which I alone know about. I had noticed that in the Red Sea and the Mediterranean there existed a certain number of fish of absolutely identical species—ophidia, fiatoles, girelles, exocœti. Certain of this fact, I asked myself if there existed no communication between the two seas. If one did exist, the subterranean current must necessarily flow from the Red Sea to the Mediterranean on account of the different levels. I therefore took a great number of fish in the neighbourhood of Suez. I put a brass ring on their tails, and threw them back into the sea. A few months later, on the coast of Syria, I again took some specimens of my fish with their tell-tale ornaments. The communication between the two seas was then demonstrated. I looked for it with my *Nautilus*, discovered it, ventured into it, and before long, professor, you too will have been through my Arabic tunnel."

CHAPTER V

The Arabian Tunnel

That day I repeated to Conseil and Ned Land the part of this conversation in which they were directly interested. When I told them that in two days' time we should be in the midst of the waters of the Mediterranean, Conseil clapped his hands, but the Canadian shrugged his shoulders.

"A submarine tunnel!" he cried; "a communication between the two seas! Who ever heard of such a thing?"

"Friend Ned," answered Conseil, "had you ever heard of such a thing as the *Nautilus*? No. Yet it exists. So don't shrug your shoulders so easily, and laugh at things because you have never heard of them before."

"We shall see," answered Ned Land, shaking his head. "After all, I want to believe in this captain's passage, and Heaven grant that it may take us into the Mediterranean!"

The same evening, in 21° 30' north latitude, the *Nautilus*, floating on the surface of the sea, approached the Arabian coast I perceived Djeddah, the important trading-place of Egypt, Syria, Turkey, and India. I distinguished its buildings pretty clearly, the ships anchored along its quays, and those that their draught forced to anchor in the roadstead. The sun, low on the horizon, fell full upon the houses of the town, and showed off their whiteness. Outside, cabins of wood or reeds indicated the quarter inhabited by the Bedouins.

Soon Djeddah disappeared in the shades of evening, and the *Nautilus* sank under the slightly phosphorescent waters.

The next day, the 10th of February, several ships appeared to windward. The *Nautilus* went on with her submarine navigation; but at noon, when her bearings were taken, the sea being deserted, she went up to the sea level.

Accompanied by Ned and Conseil, I went to sit down on the platform. The coast on the east was outlined in a damp fog.

Leaning on the sides of the vessel, we were talking about

various things, when Ned Land, pointing towards a point in the sea, said—

"Do you see anything there, professor?"

"No, Ned," I replied; "but my eyes are not yours, you know."

"Look well," said Land, "over there on the starboard beam, about the height of the lantern. Don't you see a mass that moves?"

"Yes," said I, after an attentive examination. "I perceive a long black body on the surface of the water."

"Another *Nautilus*?" said Conseil.

"No," answered the Canadian, "but I am much mistaken if it is not some marine animal."

"Are there any whales in the Red Sea?" asked Conseil.

"Yes, my boy," I answered. "They are met with here sometimes."

"It is not a whale," said Ned Land, who did not lose sight of the object signalled. "Whales and I are old acquaintances, and I could not be mistaken in their gait."

"Wait," said Conseil. "The *Nautilus* is going towards it, and before long we shall know what to think about it."

The long black object was soon not a mile from us. It looked like a great rock deposited in the open sea. What was it? I could not yet determine.

"Ah, it is moving! it plunges!" cried Ned Land. "What animal can it be? It has not even a forked tail like whales or cachalots, and its fins look like stumps."

"Then——" I began.

"It is on its back now," resumed the Canadian, "and it raises its udders in the air!"

"It's a syren," cried Conseil, "a veritable syren!"

The name of syren set me on its track, and I understood that this animal belonged to the order of marine animals of which fable has made syrens—half women, half fishes.

"No," said I to Conseil, "it is not a syren, but a curious animal of which there only remain a few specimens in the Red Sea. It is a dugong."

"Order of syrenians, group of pisciforms, sub-class of mono-delphians, class of mammalia, branch of vertebrates," answered Conseil.

And when Conseil had spoken thus there was nothing more to be said.

In the meantime Ned Land was still looking. His eyes shone covetously at the sight of this animal. His hand seemed ready to harpoon it. Anyone would have thought he was awaiting the moment to throw himself into the sea to attack it in its own element.

"Oh, sir!" he said in a voice trembling with emotion, "I have never killed any of 'that.'"

All the harpooner was in that word.

At that instant Captain Nemo appeared on the platform. He perceived the dugong, understood the Canadian's attitude, and said to him—

"If you held a harpoon, Mr. Land, would it not burn your hand?"

"That it would!"

"And you would not be sorry to take up your old trade again for one day, and add that cetacean to the list of those you have already struck?"

"No, I shouldn't be sorry."

"Well, you may try."

"Thank you, sir," answered Ned Land, with eyes aflame.

"Only," continued the captain, "I advise you, in your own interest, not to miss that animal."

"Is the dugong dangerous to attack?" I asked, in spite of the Canadian's contemptuous shrug.

"Yes, sometimes," answered the captain. "That animal turns on its assailants and wrecks their boats. But for Ned Land that danger is not to be feared. His glance is prompt, his hand sure. If I recommend him not to miss the dugong it is because it is justly considered fine game, and I know that Ned Land likes good meat."

"Ah!" said the Canadian, "so that animal gives himself the luxury of being good to eat?"

"Yes, Mr. Land. Its flesh, a veritable meat, is much esteemed, and in all Malasia it is kept for princes' tables. This animal is so much hunted, that, like the lamantin, or sea-cow, it becomes more and more rare."

"Then, sir captain," said Conseil seriously, "if this one should be the last of its race, ought it not, in the interest of science, to be spared?"

"Perhaps," replied the Canadian; "but in the interest of our table it is better to pursue it."

"Do it, then, Mr. Land," answered Captain Nemo.

At that moment seven of the crew, mute and impassible as usual, came upon the platform. One was carrying a harpoon and a line similar to those employed by whale-fishers. The deck was taken off the boat, which was lifted from its niche and thrown into the sea. Six rowers took their places on the seats, and the coxswain at the helm. Ned, Conseil, and I seated ourselves aft.

"Are you not coming, captain?" I asked.

"No, sir, but I wish you much success."

The boat, rowed vigorously, went rapidly towards the dugong, which was then floating about two miles from the *Nautilus*.

When it arrived within a few cables' length of the cetacean it slackened speed, and the oars dipped noiselessly into the tranquil waters. Ned Land, harpoon in hand, went and stood at the prow. The whale-harpoon is generally fastened to a very long cord that rapidly unwinds as the wounded animal drags it away. But here the cord was not more than ten cables long, and its extremity only was fastened to a little barrel to float on the surface and indicate the course of the dugong under water.

I rose and distinctly observed the Canadian's adversary. The dugong was very much like a lamantin. Its oblong body terminated in a much-elongated tail, and its lateral fins by veritable claws. The difference between it and the lamantin was that its upper jaw was armed with two long and pointed teeth that formed divergent defences on either side.

The dugong that Ned Land was preparing to attack was of colossal dimensions, not less than eight yards long. It was not moving, and seemed to be sleeping on the surface of the water, a circumstance that made its capture easier.

The boat prudently approached to within three cables' length of the animal. The oars remained suspended on their rowlocks. I half rose. Ned Land, his body thrown slightly backward, brandished his harpoon in his experienced hand.

Suddenly a hissing sound was heard, and the dugong disappeared. The harpoon, launched with force, had doubtless only struck the water.

"The devil!" cried the Canadian in a rage. "I have missed it!"

"No," I said, "the animal is wounded; there is its blood, but your instrument did not remain in its body."

"My harpoon! my harpoon!" cried Ned Land.

The sailors rowed vigorously, and the coxswain guided the boat towards the floating barrel. When the harpoon was fished up again the boat began to pursue the animal.

The dugong came up to the surface of the sea to breathe from time to time. Its wound had not weakened it, for it moved along with extreme rapidity. The boat, rowed by vigorous arms, flew on its track. Several times it approached to within a few cables, and the Canadian made ready to strike; but the dugong escaped by a rapid plunge, and it was impossible to reach it.

Ned Land's anger may be imagined. He launched the most energetic oaths in the English language at the animal.

They pursued it thus without ceasing for an hour, and I was beginning to believe that it would be very difficult to catch it, when the animal was taken with an unfortunate idea of vengeance that it was destined to repent. He turned upon the boat to assail it in return.

This manœuvre did not escape the Canadian.

"Attention!" said he.

The coxswain pronounced several words in his strange language, and he was doubtless warning his men to keep on their guard.

The dugong stopped within twenty feet of the boat, roughly took in air with his vast nostrils, situated, not at the extremity, but at the upper part of its snout; then, taking a spring, he rushed upon us.

The boat could not avoid the shock; half overturned, it embarked one or two tons of water we were obliged to empty; but, thanks to the skill of the coxswain, it righted itself. Ned Land, clinging to the bows, belaboured the gigantic animal with blows from his harpoon; the creature's teeth were buried in the gunwale, and it lifted the whole thing out of the water like a lion a roebuck. We were thrown over one another, and I hardly know how the adventure would have ended had not the Canadian, still enraged with the beast, at last struck it in the heart. I heard its teeth grind on the iron plate, and the dugong disappeared, dragging the harpoon with it. But the barrel soon returned to the surface, and a few instants afterwards the body of the animal appeared, turned over on its back. The boat went up to it, took it in tow, and rowed towards the *Nautilus*.

They were obliged to use tackle of enormous strength to hoist up the dugong on to the platform. It weighed 10,000lbs. They cut it up under the eyes of the Canadian, who wanted to follow all the details of the operation. The same day the steward served me at dinner with some slices of the flesh skilfully prepared by the ship's cook. I thought it excellent, superior to veal, if not to beef.

The next day, the 11th of February, the pantry of the *Nautilus* was enriched by some more delicate game. A flight of sea-swallows swooped down on the *Nautilus*. It was a species of *sterna nilotica*, peculiar to Egypt, the beak of which is black, the head grey and speckled, the eye surrounded with white dots, the back, wings, and tail grey, the stomach and throat white, the legs red. They also took some dozens of Nile ducks, wild birds of delicious flavour, the neck and back of which are white, with black spots.

The speed of the *Nautilus* was then moderate. I noticed that the Red Sea became less and less salt as we drew nearer to Suez.

About 5 p.m. we sighted the Cape of Ras-Mohammed. It is the cape that forms the extremity of Arabia Petræa, lying between the Gulf of Suez and the Gulf of Acabah. The *Nautilus* entered the Straits of Jubal, that lead to the Gulf of Suez. I distinctly perceived a high mountain between the two gulfs. It was Mount Horeb, the Sinai at the top of which Moses saw God face to face, and which the mind pictures as incessantly crowned with lightning.

At 6 p.m. the *Nautilus*, sometimes floating, sometimes submerged, passed by Tor, seated on a bay, the waters of which seemed of a reddish tint, as Captain Nemo had said. Then night fell in the midst of a deep silence, sometimes broken by the cries of the pelican and other night birds, the noise of the waves beating on the rocks, or the far-off panting of some steamer beating the waters of the gulf with its noisy paddles.

From eight to nine o'clock the *Nautilus* kept at some yards below the water. According to my calculations we were very near Suez. Through the panels of the saloon I perceived the rocks lighted up by our electric light. It seemed to me that the passage grew gradually narrower.

At a quarter-past nine the boat went up again to the surface, and I ascended to the platform. Impatient to go through the captain's tunnel I could not keep still, and wanted to breathe the fresh air of night.

Soon, in the darkness, I perceived a pale light, half-discoloured by the mist, shining about a mile off.

"A lightship," said someone near me.

I turned and recognised the captain.

"It is the Suez lightship," he continued. "We shall not be long before we reach the orifice of the tunnel."

"It cannot be very easy to enter it."

"No. And I am in the habit of keeping in the helmsman's cage to direct the manœuvre myself. And now, if you will go down, M. Aronnax, the *Nautilus* will sink under the waves, and will not come up to the surface again till it has been through the Arabian Tunnel."

I followed Captain Nemo. The panels were shut, the reservoirs of water filled, and the apparatus sank about thirty feet. As I was about to enter my room the captain stopped me.

"Professor," said he, "should you like to accompany me in the pilot's cage?"

"I dared not ask it of you," I answered.

"Come, then. You will thus see all that can be seen of that navigation at the same time subterrestial and submarine."

Captain Nemo conducted me to the central staircase. About half-way up he opened a door, went along the upper waist, and arrived at the pilot's cage, which, my readers know, rose from one end of the platform.

It was a cabin, six feet square, something like those occupied by the helmsmen of the Mississippi or Hudson steamboats. In the midst was a wheel, vertically stationed, working into the truss of the helm that ran as far as the aft of the *Nautilus*. Four light-ports, made of lenticular glasses, were fixed in the sides of the cabin, and allowed the man at the helm to see in every direction.

This cabin was dark, but my eyes soon became accustomed to the obscurity, and I perceived the pilot, a vigorous man, whose hands were leaning on the fellies of the wheel. Outside the sea seemed brilliantly lighted up by the lantern that was shining behind the cabin at the other extremity of the platform.

"Now," said Captain Nemo, "we must seek our passage."

Electric wires put the helmsman's cage into communication with the engine-room, and from thence the captain could give simultaneously to his *Nautilus* both direction and movement. He pressed a metal knob, and immediately the speed of the screw was much diminished.

I watched in silence the high wall that we were moving along at that moment; it was the immovable foundation of the sand-bed on the coast. We followed it thus for an hour at some yard distance only. Captain Nemo did not look away from the compass, hung by two concentric circles in the midst of the cabin. At a sign the helmsman modified every instant the direction of the *Nautilus*.

I had placed myself at the triboard port-glass, and perceived magnificent substructures of coral, zoophytes, sea-wrack, and crustaceans waving their enormous claws that they passed out from the confractuosities of the rock.

At 10.15 p.m. Captain Nemo took the helm himself. A wide gallery, black and deep, opened before us. The *Nautilus* entered it boldly. An unaccustomed rumbling was heard along the sides. It was the waters of the Red Sea that the slope of the tunnel was precipitating into the Mediterranean. The *Nautilus* followed the torrent with the speed of an arrow, notwithstanding the efforts of the machine that, in order to resist it, beat the waves backwards.

On the narrow walls of the passage I saw nothing but brilliant lines, furrows of fire traced by the speed under the electric light. My heart beat wildly, and I passed my hand to it to stay its palpitations.

At 10.35 p.m. Captain Nemo let go the helm, and, turning towards me—

"The Mediterranean!" said he.

In less than twenty minutes the *Nautilus*, carried along by the torrent, had cleared the Isthmus of Suez.

CHAPTER VI

The Grecian Archipelago

The next day, the 12th of February, at daybreak, the Nautilus went up to the surface of the sea. I rushed up to the platform. At three miles to the south was the vague outline of Pelusium. A torrent had carried us from one sea to another. But the tunnel, so easy to descend, must be impossible to ascend.

About seven o'clock Ned and Conseil joined me. These two inseparable companions had slept tranquilly, thinking no more of the *Nautilus'* feat.

"Well, Mr. Naturalist," asked the Canadian in a slightly jeering tone, "what about the Mediterranean?"

"We are on its surface, friend Ned."

"What!" said Conseil, "last night——"

"Yes, last night itself, in a few minutes, we cleared the insuperable isthmus."

"I don't believe it," said the Canadian.

"And you are wrong, Land," I resumed. "The low coast rounding off towards the south is the Egyptian coast."

"You won't take me in," said the obstinate Canadian.

"But it must be true," said Conseil, "or monsieur would not say so."

"Besides, Ned, Captain Nemo did the honours of his tunnel, and I was near him in the helmsman's cage whilst he guided the *Nautilus* through the narrow passage himself."

"You hear, Ned?" said Conseil.

"And you who have such good eyes," I added—"you, Ned, can see the piers of Port Saïd stretching out into the sea."

The Canadian looked attentively.

"Yes," said he, "you are right, professor, and your captain is a clever man. We are in the Mediterranean. Good. Well, now let us talk, if you please, about our own concerns, but so that no one can hear."

I saw very well what the Canadian was coming to. In any case

I thought it better to talk about it, as he desired, and we all three went and sat down near the lantern-house, where we were less exposed to be wet by the spray from the waves.

"Now, Ned, we are ready to hear you," said I. "What have you to tell us?"

"What I have to tell you is very simple," answered the Canadian. "We are in Europe, and before Captain Nemo's caprice drags us to the bottom of the Polar Seas, or takes us back to Oceania, I want to leave the *Nautilus*."

I must acknowledge that a discussion with the Canadian on the subject always embarrassed me.

I did not wish to trammel the liberty of my companions in any way, and yet I felt no desire to leave Captain Nemo. Thanks to him and his apparatus, I was each day completing my submarine studies, and I was writing my book on submarine depths again in the very midst of its element. Should I ever again meet with such an opportunity of observing the marvels of the ocean? No, certainly. I could not, therefore, reconcile myself to the idea of leaving the *Nautilus* before our cycle of investigations was accomplished.

"Friend Ned," I said, "answer me frankly. Are you dull here? Do you regret the destiny that has thrown you into the hands of Captain Nemo?"

The Canadian remained for some moments without answering. Then crossing his arms—

"Frankly," he said, "I do not regret this voyage under the seas. I shall be glad to have made it; but to have made it, it must come to an end. That is my opinion."

"It will come to an end, Ned."

"Where and when?"

"I do not know where, and I can't say when, or rather I suppose it will end when these seas have nothing further to teach us. All that begins has necessarily an end in this world."

"I think like monsieur," answered Conseil, "and it is quite possible that after going over all the seas of the globe Captain Nemo will give us our discharge."

"Our discharge! (*la volée*)" cried the Canadian. "A drubbing (*une volée*) you mean!"

"We must not exaggerate, Land," I resumed. "We have nothing to fear from the captain, but I am not of Conseil's opinion either. We are acquainted with the secrets of the *Nautilus*, and I have no hope that its commander, in order to set us at liberty, will resign himself to the idea of our taking them about the world with us."

"Then what do you hope?" asked the Canadian.

"That circumstances will happen of which we can and ought to take advantage, as well in six months' time as now."

"Phew!" said Ned Land. "And where shall we be in six months, if you please, Mr. Naturalist?"

"Perhaps here, perhaps in China. You know that the *Nautilus* is a quick sailer. It crosses oceans like a swallow the air, or an express a continent. It does not fear frequented seas. How do we know that it will not rally round the coasts of France, England, or America, where we can attempt to escape as advantageously as here?"

"M. Aronnax," answered the Canadian, "your premises are bad. You speak in the future tense: 'We shall be there! we shall be here!' I speak in the present: 'We are here, and we must take advantage of it.'"

I was closely hemmed in by Ned Land's logic, and felt myself beaten on that ground. I no longer knew what arguments to use.

"Sir," Ned went on, "let us suppose, for the sake of argument, that Captain Nemo were to offer you your liberty today, should you accept it?"

"I do not know," I replied.

"And if he were to add that the offer he makes today he would not renew later on, should you accept?"

I did not answer.

"And what do you think about it, friend Conseil?" asked Ned Land.

"I have nothing to say. I am absolutely disinterested in the question. Like my master and Ned, I am a bachelor. No wife,

251

relations, nor children expect my return. I am at monsieur's service. I think like monsieur, I say what monsieur says, and you must not depend upon me to make a majority. Two persons only are concerned; monsieur on one side, Ned Land on the other. That said, I listen, and am ready to count for either."

I could not help smiling at seeing Conseil annihilate his personality so completely. The Canadian must have been enchanted not to have him against him.

"Then, sir," said Ned Land, "as Conseil does not exist, we have only to speak to each other. I have spoken, you have heard me. What have you to answer?"

It was evident that I must sum up, and subterfuges were repugnant to me.

"Friend Ned," I said, "this is my answer. You are right and I am wrong. We must not depend upon Captain Nemo's goodwill. The commonest prudence forbids him to set us at liberty. On the other hand, prudence tells us that we must profit by the first opportunity of leaving the *Nautilus*."

"Very well, M. Aronnax, that is wisely spoken."

"Only," I said, "I have but one observation to make—the occasion must be serious. Our first attempt must succeed, for if it fail we shall not find another opportunity of attempting it again, and Captain Nemo would not forgive us."

"That's true enough," answered the Canadian. "But your observation applies to every attempt at flight, whether it be made in two years' or two days' time. Therefore the question is still the same; if a favourable opportunity occurs, we must seize it."

"Agreed. And now, friend Ned, will you tell me what you mean by a favourable opportunity?"

"For instance, a dark night when the *Nautilus* would be only a short distance from some European coast."

"Then you would attempt to escape by swimming?"

"Yes, if we were sufficiently near the coast, and the vessel were on the surface; but if we were far off, or if the vessel were under water——"

"And in that case?"

"In that case I should try to take possession of the boat. I know how it is worked. We would get into the interior of it, undo the bolts, and get up to the surface without even the helmsman seeing us."

"Well, Ned, look out for that opportunity; but do not forget that a failure would be fatal to us."

"I will not forget it, sir."

"And now, Ned, should you like to know what I think of your plan?"

"Yes, M. Aronnax."

"Well, I think—I do not say I hope—that so favourable an opportunity will not occur."

"Why?"

"Because Captain Nemo cannot be unaware that we have not renounced the hope of recovering our liberty, and will keep watch above all in European seas."

"I am of monsieur's opinion," said Conseil.

"We shall see," answered Ned Land, shaking his head in a determined manner.

"And now, Ned Land," I added, "we must leave it there. Not another word on this subject. The day you are ready you will inform us and we shall follow you. I leave it entirely to you."

This conversation, that was destined to have such grave consequences later on, ended thus. I ought now to say that facts seemed to confirm my previsions, to the Canadian's great despair. Did Captain Nemo distrust us in these frequented seas, or did he merely wish to keep out of sight of the numerous ships of all nations that plough the Mediterranean? I do not know, but he generally kept under water and a good distance from land. When the *Nautilus* rose to the surface nothing but the helmsman's cage emerged, and it went to great depths, for between the Grecian Archipelago and Asia Minor the sea is more than 2,000 yards deep.

I only made acquaintance with the Island of Carpathos, one of the Sporades, by these lines of Virgil that Captain Nemo quoted to me whilst placing his finger on a point of the planisphere:—

"Est in Carpathio Neptuni gurgite vates,
Cæruleus Proteus——"

It was, in fact, the ancient sojourn of Proteus, the old shepherd of Neptune's flocks, now the Island of Scarpanto, situated between Rhodes and Crete. I only saw its granite substructure through the saloon windows.

The next day, the 14th of February, I resolved to spend some hours in studying the fish of the archipelago; but for some motive or other the panels remained hermetically closed. By taking the direction of the *Nautilus* I saw that it was making towards the Island of Crete. At the epoch I had embarked on board the *Abraham Lincoln*, that island had just revolted against Turkish despotism. But what had become of the insurrection since I knew nothing, and Captain Nemo, cut off as he was from all communication with land, could not inform me.

I therefore made no allusion to this event when in the evening I was alone with him in the saloon. Besides, he seemed taciturn and preoccupied. Then, contrary to his custom, he ordered the panels of the saloon to be opened, and going from one to another he attentively observed the mass of water, for what purpose I could not guess, and on my side I employed my time in studying the fish that passed before my eyes.

Amongst others I noticed some *gobies aphyses*, mentioned by Aristotle, and vulgarly called "sea-loach," which are more particularly met with in the salt water near the Nile Delta. Near them some half-phosphorescent sea-bream displayed themselves, a kind of sparus that the Egyptians ranked amongst their sacred animals, whose arrival in the waters of their river announced a fertile overflow, and was celebrated by religious ceremonies. I also noticed some cheilines, about nine inches long, a bony fish with transparent scales, whose livid colour is mixed with red spots; these are great eaters of marine vegetation, which gives them an exquisite flavour; these cheilines were much sought after by the *gourmets* of ancient Rome, and their entrails cooked with the soft row of lampreys, peacocks' brains, and tongues of phenicoptera, composed the divine dish that delighted Vitellius.

Another inhabitant of these seas drew my attention, and brought back the remembrance of antiquity to my mind. This was the remora that journeys about fastened on to a shark's belly; according to the ancients, this little fish, by holding on to a ship's bottom, could stop its movements; and one of them, by keeping back Antony's ship during the battle of Actium, helped Augustus to gain the victory. On what slight threads hang the destinies of nations! I noticed, too, some admirable anthiæ that belonged to the order of lutjans, a fish held sacred by the Greeks, who attributed to them the power of driving marine monsters out of the waters they frequented; their name signifies *flower*, and they justify this appellation by their play of colours, their shades comprising the whole gamut of reds, from the palest pink to the depth of the ruby, and the fugitive tints that clouded their dorsal fins. I could not take my eyes off these wonders of the sea, when they were suddenly struck with an unexpected apparition. In the midst of the waters a man appeared, a diver, wearing in his belt a leather purse. It was a living man, swimming vigorously, occasionally disappearing to take breath on the surface, then plunging again immediately. I turned to Captain Nemo, and exclaimed in an agitated voice—

"A man! a shipwrecked man! He must be saved at any price!"

The captain did not answer, but came and leaned against the window.

The man had approached, and with his face flattened against the glass, he was looking at us.

To my profound stupefaction Captain Nemo made a sign to him. The diver answered him with his hand, immediately went up again to the surface of the sea, and did not appear again.

"Don't be uneasy," said the captain to me. "It is Nicholas of Cape Matapan, surnamed the Pesce. He is well known in all the Cyclades. A bold diver! Water is his element, and he lives in it more than on land, going constantly from one island to another, and even as far as Crete."

"Do you know him, captain?"

"Why not, M. Aronnax?"

That said, Captain Nemo went towards a piece of furniture placed near the left panel of the saloon. Near this piece of furniture I saw an iron safe, on the lid of which was a brass plate with the initials of the *Nautilus*, and its motto, "*Mobilis in Mobile*," upon it.

At that moment the captain, without taking further notice of my presence, opened the piece of furniture, which contained a great number of ingots.

They were ingots of gold. From whence came this precious metal that represented an enormous sum? Where did the captain get this gold, and what was he going to do with it?

I did not speak a word. I looked. Captain Nemo took these ingots, one by one, and arranged them methodically in the safe, which he entirely filled. I estimated that it then contained more than 2,000lbs. weight of gold—that is to say, nearly £200,000.

The safe was securely fastened, and the captain wrote an address on the lid in what must have been modern Greek characters.

This done, Captain Nemo pressed a knob, the wire of which communicated with the quarters of the crew. Four men appeared, and, not without some trouble, pushed the safe out of the saloon. Then I heard them pulling it up the iron staircase with pulleys.

Then Captain Nemo turned to me.

"Did you speak, professor?"

"No, captain."

"Then, sir, if you allow me, I will wish you good-night."

Upon which Captain Nemo left the saloon.

I went back to my room very curious, as may be believed. I tried in vain to sleep. I tried to find what connection there could be between the diver and the safe filled with gold. I soon felt by its pitching and tossing that the *Nautilus* was back on the surface of the water.

Then I heard a noise of steps on the platform. I understood that they were unloosening the boat and launching it on the sea. It struck for an instant against the sides of the *Nautilus*, and then the noise ceased.

Two hours afterwards the same noise, the same movements, were repeated. The boat, hoisted on board, was replaced in its socket, and the *Nautilus* sank again under the waves.

Thus, then, the gold had been sent to its address. To what point of the continent? Who was Captain Nemo's correspondent?

The next day I related to Conseil and the Canadian the events of the preceding night, which had excited my curiosity to the highest pitch. My companions were no less surprised than I.

"But where does he find all that gold?" asked Ned Land.

To that there was no answer possible. I went to the saloon after breakfast and began to work. Until 5 p.m. I wrote out my notes. At that moment—ought I to attribute it to a feeling of my own?—I felt extremely hot, and I was obliged to take off my garment of byssus—an incomprehensible fact, for we were not in high latitudes, and besides, when the *Nautilus* was submerged, it ought to experience no elevation of temperature. I looked at the manometer. It indicated a depth of sixty feet, to which atmospheric heat cannot reach.

I went on with my work, but the heat became intolerable.

"Can the vessel be on fire?" I asked myself.

I was going to leave the saloon when Captain Nemo entered. He approached the thermometer, corrected it, and said—

"Forty-two degrees" (centigrade).

"I feel it, captain," I answered, "and if the heat augments we cannot bear it."

"The heat will not augment unless we choose."

"Then you can moderate it as you please?"

"No, but I can get away from the focus that produces it."

"Then it is exterior?"

"Certainly. We are floating in boiling water."

"Is it possible?" I cried.

"Look!"

The panels opened, and I saw the sea entirely white round the *Nautilus*. A sulphurous smoke was curling amongst the waves that boiled like water in a copper. I placed my hand on one of the panes of glass, but the heat was so great that I was obliged to withdraw it.

"Where are we?" I asked.

"Near the Island of Santorin, professor," replied the captain, "and precisely in the channel that separates Nea-Kamenni from Pali-Kamenni. I wished to show you the curious spectacle of a submarine eruption."

"I thought," said I, "that the formation of these new islands was ended."

"Nothing is ever ended in volcanic places," replied Captain Nemo. "The globe is always being worked there by subterranean fires. Already, in the 19th year of our era, according to Cassiodorus and Pliny, a new island, Theia (the divine), appeared in the very place where islets have recently been formed. Then it sank again under the waves, came up again in the year '69, and again sank under the waves. Since that epoch till our own days, the Plutonian work has been suspended. But on February 3rd, 1866, a new islet, which they named George Island, emerged from the sulphurous vapour near Nea-Kamenni, and joined itself to it on the 6th of the same month. Seven days after, on the 13th of February, the Island of Aphroessa appeared, leaving between itself and Nea-Kamenni a channel ten yards broad. I was in these seas when the phenomenon occurred, and I could, therefore, watch all its different phases. The Island of Aphroessa, round in form, measured three hundred feet in diameter, and thirty feet in height. It was composed of black and vitreous lava, mixed with fragments of felspar. And lastly, on the 10th of March a smaller islet called Reka showed itself near Nea-Kamenni, and since then these three joined together have formed one single island."

"Then what channel are we in now?"

"Here it is now," answered Captain Nemo, showing me a map of the archipelago. "You see I have put in the new islets."

"But one day this channel will be filled up?"

"Very likely, M. Aronnax, for since 1866 eight little islands of lava have risen opposite Port Saint Nicholas, in the Island of Palea-Kamenni. It is evident, therefore, that Nea and Palea will be joined soon. If, in the Pacific, it is the infusoria that form continents, here it is eruptive phenomena. See, sir, see the work that is going on under these waves."

I returned to the window. The *Nautilus* was no longer moving. The heat was growing intolerable. From white the sea was getting red, a colouration due to the presence of salts of iron. Notwithstanding the saloon's being hermetically closed, an unbearable sulphurous smell pervaded it, and I perceived scarlet flames the brilliancy of which killed the electric light.

I was in a bath of perspiration, choking, and nearly broiled.

"We cannot remain any longer in this boiling water," I said to the captain.

"No, that would not be prudent," answered the unmoved Nemo.

An order was given. The *Nautilus* tacked about, and left the furnace it could not with impunity set at defiance. A quarter of an hour later we were breathing on the surface of the waves.

The thought then occurred to me that if Ned Land had chosen that part of the sea for our flight we should not have come out of it alive.

The next day, the 16th of February, we left this basin, which, between Rhodes and Alexandria, is more than 1,500 fathoms deep, and the *Nautilus*, passing within sight of Cerigo, left the Grecian Archipelago after doubling Cape Matapan.

CHAPTER VII

The Mediterranean in Forty-Eight Hours

The Mediterranean, the blue sea *par excellence*, "the great sea" of the Hebrews, the "sea" of the Greeks, the *mare nostrum* of the Romans, bordered with orange-trees, aloes, cactus, maritime pines, made fragrant with the perfume of myrtles, framed in rude mountains, saturated with a pure and transparent air, but incessantly worked by underground fires, is a perfect battle-field, in which Neptune and Pluto still dispute the empire of the world. It is there, upon its banks and waters, says Michelet, that man is renewed in one of the most powerful climates of the world. But, although it is so beautiful, I could only take a rapid glance at its basin, which covers a superficial area of two millions of square kilometers. Even Captain Nemo's knowledge was lost to me, for the enigmatical personage did not once appear during our rapid passage. I estimated at about six hundred leagues the course of the *Nautilus* under the waves of this sea, and it accomplished this voyage in twice twenty-four hours. Starting on the morning of the 16th of February from the Grecian seas, we had cleared the Straits of Gibraltar by sunrise on the 18th.

It was evident to me that this Mediterranean, inclosed by the countries which he wished to avoid, was distasteful to Captain Nemo. Its waves and breezes recalled too many memories, if not too many regrets. He had not here that liberty of movement, that independence of manœuvre, that he had in the ocean, and his *Nautilus* was cramped between the shores of Africa and Europe.

Our speed was now twenty-five miles an hour, or twelve leagues of four kilometers. It is useless to say that Ned Land, notwithstanding his great wish, was obliged to renounce his projects of flight. He could not use a boat that was being dragged along at the rate of thirteen yards a second. To leave the *Nautilus* then would be like jumping out of a train going at the same speed, as imprudent a thing as could possibly be attempted. Besides, our apparatus only went up to the surface at night in order to renew its provision of air, and it was guided entirely by the compass and log.

I therefore only saw of the Mediterranean what passengers by an express see of the country that is flying before their eyes—that is to say, the distant horizon, and not the nearer objects which pass like a flash of lightning. However, Conseil and I could notice some of the Mediterranean fish, the power of whose fins would keep them for some moments in sight of the *Nautilus*. We lay in wait for them before the windows of the saloon, and our notes allow me to write out in few words the icthyology of this sea.

Of the different fish that inhabit it, I saw some, caught a glimpse of others, without speaking of those that the speed of the *Nautilus* hid from my eyes. I hope I may be allowed to classify them according to this fantastic classification. It will better allow me to give my rapid observations.

Amidst the mass of waters brightly lighted up by the electric lamp glided some of those lampreys, a yard long, that are common to almost every climate; some of the oxyrhynchi, a sort of skate, five feet wide, with white belly and grey spotted back, spreading out like large shawls, carried along by the currents. Other skates passed so quickly that I could not tell if they deserved the name of eagles, given them by the Greeks, or the qualification of rats, toads, and bats, which modern fishermen have given them. A few milander-sharks, twelve feet long, and particularly dreaded by plungers, struggled with them for speed. Sea-foxes, eight feet long, endowed with wonderful sense of smell, appeared like great blue shadows. Dorades of the gilt-head kind, some of which measured at least thirty-nine inches, showed themselves in their blue and silver dress, bordered with fine stripes that showed well against the sombre tint of their fins; fish sacred to Venus, the eyes of which are encased in gold sockets, a precious species, patronising all waters, salt and fresh, an inhabitant of rivers, lakes, and oceans, living under all climates, supporting all temperatures, and whose race, that ascends to the geographical epochs of the globe, has kept its primitive beauty. Magnificent sturgeons, from ten to twelve yards long, animals of great speed, striking the glass of the panels with their strong tails, showing their bluish back with little brown spots; they resemble sharks, but are not so strong, and are met with in all seas; in the spring they like to go up large rivers, to struggle against the currents of the Volga, Danube, Po, Rhone, Loire, and Oder, and feed on herrings, mackerel, salmon, and cod; although they belong to the cartilaginous class, they are delicate food; they are eaten fresh, dried, salted, and were formerly carried in triumph on to the table of Lucullus. But of these different inhabitants of the Mediterranean those that I could observe to the greatest advantage belonged to the 63rd genus of bony fish. They were sombre tunnies with blue-black backs, belly cuirassed with silver, and whose dorsal fins threw out gleams of gold. They have the reputation of following ships for the sake of their shade under tropical skies, and they accompanied the *Nautilus*, as they formerly accompanied the vessels of La Pérouse. For many long hours they tried to keep up with our apparatus. I was never tired of admiring these animals, veritably fashioned for speed, their small heads, their lithe and fusiform bodies that in some of them were more than three yards long, their pectoral fins endowed with remarkable vigour, and their forked caudals. They swam in a triangle, like certain flocks of birds, whose rapidity they equalled, which made the ancients say that they were acquainted with geometry and strategy. But still they do not escape the pursuit of the Provençals, who esteemed them as highly as the inhabitants of the Propontis and Italy did, and these precious but blind and giddy animals perish by thousands in the Marseillaise nets.

I quote from memory only the Mediterranean fish that Conseil and I only caught a glimpse of. They were the whitish gymnotus, that passed like indiscernible vapours, conger-eels, serpents from three to four yards long, adorned with green, blue, and yellow; cod, three feet long, the liver of which forms a delicate dish; cœpoles-tænia, that float like fine sea-wrack; trygles, called by poets lyre-fish and sailors whistling fish, the mouth of which is adorned with two triangular and toothed blades shaped like old Homer's instrument; swallow-trygles, swimming with the rapidity of the bird from whom they take their name; aloses, ornamented with black, grey, brown, blue, yellow, and green spots, that are sensible to the silvery sound of bells; and splendid turbots, those sea-pheasants, a sort of lozenge with yellow fins specked with brown, and the left side of which is generally marked brown and yellow; lastly, troops of admirable red-mullet, veritable ocean birds of Paradise, which the Romans paid as much as ten thousand sesterces each for, and that they had killed at table so as to be able to watch their cruel changes of colour from the cinnabar red of life to the pale white of death.

And if I could not observe mullets, balisters, retrodons, hippocamps, jouans, trumpet-fish, blennies, surmullets, wrass, smelts, mugil, anchovies, pagels, bogues, garfish, nor any of the principal representatives of the order of pleuronects or flat-fish, dabs, flez, plaice, soles, flounders, common to the Atlantic and Mediterranean, the bewildering speed of the *Nautilus* across these opulent waters was the cause.

As to the marine mammifers, I think I saw, as we passed the entrance to the Adriatic, two or three cachalots furnished with the dorsal fin of the genus physetera, a few dolphins of the genus globicephali, peculiar to the Mediterranean, with the back of the head striped in small clear lines, and also a dozen seals with white stomachs and black hair, known under the name of *monks*, and that really look like Dominicans three yards long.

On his side Conseil thought he saw a turtle six feet across, ornamented with salient bones in a longitudinal direction. I regretted not seeing this reptile, for, from Conseil's description of it, I thought it must have been a lute which forms a rather rare species. For my own part, I only remarked a few cacouans with long carapaces.

As to zoophytes, I was for some instants able to admire a beautiful orange galeolaria that had fastened itself to the triboard panel; it was a long tenuous filament, spreading out into infinite branches and terminating by the finest lace that the rivals of Arachne could ever have woven. Unfortunately, I could not take this admirable specimen, and no other Mediterranean zoophyte would have offered itself to my observation if the *Nautilus*, during the evening of the 16th, had not singularly slackened speed under the following circumstances:—

We were then passing between Sicily and the coast of Tunis. In the narrow space between Cape Bon and the Straits of Messina, the bottom of the sea rises almost abruptly. There a sort of ridge has formed, on which there is only about eight fathoms of water, whilst on either side the depth is about ninety fathoms. The *Nautilus* was therefore obliged to be steered prudently in order not to strike against the submarine barrier.

I showed Conseil, on the chart of the Mediterranean, the spot where this reef is situated.

"It is like a veritable isthmus," said Conseil, "joining Europe to Africa."

"Yes, my boy," I answered, "it entirely barricades the Straits of Syria, and Smith's soundings have proved that in former times the continents were joined between Cape Boco and Cape Furina."

"I can quite believe that," answered Conseil.

"I may add," I continued, "that a similar barrier exists between Ceuta and Gibraltar, which, in geological times, closed in the whole Mediterranean."

"What if some volcanic outburst should one day raise these barriers above the waves!"

"That is hardly probable, Conseil."

"But if such a phenomenon were really to happen it would be a bad thing for Monsieur de Lesseps, who is giving himself so much trouble to pierce his isthmus."

"Yes, it would; but I repeat, Conseil, it will not happen. The violence of the subterranean forces goes on diminishing. The volcanoes, so numerous in the early days of the world's history, are gradually being extinguished; the interior heat is growing weaker, the temperature of the lower strata of the globe is lowered in an appreciable degree each century, and to the detriment of our globe, for this heat is its life."

"But the sun——"

"The sun is insufficient, Conseil. Can it put heat into a corpse?"

"Not that I know of."

"Well, my friend, the earth will one day be this cold corpse. It will become uninhabitable, and will be uninhabited like the moon, which long ago lost her vital heat."

"In how many centuries?" asked Conseil.

"In some hundreds of thousands of years, my boy."

"Then," answered Conseil, "we have time to finish our voyage if Ned Land does not interfere with it."

And Conseil, reassured, returned to the study of the high bottom that the *Nautilus* was skirting at moderate speed.

There on a rocky and sandy soil blossomed quite a living flora of sponges, holithuria, hyaline cydippes ornamented with reddish cyrrhæ, which emit a slight phosphorescence; beroës, commonly known under the name of sea-cucumbers, and, bathed in the glitter of a solar spectrum, ambulant comatulæ, more than a yard across, the purple from which reddened the waters, arborescent euryales of the greatest beauty, pavonaceæ with long stalks, a great number of edible echinus of varied species, and green sea-anemones with grey trunks and brown discs, lost in their olive-coloured tentacles.

Conseil had paid more particular attention to the molluscs and articulates, and although his nomenclature is rather dry, I will not wrong the brave fellow by omitting his personal observations.

In the branch of molluscs he cited numerous pectiniform scallops, asses'-feet spondylus that heap themselves on each other; triangular donaces, tridented hyallæ, with yellow fins and transparent shells; orange-tinted pleurobranches, eggs dotted with greenish spots; aplysiæ, known under the name of sea-hares; dolabellæ, fleshly acerose, ombrellæ, peculiar to the Mediterranean; sea-ears, the shell of which produces a much-esteemed kind of mother-of-pearl; flammulated petronclæ, anomies that the Languedocians are said to have preferred to oysters; clovis, so dear to the Marseillais; double praïres, white and fat, some of those clams that abound on the coasts of North America, and for which there is so large a sale in New York; opercular combs of variegated colours; lithodonces, buried in their holes, the peppery taste of which I much liked; furrowed venericards, the shell of which has a convex summit and salient sides; cynthies bristling with scarlet tubercules; carnieres with bent back, points like light gondolas; crowned feroles, atlantes with spiral-form shells, grey thetys, spotted with black, and covered with a fringed mantilla; eolides like small snails, cavolines climbing on their back; auriculæ, and, amongst others, the mysotis auricula, with an oval shell; fawn-coloured scalaries, littorines, panthuræ, cineraïræ, petricolæ, lamellairæ, cabochons, pandoræ, &c. As to the articulates, Conseil has, in his notes, very rightly divided them into six classes, of which three belong to the marine world. These three are the crustaceans, cirrhopodeans, and annelides.

The crustaceans are subdivided into nine orders, and the first of these orders comprehends the decapods—that is to say, the animals whose head and thorax are generally joined together, and whose buccal apparatus is composed of several pairs of limbs, and that possess four, five, or six pairs of ambulatory claws. Conseil had followed the method of our master, Milne-Edwards, who makes three sections of deca-pods—the brachyoures, macroures, and anomoures. These names are slightly barbarous, but they are just and precise. Amongst the macroures, Conseil cites the amathies, the forehead of which is armed with two great divergent points; the inachus scorpion, which—I do not know why—symbolised wisdom to the Greeks; lambres-massena, lambres-spinimanes, probably lost on this high bottom, for they generally live in greath depths; schantes, pilumnes, rhomboïdes, granulous calappiens—very easy to digest, observes Conseil—edented corystes, ebalies, cymopolies, woolly dorripes, &c. Amongst the macroures, subdivided into five families, the cuirassiers, foirisseurs, astaciens, slicoques, and chyzopodes, he cites the common spring-lobster, the flesh of the female being much esteemed, the scyllares-ours, or sea-grasshopper, and all sorts of edible species; but he says nothing of the subdivision of the astaciens, which comprehends the lobster, for the spring-lobster is the only lobster of the Mediterranean. Lastly, amongst the anomoures he saw common drocines sheltered behind the abandoned shell they take possession of; homoles with thorny foreheads, hermit bernards, porcelains, &c.

There Conseil's work stopped. Time had failed him for completing the class of crustaceans by the examination of the stomapods, amphipods, homopods, isopods, trilobites, branchiapods, ostracodes, and entomostraceans. And to terminate the study of marine articulates, he ought to have mentioned the eyrrhopods that include the cyclops, argules, and the class of annelides, that he would not have failed to divide into tubicoles and dorsibranches. But the *Nautilus* having passed the ridge of the Lybian Strait, went at its usual speed in deeper water. From that time we saw no more molluscs, no more articulates, no more zoophytes; only a few large fish that passed like shadows.

During the night between the 16th and 17th of February we entered the second Mediterranean basin, the greatest depths of which are found at 1,500 fathoms. The *Nautilus*, under the action of its screw, gliding over its inclined planes, sank into the lowest depths of the sea.

There, instead of natural marvels, the mass of waters offered me many touching and terrible scenes. In fact, we were then crossing all that part of the Mediterranean so fertile in disasters. From the Algerian coast to the shores of Provence, how many vessels have been wrecked, how many ships have disappeared! The Mediterranean is only a lake compared to the vast liquid plains of the Pacific, but it is a capricious lake with changing waters, today propitious and caressing to the fragile tartan that seems to float between the double ultramarine of sea and sky, tomorrow tempestuous, agitated by winds, breaking up the strongest ships by the precipitate blows of its short waves.

In that rapid course across the great depths what wrecks I saw lying on the ground! some already encrusted with coral, others simply covered with a layer of rust, anchors, cannons, bullets, iron tackle, screws, pieces of engines, broken cylinders, crushed boilers, and hulls floating in mid-water, some upright, some overturned.

Amongst these wrecks some had been caused by collision, others had struck upon some granite rock. I saw some that had sunk straight down with upright masts, and rigging stiffened by the water. They seemed to be at anchor in an immense roadway, only awaiting the time of starting. When the *Nautilus* passed amongst them, and enveloped them with its electric light, it seemed as if they would salute our vessel with their colours, and give the orders. But no; nothing but the silence of death reigned in the field of catastrophes!

I observed that the bottom of the Mediterranean was more encumbered with these wrecks as the *Nautilus* approached the Straits of Gibraltar. The coasts of Africa and Europe are then nearer each other, and in the narrow space collisions are frequent. I saw there numerous iron keels, the fantastic ruins of steamers, some lying down, others upright, like formidable animals. One of these boats with open sides, bent funnel, wheels of which only the mounting remained, the helm separated from the sternpost, and still held by an iron chain, its stern eaten away by marine salts, presented a terrible spectacle! How many existences did this shipwreck destroy! How many victims swallowed up by the waves! Had any sailor on board survived to relate the terrible disaster, or did the waves still keep the fatal secret? I do not know why, but it came into my head that this boat must be the *Atlas* that had totally disappeared for twenty years, and of which nothing had ever been heard! Ah, what a fatal history would be that of these Mediterranean depths, this vast charnel-house where so many riches have been lost, and so many victims have met with their death!

In the meantime the *Nautilus*, indifferent and rapid, journeyed at full speed amidst these ruins. On the 18th of February, about 3 a.m., it was at the entrance to the Straits of Gibraltar.

There two currents exist—an upper current, long since known, that conveys the waters of the ocean into the Mediterranean basin, and a lower counter-current, of which reasoning has now shown the existence. For the volume of water in the Mediterranean, incessantly increased by the Atlantic current and the rivers that flow into it, must raise the level of the sea every year, for its evaporation is insufficient to restore the equilibrium. As this is not the case, we must naturally admit the existence of a lower current that pours through the Straits of Gibraltar, the overplus of the Mediterranean into the Atlantic.

We proved this fact. The *Nautilus* profited by this counter-current. It rushed rapidly through the narrow passage. For an instant I caught a glimpse of the admirable ruins of the temple of Hercules, sunk, according to Pliny and Avienus, with the low island on which it stood, and a few minutes later we were afloat on the waves of the Atlantic.

CHAPTER VIII

Vigo Bay

The Atlantic!—that vast extent of water the superficial area of which covers twenty-five millions of square miles, nine thousand miles long, with a mean breadth of two thousand seven hundred miles. An important ocean almost unknown to the ancients, except, perhaps, to the inhabitants of Carthage, those Dutchmen of antiquity who, in their commercial peregrinations, followed the western coasts of Europe or Africa! An ocean whose parallel winding shores embrace an immense perimeter, watered by the largest rivers in the world, the Saint Lawrence, the Mississippi, Amazon, La Plata, Orinoco, Niger, Senegal, Elba, Loire, and Rhine, which bring down the waters of the most civilised as well as those of the most savage countries! A magnificent plain, incessantly ploughed by ships of all nations, sheltered under the flags of every nation, and terminated by the two terrible points, dreaded by navigators, Cape Horn and the Cape of Tempests.

The *Nautilus* was culling its waters under her sharp prow after having accomplished nearly ten thousand leagues in three months and a half, a distance greater than one of the great circles of the earth. Where were we going now, and what had the future in store for us?

The *Nautilus* once out of the Straits of Gibraltar came up to the surface again, and our daily walks on the platform were thus restored to us.

I immediately went up there, accompanied by Ned Land and Conseil. At a distance of twelve miles, Cape Vincent, which forms the S.W. point of the Spanish peninsula, was dimly to be seen. It was blowing a rather strong gale. The sea was rough. It made the *Nautilus* rock violently. It was almost impossible to keep on the platform, which enormous seas washed at every moment. We therefore went down again after taking in some mouthfuls of fresh air.

I went back to my room, and Conseil returned to his cabin, but the Canadian, with a preoccupied air, followed me. Our rapid passage across the Mediterranean had prevented him putting his projects into execution, and he did not hide his disappointment.

When the door of my cabin was shut, he sat down and looked at me in silence.

"Friend Ned," I said, "I understand you, but you have nothing to reproach yourself with. To have attempted to leave the *Nautilus* while it was going at that rate would have been madness."

Ned Land answered nothing. His compressed lips and frowning brow indicated the violent possession this fixed idea had taken of his mind.

"Well," said I, "we need not despair yet. We are going up the coast of Portugal. France and England are not far off, where we should easily find a refuge. If the *Nautilus*, once out of the Straits of Gibraltar, had gone southward, if it had carried us towards those regions where land is wanting, I should share your uneasiness. But now we know that Captain Nemo does not avoid civilised seas, and in a few days I think we can act with some security."

Ned Land looked at me more fixedly still, and at length he opened his lips.

"It is for tonight," said he.

I started. I must acknowledge I was little prepared for this communication. I wanted to answer the Canadian, but words would not come.

"We agreed to wait for an opportunity," said Ned Land. "I have that opportunity. This night we shall only be a few miles off the Spanish coast. The night will be dark. I have your word, M. Aronnax, and I depend upon you."

As I still was silent, the Canadian rose, and coming nearer to me said—

"This evening, at 9 o'clock. I have told Conseil. At that time Captain Nemo will be shut up in his room, and probably in bed. Neither the engineers nor any of the crew can see us. Conseil and I will go to the central staircase. You, M. Aronnax, must remain in the library not far off, and await our signal. The oars, mast, and sail are in the boat, and I have even succeeded in putting some provisions into it. I procured an English wrench to unscrew the bolts that fasten the boat to the hull of the *Nautilus*. Thus everything is ready for tonight."

"The sea is bad."

"That I allow," answered the Canadian, "but we must risk that. Liberty is worth paying for. Besides, the boat is solid, and a few miles with the wind in our favour are not of any consequence. Who knows if tomorrow we shall not be a hundred leagues out? If circumstances favour us we shall land, living or dead, on some point of solid ground between 10 and 11 o'clock. Then tonight, by the grace of God!"

Thereupon the Canadian withdrew, leaving me almost stunned. I had imagined that when the matter turned up I should have time to reflect and discuss it. My stubborn companion had not allowed me to do that. And, after all, what could I have said to him? Ned Land was quite right. It was almost an occasion, and he took advantage of it. Could I take back my word, and assume the responsibility of compromising, by personal interest, the future of my companion? Tomorrow Captain Nemo might carry us far away from any land.

At that moment a rather strong hissing sound informed me that the reservoirs were being filled, and then the *Nautilus* sank under the waves of the Atlantic.

I remained in my room. I wished to avoid the captain in order to hide from his eyes the emotion I was labouring under. It was a sad day I passed thus between the desire of being free again and the regret of abandoning the marvellous *Nautilus*, leaving my submarine studies unfinished! To leave my ocean, "my Atlantic," as I liked to call it, thus, without having observed its lowest strata, or learnt from it those secrets that the Indian seas and the Pacific had taught me! My romance had fallen from my hand while I was yet at the first volume, my dream was interrupted at its most delightful moment! What wretched hours passed thus, sometimes seeing myself safely on board with my companions, sometimes wishing, in spite of my reason, that some unforeseen circumstance would prevent the realisation of Ned Land's projects!

Twice I went into the saloon. I wished to consult the compass, and to see if the *Nautilus* was approaching or going farther away from the coast. But no. The *Nautilus* kept constantly in the Portuguese waters. It was making for the north along the shores of the ocean.

I was, therefore, obliged to make up my mind to it, and prepare for flight. My baggage was not heavy, and consisted of my notes, nothing more. I asked myself what Captain Nemo would think of our flight, what uneasiness it might cause him, what harm it might do him, and what he would do in case it was discovered or it failed. Certainly I had no fault to find with him—on the contrary. Hospitality was never given more freely than his. In leaving him I could not be accused of ingratitude. No oath bound us to him. He counted upon the force of circumstances alone, and not upon our word, to keep us with him for ever. But his intention, openly avowed, of keeping us eternally prisoners on board his vessel justified our attempts.

I had not seen the captain again since our visit to the Island of Santorin. Would chance bring me into his presence before our departure? I both desired and feared it might. I listened if I could hear him walking in the room next to mine. No noise reached my ear. There could be no one in the room.

Then I asked myself if the strange personage was on board at all. Since the night during which the boat had left the *Nautilus* on a mysterious mission, my ideas about him were slightly modified. I thought, whatever he might say about it, that Captain Nemo must have kept up some sort of communication with land. Did he never leave the *Nautilus*? Entire weeks had passed without my having seen him. What was he doing during that time? and while I thought him a prey to fits of misanthropy, was he not far off accomplishing some secret act the nature of which had thus far escaped me?

All these ideas, and a thousand more, assailed me at once. The field of conjectures could not be but infinite in our strange situation. I felt an insupportable discomfort. That day of waiting seemed to me eternal. The hours struck too slowly for my impatience.

My dinner was served as usual in my room. I ate little, being too much preoccupied. I left the table at seven o'clock. A hundred and twenty minutes—I counted them—still separated me from the time when I was to join Ned Land. My agitation redoubled. My pulse beat violently. I could not remain immobile. I walked about, hoping to calm the trouble of my mind by movement. The idea of failing in our bold enterprise was the least painful of my thoughts; but at the idea of seeing our project discovered before leaving the *Nautilus*, and of being brought before Captain Nemo, irritated, or, what would have been worse, saddened by my leaving him, my heart palpitated.

I wished to see the saloon for the last time. I went by the waist, and entered that museum where I had passed so many useful and agreeable hours. I looked at all these riches and treasures like a man on the eve of eternal exile, and who is going away never to return. These marvels of nature, these masterpieces of art, amongst which for so many days my life had been concentrated, I was going to leave them for ever. I should have liked to look through the windows across the waters of the Atlantic; but the panels were hermetically shut, and an iron sheet separated me from that ocean which I did not know as yet.

As I moved thus about the saloon I reached the door, let into the angle, which opened into the captain's room. To my great astonishment this door was ajar. I drew back involuntarily. If Captain Nemo was in his room he could see me. However, hearing no noise, I drew near it. The room was empty. I pushed open the door and entered. Still the same severe monk-like aspect.

At that moment some prints, hung up, that I had not noticed during my first visit, struck me. They were portraits, portraits of great historical men whose existence was but a perpetual devotion to one great humane idea: Kosciusko, the hero who fell to the cry of "Finis Poloniæ!"; Botzaris, the Leonidas of modern Greece; O'Connell, the defender of Ireland; Washington, the founder of the American Union; Manin, the Italian patriot; Lincoln, who fell by the hand of a slave-owner; and, lastly, that martyr to the freedom of the black race, John Brown, hanging on his gallows as Victor Hugo's pencil has so terribly drawn him.

What tie could exist between these heroic souls and the soul of Captain Nemo? Could I at last, from that assemblage of portraits, find out the mystery of his existence? Was he the champion of oppressed nations, the liberator of slaves? Had he figured in the last social or political commotions of this century? Had he been one of the heroes of the terrible American war?—a war lamentable, but for ever glorious.

Suddenly the clock struck eight. The first stroke awoke me to reality. I trembled as if some invisible eye could see to the bottom of my thoughts, and I rushed out of the room.

There I glanced at the compass. Our course was still north. The log indicated moderate speed, the manometer a depth of about sixty feet. Circumstances, therefore, were favouring the Canadian's project.

I went back to my room and clothed myself warmly in my sea-boots, sealskin cap, and vest of byssus lined with sealskin. I was ready. I waited. The vibration of the screw alone disturbed the profound silence that reigned on board. I listened attentively. Would not a shout tell me all at once that Ned Land had been caught in his effort to escape? A mortal dread took possession of me. I tried in vain to regain my *sang-froid*.

At a few minutes to nine o'clock I put my ear against the captain's door. No sound. I left my room and went back to the saloon, which was insufficiently lighted, but empty.

I opened the door communicating with the library. The same insufficient light, the same solitude. I went and placed myself near the door that opened into the cage of the central staircase, and awaited Ned Land's signal.

At the moment the vibration from the screw sensibly diminished, then ceased altogether. Why was this change made in the working of the *Nautilus*? Whether this halt would be favourable to or against Ned Land's plans I could not tell.

The silence was only broken by the beatings of my heart.

Suddenly I felt a slight shock. I understood that the *Nautilus* had just stopped on the bottom of the ocean. My anxiety increased. The Canadian's signal did not reach me. I wanted to go to Ned Land and beg him to put off his attempt. I felt that something was changed in our usual navigation.

At that moment the saloon door opened, and Captain Nemo appeared. He perceived me, and said without further preamble, in an amiable tone—

"Ah, professor, I was looking for you. Do you know your Spanish history?"

Anyone knowing the history of his own country thoroughly under the same conditions of mental worry and anxiety, would not be able to quote a single word of it.

"Well," continued Captain Nemo, "you heard my question. Do you know the history of Spain?"

"Very badly," I replied.

"That is like *savants*," said the captain, "they know nothing. Well, sit down," added he, "and I will relate a curious episode of that history to you."

The captain stretched himself upon a divan, and I mechanically took a place beside him, with my back to the light.

"Professor," he said, "give me all your attention. This history will interest you in some sort, for it will answer a question that doubtless you have not been able to solve."

"I hear, captain," said I, not knowing what my interlocutor was driving at, and wondering whether it had anything to do with our projects of flight.

"Professor," resumed the captain, "if you have no objection we will go as far back as 1702. As you know, your king, Louis XIV, thinking that the gesture of a potentate was sufficient to make the Pyrenees sink into the ground, had imposed his grandson, the Duke of Anjou, on the Spaniards. This prince, who reigned more or less badly under the name of Philip V, had a strong party against him from without.

"In fact, the year before, the Royal houses of Holland, Austria, and England had concluded a treaty of alliance at the Hague, for the aim of taking the crown of Spain from Philip V and placing it on the head of an archduke, to whom they gave the premature title of Charles III.

"Spain had this coalition to resist. But she was nearly destitute of soldiers and sailors. However, money would not be wanting, provided that their galleons, loaded with gold and silver from America, could enter her ports. Now, towards the end of 1702 she was expecting a rich convoy which France had sent, a fleet of twenty-three vessels, commanded by the Admiral Château-Renaud to escort, for the combined fleets were then scouring the Atlantic.

"This convoy was bound for Cadiz; but the admiral, having learnt that the English fleet was cruising in the neighbourhood, resolved to make for a French port.

"The Spanish commanders of the convoy protested against this decision. They wished to be accompanied to a Spanish port, and if not to Cadiz, to Vigo Bay, situated on the N.W. coast of Spain, which was not blockaded.

"The Admiral Château-Renaud was weak enough to obey this injunction, and the galleons entered Vigo Bay.

"Unfortunately, this bay is an open roadstead that cannot be in the least defended. They were, therefore, obliged to hasten the unloading of the galleons before the arrival of the combined fleets, and there would have been plenty of time to do it in, but for a miserable question of rivalry that arose suddenly.

"You are following the links of these facts?" said the captain.

"Perfectly," said I, not knowing why I was receiving this lesson in history.

"Then I continue. This is what happened. The merchants of Cadiz had a privilege by which they were to receive all the merchandise that came from the East Indies, and the landing of the ingots form the galleons at the port of Vigo was a contravention of their rights. They made complaints at Madrid, and obtained from the feeble Philip V the order to make the convoy remain without unloading in the roadstead of Vigo until the enemy's fleets should be out of the way.

"Now whilst this decision was being arrived at, on the 22nd of October, 1702, the English ships arrived in Vigo Bay. The Admiral Château-Renaud, notwithstanding his inferior forces, fought courageously. But when he saw that the riches of the convoy were about to fall into the hands of enemies, he burnt and scuttled the galleons that went to the bottom with their immense treasures."

Captain Nemo stopped. I acknowledged that I did not perceive as yet how his story could interest me.

"Well?" I asked him.

"Well, M. Aronnax," answered Captain Nemo, "we are in Vigo Bay, and it rests with yourself whether you will penetrate into its mysteries."

The captain rose and begged me to follow him. I had had time to recover myself. I obeyed. The saloon was dark, but across the transparent panes glittered the sea. I looked.

For a radius of half-a-mile round the *Nautilus* the waters seemed impregnated with electric light, the sandy bottom clear and distinct. Some of the crew, clothed in their bathing dresses, were at work emptying half-rotten casks, splintered cases, amidst still blackened spars. From these cases and casks escaped ingots of gold and silver, cascades of piastres and jewels. The sand was strewed with them. Then, loaded with their previous booty, these men returned to the *Nautilus*, deposited their load, and went back to continue their inexhaustible gold and silver fishery.

278

I understood. It was the battle-field of the 22nd of October, 1702. In this very place the galleons laden for the Spanish government had sunk. Here Captain Nemo came, according to his needs, to encase the millions with which he ballasted his *Nautilus*. It was for him, and for him alone, that America had given up her precious metals. He was the direct heir, without anyone to share, of these treasures taken from the Incas and Ferdinand Cortez' conquered people.

"Did you know, professor," he asked me, smiling, "that the sea contained such riches?"

"I knew," I answered, "that the silver held in suspension in the sea is estimated at two millions of tons."

"Doubtless, but in order to extract the silver the expense would be greater than the profit. Here, on the contrary, I have only to pick up what men have lost, not only in this Vigo Bay, but in a thousand other scenes of shipwreck, all marked on my marine chart. Now do you understand why I am so many times a millionaire?"

"Yes, captain. But allow me to tell you that in your work in Vigo Bay you have only been beforehand with a rival company."

"What company, pray?"

"A company that has received from the Spanish government the privilege of seeking the shipwrecked galleons. The shareholders are tempted by the bait of an enormous profit, for they estimate the value of these shipwrecked treasures at five hundred millions of francs."

"Five hundred millions!" answered Captain Nemo; "they were that much once, but are so no longer."

"Just so," said I, "and a warning to the shareholders would be an act of charity. Who knows, however, if it would be well received? What speculators regret, above all, generally, is less the loss of money than that of their insane hopes. I pity them, after all, less than the thousands of unfortunates to whom so much wealth, well distributed, would have been profitable, whilst it is for ever lost to them."

I had no sooner expressed this regret than I felt it must have wounded Captain Nemo.

"Lost to them!" he answered, getting animated. "Do you think, then, that this wealth is lost when it is I that gather it? Do you think I give myself the trouble to pick up these treasures for myself? Who says that I do not make a good use of them? Do you believe that I ignore the existence of suffering beings, of races oppressed in this world, of miserable creatures to solace, of victims to revenge? Do you not understand—"

Captain Nemo stopped, regretting, perhaps, having said so much. But I had guessed. Whatever might be the motives that had forced him to seek independence under the seas, he was still a man! His heart still beat for the sufferings of humanity, and his immense charity was given to oppressed races, as well as to individuals.

And I then understood to whom the millions were sent by Captain Nemo, while the *Nautilus* was cruising in the waters of revolted Crete.

CHAPTER IX

A Vanished Continent

On the morning of the next day, the 19th of February. I saw the Canadian enter my room. I was expecting his visit. He looked much disappointed.

"Well, sir," he said to me.

"Well, Ned, luck was against us yesterday."

"Yes, that captain must stop at the very time we were going to escape from his vessel."

"Yes, Ned, he had business with his banker."

"His banker?"

"Yes, or rather his bank. I mean by that this ocean, where his wealth is in greater safety than it would be in the coffers of a state."

I then related to the Canadian the incident of the preceding evening, in the secret hope of making him wish not to leave the captain; but the only result of my account was an energetic regret expressed by Ned at not being able to take a walk on the Vigo battle-field on his own account.

"But all is not over," he said. "It is only one harpoon-throw lost. Another time we shall succeed, and this very evening, if necessary——"

"What is the direction of the *Nautilus*?" I asked.

"I do not know," answered Ned.

"Well, at noon we shall find our bearings."

The Canadian returned to Conseil. As soon as I was dressed I went into the saloon. The compass was not reassuring. The direction of the *Nautilus* was S.S.W. We were turning our backs on Europe.

I waited impatiently for our bearings to be taken. About 11.30 a.m. the reservoirs were emptied, and our apparatus went up to the surface of the ocean. I sprang upon the platform. Ned Land preceded me there.

There was no land in sight. Nothing but the immense sea. A

few sails on the horizon, doubtless those that go as far as San Roque in search of favourable winds for doubling the Cape of Good Hope. The weather was cloudy. A gale was springing up.

Ned, in a rage, tried to pierce the misty horizon. He still hoped that behind the mist stretched the land so much desired.

At noon the sun appeared for an instant. The first officer took advantage of the gleam to take the altitude. Then, the sea becoming rougher, we went down again, and the panel was closed.

An hour afterwards, when I consulted the map, I saw that the position of the *Nautilus* was indicated upon it by 16° 17' long. and 33° 22' lat., at 150 leagues from the nearest coast. It was no use to dream of escaping now, and I leave Ned Land's anger to be imagined when I informed him of our situation.

On my own account I was not overwhelmed with grief. I felt relieved from a weight that was oppressing me, and I could calmly take up my habitual work again.

That evening, about 11 p.m., I received the very unexpected visit of Captain Nemo. He asked me very graciously if I felt fatigued from sitting up so late the night before. I answered in the negative.

"Then, M. Aronnax, I have a curious excursion to propose to you."

"What is it, captain?"

"You have as yet only been on the sea-bottom by daylight. Should you like to see it on a dark night?"

"I should like it much."

"It will be a fatiguing walk, I warn you. You will have to go far, and climb a mountain. The roads are not very well kept in repair."

"What you tell me makes me doubly curious. I am ready to follow you."

"Come, then, professor. We will go and put on our diving dresses."

When we reached the ward-room I saw that neither my companions nor any of the crew were to follow us in our excursion. Captain Nemo had not even asked me to take Ned or Conseil.

In a few minutes we had put on our apparatus. They placed on our backs the reservoirs full of air, but the electric lamps were not prepared. I said as much to the captain.

"They would be of no use to us," he answered.

I thought I had not heard aright, but I could not repeat my observation, for the captain's head had already disappeared under its metallic covering. I finished harnessing myself, felt that someone placed an iron spiked stick in my hand, and a few minutes later, after the usual manœuvre, we set foot on the bottom of the Atlantic, at a depth of 150 fathoms.

Midnight was approaching. The waters were in profound darkness, but Captain Nemo showed me a reddish point in the distance, a sort of large light shining about two miles from the *Nautilus*. What this fire was, with what fed, why and how it burnt in the liquid mass, I could not tell. Anyway it lighted us, dimly it is true, but I soon became accustomed to the peculiar darkness, and I understood, under the circumstances, the uselessness of the Ruhmkorff apparatus.

Captain Nemo and I walked side by side directly towards the light. The flat soil ascended gradually. We took long strides, helping ourselves with our sticks, but our progress was slow, for our feet often sank in a sort of mud covered with seaweed and flat stones.

As we went along I heard a sort of pattering above my head. The noise sometimes redoubled, and produced something like a continuous shower. I soon understood the cause. It was rain falling violently and crisping the surface of the waves. Instinctively I was seized with the idea that I should be wet through. By water, in water! I could not help laughing at the odd idea. But the truth is that under a thick diving dress the liquid element is no longer felt, and it only seems like an atmosphere rather denser than the terrestrial atmosphere, that is all.

After half-an-hour's walking the soil became rocky. The medusæ, the microscopic crustaceans, the pennatules slightly lighted us with their phosphorescent gleams. I caught a glimpse of heaps of stones covered by some millions of zoophytes and thickets of seaweed. My foot often slipped upon this viscous carpet of seaweed, and without my stock I should have fallen several times. Turning, I still saw the white light of the *Nautilus* beginning to gleam in the distance.

The heaps of stones of which I have just spoken were heaped on the bottom of the ocean with a sort of regularity I could not explain to myself. I perceived gigantic furrows which lost themselves in the distant darkness, the length of which escaped all valuation. Other peculiarities presented themselves that I did not know how to account for. It seemed to me that my heavy leaden shoes were crushing a litter of bones that cracked with a dry noise. What, then, was this vast plain I was thus moving across? I should have liked to question the captain, but his language by signs, that allowed him to talk to his companions when they followed him in his submarine excursions, was still incomprehensible to me.

In the meantime the reddish light that guided us increased and inflamed the horizon. The presence of this fire under the seas excited my curiosity to the highest pitch. Was it some electric effluence? Was I going towards a natural phenomenon still unknown to the *savants* of the earth? Or—for this thought crossed my mind—had the hand of man any part in the conflagration? Had it lighted this fire? Was I going to meet in this deep sea companions and friends of Captain Nemo living the same strange life, and whom he was going to see? All these foolish and inadmissible ideas pursued me, and in that state of mind, ceaselessly excited by the series of marvels that passed before my eyes, I should not have been surprised to see, at the bottom of the sea, one of the submarine towns Captain Nemo dreamed of.

Our road grew lighter and lighter. The white light shone from the top of a mountain about eight hundred feet high. But what I perceived was only a reflection made by the crystal of the water. The fire, the source of the inexplicable light, was on the opposite side of the mountain.

Amidst the stony paths that furrowed the bottom of the Atlantic Captain Nemo went on without hesitating. He knew the dark route, had doubtless often been along it, and could not lose himself in it. I followed him with unshaken confidence. He appeared, whilst walking before me, like one of the sea genii, and I admired his tall stature like a black shadow on the luminous background of the horizon.

It was one o'clock in the morning. We had reached the first slopes of the mountain. But the way up led through the difficult paths of a vast thicket.

Yes, a thicket of dead trees, leafless, sapless, mineralised under the action of the water, overtopped here and there by gigantic pines. It was like a coal-bed, still standing, holding by its roots to the soil that had given way, and whose branches, like fine black paper-cuttings, stood out against the watery ceiling. My readers may imagine a forest on the side of the Harz Mountains, but forest and mountain sunk to the bottom of the sea. The paths were encumbered with seaweed and fucus, amongst which swarmed a world of crustaceans. I went on climbing over the rocks, leaping over the fallen trunks, breaking the sea-creepers that balanced from one tree to another, startling the fish that flew from branch to branch. Pressed onwards, I no longer felt any fatigue. I followed my guide, who was never fatigued.

What a spectacle! How can I depict it? How describe the aspect of the woods and rocks in this liquid element, their lower parts sombre and wild, the upper coloured with red tints in the light which the reverberating power of the water doubled? We were climbing rocks which fell in enormous fragments directly afterwards with the noise of an avalanche. Right and left were deep dark galleries where sight was lost. Here opened vast clearings that seemed made by the hand of man, and I asked myself sometimes if some inhabitant of these submarine regions was not about to appear suddenly.

But Captain Nemo still went on climbing. I would not be left behind. My stick lent me useful aid. A false step would have been dangerous in these narrow paths, hollowed out of the sides of precipices; but I walked along with a firm step without suffering from vertigo. Sometimes I jumped over a crevice the depth of which would have made me recoil on the glaciers of the earth; sometimes I ventured on the vacillating trunks of trees thrown from one abyss to another without looking under my feet, having only eyes to admire the savage sites of that region. There, monumental rocks perched on these irregularly-cut bases seemed to defy the laws of equilibrium. Between their stony knees grew trees like a jet of water under strong pressure, sustaining and sustained by the rocks. Then, natural towers, large scarps cut perpendicularly like a fortress curtain, inclining at an angle which the laws of gravitation would not have authorised on the surface of the terrestrial regions.

And did I not myself feel the difference due to the powerful density of the water, when, notwithstanding my heavy garments, my brass headpiece, my metal soles, I climbed slopes impracticably steep, clearing them, so to speak, with the lightness of an isard or a chamois?

I feel that this recital of an excursion under the sea cannot sound probable. I am the historian of things that seem impossible, and that yet are real and incontestable. I did not dream. I saw and felt.

Two hours after having quitted the *Nautilus* we had passed the trees, and a hundred feet above our heads rose the summit of the mountain, the projection of which made a shadow on the brilliant irradiation of the opposite slope. A few petrified bushes were scattered hither and thither in grimacing zigzags. The fish rose in shoals under our footsteps like birds surprised in the tall grass. The rocky mass was hollowed out into impenetrable confractuosities, deep grottoes, bottomless holes, in which I heard formidable noises. My blood froze in my veins when I perceived some enormous antenna barricading my path, or some frightful claw shutting up with noise in the dark cavities. Thousands of luminous points shone amidst the darkness. They were the eyes of gigantic crustaceans, giant lobsters setting themselves up like halberdiers, and moving their claws with the clanking sound of metal; titanic crabs pointed like cannon on their carriages, and frightful squid, intertwining their tentacles like a living nest of serpents.

What was this exorbitant world that I did not know yet? To what order belonged these articulates to which the rock formed a second carapace? Where had Nature found the secret of their vegetating existence, and for how many centuries had they lived thus in the lowest depths of the ocean?

But I could not stop. Captain Nemo, familiar with these terrible animals, paid no attention to them. We had arrived at the first plateau, where other surprises awaited me. There rose picturesque ruins which betrayed the hand of man, and not that of the Creator. They were vast heaps of stones in the vague outlines of castles and temples, clothed with a world of zoophytes in flower, and, instead of ivy, seaweed and fucus clothed them with a vegetable mantle.

But what, then, was this portion of the globe swallowed up by cataclysms? Who had placed these rocks and stones like dolmens of anti-historical times? Where was I? where had Captain Nemo's whim brought me to?

I should have liked to question him. As I could not do that, I stopped him. I seized his arm. But he, shaking his head, and pointing to the last summit, seemed to say to me—

"Higher! Still higher!"

I followed him with a last effort, and in a few minutes I had climbed the peak that overtopped for about thirty feet all the rocky mass.

I looked at the side we had just climbed. The mountain only rose seven or eight hundred feet above the plain; but on the opposite side it commanded from twice that height the depths of this portion of the Atlantic. My eyes wandered over a large space lighted up by a violent fulguration. In fact, this mountain was a volcano. At fifty feet below the peak, amidst a rain of stones and scoriæ, a wide crater was vomiting forth torrents of lava which fell in a cascade of fire into the bosom of the liquid mass. Thus placed, the volcano, like an immense torch, lighted up the lower plain to the last limits of the horizon.

I have said that the submarine crater threw out lava, but not flames. The oxygen of the air is necessary to make a flame, and it cannot exist in water; but the streams of red-hot lava struggled victoriously against the liquid element, and turned it to vapour by its contact. Rapid currents carried away all this gas in diffusion, and the lava torrent glided to the foot of the mountain, like the eruption of Vesuvius on another Torre del Greco.

There, before my eyes, ruined, destroyed, overturned, appeared a town, its roofs crushed in, its temples thrown down, its arches dislocated, its columns lying on the ground, with the solid proportions of Tuscan architecture still discernible upon them; further on were the remains of a gigantic aqueduct; here, the incrusted base of an Acropolis, and the outlines of a Parthenon; there, some vestiges of a quay, as if some ancient port had formerly sheltered, on the shores of an extinct ocean, merchant vessels and war triremes; further on still, long lines of ruined walls, wide deserted streets, a second Pompeii buried under the waters, raised up again for me by Captain Nemo.

Where was I? Where was I? I wished to know at any price. I felt I must speak, and tried to take off the globe of brass that imprisoned my head.

But Captain Nemo came to me and stopped me with a gesture. Then picking up a piece of clayey stone he went up to a black basaltic rock and traced on it the single word—

"ATLANTIS."

What a flash of lightning shot through my mind! Atlantis, the ancient Meropis of Theopompus, the Atlantis of Plato, the continent disbelieved in by Origen, Jamblichus, D'Anville, Malte-Brun, and Humboldt, who placed its disappearance amongst legendary tales; believed in by Posidonius, Pliny, Ammianus Marcellinus, Tertullian, Engel, Sherer, Tournefort,

Buffon, and d'Avezac, was there before my eyes bearing upon it the unexceptionable testimony of its catastrophe! This, then, was the engulphed region that existed beyond Europe, Asia, and Lybia, beyond the columns of Hercules, where the powerful Atlantides lived, against whom the first wars of Ancient Greece were waged!

The historian who put into writing the grand doings of the heroic times was Plato himself. His dialogue of Timotheus and Critias was, thus to speak, written under the inspiration of Solon, poet and legislator.

One day Solon was talking with some wise old men of Saïs, a town already eight hundred years old, as the annals engraved on the sacred wall of its temples testified. One of these old men related the history of another town, a thousand years older. This first Athenian city, nine hundred centuries old, had been invaded and in part destroyed by the Atlantides. The Atlantides, said he, occupied an immense continent, larger than Africa and Asia joined together, which covered a surface between the twelfth and fortieth degree of north latitude. Their dominion extended even as far as Egypt. They wished to impose it upon Greece, but were obliged to retire before the indomitable resistance of the Hellenes. Centuries went by. A cataclysm occurred with inundations and earthquakes. One night and one day sufficed for the extinction of this Atlantis, of which the highest summits, the Madeiras, Azores, Canaries, and Cape Verd Islands still emerge.

Such were the historical souvenirs that Captain Nemo's inscription awoke in my mind. Thus, then, led by the strangest fate, I was treading on one of the mountains of this continent! I was touching with my hand these ruins a thousand times secular and contemporaneous with the geological epochs. I was walking where the contemporaries of the first man had walked. I was crushing under my heavy soles the skeletons of animals of fabulous times, which these trees, now mineralised, formerly covered with their shade.

Ah! why did time fail me? I should have liked to descend the abrupt sides of this mountain, and go over the whole of the immense continent that doubtless joined Africa to America, and to visit the great antediluvian cities. There, perhaps, before my gaze, stretched Makhimos the warlike, Eusebius the pious, whose gigantic inhabitants lived entire centuries, and who were strong enough to pile up these blocks which still resisted the action of the water. One day, perhaps, some eruptive phenomenon would bring these engulphed regions back to the surface of the waves. Sounds that announced a profound struggle of the elements have been heard, and volcanic cinders projected out of the water have been found. All this ground, as far as the Equator, is still worked by underground forces. And who knows if in some distant epoch, increased by the volcanic dejections, and by successive strata of lava, the summits of ignivome mountains will not appear on the surface of the Atlantic?

Whilst I was thus dreaming, trying to fix every detail of the grand scene in my memory, Captain Nemo, leaning against a moss-covered fragment of ruin, remained motionless as if petrified in mute ecstasy. Was he dreaming about the long-gone generations and asking them the secret of human destiny? Was it here that this strange man came to refresh his historical memories and live again that ancient existence?—he who would have no modern one. What would I not have given to know his thoughts, to share and understand them!

We remained in the same place for a whole hour, contemplating the vast plain in the light of the lava that sometimes was surprisingly intense. The interior bubblings made rapid tremblings pass over the outside of the mountain. Deep noises, clearly transmitted by the liquid medium, were echoed with majestic amplitude.

At that moment the moon appeared for an instant through the mass of waters and threw her pale rays over the engulphed continent. It was only a gleam, but its effect was indescribable. The captain rose, gave a last look at the immense plain, and then, with his hand, signed to me to follow him.

We rapidly descended the mountain. When we had once passed the mineral forest I perceived the lantern of the *Nautilus* shining like a star. The captain walked straight towards it, and we were back on board as the first tints of dawn whitened the surface of the ocean.

CHAPTER X

Submarine Coalfields

The next day, the 20th of February, I awoke very late. The fatigues of the previous night had prolonged my sleep until eleven o'clock. I dressed promptly. I was in a hurry to know the direction of the *Nautilus*. The instruments informed me that it was running southward at a speed of twenty miles an hour and a depth of fifty fathoms.

Conseil entered. I gave him an account of our nocturnal excursion, and the panels being opened, he could still get a glimpse of the submerged continent.

In fact, the *Nautilus* was moving only five fathoms from the soil of the Atlantis plain. It was flying like a balloon before the wind above terrestrial prairies; but it would be more according to fact to say that we were in this saloon like being in a carriage of an express train. In the foreground were fantastically-shaped rocks, forests of trees transformed from the vegetable to the mineral kingdom whose immovable outlines appeared under the waves. There were also stony masses, buried under a carpet of axides and anemones, bristling with long vertical hydrophytes; then blocks of lava strangely twisted that attested the fury of the underground expansions.

Whilst these strange sites shone under our electric fires I related the history of the Atlantides to Conseil, which, from an imaginary point of view, has inspired Bailly with so many charming pages. I told him all about the wars of these heroic peuplades. I discussed the question of the Atlantis as a man who has no doubts left on the subject. But Conseil did not pay much attention to my historical lesson, and I soon saw why.

Numerous fishes were attracting his attention, and when fish were passing Conseil was always lost in an abyss of classification and left the real world. In that case all I had to do was to follow him and go on with our ichthyological studies.

But these Atlantic fish did not much differ from those we had observed elsewhere. They were rays of gigantic size, five yards long, and endowed with great muscular strength, which allows them to spring up out of the waves; sharks of many kinds—amongst others a glaucus, fifteen feet long, with sharp triangular teeth, whose transparency rendered it almost invisible in the water; brown sagræ; prism-shaped humantins, cuirassed in a tuberculous skin; sturgeons, similar to their Mediterranean congeners; horn-fish, a foot and a-half long, of yellow-brown colour, with little grey fins, without teeth or tongue, as fine and supple as serpents.

Amongst the bony fish Conseil remarked some blackish makairas three yards long, armed at the upper jaw with a piercing sword; brilliant-coloured vivers, known in Aristotle's time as sea-dragons, which their dorsal darts rendered it difficult to seize; then coryphænes, with brown backs marked with blue stripes and framed in a border of gold; beautiful dorades; lunachrysostons—a sort of discs with azure shades, which, when shone upon by the solar rays, looked like silver spots; and lastly, swordfish, eight yards long, swimming in shoals, bearing yellowish scythe-shaped fins and blades six feet long—intrepid animals more herbivorous than piscivorous, who obey the least sign from their females, like hen-pecked husbands.

But whilst I was observing these different specimens of marine fauna, I did not grow tired of walking the long plains of Atlantis. Sometimes the capricious undulations of the ground forced the *Nautilus* to slacken speed whilst it glided, with all the skill of a cetacean, amongst the narrow passes between the hills. If the labyrinth proved inextricable the apparatus rose like a balloon, and, once the obstacle cleared, it went on its rapid way some yards above the bottom—admirable and charming navigation that recalled the manœuvres of a balloon journey, with this difference, however, that the *Nautilus* passively obeyed the hand of its helmsman.

About 4 p.m. the ground, generally composed of thick mud and mineralised branches, gradually changed; it became more rocky and appeared strewn with conglomerations of basaltic tufa, with pieces of lava and sulphurous obsidians. I thought that a mountainous region would soon succeed the long plains, and in fact, during certain evolutions of the *Nautilus*, I perceived the southern horizon bounded by a high wall that seemed to close all issue. Its summit evidently passed above the level of the ocean. It must be a continent, or at least an island—either one of the Canaries or one of the Cape Verd Islands. Our bearings not having been taken—perhaps purposely—I was ignorant of our whereabouts. In any case such a wall appeared to me to mark the end of that Atlantis of which, after all, we had seen so little.

The night did not put a stop to my observations. Conseil had gone to his cabin. The *Nautilus*, slackening speed, fled over the confused masses on the ground, sometimes almost touching them as to rest on them, sometimes going up whimsically to the surface of the waves. I then caught a glimpse of some bright constellations through the crystal waters, and precisely five or six of those zodiacal stars that hang in the trail of Orion.

I should have remained much longer at my window, admiring the beauties of sea and sky, but the panels were shut. At that moment the *Nautilus* was close to the high wall. What it would do now I could not guess. I went to my room. The *Nautilus* did not move. I went to sleep with the firm intention of waking after a few hours' slumber.

But the next day it was eight o'clock when I returned to the saloon. I looked at the manometer. It showed me that the *Nautilus* was floating on the surface of the ocean. I heard, besides, a noise of footsteps on the platform. However, no rolling betrayed to me the undulation of the upper waves.

I went up as far as the panel. It was open. But instead of the broad daylight I expected I was surrounded by profound darkness. Where were we? Had I made a mistake? Was it still night? No—there was not a star shining, and no night is so absolutely dark.

I did not know what to think when a voice said to me—

"Is that you, professor?"

"Ah, Captain Nemo," I answered; "where are we?"

"Under the ground, professor."

"Under ground!" I cried, "and the *Nautilus* still floating?"

"Yes; it floats still."

"But I do not understand."

"Wait a few minutes. Our lantern is going to be lighted, and if you want a light on the subject you will soon be satisfied."

I set foot on the platform and waited. The darkness was so complete that I did not even see Captain Nemo. However, in looking at the zenith exactly above my head, I thought I could perceive a vague light—a sort of twilight—that filled a circular hole. At that moment the lantern was suddenly lighted, and its brilliancy made the vague light vanish.

I looked after having closed my eyes for an instant, dazzled by the electric flame. The *Nautilus* was stationary, near a bank something like a quay. The sea on which it was riding was a lake imprisoned in a circle of walls which measured two miles in diameter, or six miles round. Its level—the manometer indicated it—could only be the same as the exterior level, for a communication naturally existed between this lake and the sea. The high walls, inclined at the base, were rounded like a vault, and made a vast tundish upside down, the height of which was about 1,200 feet. At the summit was a circular orifice through which I had seen the vague light evidently made by daylight.

Before examining the interior dispositions of this enormous cavern more attentively, before asking myself if it was the work of man or Nature, I went up to Captain Nemo.

"Where are we?" I said.

"In the very heart of an extinct volcano," he answered, "a volcano the interior of which has been invaded by the sea after some convulsion of the ground. Whilst you were asleep, professor, the *Nautilus* penetrated into this lagoon by a natural channel opened at a depth of five fathoms below the surface of the ocean. This is its port, a sure, convenient, and mysterious port, sheltered from all the winds of heaven. Find me on the coasts of your continents or islands a roadstead that equals this assured refuge against the fury of tempests."

"You certainly are in safety here, Captain Nemo. Who could get at you in the heart of a volcano? But did I not perceive an aperture at its summit?"

"Yes, a crater, a crater formerly filled with lava, smoke, and flames, which now gives entrance to the life-giving air we are breathing."

"But what volcanic mountain is this, then?"

"It belongs to one of the numerous islets with which this sea is strewn. A simple rock for ships, for us an immense cavern. I discovered it by accident, and accident has done me a good service."

"But could not someone descend by the orifice that forms the crater of the volcano?"

"Not more than I could go up through it. For about a hundred feet the base of the mountain is practicable, but above the sides overhang and could not be climbed."

"I see, captain, that Nature serves you everywhere and always. You are in safety on this lake, and no one but you can visit its waters. But what do you want with such a refuge? The *Nautilus* needs no port?"

"No, professor, but it needs electricity, the elements to produce electricity, sodium to feed these elements, coal to make its sodium, and coalfields to extract the coal. Now here it happens that the sea covers entire forests that were buried in geological epochs; now mineralised and formed into coal they are an inexhaustible mine to me."

"Then your men here, captain, do miners' work?"

"Precisely. These mines extend under the water like the coalfields of Newcastle. It is here that, clad in their bathing dresses, pickaxe and spade in hand, my men go to extract the coal that I do not even ask for from the mines of earth. When I burn this fuel for the fabrication of sodium, the smoke that escapes through the crater gives it once more the appearance of an active volcano."

296

"Shall we see your companions at work?"

"Not this time, at least, for I am in a hurry to continue our voyage round the submarine world. So I shall content myself with taking some of the reserves of sodium that I possess. One day will suffice to embark them, and then we shall continue our voyage. If, therefore, you wish to inspect this cavern and make the tour of the lake, take advantage of today, M. Aronnax."

I thanked the captain and went to look for my two companions, who had not yet left their cabin. I invited them to follow me without telling them where they were.

They came up on to the platform. Conseil, whom nothing astonished, thought it quite natural to wake up under a mountain after going to sleep under the sea. But Ned Land's only idea was to try and find out whether the cavern had any other issue.

After breakfast, about 10 a.m., we descended on the bank.

"Here we are once more on land," said Conseil.

"I don't call this land," answered the Canadian. "And, besides, we are not upon but underneath."

Between the foot of the mountain slopes and the waters of the lake ran a sandy shore, which in its widest part measured five hundred feet. Upon this it was easy to make the tour of the lake. But the base of the slopes formed an irregular soil, on which lay, in picturesque heaps, volcanic blocks and enormous pieces of pumice-stone. All these disintegrated masses, covered under the action of subterranean fires with polished enamel, shone in the lantern's electric flames. The micaceous dust of the shore that rose under our footsteps flew up like a cloud of sparks.

The ground gradually rose from the water, and we soon reached long and sinuous slopes, veritable ascents that allowed us to climb by degrees, but we were obliged to walk prudently amongst the conglomerates that no cement joined together, and our feet slipped on the glassy trachyte formed of crystal, felspar, and quartz.

The volcanic nature of this enormous excavation was proved on all sides. I pointed it out to my companions.

"Can you picture to yourselves," I asked them, "what this enormous tundish must have been like when filled with boiling lava, and the level of the incandescent liquid rose to the orifice of the mountain like molten metal on the sides of a furnace?"

"I can picture it to myself perfectly," answered Conseil. "But will monsieur tell me why the Great Smelter suspended His operation, and how it is that the furnace is replaced by the tranquil waters of a lake?"

"It is very likely, Conseil, because some convulsion made that opening under the surface of the ocean which gave ingress to the *Nautilus*. Then the waters of the Atlantic rushed into the interior of the mountain. There was a terrible struggle between the two elements, a struggle that terminated to the advantage of Neptune. But many centuries have elapsed since then, and the submerged volcano is changed into a peaceful grotto."

"Very well," replied Ned Land. "I accept the explanation, but I regret in our interest that the opening of which you speak did not take place above the sea-level."

"But, friend Ned," replied Conseil, "if this passage had not been submarine the *Nautilus* could not have gone through it."

"And I may add, Ned," said I, "that the waters would not have rushed under the volcano, and that the volcano would have remained a volcano. Therefore your regrets are wasted."

Our ascension continued. The slopes became steeper and narrower. Sometimes profound excavations lay in the way which we were obliged to cross. Overhanging masses had to be avoided. We crawled on our hands and knees. But by the help of Conseil's skill, and the Canadian's strength, we overcame all obstacles.

At a height of about ten feet the nature of the ground changed. To the conglomerates and trachytes succeeded black basalts, some spread in layers full of bubbles; some forming regular prisms, placed like a colonnade supporting the spring of an immense vault, an admirable specimen of natural architecture. Then, amongst these basalts lay serpent-like streams of cooled lava, encrusted with bituminous stripes, and, in some places, lay wide carpets of sulphur. A more powerful light, shining through the upper crater, shed a vague glimmer over all these volcanic dejections buried for ever in the heart of the extinct mountain.

However, our ascent was soon stopped at a height of about 250 feet by impassable obstacles. There was quite a vaulted arch overhanging us, and our ascent was exchanged for a circular walk. Here the vegetable kingdom began to struggle with the mineral kingdom. A few shrubs and even trees grew out of the anfractuosities of the sides. I recognised some euphorbias, with their caustic sap running. Heliotropes quite incapable of justifying their name, since the solar rays never reached them, sadly drooped their clusters of flowers, both their colour and perfume half-faded. Here and there chrysanthemums grew timidly at the foot of aloes with long and sickly-looking leaves. But amongst the lava streams I perceived little violets, still slightly scented, and I admit that I smelt them with delight. Perfume is the soul of flowers, and the sea-flowers—the splendid hydrophytes—have no soul!

We had arrived at the foot of a thicket of robust dragontrees which had pushed aside the rocks by the effort of their muscular roots, when Ned Land exclaimed—

"Why, here's a nest of bees, sir!"

"A nest?" replied I, with a gesture of perfect incredulity.

"Yes, a nest," repeated the Canadian; "and the bees are buzzing all about it."

I approached and was forced to surrender to evidence. There, at the orifice of a hole in the trunk of a dragon-tree, were several thousands of the industrious insects so common in all the Canaries, and whose produce is so particularly esteemed.

The Canadian naturally wished to make a provision of honey, and it would have been churlish of me to refuse it. He lighted a quantity of dry leaves, mixed with sulphur, by means of a spark from his flint, and began to smoke out the bees. The buzzing gradually ceased, and the hive eventually yielded several pounds of perfumed honey, with which Ned Land filled his haversack.

"When I have mixed this honey with some artocarpus paste," said he, "I shall be able to offer you a delicious cake."

"It will be as good as gingerbread," said Conseil.

"Gingerbread let it be," said I; "but let us go on with our interesting walk."

At certain turns of the path we were following, the lake appeared in its whole extent. The lantern lighted up the whole of its peaceful surface that knew neither ripple nor wave. The *Nautilus* kept perfectly still. On the platform and the shore the ship's crew were working like black shadows clearly cut against the luminous atmosphere.

At that moment we were rounding the highest crest of the first layers of rock that upheld the roof. I then saw that bees were not the only representatives of the animal kingdom in the interior of this volcano. Birds of prey hovered and turned here and there in the darkness, or fled from their nests perched on the points of rock. There were sparrowhawks with white breasts and screaming kestrels. Down the slopes also scampered, with all the rapidity of their long stilts, fine fat bustards. I leave it to be imagined if the covetousness of the Canadian was roused at the sight of this savoury game, and if he did not regret not having a gun in his hands. He tried to substitute stones for lead, and after several fruitless attempts he succeeded in wounding a magnificent bird. To say that he risked his life twenty times before hitting it is but the truth; but he managed so well that the animal was deposited with the honeycombs in his bag.

We were now obliged to descend towards the shore, the crest becoming impracticable. Above us the gaping crater looked like the wide mouth of a well. From this place the sky could be clearly seen, and I saw the dishevelled clouds running before the west wind touching the summit of the mountain with their misty fringes—a certain proof that these clouds were low ones, for the volcano did not rise more than 800 feet above the sea level.

Half-an-hour after the Canadian's exploit we had reached the inner shore. Here the flora was represented by large carpets of rock samphire, a little umbelliferous plant, a very good preserve, which also bears the names of "pierce-stone," "pass-stone," and "sea-fennel." Conseil gathered some bundles of it. The fauna might be counted by thousands of crustacea of all sorts—lobsters, crabs, palæmons, spider-crabs, chameleon shrimps, and a large number of shells, rock-fish, and limpets.

At that place opened a magnificent grotto. My companions and I were delighted to lie down on its fine sand. The fire had polished its enamelled and sparkling sides all dusted over with mica. Ned Land tapped the walls to try and find out their thickness. I could not help smiling. The conversation then turned upon the eternal projects of flight; and I thought I would, without saying too much, give him the hope that Captain Nemo had only come down south to renew his provision of sodium. I therefore hoped that now he would go near the coasts of Europe and America, which would allow the Canadian to renew with more success his former abortive attempt.

We had been lying for an hour in this charming grotto. The conversation, animated at first, was then languishing. We began to feel sleepy, and as I saw no reason why I should not give way to slumber, I fell fast asleep. I was dreaming (one does not choose one's dreams) that my existence was reduced to the vegetating life of a simple mollusc. It seemed to me that this grotto formed the double valve of my shell. All at once I was awakened by Conseil's voice.

"Look out!—look out!" cried the worthy fellow.

"What is it?" I asked, raising my head.

"The water is coming up to us!"

I rose. The water was rushing like a torrent into our retreat, and as we certainly were not molluscs, we were obliged to fly.

In a few minutes' time we were in safety on the summit of the grotto itself.

"What was it?" asked Conseil. "Some new phenomenon?"

"No, my friends," replied I; "it was the tide, the tide that almost caught us as it did Walter Scott's hero! The ocean outside rises, and, by a natural law of equilibrium, the level of the lake rises likewise. We have escaped with a bath. Let us go to the *Nautilus* and change our clothes."

Three-quarters of an hour later we had ended our circular walk, and were back on board. The men of the crew were then finishing taking the sodium on board, and the *Nautilus* could have started at once.

But Captain Nemo gave no order. Perhaps he meant to wait for night, and go out secretly by his submarine passage.

However that may be, the next day the *Nautilus*, having left its moorings, was navigating far from all land, and a few yards beneath the waves of the Atlantic.

CHAPTER XI

The Sargasso Sea

The direction of the *Nautilus* had not been changed. All hope of returning to the European seas must for the present be given up. Captain Nemo kept to the south. Where was he taking us to? I dared not imagine.

That day the *Nautilus* crossed a singular part of the Atlantic Ocean. Everyone knows of the existence of that great current of warm water known under the name of the Gulf Stream. After leaving the Gulf of Florida it goes towards Spitzbergen; but some time after quitting the Gulf of Mexico, about the 44th degree of north latitude, this current divides into two arms, the principal one going towards the coasts of Ireland and Norway, whilst the second bends southward abreast of the Azores; then striking against the African shores and describing a long oval, it comes back towards the Antilles.

Now this second arm (it is rather a collar than an arm) surrounds with its circles of warm water that portion of the cool, quiet, immovable ocean called the Sargasso Sea. A perfect lake in full Atlantic, the waters of the great current take no less than three years to go round it.

The Sargasso Sea, properly speaking, covers all the submerged part of Atlantis. Certain authors have even stated that the numerous herbs with which it is strewn are torn from the prairies of that ancient continent. It is more probable, however, that these herbs, sea-wrack and fucus, carried away from the shores of Europe and America, are brought to this zone by the Gulf Stream. That was one of the reasons that brought Columbus to suppose the existence of a new world. When the ships of this bold navigator arrived at the Sargasso Sea they sailed with difficulty amidst the herbs that impeded their course to the great terror of their crews, and they lost three long weeks crossing it.

Such was the region the *Nautilus* was now visiting, a veritable prairie, a thick carpet of sea-wrack, fucus, and tropical berries, so thick and compact that the stem of a vessel could hardly tear its way through it. And Captain Nemo, not wishing to entangle his screw in that herby mass, kept at a depth of some yards beneath the surface of the waves.

The name "Sargasso" comes from the Spanish "sargazzo," that signifies varech. This varech, or kelp, or berry-plant, principally forms this immense bank. The reason given by the learned Maury, the author of the *Physical Geography of the Sea*, for the presence of these hydrophytes in the peaceful basin of the Atlantic is the following:—

"The explanation that may be given," said he, "seems to me to result from an experiment known by everyone. If some fragments of cork, or other floating bodies, are placed in a vessel of water, and a circular movement is given to the water, the scattered fragments will be seen united in a group in the centre of the liquid surface—that is to say, at the least agitated point. In the phenomenon that occupies us the vessel is the Atlantic, the Gulf Stream is the circular current, and the Sargasso Sea the central point where the floating bodies unite."

I am of the same opinion as Maury, and I have been able to study this phenomenon in the special sea into which vessels rarely penetrate. Above us floated products of all kinds, entangled amidst these brownish herbs; trunks of trees, from the Andes or the Rocky Mountains, floated down the Amazon or the Mississippi; numerous spars, the remains of keels or ships' bottoms, side planks stove in, and so weighted with shells and barnacles that they could not rise to the surface of the ocean. And time will one day justify another of Maury's opinions, that these substances thus accumulated for ages will become mineralised under the action of the water, and will then form inexhaustible coalfields—a precious reserve prepared by far-seeing Nature for the time when men have exhausted the mines of the continents.

Amidst this inextricable tissue of herbs and fucus I noticed some charming pink stella alcyons, actiniæ with their long tentacles, green, red, and blue medusæ, and particularly

Cuvier's large rhyostoms, whose bluish umbrella is festooned with violet.

All that day of February 22nd was passed in the Sargasso Sea, where the fish that feed on marine plants and crustaceans find abundant food. The next day the ocean had resumed its accustomed aspect.

From that date, for nineteen days, from the 23rd of February to the 12th of March, the *Nautilus*, keeping in the midst of the Atlantic, carried us along at a constant speed of one hundred leagues in twenty-four hours. Captain Nemo evidently intended to accomplish his submarine programme, and I had no doubt that after doubling Cape Horn he meant to go back into the South Pacific.

Ned Land had therefore cause to fear. In these wide seas, destitute of islands, leaving the vessel could not be attempted. Neither were there any means of opposing Captain Nemo's will. The only thing to do was to submit; but that which could no longer be expected from force or ruse I liked to think might be obtained by persuasion. This voyage ended, would not Captain Nemo consent to give us liberty if we swore never to reveal his existence?—an oath of honour which we should have kept. But that delicate question must be discussed with the captain. But would this request for liberty be well received? Had he not himself declared at the very beginning, in the most formal manner, that the secret of his life required our perpetual imprisonment on board the *Nautilus*? Would not my silence of the last four months appear to him a tacit acceptation of the situation? Would not a return to this subject give rise to suspicions that might be prejudicial to our projects if some favourable circumstance should cause us to renew them? I turned over all these reasons, weighed them in my mind, and submitted them to Conseil, who was no less embarrassed than I. On the whole, although I am not easily discouraged, I understood that the chances of ever seeing my fellows again were diminishing from day to day; above all, now that Captain Nemo was boldly rushing to the very south of the Atlantic.

During the above-mentioned nineteen days no particular incident occurred. I saw little of the captain. He was working. I often found books in the library that he had left open, and especially works of natural history. My book on the submarine depths was covered by him with notes in the margin that sometimes contradicted my theories and systems. But the captain contented himself with thus revising my work, and it was rare that he discussed it with me. Sometimes I heard the melancholy tones of his organ, which he played with much expression, but at night only, amidst the most secret obscurity, when the *Nautilus* was sleeping in the deserts of the ocean.

During this part of the voyage we went along for whole days on the surface of the waves. The sea was abandoned. A few sailing vessels only were to be seen, bound for the Indies, and making for the Cape of Good Hope. One day we were pursued by the boats of a whaler that had doubtless taken us for some enormous whale of great value. But Captain Nemo did not wish the brave fellows to lose their time and trouble, and he ended the pursuit by plunging under the water. This incident seemed greatly to interest Ned Land. I do not think I am mistaken in saying that the Canadian regretted that our iron-plated cetacean could not be struck dead by the harpoon of the fishers.

The fish observed by Conseil and me during this period differed little from those we had already studied under other latitudes. The principal were some specimens of the terrible cartilaginous class, divided into three sub-classes, which count no less than thirty-two species—striped dog-fish, five yards long, with depressed heads wider than their bodies, round caudal fins, and seven large black parallel and longitudinal bands down their backs; sapphirine dog-fish, of under-grey colour, pierced with seven gill-openings, and furnished with a single dorsal fin placed in about the middle of the body.

Hound-fish also passed, as voracious as fish could be. The accounts fishermen give of them may be disbelieved, but they say that the head of a buffalo and an entire calf have been found in the body of one of these animals; in another, two tunny-fish and a sailor in uniform; in another, a soldier and his sword; and lastly, in another, a horse and his rider. All this certainly is not an article of faith. All I can affirm is that the nets of the *Nautilus* never caught one of these animals, so that I could not verify their voracity.

Elegant and playful shoals of dolphins accompanied us for whole days. They went in bands of five and six, hunting in packs like wolves; they are no less voracious than hound-fish, if I may believe a Copenhagen professor who drew from the stomach of a dolphin thirteen porpoises and fifteen seals. Dolphins belong to the largest known species of grampus, and are sometimes more than twenty-four feet long. This family of delphinians counts six classes, and those I perceived belonged to the class of delphinorinques, remarkable for their excessively narrow snouts, four times as long as the cranium. Their bodies, measuring three yards, black on the top, were underneath of a pinky-white, with a few rare and little spots.

I may also mention in these seas some curious specimens of fish belonging to the order of acanthopterigians and the family of scienoides. Some authors—greater poets than naturalists—pretend that these fish sing melodiously, and that their united voices form a concert that no chorus of human voices could equal. I do not say that it is not so, but these syrens gave us no serenade on our passage, which I regret.

In short, to end with, Conseil classified a great quantity of flying-fish. Nothing was more curious than to see the dolphins give chase to them with marvellous precision. However high it flew, whatever trajectory it described—even over the *Nautilus*—the unfortunate fish always found a dolphin's mouth open to receive it. They were kite-gurnards with luminous mouths, which during the night, after having striped the atmosphere with fire, plunged into the dark waters like so many shooting-stars.

Until the 13th of March our navigation went on under the same conditions. That day the *Nautilus* was employed in sounding experiments that greatly interested me.

We had then come nearly 13,000 leagues since our departure from the high seas of the Pacific. Our bearings gave us 45° 37' south lat, and 37° 53' west long. It was the spot where Captain Denham, of the *Herald*, ran out 7,000 fathoms of line without finding the bottom. There, too, Lieutenant Parker, of the American frigate *Congress*, was not able to reach the submarine depths with a line of 7,600 fathoms.

Captain Nemo resolved to send his *Nautilus* to the very bottom in order to verify these different soundings. I prepared to take notes of the result. The saloon panels were opened, and the manœuvres necessary to reach such prodigious depths were begun.

It will be readily imagined that the filling of the reservoirs would not suffice. They would probably not have sufficiently increased the specific weight of the *Nautilus*. Besides, to go up again it would have been necessary to get rid of the extra stock of water, and the pumps would not have been powerful enough to conquer the exterior pressure.

Captain Nemo resolved to seek the oceanic bottom by a sufficiently elongated diagonal by means of his lateral planes, which were inclined at an angle of 45° with the water-lines of the *Nautilus*. Then the screw was worked at its maximum of speed, and its quadruple branch beat the water with indescribable violence.

Under this powerful propulsion the hull of the *Nautilus* vibrated like a sonorous wire and sank regularly under the water. The captain and I, in the saloon, followed the needle of the manometer that rapidly moved. We had soon passed the habitable zone where most of the fish dwell. Some can only live on the surface of seas or rivers, whilst others, less numerous, inhabit greater depths. Amongst these latter I noticed the hexanch, a species of sea-hound, furnished with six gills; the enormous-eyed telescope; the cuirassed malarmat, with grey thorax, black pectorals which protected his chest-plate of pale red bony plates; and lastly, the grenadier, which, living at a depth of six hundred fathoms, supports a pressure of a hundred and twenty atmospheres.

I asked Captain Nemo if he had ever seen fish at greater depths.

"Rarely," he replied. "But in the actual state of science what do they know or suppose?"

"They know that as we sink lower in the ocean vegetable life disappears before animal life. They know that where animated life is still encountered not a single hydrophyte exists. They know that pelerines and oysters live in 1,000 fathoms, and that McClintock, the hero of the Polar Seas, drew up a star-fish alive from a depth of 1,250 fathoms. They know that the crew of the Royal Navy *Blue Dog* drew up a sea-star from a depth of 2,620 fathoms, or more than a league. But perhaps, Captain Nemo, you will tell me they know nothing?"

"No, professor," answered the captain, "I shall not be so rude. I shall only ask you how you explain the fact that animals can live at such a depth."

"I explain it by two reasons," I replied. "First, because the vertical currents determined by the difference of saltness and density in water produce a movement that is sufficient to keep up the rudimentary life of asteria and encrines."

"Right," said the captain.

"And also because, if oxygen is the basis of life, it is known that the quantity of oxygen dissolved in sea-water augments, instead of diminishing, with its depth, and that the pressure of the lowest depth contributes to compress it there."

"Ah, they know that?" answered Captain Nemo in a slightly surprised tone. "Well, professor, they do right to know it, for it is the truth. I may add that the air-bladder of fish contains more azote than oxygen when caught on the surface of the water, and more oxygen than azote when taken from greater depths, which fact gives reason to your system. But let us continue our observations."

I looked at the manometer. The instrument indicated a depth of 3,000 fathoms. Our submersion had lasted an hour. The

Nautilus, gliding on its inclined planes, was still sinking. The solitary water was admirably transparent and of a diaphaneity that nothing could depict. An hour later we were at a depth of 6,500 fathoms—about three leagues and a quarter—and still there was no sign of the bottom.

However, at a depth of 7,000 fathoms 1 perceived some blackish summits rise amidst the waters. But these summits might belong to mountains as high as the Himalayas or Mont Blanc, higher even, and the depth of these abysses remains unknown.

The *Nautilus* sank still lower, in spite of the powerful pressure it endured. I felt the steel plates tremble under the jointures of their bolts; its bars bent; its partitions groaned; the windows of the saloon seemed to curve under the pressure of the water. And the apparatus would doubtless have been crushed in, if, as the captain said, it had not been as capable of resistance as a solid block.

Whilst skirting the declivity of these rocks, lost under the water, I still saw some shells, serpulæ, and spinorbis, still living, and some specimens of asteriads.

But soon these last representatives of animal life disappeared, and below three leagues the *Nautilus* passed the limits of submarine existence, like a balloon that rises above the respirable atmosphere. We had reached a depth of 8,000 fathoms—four leagues—and the sides of the *Nautilus* then supported a pressure of 1,600 atmospheres—that is to say, 3,200 lbs. on each square centimetre of its surface.

"What a situation!" I cried. "To traverse these deep regions to which man has never reached! Look, captain, look at those magnificent rocks, those uninhabited grottoes, those last receptacles of the globe where life is no longer possible! What unknown sites, and why must we be forced to keep nothing of them but the remembrance?"

"Should you like to take away anything better than the remembrance?" asked Captain Nemo.

"What do you mean?"

"I mean that nothing is easier than to take a photographic view of this submarine region!"

I had not time to express the surprise that this fresh proposition caused me before, at an order from Captain Nemo, a camera was brought into the saloon. Through the wide-opened panels the liquid, lighted up by electricity, was distributed with perfect clearness. No shade, not a gradation, was to be seen in our manufactured light. The sun would not have been more favourable to an operation of this nature. The *Nautilus*, under the propulsion of its screw, mastered by the inclination of its planes, remained motionless. The camera was pointed at these sites on the oceanic bottom, and in a few seconds we had obtained an exceedingly pure negative.

The positive I give here. Here may be seen the primordial rocks that have never known the light of heaven, the lower granites that form the powerful foundation of the globe, the profound grottoes dug out of the stony mass, the outlines of such incomparable clearness, the border-lines of which stand out black as if due to the brush of certain Flemish artists. Then, beyond, an horizon of mountains, an admirable undulated line composing the background of the landscape. I cannot describe the effect of these smooth black polished rocks, destitute of moss, without a stain, and with such strange forms solidly resting on the carpet of sand that sparkled in the electric light.

However, after Captain Nemo had terminated his operation, he said to me—

"We must go up again now, professor. It would not do to expose the *Nautilus* too long to such pressure."

"Go up again!" I expostulated.

"Hold tight."

I had not time to understand why the captain gave me this caution before I was thrown upon the carpet.

At a signal from the captain the screw had been shipped, the planes raised vertically, and the *Nautilus*, carried up like a balloon into the air, shot along with stunning rapidity. It cut through the water with a sonorous vibration. No detail was visible. In four minutes it had cleared the four leagues that separated it from the surface of the ocean, and after emerging like a flying fish it fell again, making the waves rebound to an enormous height.

CHAPTER XII

Cachalots and Whales

During the night, from the 13th to the 14th of March, the *Nautilus* resumed her southerly direction. I thought that, once abreast of Cape Horn, the head would be turned westward, so as to make for the seas of the Pacific, and so complete its voyage round the world. Nothing of the kind was done, however, and the vessel kept on its way to the austral regions. Where was it going? To the Pole? That was madness! I began to think that the daring of the captain justified Ned Land's fears.

For some time past the Canadian had not spoken to me about his projects of flight. He had become less communicative, almost silent. I could see how much this prolonged imprisonment was weighing upon him. I felt how his anger was accumulating. When he met the captain his eyes lighted up with sombre fire, and I always feared that his natural violence would lead him into some extreme.

That day, the 14th of March, Conseil and he came into my room to find me. I asked them the reason for their visit.

"I have a simple question to ask you, sir," answered the Canadian.

"Speak, Ned."

"How many men do you think there are on board the *Nautilus*?"

"I cannot say, my friend."

"It seems to me," concerned Ned Land, "that it would not take a large crew to work it."

"Certainly, under existing circumstances, ten men ought to be enough."

"Well," said the Canadian, "why should there be any more?"

"Why?" I replied.

I looked fixedly at Ned Land, whose intentions were easy to guess.

"Because," I added, "if my surmises are correct, if I understand the captain's existence rightly, the *Nautilus* is not only a vessel. It must also be a place of refuge for those who, like its commander, have ceased all communication with land."

"Perhaps so," said Conseil; "but after all the *Nautilus* can only contain a certain number of men, and monsieur might estimate their maximum?"

"How so, Conseil?"

"By calculating. Given the size of the vessel, which monsieur knows, and consequently the quantity of air it contains; knowing also how much each man needs to breathe, and comparing these results with the necessity the *Nautilus* is under to go up to the surface every twenty-four hours——"

Conseil did not finish his sentence, but I saw what he wanted to say.

"I understand you," said I; "but that calculation, though simple enough, can only give us a very uncertain result."

"Never mind that," said Ned Land, insisting.

"Here is the calculation, then," said I. "In one hour each man consumes the oxygen contained in 100 litres of air, or in twenty-four hours the oxygen contained in 2,400 litres. We must, therefore, find out how many times 2,400 litres of air the *Nautilus* contains."

"Precisely," said Conseil.

"The capacity of the *Nautilus* is 1,500 tons, and one ton holding 1,000 litres, the *Nautilus* contains 1,500,000 litres of air, which divided by 2,400——"

I calculated rapidly with a pencil.

"——gives a quotient of 625, which is the same as saying that the air contained in the *Nautilus* could, strictly speaking, suffice 625 men during twenty-four hours."

"Six hundred and twenty-five!" repeated Ned.

"But be you sure," I added, "that all of us, passengers, sailors, and officers included, do not form a tenth part of that number."

"Still too many for three men!" murmured Conseil.

"Therefore, my poor Ned, I can only preach patience to you."

"And even more than patience," answered Conseil—"resignation too."

Conseil had used the right word.

"After all," he continued, "Captain Nemo cannot always go southward! He must stop somewhere, if only before an ice-bank, and afterwards he will return to more civilised seas! It will then be time to return to Ned Land's projects."

The Canadian shook his head, passed his hand across his forehead, and left the room without answering.

"Will monsieur allow me to make one observation?" said Conseil. "That poor Ned thinks of everything he cannot have. Everything in his past life comes back to him. Everything we are forbidden seems to him regrettable. His old recollections oppress him and make him heartsick. It is easy to understand. What has he to do here? Nothing. He is not learned like monsieur, and cannot have the same taste for the beauties of the sea as we have. He would risk all to be able once more to enter a tavern in his own country."

It is certain that the monotonous life on board must appear insupportable to the Canadian, accustomed as he was to a free and active life. The events he could take an interest in were rare. However, that day an event did happen that recalled the bright days of the harpooner.

About 11 a.m. the *Nautilus*, being then on the surface of the ocean, fell in with a troop of whales—an encounter that did not surprise me, for I knew that these animals, hunted to death, had taken refuge in the high latitudes.

The part played by the whale in the marine world, and its influence upon geographical discoveries, have been con-siderable. It was the whale that dragged in its wake, first Basques, then Asturians, English, and Dutch, emboldened them against the dangers of the ocean, and led them from one extremity of the world to the other. Whales like to frequent the boreal and austral seas. Ancient legends even pretend that these cetaceans led fishermen to within seven leagues of the North

315

Pole. If the fact is false it will one day be true, and it is thus probable that whilst pursuing whales in the Arctic and Antarctic regions men will reach this unknown point of the globe.

We were seated on the platform, with a quiet sea. The month of October in those latitudes gave us some beautiful autumnal days. It was the Canadian—he could not be mistaken—who signalled a whale on the eastern horizon. Looking attentively, we could see its black back rise and fall above the waves at five miles' distance from the *Nautilus*.

"Ah!" cried Ned Land, "if I was on board a whaler now what pleasure that sight would give me! It is one of large size. Look with what strength its blow-holes throw up columns of air and vapour! Confound it all! Why am I chained to this piece of iron?"

"What, Ned!" said I, "you have not yet got over your old fishing ideas?"

"Can a whale-fisher ever forget his old trade, sir? Can he ever tire of the emotions of such a chase?"

"Have you never fished in these seas, Ned?"

"Never, sir. Only in the Arctic Seas, and as much in Behring as in Davis Straits."

"Then the austral whale is still unknown to you. It is the Greenland whale you have hunted up till now; it would not venture to pass through the warm water at the equator."

"Ah, professor, what are you talking about?" replied the Canadian in a passably incredulous tone.

"About what really exists."

"Well, all I know is that I myself in '65—that is, two years and a half ago—I harpooned a whale near Greenland that carried in its side a pointed harpoon of a Behring whaler. Now I ask you, sir, how could it, after being struck on the west coast of America, come to the east coast to be killed unless it had either doubled Cape Horn or the Cape of Good Hope, and so crossed the equator?"

"I think like Ned," said Conseil, "and I await monsieur's answer."

"Monsieur will answer you, my friend, that whales are

localised, according to their kinds, in certain seas that they do not leave. And if one of these creatures went from Behring to Davis Straits, it must be simply because there is a passage from one sea to the other, either on the coasts of America or Asia."

"Must I believe you?" asked the Canadian, winking.

"Monsieur must be believed," answered Conseil.

"In that case, as I have never fished in these seas, I do not know what sort of whales frequent them."

"I have told you so, Ned."

"More reason for making their acquaintance," said Conseil.

"Look! look!" cried the Canadian excitedly. "It is coming nearer! It is coming up to us! It sets me at defiance! It knows I can do nothing to it!"

Ned stamped. His hand trembled as he brandished an imaginary harpoon.

"Are these whales as big as those in the north seas?" he asked.

"About the same, Ned."

"Because I have seen large whales, sir—whales a hundred feet long. I have even been told that the Hullamoch and Umgallick, of the Aleutian Islands, are sometimes a hundred and fifty feet long."

"That seems to me exaggerated. These creatures are only balænopterons, furnished with dorsal fins, and, like cachalots, are generally much smaller than the ordinary whale."

"Ah!" cried the Canadian, whose eyes never left the ocean, "it is coming nearer; it is coming into the water of the *Nautilus*."

Then resuming the conversation—

"You speak of the cachalot," said he, "as though it was a small creature. They talk, however, of gigantic ones. They are intelligent cetaceans. Some of them, they say, cover themselves with sea-wrack and fucus. They are taken for islands. People encamp on them, settle, light fires——"

"And build houses," said Conseil.

"Yes, joker," answered Ned Land. "Then one fine day the animal plunges and drags all its inhabitants to the bottom of the sea."

317

"Like the voyages of Sinbad the sailor," replied I, laughing. "Ah, Ned, it appears that you like extraordinary tales! What cachalots yours are! I hope you do not believe in them."

"Mr. Naturalist," answered the Canadian seriously, "every thing about whales may be believed. What a rate this one is going at! They make out that these creatures can go round the world in a fortnight."

"I do not contradict the statement."

But what you very likely do not know, M. Aronnax, is that, in the beginning of the world, whales went along more rapidly still."

"Really, Ned! How so?"

"Because then their tails were like fishes' tails—that is to say, that compressed vertically they struck the water from right to left and from left to right. But the Creator, perceiving that they went along too quickly, bent their tails, and from that time they beat the water from top to bottom to the detriment of their speed."

"Good, Ned," said I, adopting one of his expressions; "must I believe you?"

"Not altogether," answered Ned Land, "and not more than if I told you that there exist whales three hundred feet long, and weighing a hundred thousand pounds."

"That is a good deal, certainly," I said. "Still it must be acknowledged that there are cetaceans of extraordinary development, since they can give as much as a hundred and twenty tons of oil."

"As to that, I have seen it," said the Canadian.

"I readily believe it, Ned, as I believe that some whales are as large as a hundred elephants. Judge of the effect of such a mass hurled at full speed."

"Is it true," asked Conseil, "that they can sink ships?"

"Not ships, I believe," answered I. "Still it is related that in 1820, precisely in these southern seas, a whale threw itself upon the *Essex* and sent her backward at the rate of fourteen feet a second. The water rushed in aft, and the *Essex* sank almost immediately."

Ned looked at me with a bantering air.

"For my part," said he, "I have had a blow from a whale's tail—in my boat, of course. My companions and I were thrown up to a height of twenty feet. But mine was only an infant whale in comparison to yours."

"Do those animals live a long time?" asked Conseil.

"A thousand years," answered the Canadian unhesitatingly.

"How do you know that, Ned?"

"Because they say so."

"But what makes them say so?"

"Because they know."

"No, Ned, they do not know, but they suppose it, and for this reason. Four hundred years ago, when fishermen pursued whales for the first time, those animals were of larger size than they are now. It is, therefore, logically supposed that the inferiority of actual whales comes from their not having had time to reach their complete development. This is what made Buffon say that cetaceans could and must live a thousand years. Do you understand?"

Ned Land was not listening. The whale was drawing nearer. He devoured it with his eyes.

"Ah!" cried he, "it is not one whale, but ten, twenty, a whole troop of them! And I can't do anything! I'm bound hand and foot!"

"But, friend Ned," said Conseil, "why not ask the captain's permission to pursue them?"

Conseil had not finished his sentence before Ned Land had lowered himself through the panel, and was running to seek the captain. A short time afterwards both appeared on the platform.

Captain Nemo looked at the troop of cetaceans that were playing on the waters about a mile from the *Nautilus*.

"They are austral whales," said he. "There's the fortune of a fleet of whalers there."

"Well, sir," asked the Canadian, "can't I pursue them just to prevent myself forgetting my old trade of harpooner?"

"What is the use?" answered Captain Nemo. "We have no use for whale-oil on board."

"But, sir," resumed the Canadian, "you allowed us to pursue a dugong in the Red Sea!"

"That was to procure fresh meat for my crew. Here it would only be for the pleasure of killing. I know that it is a privilege reserved to man, but I do not approve of such murderous pastime. By destroying the austral as well as the ordinary whale, both inoffensive creatures, people like you, Ned Land, commit a blamable action. It is thus they have depopulated the whole of Baffin's Bay, and they will annihilate a class of useful animals. Therefore let the unfortunate cetaceans alone. They have quite enough of their natural enemies, the cachalots, swordfish, and saw-fish, without your interfering."

I leave the Canadian's face during this moral lecture to be imagined. It was a waste of words to give such reasons to a sportsman. Ned Land looked at Captain Nemo, and evidently did not understand what he meant. However, the captain was right. The barbarous and inconsiderate greed of the fishermen will one day cause the last whale to disappear from the ocean.

Ned Land whistled "Yankee Doodle" between his teeth, and turned his back upon us.

However, Captain Nemo looked at the troop of cetaceans, and addressing me—

"I was right in saying whales had enough natural enemies. They will have plenty to do before long. Do you see those black moving points, M. Aronnax, about eight miles to leeward?"

"Yes, captain," I replied.

"They are cachalots—terrible animals that I have sometimes met with in troops of two or three hundred. As to those cruel and mischievous creatures, it is right to exterminate them."

The Canadian turned quickly at these last words.

"Well, captain," I said, "in the interest of the whales there is still time."

"It is useless to expose oneself, professor. The *Nautilus* will suffice to disperse these cachalots. It is armed with a steel spur that I imagine is quite worth Mr. Land's harpoon."

The Canadian did not repress a shrug of the shoulders. Attack cetaceans with a prow! Who had ever heard of such a thing?

"Wait, M. Aronnax," said Captain Nemo. "We will show you a hunt you have never seen before. I have no pity for such ferocious cetaceans. They are all mouth and teeth."

Mouth and teeth! The macrocephalous cachalot, or spermaceti whale, could not be better described; it is sometimes more than seventy-five feet long. Its enormous head takes up one-third of its entire body. Better armed than the whale, whose upper jaw is only furnished with whalebone, it is supplied with twenty-five large tusks, about three inches long, cylindrical, and conical at the top, which weigh two pounds each. It is in the upper part of this enormous head, in great cavities divided by cartilages, that from six to eight hundred pounds of the precious oil called spermaceti is found. The cachalot is an ugly animal, more of a tadpole than a fish, according to Frédol's description. It is badly formed, the whole of the left side being what we might call a "failure," and seeing little except with the right eye.

In the meantime the formidable troop was drawing nearer. They had perceived the whales, and were preparing to attack them. One could prophesy beforehand that the cachalots would be victorious, not only because they were better built for attack than their inoffensive adversaries, but also because they could remain longer under the waves without rising to the surface.

There was only just time to go to the help of the whales when the *Nautilus* came up to them. The *Nautilus* sank; Conseil, Ned, and I took our places at the windows of the saloon. Captain Nemo joined the helmsman in his cage to work his apparatus as an engine of destruction. I soon felt the vibration of the screw increase and our speed become greater.

The combat between the cachalots and whales had already

begun when the *Nautilus* reached them. It was worked so as to divide the cachalots, who at first showed no fear at the sight of the new monster joining in the conflict. But they soon had to guard against its blows.

What a struggle! Ned Land himself, soon enthusiastic, ended by clapping his hands. The *Nautilus* was now nothing but a formidable harpoon, brandished by the hand of its captain. It hurled itself against the fleshy mass, cut it through from end to end, leaving behind it two quivering halves of an animal. It did not feel the formidable blows on its sides from the cachalots' tails, nor the shocks it produced itself. One cachalot exterminated, it ran to another, tacked on the spot that it might not miss its prey, going backwards and forwards obedient to its helm, plunging when the cetacean dived into deep water, coming back with it to the surface, striking it in front or sideways, cutting or tearing in all directions and at any pace, piercing it through with its terrible spur.

What carnage! What a noise on the surface of the waves! What sharp hissing and snorting, peculiar to these animals when frightened! Amidst these generally peaceful waters their tails made perfect billows.

For an hour this Homeric massacre went on, which the cachalots could not escape. Ten or twelve of them tried several times to crush the *Nautilus* under their mass. We saw through the window their enormous mouths, paved with teeth, and their formidable eyes. Ned Land, who could no longer contain himself, threatened and stormed at them. We could feel them clinging to our vessel, like dogs worrying a wild boar in a copse. But the *Nautilus*, forcing its screw, carried them hither and thither, or to the upper level of the waters, in spite of their enormous weight or powerful hold.

At last the mass of cachalots was broken up, the waves became quiet again, and I felt that we were rising to the surface of the ocean. The panel was opened, and we rushed on to the platform.

The sea was covered with mutilated bodies. A formidable

explosion could not have divided or cut up these fleshy masses more effectually. We were floating amidst gigantic bodies, bluish on the back, whitish underneath, covered with enormous protuberances. Some terrified cachalots were flying away on the horizon. The waves were dyed red for several miles round, and the *Nautilus* was floating in a sea of blood.

Captain Nemo joined us.

"Well, Mr. Land?" said he.

"Well, sir, answered the Canadian, whose enthusiasm had calmed down, "it is a terrible spectacle, certainly. But I am not a butcher—I am a hunter, and this is only butchery."

"It is a massacre of mischievous animals," replied the captain, "and the *Nautilus* is not a butcher's knife."

"I like my harpoon better," answered the Canadian.

"Each to his arm," replied the captain, looking fixedly at Ned Land.

I feared that the Canadian would give way to some act of violence that would have deplorable consequences. But his anger was averted by the sight of a whale which the *Nautilus* had just come up with.

The animal had not been able to escape the cachalots' teeth. I recognised the South Sea whale by its flat head, which is quite black. Anatomically it is distinguished from the white whale and the ice-whale by the soldering of the seven conical vertebræ and its having two more ribs than its congeners. The unfortunate cetacean was lying on its side, its belly riddled with holes from the bites, and quite dead. From its mutilated fin still hung a young whale that it had not been able to save from the massacre. Its open mouth let the water run in and out, which murmured through the whale's bones like waves breaking on the shore.

Captain Nemo steamed the *Nautilus* close to the body of the animal. Two of his men mounted on the whale's side, and I saw, not without astonishment, that they were drawing from its udders all the milk they contained—that is to say, about two or three tons.

The captain offered me a cup of this milk, which was still

warm. I could not help showing him my repugnance to this drink. He assured me that it was excellent, and not to be distinguished from cow's milk.

I tasted it, and was of his opinion. It was a useful reserve for us, for this milk under the form of butter or cheese would make an agreeable variety to our daily food.

From that day I noticed, with uneasiness, that Ned Land's ill-will for the captain increased, and I resolved to watch the Canadian's doings and gestures very closely.

CHAPTER XIII

The Ice-Bank

The *Nautilus* resumed her imperturbable southwardly course, following the fiftieth meridian with considerable speed. Did it mean, then to reach the Pole? I did not think so, for hitherto every attempt to reach that point had failed. The season, besides, was far advanced, for in the Antarctic regions the 13th of March corresponds to the 13th of September of Arctic regions, which begins the equinoctial period.

On the 14th of March I perceived floating ice by 55° of latitude—merely pale *débris* from twenty to twenty-five feet long, forming reefs over which the sea curled. The *Nautilus* kept on the surface of the ocean. Ned Land, who had already fished in the Arctic seas, was familiar with the spectacle of icebergs. Conseil and I were admiring it for the first time.

In the air, towards the southern horizon, stretched a white band of dazzling aspect. English whalers have given it the name of "ice-blink." However thick the clouds may be, they cannot hide it; it announces the presence of an ice-pack or bank.

In fact, larger blocks soon appeared, the brilliancy of which was modified according to the caprices of the mist. Some of these masses showed green veins, as if the long undulating lines had been traced by sulphate of copper. Others, like enormous amethysts, let the light shine through them. Some reflected the rays of the sun upon a thousand crystal facets. Others, shaded with vivid calcareous tints, would have sufficed for the construction of a whole town in marble.

The more we went down south the more these floating islands gained in number and importance. The Polar birds rested on them by thousands; petrels, danners, and puffins deafened us with their cries. Some of them took the *Nautilus* for the body of a whale, came upon it to rest, and pecked its sonorous plates with their beaks.

During this navigation amidst the ice Captain Nemo often kept on the platform. He attentively observed these solitary regions. I saw his calm look sometimes change to an animated one. Did he say to himself that in these Polar seas, interdicted to man, he was at home, master of unbounded space? Perhaps—but he did not speak. He remained motionless, only coming to himself when his steersman's instincts were uppermost. Then, directing his *Nautilus* with consummate skill, he cleverly avoided the shock of those masses, some of which were several miles long and from 200 to 300 feet high. The horizon often appeared entirely closed up. At the height of the sixtieth degree of latitude all passage had disappeared. But Captain Nemo, by careful search, soon found some narrow opening through which he audaciously glided, knowing well, however, that it closed up behind him.

It was thus that the *Nautilus*, steered by this skilful hand, passed all these icebergs, classified according to their form or size with a precision that enchanted Conseil—icebergs, ice-fields, packs, called "palchs" when they are circular, and "streams" when they are formed of long pieces.

The temperature was rather low. The thermometer, exposed to the exterior air, indicated two or three degrees below zero. But we were warmly dressed in furs that seals or Polar bears had furnished us with. The interior of the *Nautilus*, regularly heated by its electrical apparatus, defied the most intense cold. Besides, it had only to sink some yards below the surface to find a supportable temperature. Two months earlier we should have experienced perpetual daylight in these latitudes; but we had already three or four hours' night, and by-and-by there would be six months of darkness in these circumpolar regions.

On the 15th of March we passed the latitude of the New Shetland and New Orkney Islands. The captain informed me that formerly numerous tribes of seals inhabited them; but the English and American whalers, in their rage for destruction, massacred even mothers with young, and left the silence of death where life and animation formerly existed.

On the 16th of March, about 8 a.m., the *Nautilus*, following the fifty-fifth meridian, crossed the Antarctic Polar Circle. Ice surrounded us on every side and closed the horizon. Still Captain Nemo went through one passage after another, and still more southward.

"Where can he be going to?" I asked.

"He is following his nose," answered Conseil. "After all, when he cannot go any farther he will stop."

"I would not swear to that!" I answered. And, to tell the truth, I must acknowledge that this adventurous excursion did not displease me. I cannot express my astonishment at the beauties of these new regions. The ice took most superb forms. Here the grouping formed an Oriental town, with its innumerable minarets and mosques; there an overturned city, looking as if thrown to the earth by some earthquake—aspects incessantly varied by the oblique rays of the sun or lost in the grey mists amidst snowstorms. Detonations and ice-slips were heard on all sides—great overthrows of icebergs that changed the scene like the landscape of a diorama.

When the *Nautilus* was submerged at the moment that these equilibriums were disturbed, the noise was propagated under the water with frightful intensity, and the fall of the masses created fearful eddies as far as the greatest depth of the ocean. The *Nautilus* then pitched and tossed like a ship given up to the fury of the elements.

Often, seeing no issue, I thought we were definitely prisoners; but instinct guided him, and on the slightest indication Captain Nemo discovered new passages. He never made a mistake in observing the slender threads of bluish water that furrowed the ice-fields. I did not doubt that he had already steered his *Nautilus* in the Antarctic seas.

However, on the 16th of March ice-fields absolutely barricaded the road. It was not yet the ice-bank, but vast ice-fields cemented by the cold. This obstacle could not stop Captain Nemo, and he threw himself against the ice-field with frightful violence. The *Nautilus* entered the brittle mass like a wedge, and split it up with a frightful cracking noise. It was the ancient battering-ram hurled by infinite power. Pieces of ice, thrown high in the air, fell in hail around us. By its single power of impulsion our apparatus made a canal for itself. Sometimes by the force of its own impetus it fell on the ice-field and crushed it with its weight, or, deeply engaged in the ice, it divided it by a simple pitching movement that opened up wide fissures in it.

Violent showers assailed us during these days. During certain thick fogs we could not see from one end of the platform to another. The wind veered round to every point of the compass; the snow accumulated in such hard heaps that it had to be broken up with a pickaxe. The temperature of 5° below zero covered the exterior of the *Nautilus* with ice. A rigged vessel could not have been worked there, for all rigging would have been frozen to the pulleys. A vessel without sails, with electricity for its motive power, that did without coal, could alone brave such high latitudes.

Under these conditions the barometer generally kept very low. It even fell to 73° 5'. The indications of the mariner's compass could no longer be relied upon. Its needles indicated contradictory directions whilst approaching the southern magnetic pole, which must not be confounded with the south of the globe. In fact, according to Hansten, this pole is situated nearly by 70 of lat. and 130° of long., and, according to Duperrey, by 130° of long. and 70° 30' of lat. It was then necessary to make numerous observations on the compass, placed in different parts of the ship, and taking an average. But often the reckoning had to be consulted to know our whereabouts—a very unsatisfactory method amidst the sinuous pass whose landmarks so incessantly changed.

At length, on the 18th of March, after many useless assaults, the *Nautilus* was positively blocked up. It was no longer stopped by either streams, packs, or ice-fields, but an interminable and immovable barrier, formed by icebergs soldered together.

"The ice-bank!" said the Canadian to me.

I understood that to Ned Land, like all the navigators who had preceded us, this was an insuperable obstacle. The sun having appeared for an instant about noon, the captain took a pretty exact observation, which gave our bearings by 51° 30' of long. and 67° 39' of south lat. It was already a very high point in these Antarctic regions.

There was no longer the slightest appearance of sea or liquid surface before our eyes. Under the prow of the *Nautilus* stretched a vast plain covered with confused blocks, looking like the surface of a river some time before the breaking up of the ice, but on a gigantic scale. Here and there sharp peaks and slender needles rising to a height of two hundred feet; farther, a line of cliffs with precipitous sides, covered with greyish tints, vast mirrors that reflected a few rays of the sun, half-drowned in the mists. Then over this desolate scene a savage silence, scarcely broken by the flapping of petrels' or puffins' wings. All was then frozen, even sound.

The *Nautilus* was then obliged to stop in its adventurous course amidst the ice-fields.

"Sir," said Ned Land to me one day," if your captain goes any farther——"

"Well?"

"He will be a clever man."

"Why, Ned?"

"Because no one can pass the ice-bank. He is powerful, your captain, but, confound it! he is not more powerful than Nature, and where it has put limits he must stop whether he likes it or not."

"That's certain, Ned Land, and yet I should like to know what is behind that ice-bank! A wall; that is what irritates me the most."

"Monsieur is right," said Conseil. "Walls have only been invented to irritate *savants*. There ought to be walls nowhere."

"Well," said the Canadian, "it is well known what is behind the ice-bank."

"What?" I asked.

"Ice, ice, and nothing but ice!"

"You are certain of that fact, Ned," I replied, "but I am not. That is why I should like to go and see."

"Well, professor," answered the Canadian, "give up the idea. You have reached the ice-bank, which is already sufficient, and you won't go any further, either you, your Captain Nemo, or his *Nautilus*. And whether he likes it or no, we will have to go up north again—that is to say, to the country of honest folks."

I ought to acknowledge that Ned was right, and until vessels are made to navigate on ice-fields they must stop at the ice-bank.

In fact, notwithstanding all its efforts, notwithstanding the powerful means employed to break up the ice, the *Nautilus* was reduced to immobility. Generally, if you cannot go any farther, all you have to do is to go back. But here going back was as impossible as going on, for the passages had closed up behind us, and if our apparatus remained stationary long it would soon be blocked up. That is what happened about 2 p.m., and the young ice formed on its sides with astonishing rapidity. I was forced to acknowledge that Captain Nemo's conduct was more than imprudent. I was at that moment on the platform. The captain, who had been observing the situation for some minutes, said to me—

"Well, professor, what do you think of it?"

"I think we are caught, captain."

"Caught? What do you mean by that?"

"I mean that we cannot go either backwards or forwards, nor on either side. I believe that is what may be called caught, at least, on inhabited continents."

"Then, M. Aronnax, you do not think the *Nautilus* can be set free?"

"Not easily, captain, for the season is already too far advanced for you to depend upon the breaking up of the ice."

"Ah, professor!" answered the captain in an ironical tone, "you are always the same! You only see obstacles and difficulties. But I affirm to you that not only will the *Nautilus* be set free, but it will go farther still!"

"Farther south?" I asked, looking at the captain.

"Yes, sir, it will go to the Pole."

"To the Pole!" I cried, unable to restrain a movement of incredulity.

"Yes," replied the captain coldly, "to the Antarctic Pole, to that unknown point where all the meridians of the globe meet. You know whether I do all I please with the *Nautilus*."

Yes, I knew it. I knew that man pushed boldness to temerity. But was it not an enterprise absolutely insane, and that none but the brain of a madman would have conceived?

It then came into my head to ask Captain Nemo if he had already discovered this Pole, which no human being had set foot upon.

"No, professor," he answered, "and we will discover it together. There, where so many have failed, I shall not fail. I have never brought my *Nautilus* so far south; but, I repeat, it shall go farther still."

"I wish to believe you, captain," said I in a slightly ironical tone. "I do believe you! There is no obstacle before us! We will break up that ice-bank, and if it resists, we will give the *Nautilus* wings so that we can pass over it!"

"Over it, professor?" answered Captain Nemo tranquilly. "No, not over it, but under it."

"Under it!" I cried.

A sudden revelation of the captain's projects illuminated my mind. I understood. The marvellous qualities of the *Nautilus* would again be of service in this superhuman enterprise.

"I see that we begin to understand each other, professor," said the captain, half smiling. "You already catch a glimpse of the possibility—I say of the success—of this attempt. What is impracticable to an ordinary ship is easy to the *Nautilus*. If a continent emerges at the Pole, it will stop before that continent. But if, on the contrary, the Pole is bathed by the open sea, the *Nautilus* will go to the Pole itself."

"It is certain," said I, carried along by the captain's reasoning, "that though the surface of the sea is solidified by ice, its depths are free on account of the providential reason that has placed the maximum of density of sea-water at a superior degree to its congelation. And if I am not mistaken, the submerged part of this ice-bank is to the emerged part as four is to one."

"About that, professor. For every foot that icebergs have above the sea they have three below. Now as these mountains of ice are 300 feet high, they are not more than 900 deep. Well, what is 900 feet to the *Nautilus*?"

"Nothing, captain."

"It might even go and seek at a greater depth the uniform temperature of sea-water, and there we could brave with impunity the thirty or forty degrees of cold on the surface."

"True, sir, very true," I answered, getting animated.

"The only difficulty," continued Captain Nemo, "will be to remain submerged for several days without renewing the air."

"Is that all?" I replied. "The *Nautilus* contains vast reservoirs; we will fill them, and they will furnish us with all the oxygen we shall want."

"Well imagined, M. Aronnax," said the captain, smiling. "But I did not wish you to accuse me of foolhardiness, so I submit all objections to you beforehand."

"Have you any more to make?"

"One only. It is possible that if sea exists at the South Pole, that sea may be entirely frozen over, and consequently we cannot go up to the surface."

"Well, sir, do you forget that the *Nautilus* is armed with a powerful prow, and can we not hurl it diagonally against the ice-fields, which will open at the shock?"

"Ah, professor, you have some good ideas today!"

"Besides, captain," said I, getting more and more enthusiastic, "why should we not find an open sea at the South as well as at the North Pole? The cold poles and the poles of the globe are not the same either in the boreal or austral hemispheres, and until we get proofs to the contrary we may suppose there is either a continent or an ocean free from ice at these two points of the globe."

"I think so too, M. Aronnax," answered Captain Nemo. "I will only observe to you that after uttering so many objections to my scheme, you now crush me with arguments in favour of it."

Captain Nemo spoke truly. I had come to rival him in audacity! It was I who was dragging him to the Pole! I outdistanced him. But no, poor fool! Captain Nemo knew the for and against better than you, and was amusing himself with seeing you carried away by your dreams of the impossible.

In the meantime he had not lost an instant. At a signal the first officer appeared. These two men spoke rapidly in their incomprehensible language, and whether it was that the first officer had been told of it beforehand, or that he found the scheme practicable, he manifested no surprise.

But he did not show more impassiveness than Conseil when I told the worthy fellow of our intention of going as far as the South Pole. An "As monsieur pleases" answered my communication, and with that I was obliged to content myself. As to Ned Land, he shrugged his shoulders up as high as they would go.

"I am sorry for you and your captain, M. Aronnax," said he.

"But we shall go to the Pole, Ned!"

"Possibly, but you won't come back!"

The preparations for this audacious attempt were now begun. The powerful pumps of the *Nautilus* were working air into the reservoirs, and storing it at high pressure. About four o'clock Captain Nemo informed me that the panels of the platform were going to be closed. I threw a last look at the thick ice-bank we were going to pass. The weather was clear, the atmosphere pure, and the cold very piercing, twelve degrees below zero; but the wind had lulled, and this temperature did not seem unbearable.

About ten men got up on the sides of the *Nautilus*, and, armed with pickaxes, broke the ice round the hull, which was soon set free. This was a speedy operation, for the young ice was still thin. We all went back into the interior. The usual reservoirs were filled with the liberated water, and the *Nautilus* soon sank.

I had taken my place with Conseil in the saloon. Through the open window we watched the different depths of the Southern Ocean. The thermometer rose. The needle of the manometer deviated on its dial.

At a depth of nine hundred feet, as Captain Nemo had foreseen, we were floating under the undulated surface of the ice-bank. But the *Nautilus* sank lower still. It reached a depth of four hundred fathoms. The temperature of the water, which gave 12° on the surface, was now only 10°. Two degrees were already gained. Of course the temperature of the *Nautilus*, raised by its heating apparatus, kept up to a much superior degree. All the manœuvres were accomplished with extraordinary precision.

"We shall pass it, if monsieur will allow me to say so," said Conseil.

"I count upon it," I answered in a tone of profound conviction.

Under the sea, the *Nautilus* had gone the direct road to the Pole straight along the fifty-second meridian. There remained from 67° 30' to 90°, twenty-two and a half degrees—to cross—that is to say, rather more than five hundred leagues. The *Nautilus* went at an average speed of twenty-six miles an hour—that of an express train (a *French* express). If it kept it up forty hours that time would be enough to reach the Pole.

During a part of the night the novelty of the situation kept us at the window. The sea was lighted up by the electric lantern. Fish did not sojourn in these imprisoned waters. They only used them as a passage to go from the Antarctic Ocean to the open sea at the Pole. Our speed was rapid. We felt it by the vibrations of our long steel hull.

About 2 a.m. I went to take a few hours' rest. Conseil did the same. Going through the waist I did not meet Captain Nemo. I supposed that he was in the helmsman's cage.

The next day, March 19th, at 5 a.m., I went back to my station in the saloon. The electric log indicated that the speed of the *Nautilus* had only been moderate. It was then going up towards the surface, but prudently, by slowly emptying its reservoirs.

My heart beat quickly. Were we going to emerge and find the free atmosphere of the Pole?

No. A shock told me that the *Nautilus* had struck against the bottom of the ice-bank, still very thick, to judge by the dulness of the sound. We had struck at a depth of 1,000 feet. That gave 2,000 feet above us, 1,000 feet of which emerged. The ice-bank, therefore, was higher than it was on its border—a not very reassuring fact.

During that day the *Nautilus* several times recommenced the same experiment, and always struck against the wall that hung above it like a ceiling. At certain moments it met it at a depth of five hundred fathoms. Sometimes it was double the height it was where the *Nautilus* sank.

I carefully noted these different depths, and thus obtained a submarine profile of this chain.

In the evening no change had occurred in our situation. Still ice between two and three hundred fathoms deep—an evident diminution, but what thickness there still was between us and the surface of the ocean!

It was then 8 p.m. According to the daily custom on board the air ought to have been renewed four hours before. I did not suffer from it much, although Captain Nemo had not yet drawn upon his reservoirs for a supplement of oxygen.

My sleep was restless that night. Hope and fear besieged me by turns. I rose several times. The gropings of the *Nautilus* were still going on. About 3 a.m. I noticed that the lower surface of the ice-bank was met with at a depth of only twenty-five fathoms. A hundred and fifty feet next separated us from the surface of the water. The ice-bank was gradually becoming an ice-field. The mountain was becoming a plain.

My eyes no longer left the manometer. We were still ascending, diagonally following the brilliant surface that shone under the rays of the electric lamp. The ice-bank was getting lower above and below in long slopes. It got thinner from mile to mile.

At last, at 6 a.m. on this memorable 19th of March, the door of the saloon opened. Captain Nemo appeared.

"The open sea!" he said.

CHAPTER XIV

The South Pole

I rushed upon the platform. Yes! There lay the open sea. A few pieces of ice and moving icebergs were scattered about; in the distance a long stretch of sea; a world of birds in the air, and myriads of fish in the waters, which, according to their depth, varied from intense blue to olive green. The thermometer marked three degrees centigrade above zero. It was like a relative spring inclosed behind this ice-bank, whose distant masses were outlined on the northern horizon.

"Are we at the Pole?" I asked the captain, with a palpitating heart.

"I do not know yet," he answered. "At noon we will take our bearings."

"But will the sun show itself through these mists?" said I, looking at the grey sky.

"However little it shows, it will be enough for me," answered the captain.

About ten miles south of the *Nautilus* a solitary island rose to a height of six hundred feet. We were bearing down upon it, but prudently, for the sea might be strewn with reefs.

An hour afterwards we had reached the islet. Two hours later we had been round it. It measured from four to five miles in circumference. A narrow channel separated it from a considerable stretch of land, perhaps a continent, the limits of which we could not perceive. The existence of this land seemed to prove Maury's hypothesis. The ingenious American has, in fact, remarked that between the South Pole and the 60th parallel the sea is covered with floating icebergs of enormous dimensions, which are never met with in the North Atlantic. From this fact he drew the conclusion that the Antarctic circle incloses a considerable quantity of land, as icebergs cannot form in the open sea, but only on coasts. According to his calculations, the mass of icebergs that surround the austral pole forms a vast cape, the width of which must reach three hundred miles.

The *Nautilus*, for fear of being stranded, had stopped at three cables' length from a beach, over which rose a superb heap of rocks. The boat was launched. The captain, two of his men carrying the instruments, Conseil, and I embarked. It was 10 a.m. I had not seen Ned Land. The Canadian, doubtless, did not wish to acknowledge himself in the wrong in the presence of the South Pole.

A few strokes of the oars brought the boat on to the sand, where it stranded. As Conseil was going to jump out I stopped him.

"Captain Nemo," said I, "to you belongs the honour of first setting foot on this land."

"Yes, professor," answered the captain, "and I do not hesitate to do so, because, until now, no human being has left the imprint of his footsteps upon it."

That said he jumped lightly on to the sand. Keen emotion made his heart beat faster. He climbed a rock which overhung, forming a small promontory, and there, with his arms crossed, mute and motionless, he seemed to take possession with an eager look of these southern regions. After five minutes passed in this rapt contemplation he turned towards us.

"When you are ready, professor," he called to me.

I disembarked, followed by Conseil, leaving the two men in the boat.

For some distance the soil was composed of a reddish tufa, as if it had been made of crushed bricks. Scoriæ, lava streams, and pumice-stone covered it. Its volcanic origin could not be mistaken. In certain places some slight curls of smoke attested that the interior fires still kept their expansive force. Still, when I had climbed a high cliff, I saw no volcano within a radius of several miles. It is known that in these Antarctic countries James Ross found the craters of the Erebus and Terror in full activity on the 167th meridian, and in lat. 77° 32'.

The vegetation of this desolate continent seemed to me very restricted. Some lichens of the species *Unsnea melanoxantha* were spread upon the black rocks, certain microscopic plantlets, rudimentary diatomas, a sort of cells placed between two quartz shells, long purple and crimson fucus, supported on small natatory bladders, and which the tide threw upon the shore, composed the whole meagre flora of the region.

The shore was scattered over with molluscs, small mussels, limpets, heart-shaped buccards, and particularly clios with oblong membraneous bodies, the heads of which were formed of two rounded lobes. I also saw myriads of northern clios, one inch and a quarter long, of which whales swallow a world in one mouthful. Charming pteropods, veritable sea-butterflies, animated the free waters on the skirts of the shore.

In the shallows, amongst other zoophytes, appeared some coralline arborescences, those which, according to James Ross, live in the Antarctic seas at a depth of five hundred fathoms; and small halcyons belonging to the species *Procellaria pelagica*, as well as a great number of asteriads pecular to these climates, and sea-stars studded the soil.

But in the air life was superabundant. There thousands of birds of all kinds fluttered and flew about, deafening us with their cries. Others crowded the rocks, gazing at us, as we passed, without fear, and pressing familiarly under our feet. There were penguins as agile and supple in the water, where they are sometimes taken for rapid bonitoes, as they are heavy and clumsy on land. They uttered harsh sounds, and formed numerous assemblies, sober in gesture, but prodigal of clamour.

Amongst the birds I noticed the chionis of the long-legged family, as large as pigeons, white, with short conical beaks, and a red circle round the eye. Conseil made a provision of them, for, suitably dressed, they make an agreeable dish. In the air passed albatrosses, the expanse of whose wings measured at least four yards and a half, justly called ocean vultures; gigantic petrels; amongst others the *quebrante-huesos*, with arched wings, that are great seal-eaters; damiers, a kind of small duck, the top of whose body is black and white; and, lastly, a whole series of petrels, some whitish, with brown-bordered wings, others blue, and special to the Antarctic seas, "which are so oily," I said to Conseil, "that the inhabitants of the Feroë Islands content themselves with putting a wick inside them, and then lighting it."

"A little more," said Conseil, "and they would be perfect lamps. Ah, why did not Nature supply the wick?"

About a half-a-mile farther on the soil was riddled with ruffs' nests; it was a sort of laying ground from which many birds issued. Captain Nemo had some hundreds killed, for their blackish flesh is very good. They uttered a cry like the braying of an ass, were about the size of a goose, slate-colour on the body, white underneath, with a yellow cravat round their throats. They let themselves be killed with stones without trying to escape.

In the meantime the mist was not rising, and at 11 a.m. the sun had not yet made its appearance. Its absence made me uneasy. Without it there was no observation possible. How, then, could we settle whether we had reached the Pole?

When I rejoined Captain Nemo I found him silently leaning against a rock, and looking at the sky. He seemed impatient and vexed. But there was no help for it. This powerful and audacious man could not command the sun as he did the sea.

Twelve o'clock came without the sun having showed itself for a single instant. Even the place it occupied behind the curtain of mist could not be distinguished. The mist soon after dissolved in snow.

"We must wait till tomorrow," said the captain simply, and we went back to the *Nautilus* amidst the snow.

During our absence the nets had been set, and I noticed with interest the fish that had just been caught. The Antarctic seas are a refuge to a great number of migratory fish that fly from the tempests of the less elevated zones to fall under the teeth of seals and sea-hogs. I noticed several austral bull-heads three inches long, a species of whitish cartilaginous fish, crossed with pale bands, and armed with darts; also Antarctic chimera three feet long, a very elongated body, white skin, silvery and smooth, with a rounded head, a back furnished with three fins, the snout ending in a trumpet that curled back towards the mouth. I tasted them, and found them insipid, notwithstanding Conseil's opinion, who found them very good.

The snow-storm lasted until the next day. It was impossible to keep upon the platform. From the saloon, where I was taking notes of the incidents of this excursion, to the Polar continent, I heard the cries of petrels and albatrosses playing amidst the tempest. The *Nautilus* did not remain motionless, and, coasting the continent, it went about ten miles farther south in the sort of twilight that the sun left as it skirted the horizon.

The next day, the 20th of March, the snow had ceased. It was slightly colder. The thermometer indicated two degrees below zero. The mists rose, and I hoped it would be possible to take an observation that day.

Captain Nemo not having yet appeared, the boat took Conseil and me to the land. The nature of the soil was the same—volcanic. Everywhere traces of lava, scoriæ, basalts, but no trace of the crater from which they issued. Here, as there, myriads of birds animated this part of the Polar continent. But they divided this empire with vast troops of marine mammalia, who looked at us with their soft eyes. They were seals of different sorts, some lying on the ground, some on floating pieces of ice, several coming out of the sea or plunging into it. They did not run away at our approach, never having had to do with man, and I counted enough for the provisioning of some hundreds of ships.

"Faith," said Conseil, "it is a good thing that Ned Land did not accompany us!"

"Why so, Conseil?"

"Because the rabid sportsman would kill all the seals."

"All is saying a great deal, but I do not really think we could have prevented him killing some of these magnificent cetaceans, which would have offended Captain Nemo, for he does not uselessly spill the blood of inoffensive creatures."

"He is right."

"Certainly, Conseil. But have you not already classified some specimens of this marine fauna?"

"Monsieur knows very well that I am not strong in practice. When monsieur has told me the names of these creatures——"

"They are seals and walruses."

"Two genera belonging to the family of pinnipeds," said my learned Conseil at once, "order of carnassiers, group of unguis, sub-class of mondelphians, class of mammalia, branch of vertebrata."

"Right, Conseil," I answered; "but these two genera—seals and walruses—are divided into species, and unless I am mistaken we shall have an opportunity of observing them here. Let us go on."

It was 8 a.m. We had four hours to employ before the sun could be usefully observed. I guided our steps towards a vast bay that was hollowed out of the granitic cliff of the shore.

There I may say that as far as the eye could reach, land and ice were covered with marine mammalia, and I looked involuntarily for old Proteus, the mythological shepherd who watched over these immense flocks of Neptune. There were more seals than anything else, forming distinct groups, male and female, the father watching over his family, the mother suckling her little ones, some already strong enough to go a few steps. When they wish to move from place to place they take little jumps, made by the contraction of their bodies, and helped awkwardly by their one imperfect fin, which, as with the lamantin, their congener forms a perfect fore-arm. I ought to say that in the water, their element *par excellence*, these animals, with their mobile dorsal spine, with smooth and close skin and webbed feet, swim admirably. When resting on the earth they take the most graceful attitudes. Thus the ancients, observing their soft and expressive looks, which cannot be surpassed by the most beautiful look a woman can give—their clear, voluptuous eyes, and their charming positions, turning them into poetry, metamorphosed the males into tritons and the females into syrens.

I made Conseil notice the large development of the lobes of the brain in these interesting creatures. No mammal, except man, has so much cerebral matter. Seals are capable of receiving a certain amount of education, are easily tamed, and I think, with other naturalists, that if properly trained they might render good service as fishing-dogs.

The greater part of these seals slept on the rocks or sand. Amongst those seals, properly so called, which have no external ears—in which they differ from the otter, whose ears are prominent—I noticed several varieties of stenorhynchi, about nine feet long, with white coats, bull-dog heads armed with ten teeth in either jaw, four incisive ones top and bottom, and two large canine teeth in the form of a *fleur-de-lys*. Amongst them glided marine elephants—a sort of seals with short and mobile trunks (the giants of the species), which on a circumference of twenty feet measured ten metres. They made no movement at our approach.

"Are they dangerous animals?" asked Conseil.

"No," I answered, "unless they are attacked. When a seal is defending its young its fury is terrible, and it is not rare for it to break fishing-boats in pieces."

"It has the right to do it."

"I do not say no."

Two miles farther on we were stopped by a promontory which sheltered the bay against the south winds. It fell straight down into the sea, and was covered with foam from the waves. Beyond we heard formidable bellowings such as a troop of oxen might have uttered.

"Good," said Conseil; "are we in for a bull's concert?"

"No," said I, "but a walrus's concert."

"Are they fighting?"

"Either fighting or playing."

"If monsieur pleases we must see that."

"We must, Conseil."

And we crossed the black rocks, amidst unforeseen landslips and over stones that the ice made very slippery. More than once I slipped at the expense of my loins. Conseil, more prudent or steadier, hardly stumbled, and helped me up again, saying—

"If monsieur would be good enough to walk with his legs farther apart, monsieur would keep his equilibrium better."

After we had reached the top of the promontory I perceived a vast white plain covered with walruses. They were playing and howling with joy, and not anger.

Walruses resemble seals in the form of their bodies and the disposition of their limbs. But both canine and incisive teeth are wanting in their lower jaw, and the upper canines are two defences a yard long which measure twelve inches at the circumference of their alveolus. These tusks—made of compact ivory, not striated, harder than that of elephants and less subject to go yellow—are much sought after. Accordingly walruses are much hunted, and their destroyers, massacring indiscriminately females with young and young ones, destroy more than four thousand every year.

Passing near these curious animals I had full leisure to observe them, for they did not disturb themselves. Their skins were thick and rugged, of a fawn-colour inclining to red; their hair was short and scanty; some were twelve feet long. Quieter and less timid than their congeners of the north, they did not confide to picked sentinels the care of watching the approaches to their encampment.

After having examined this city of walruses I thought of retracing my steps. It was eleven o'clock, and if Captain Nemo found he could take an observation I wished to be present at his operation. However, I hardly hoped that the sun would show itself that day; piled-up clouds on the horizon hid him from our sight. It seemed as if the jealous planet would not reveal to human beings this unattainable point of the globe.

However, I thought of returning to the *Nautilus*. We were following a narrow track that ran up to the summit of the cliff.

At half-past eleven we had reached the spot where we landed. The stranded boat had landed the captain. I perceived him standing on a block of basalt. His instruments were by him. His eyes were fixed on the northern horizon, above which the sun was describing his elongated curve.

I stood near him and waited without speaking. Twelve o'clock came, and, like the day before, the sun did not appear.

It was fate. We still wanted an observation. If it were not taken tomorrow we must definitely renounce taking our position.

In fact, we were at the 20th of March. The next day, the 21st, was the day of the equinox, and the refraction not counting, the sun would disappear below the horizon for six months, and with its disappearance the long Polar night would begin. Since the September equinox it had been above the northern horizon, rising by elongated spirals until the 21st of December. At that epoch, the summer solstice of these austral countries, it had begun to sink, and the next day it would shoot forth its last rays.

I communicated my observations and fears to Captain Nemo.

"You are right, M. Aronnax," said he; "if tomorrow I do not obtain the height of the sun I cannot do it again for six months. But just because the chances of my navigation have brought me into these seas on the 21st of March, my point will be easy to take if the sun will reveal himself at noon."

"Why, captain?"

"Because while the sun is describing such elongated curves it is difficult to take its exact height above the horizon, and the instruments are liable to commit grave errors."

"How shall you proceed, then?"

"I shall only use my chronometer," answered Captain Nemo "If tomorrow, the 21st of March, at noon, the sun's disc, allowing for refraction, is exactly cut by the northern horizon, it is because I am at the South Pole."

"That is certain," said I; "yet that affirmation is not mathematically rigorous, because the equinox does not necessarily begin at twelve o'clock."

"Doubtless, professor; but there will not be an error of a hundred yards, and that is all we require. Till tomorrow, then."

Captain Nemo returned on board. Conseil and I remained till five o'clock, walking about the shore, observing and studying. I found nothing curious but a penguin's egg of remarkable size that an amateur would have paid £40 for. Its fawn colour, and the stripes and characters that covered it like so many hieroglyphics, made it a curiosity. I entrusted it to Conseil, and the prudent, sure-footed fellow, holding it like a piece of china porcelain, brought it to the *Nautilus* intact.

There I placed the rare egg under one of the glass cases of the museum. I supped with appetite off an excellent morsel of seal's liver, the taste of which was like pork. Then I went to bed, not without having invoked, like a Hindoo, the favour of the radiant planet.

The next day, the 21st of March, at 5 a.m., I went up on to the platform and found Captain Nemo there.

"The weather is clearing up a little," said he; "I have great hopes of it. After breakfast we will land and choose a post of observation."

This agreed upon, I went to Ned Land and tried to persuade him to come with me. The obstinate Canadian refused, and I saw that his taciturnity, like his bad temper, increased every day. After all I did not much regret his obstinacy in this circumstance. There were really too many seals on land, and such a temptation should not be placed before the un- reflecting fisher.

Breakfast over, I landed. The *Nautilus* had gone forty miles farther south still during the night. It was at a good league from the coast, which rose to an abrupt peak of 1,600 feet. The boat carried also Captain Nemo, two of his crew, and the instruments—that is to say, a chronometer, a telescope, and a barometer.

During our passage I saw numerous whales belonging to the species peculiar to the austral seas—the "right whale," which has no dorsal fin; the hump-back, or balænopteron, with reeved belly and vast whitish fins, which, in spite of its name, do not form wings; and the yellow-brown fin-back, the liveliest of cetaceans. This powerful animal makes itself heard at a great distance when it throws up its columns of air and steam into the air, which resemble torrents of smoke. These different mammalia were disporting themselves in troops in the quiet waters, and I could see that this basin of the Antarctic Pole now served as a placed of refuge to cetaceans too closely tracked by hunters.

I also noticed long whitish lines of sulpæ—a band of gregarious mollusc—and very large medusæ, swaying to the movement of the waves.

We landed at nine o'clock. The sky was getting clearer; the clouds were flying south. The mists were rising from the cold surface of the water. Captain Nemo walked towards the peak, of which he doubtless meant to make his observatory. It was a difficult ascent over the sharp lava and pumice-stones, in an atmosphere often saturated with a sulphurous smell from the smoking fissures. For a man unaccustomed to tread on land the captain climbed the steep slopes with an agility that I could not equal and that a chamois-hunter might have envied.

It took us two hours to get to the summit of this peak, which was partly porphyry and partly basalt. From there the view comprised a vast expanse of sea which on the north distinctly traced its horizon-line on the sky. At our feet lay fields of dazzling whiteness; over our heads, a pale azure free from mist. On the north lay the sun's disc, like a ball of fire, already sinking below the horizon. From the bosom of the waters rose hundreds of sparkling fountains. In the distance lay the *Nautilus*, like a cetacean asleep; behind us, on the south and east, an immense stretch of land, a chaotic heap of rocks and icebergs, the limits of which were not visible.

When Captain Nemo reached the top he carefully took its height by means of the barometer, for he would have to take it into consideration in taking his observation.

At a quarter to twelve the sun, then only seen by refraction, looked like a golden disc, shedding its last rays over these lands and seas which man had never before ploughed.

Captain Nemo, provided with a reticulated glass which, by means of a mirror, corrected the refraction, watched the sun as it disappeared gradually below the horizon describing an elongated diagonal. I held the chronometer. My heart beat quickly. If the disappearance of half the disc coincided with the noon of the chronometer, we were at the Pole itself.

"Twelve!" I cried.

"The South Pole!" answered Captain Nemo in a grave tone, giving me the glass which showed the sun cut in exactly equal halves by the horizon.

I looked at the last rays crowning the peak, and the shadows gradually mounting its slopes.

At that moment Captain Nemo, resting his hand on my shoulders, said—

"Professor, in 1600 the Dutchman Gheritk, carried along by currents and tempests, reached 64° of south latitude, and discovered the New Shetlands. In 1773, on the 17th of January, the illustrious Cook, following the 38th meridian, reached latitude 67° 30'; and in 1774, on the 30th of January, on the 109th meridian, he reached 71° 15' of latitude. In 1819 the Russian Bellinghausen reached the 69th parallel, and in 1821 the 76th by 111° of west longitude. In 1820 the Englishman Brunsfield was stopped on the 65th degree. The same year the American Morrel, whose recital is doubtful, ascending the 42nd meridian, discovered open sea in latitude 70° 14'. In 1825 the Englishman Powell could not cross the 62nd parallel. The same year a simple seal-fisher, the Englishman Weddel, reached 72° 14' of latitude on the 35th meridian, and 74° 15' on the 36th. In 1829 the Englishman Forster, commanding the *Chanticleer*, took possession of the Antarctic continent in 63° 26' of latitude and 66° 26' of longitude. In 1831 the Englishman Biscoe, on the 1st of February, discovered Enderby Land in 68° 50' of latitude; in 1832, on the 5th of February, Adelaide Land in 64° 45' of latitude. In 1838 the Frenchman Dumont d'Urville, stopped by the ice-bank in 62° 57' of latitude, sighted Louis-Philippe Land; two years later, on a new point in the south, he named, in 66° 30', on January 21st, Adelaide Land; and, eight days after, in 64° 40', Clarie Coast. In 1838 the Englishman Wilkes reached the 69th parallel on the 100th meridian. In 1839 the Englishman Balleny discovered Sabrina Land on the limits of the Polar circle. Lastly, in 1842, the Englishman James Ross, with the Erebus and Terror, on the 12th of January, in 76° 56' of latitude and 171° 7' of east longitude, discovered Victoria Land; on the 23rd of the same month he reached the 74th parallel, the highest point obtained till then; on the 27th he was in 76° 8', on the 28th in 77° 32', on the 2nd of February in 78° 4', and in 1842 he returned to the 71st degree, beyond which he could not go. I, Captain Nemo, on the 21st of March, 1868, have reached the South Pole on the 90th degree, and I take possession of this part of the globe, equal to the sixth part of known continents."

"In whose name, captain?"

"In my own, sir."

So saying, Captain Nemo unfurled a black flag, bearing an N in gold, quartered on its bunting. Then, turning towards the sun, whose last rays were lapping the horizon of the sea, he exclaimed—

"Adieu, sun! Disappear, thou radiant star! Rest beneath this free sea, and let a six months' night spread its darkness over my new domain!"

CHAPTER XV

Accident or Incident?

The next day, March 22nd, at 6 a.m., preparations for departure were begun. The last gleams of twilight were melting into night. The cold was intense. The constellations shone with wonderful intensity. In the zenith glittered that wondrous southern cross, the Polar star of Antarctic regions.

The thermometer indicated 12° below zero, and when the wind freshened it was biting. Icebergs increased on the open water. The sea seemed about to freeze all over. Numerous black patches spread over the surface announced the approaching formation of young ice. Evidently the southern basin, frozen during the six winter months, was absolutely inaccessible. What became of the whales during that period? They doubtless went to seek below the ice-bank more practicable seas. As to seals and walruses, accustomed to live in the severest climates, they remained in these frozen regions. These animals have the instinct to dig holes in the ice-fields, and keep them always opened. They come up through these holes to breathe; the birds, driven away by the cold, have emigrated northwards, and the marine mammalia remain undisputed masters of the Polar continent.

In the meantime the reservoirs of water were being filled, and the *Nautilus* was slowly sinking. It stopped at a depth of one thousand feet. It beat the waves with its screw, and advanced northwards at the rate of fifteen miles an hour. Towards evening it was already floating under the immense carapace of the ice-bank.

The panels of the saloon were closed for prudence sake, for the hull of the *Nautilus* might strike against some submerged block, so I passed that day in writing out my notes. I gave myself up to thoughts about the Pole. We had reached this inaccessible point without fatigue or danger, as if our floating carriage had glided over the rails of a railroad. And now the return had really begun. Did it reserve any fresh surprises for me? I thought it might, so inexhaustible is the series of submarine marvels! During the five months and a half that fate had thrown me on board this vessel, we had come 14,000 leagues, and during this distance, greater in extent than the terrestrial equator, how many curious or terrible incidents had varied our voyage—the hunt in the forests of Crespo, the stranding in the Torres Straits, the coral cemetery, the fisheries of Ceylon, the Arabic tunnel, the fires of Santorin, the millions of Vigo Bay, the Atlantis, the South Pole! During the night all these memories passed like a dream, not letting my brain repose for an instant.

At 3 a.m. I was awakened by a violent shock. I rose up in bed, and was listening amidst the obscurity, when I was roughly thrown into the middle of the room. The *Nautilus* had evidently made a considerable rebound after having struck.

I groped along the partition through the waist to the saloon, which was lighted up by the luminous ceiling. The furniture was all upset. Happily the windows were firmly set, and had stood fast. The pictures on the starboard side, through the vessel being no longer vertical, were sticking to the tapestry, whilst those on the larboard side were hanging a foot from the wall at their lower edge. The *Nautilus* was lying on its starboard side completely motionless.

In the interior I heard a noise of footsteps and confused voices. But Captain Nemo did not appear. At the moment I was going to leave the saloon Ned Land and Conseil entered.

"What is the matter?" said I immediately.

"I came to ask monsieur," answered Conseil.

"*Mille diables!*" cried the Canadian. "I know very well what it is. The *Nautilus* has struck, and to judge by the way it is lying, it won't come off quite so easily as in Torres Straits."

"But at least," I asked, "is it on the surface of the sea?"

"We do not know," answered Conseil.

"It is easy to find out," said I.

I consulted the manometer. To my great surprise it indicated a depth of one hundred and eighty fathoms.

"What can this mean?" I exclaimed.

"We must ask Captain Nemo," said Conseil.

"But where shall we find him?" asked Ned Land.

"Follow me," I said to my two companions.

We left the saloon. There was no one in the library, or on the central staircase, or in the ward-room. I supposed that Captain Nemo must be in the helmsman's cage. The only thing to do was to wait. We all three returned to the saloon.

I shall pass by the Canadian's recriminations in silence. He had now something to be in a rage about. I let him give off his bad-humour at his ease without answering him.

We had been thus for twenty minutes listening to the least noise in the interior of the *Nautilus*, when Captain Nemo entered. He did not seem to see us. His countenance, habitually so impassive, revealed a certain anxiety. He looked at the compass and manometer in silence, and put his finger on a point of the planisphere in that part that represented the South Seas.

I did not wish to interrupt him. When, a few instants afterwards, he turned towards me, I said to him, using an expression he had used in Torres Straits—

"An incident, captain?"

"No, professor," he replied. "An accident this time."

"Grave?"

"Perhaps."

"Is the danger immediate?"

"No."

"The *Nautilus* has run aground upon something?"

"Yes."

"How?"

"Through a caprice of Nature, not through the incapacity of man. There has not been a fault committed in our manœuvres. But no one can prevent equilibrium producing its effects. We may resist human laws, but we cannot stand against natural ones."

352

Captain Nemo chose a singular moment to utter this philosophical reflection. On the whole, his answer taught me nothing.

"May I know, sir," I asked, "the cause of this accident?"

"An enormous block of ice, a whole mountain, has turned over," he answered. "When icebergs are undermined by warmer water or reiterated shocks, their centre of gravity ascends. Then the whole thing turns over. That is what has happened. One of these blocks as it turned over struck the *Nautilus*, which was floating under the waters. Then gliding under its hull, and raising it with irresistible force, it has raised it to less dense waters, and thrown it on its side."

"But cannot the *Nautilus* be got off by employing the reservoirs so as to restore its equilibrium?"

"That is what they are doing now, sir. You can hear the pump working. Look at the needle of the manometer. It indicates that the *Nautilus* is ascending, but the block of ice is ascending with it, and until some obstacle stops its upward movement our position will not be changed."

The *Nautilus* still kept the same position. It would, doubtless, right itself when the block itself stopped. But at that moment how did we know that we should not strike against the ice-bank and so be frightfully squeezed between the two frozen surfaces?

I reflected on all the consequences of this situation. Captain Nemo did not cease to watch the manometer. The *Nautilus*, since the fall of the iceberg, had ascended about one hundred and fifty feet, but it still made the same angle with the perpendicular.

Suddenly a slight movement was felt in the hull. The *Nautilus* was evidently righting itself a little. The objects hung up in the saloon were insensibly recovering their normal position. The partitions became more vertical. No one spoke. With heightened emotion we watched the vessel right itself. The flooring became horizontal under our feet. Ten minutes went by.

"At last we are straight!" I exclaimed.

"Yes," said Captain Nemo, going towards the door of the saloon.

"But shall we get afloat again?" I asked him.

"Certainly," he answered, "since the reservoirs are not yet empty, and that when they are the *Nautilus* will ascend to the surface of the sea."

The captain went out, and I soon saw that, following his orders, they had stopped the ascension of the *Nautilus*. In fact, it would soon have struck against the bottom of the ice-bank, and it was better to keep it in the water.

"We have had a narrow escape!" then said Conseil.

"Yes. We might have been crushed between two blocks of ice, or, at least, imprisoned. And then, not being able to renew the air—— Yes, we have had a narrow escape!"

"If that is all!" murmured Ned Land.

I did not wish to begin a useless discussion with the Canadian, so did not answer him. Besides, at that moment the panels of the saloon were opened and the electric light shone through the glass panes.

We were in full water, as I have said; but at a distance of thirty feet on each side of the *Nautilus* rose a dazzling wall of ice. Above and below the same wall. Above, because the bottom of the ice-bank formed an immense ceiling. Below, because the overturned block, gliding down by degrees, had found on the lateral walls two resting-places which kept it in that position. The *Nautilus* was imprisoned in a veritable tunnel of ice, about sixty feet wide, filled with tranquil water. It would, therefore, be easy for it to go out of it by going either backwards or forwards, and finding, at some hundreds of feet lower down, a free passage under the ice-bank.

The luminous ceiling had been put out, and still the saloon was filled with intense light. It was because the powerful reflection from the walls of ice sent the light of the lantern into it with violence. I could not paint the effect of the voltaic rays of light on these capriciously-formed blocks, of which each angle, each point, each facet, threw a different light according to the veins in the ice. A dazzling mine of gems, and particularly of sapphires which crossed their blue rays with the green rays of the emeralds. Here and there opal shades of infinite softness ran amidst ardent points like so many fiery diamonds of which the eye could not sustain the brilliancy. The power of the lantern was increased a hundredfold like that of a lamp through first-class lenticular lighthouse glasses.

"Oh, how beautiful! How beautiful!" exclaimed Conseil.

"Yes!" said I. "It is an admirable sight. Is it not, Ned?"

"Yes, *mille diables!* Yes," answered Ned Land. "It is superb. I'm in a rage at being obliged to acknowledge it. No one has ever seen anything like it. But we may have to pay dearly for the sight. And I believe that here we see things God never meant us to see."

Ned was right. It was too beautiful. All at once a cry from Conseil made me turn round.

"What is the matter?" I asked.

"Let monsieur close his eyes and not look!"

So saying, Conseil quickly carried his hand to his eyes.

"But what has happened, my boy?"

"I am dazzled—blinded."

My eyes involuntarily turned to the window, but I could not bear the fire that devoured them.

I understood what had happened. The *Nautilus* had just put on full speed. All the tranquil brilliancy of the ice-walls had then changed into flashes of lightning. The fires of these myriads of diamonds were united together.

The panels of the saloon were then closed. We held our hands to our eyes, quite impregnated with the concentric flames which float before the retina when the solar rays strike it too violently. It took some time to calm the pain.

At last we lowered our hands.

"Faith, I could never have believed it," said Conseil.

"And I don't believe it yet," answered the Canadian.

"When we return to land," added Conseil, "*blasé* with so

many marvels of Nature, what shall we think of the miserable continents and little works done by the hand of man? No, the inhabited world is no longer worthy of us."

Such words from the mouth of an impassive Dutchman showed to what a boiling point our enthusiasm had reached. But the Canadian did not fail to throw cold water on it.

"The inhabited world!" said he, shaking his head. "Don't be uneasy, friend Conseil, we shall never see that again."

It was then 5 a.m. At that moment a shock took place in the bows of the *Nautilus*. I knew that its prow had struck against a block of ice. This, I thought, must be a mistaken manœuvre, for the submarine tunnel, obstructed by block, was not easily navigated. I therefore imagined that Captain Nemo, changing his direction, would turn round these obstacles, or follow the sinuosities of the tunnel. In any case our forward journey could not be quite prevented. Still, contrary to my expectation, the *Nautilus* began a decided retrograde movement.

"We are going backwards?" said Conseil.

"Yes," I answered, "the tunnel must be without issue on that side."

"And what will be done then?"

"Then," I said, "the manœuvre is very simple. We shall retrace our steps and get out by the southern orifice, that is all."

In speaking thus I wished to appear more confident than I really was. In the meantime the retrograde movements of the *Nautilus* was getting more rapid, and with reversed screw it was carrying us along with great rapidity.

"This will cause a delay," said Ned.

"What do a few hours more or less matter, so that we get out?"

"Yes," echoed Ned Land, "so that we get out."

I walked backwards and forwards for some minutes between the saloon and the library. My companions also were silent. I soon threw myself upon a divan, and took a book which my eyes ran over mechanically.

A quarter of an hour afterwards Conseil came up to me and said—

"Is what monsieur is reading very interesting?"

"Very interesting," I replied.

"I thought so. It is monsieur's book that monsieur is reading!"

"My book?"

In fact, I held in my hand the work on the *Ocean Depths*. I had not the least idea of it. I closed the book and resumed my walk. Ned and Conseil rose to go.

"Stay, my friends," I said, detaining them. "Let us remain together till we are out of this tunnel."

"As monsieur pleases," answered Conseil.

Some hours passed. I often looked at the instruments hung up on the walls of the saloon. The manometer indicated that the *Nautilus* kept at a constant depth of nine hundred feet, the compass that we were going south, the log that our speed was twenty miles an hour—an excessive speed in that narrow space. But Captain Nemo knew that he could not make too much haste, and that now minutes were worth centuries.

At twenty-five minutes past eight a second shock took place, this time at the back. I turned pale. My companions came up to me. I seized Conseil's hand. We questioned each other with a look more directly than if words had interpreted our thoughts.

At that moment the captain entered the saloon. I went to him.

"The route is barricaded on the south?" I asked.

"Yes, sir. As the iceberg turned over it closed all issue."

"Then we are blocked up?"

"Yes."

CHAPTER XVI

Want of Air

Thus there was around the *Nautilus*, above and below, an impenetrable wall of ice. We were imprisoned in the ice-bank. The Canadian struck a formidable blow on the table with his fist. Conseil said nothing. I looked at the captain. His face had regained its usual impassiveness. He had crossed his arms over his breast and was reflecting. The *Nautilus* was quite still.

The captain then spoke.

"Gentlemen," said he, in a calm voice, "there are two ways of dying under our present circumstances."

This inexplicable personage looked like a professor of mathematics stating a problem to his pupils.

"The first," he continued, "is to be crushed to death; the second is to be suffocated. I need not speak of the possibility of dying of hunger, for the provisions of the *Nautilus* will certainly outlast us."

"We cannot be suffocated, captain," I answered, "for our reservoirs are full."

"True," said Captain Nemo, "but they will only give us air for two days. Now we have already been six-and-thirty hours under water, and the heavy atmosphere of the *Nautilus* already wants renewing. In forty-eight hours our reserve will be exhausted."

"Well, captain, we must get out before forty-eight hours."

"We will try, at all events, by piercing through the wall that surrounds us."

"On which side?" I asked.

"The bore will tell us that. I am going to run the *Nautilus* on to the lower bank, and my men will put on their diving-dresses and attack the wall where it is the least thick."

"Can we have the saloon panels opened?"

"Certainly; we are no longer moving."

Captain Nemo went out. A hissing sound soon told me that the reservoirs were being filled with water. The *Nautilus* gradually sank, and rested on the ice at a depth of 175 fathoms.

"My friends," said I, 'the situation is grave, but I count on your courage and energy."

"Sir," answered the Canadian, "it is not the time to worry you with my grumbling. I am ready to do anything for the common safety."

"That is right, Ned," said I, holding out my hand to the Canadian.

"I am as handy with the pickaxe as the harpoon," he added, "and if I can be useful to the captain he may dispose of me."

"He will not refuse your aid. Come, Ned."

I led the Canadian to the room where the men of the *Nautilus* were putting on their diving-dresses. I told the captain of Ned's proposition, which was accepted. The Canadian put on his sea-costume, and was ready as soon as his companions. Each wore a Rouquayrol apparatus on his back, to which the reservoirs had furnished a contingent of pure air—a considerable but necessary diminution to the reserve of the *Nautilus*. The Ruhmkorff lamps were useless in the luminous water saturated with electric rays.

When Ned was dressed I went back to the saloon, where the panels were open, and, taking a place beside Conseil, I examined the ambient beds that supported the *Nautilus*.

Some moments after we saw a dozen men of the crew step out on to the ice with Ned Land amongst them, recognisable from his tall stature. Captain Nemo was with them.

Before beginning to dig through the walls he had them bored to discover the right direction in which to work. Long bores were sunk into the lateral walls, but after forty-five feet they were again stopped by a thick wall. It was useless to attack the ice-ceiling, for it was the ice-bank itself, which was more than 1,200 feet high. Captain Nemo then had the lower surface bored. There thirty feet of ice separated us from the water, such was the thickness of this ice-field. It was, therefore, necessary to cut away a part equal in extent to the water-line of the *Nautilus*. There were, therefore, about 7,000 cubic yards to detach in order to dig a hole through which we could sink below the ice-field.

The work was immediately begun and carried on with indefatigable energy. Instead of digging round the *Nautilus*, which would have been exceedingly difficult, Captain Nemo had an immense trench made, about eight yards from its port quarter. Then his men began simultaneously to work at it in different points of its circumference, and large blocks were soon detached from the mass. By a curious effect of specific gravity, these blocks, being lighter than water, fled up to the vault of the tunnel, which thus became thicker at the top as it became thinner at the bottom. But it was of no consequence so long as the bottom ice was so much the less thick.

After two hours of energetic work Ned Land entered exhausted. His companions and he were relieved by fresh workers, whom Conseil and I joined. The first officer of the *Nautilus* directed us.

The water seemed to me singularly cold, but I soon grew warmer with handling the pickaxe. My movements were very free, though made under a pressure of thirty atmospheres.

When I re-entered, after two hours of work, to take food and rest, I found a notable difference between the air the Rouquayrol apparatus furnished me with and the atmosphere of the *Nautilus*, already loaded with carbonic acid gas. The air had not been renewed for forty-eight hours, and its life-giving qualities were considerably weakened. However, in twelve hours we had broken off a slice of ice a yard thick, or about six hundred cubic yards. Admitting that we could go on at the same rate, it would take still five nights and four days to accomplish our task.

"Five nights and four days!" said I to my companions, "and we have only air for two days in the reservoirs."

"Without reckoning," replied Ned, "that, once out of this confounded prison, we shall still be imprisoned under the ice-bank without any possible communication with the atmosphere!"

True enough. Who could then foresee the minimum of time necessary for our deliverance? Should we not all be suffocated before the *Nautilus* could reach the surface of the waves? Was it destined to perish in this tomb of ice with all the people it contained? The situation appeared terrible, but each of us looked it in the face, and we were all decided to do our duty to the end.

As I had foreseen, during the night another slice, a yard thick, was dug off the immense alveolus. But in the morning, when, clothed in my bathing-dress, I walked in the liquid mass in a temperature of from 6° to 7° below zero, I remarked that the lateral walls were gradually approaching each other. The water away from the trench, which was not warmed by the men's work and the play of the tools, showed a tendency to solidify. In presence of this new and imminent danger what chance of safety had we, and how could we prevent the solidification of this liquid medium that would have crushed the sides of the *Nautilus* like glass?

I did not make known this new danger to my companions. Why risk the damping of that energy which they were employing in their painful toil? But when I went back on board I spoke to Captain Nemo about this grave complication.

"I know it," he said in his calm tone, which no terrible conjuncture of circumstances could modify. "It is one danger more, but I see no means of avoiding it. The only chance of safety is to work quicker than the solidification. We must be first, that is all."

"Be there first!" I ought by now to be accustomed to this way of speaking.

That day I handled the pickaxe vigorously for several hours. The work kept me up. Besides, to work was to leave the *Nautilus* and breathe the pure air drawn directly from the reservoirs and furnished by the apparatus, and to leave the impoverished and vitiated atmosphere.

Towards evening the trench had been dug another yard deeper. When I went back on board I was nearly suffocated with the carbonic acid with which the air was filled. Ah! had we not the chemical means to drive away this deleterious gas? We had abundance of oxygen—the water contained a considerable quantity—and by decompounding it with our powerful piles we could restore the vivifying fluid. I had thought of it, but what was the use, since the carbonic acid made by our respiration had invaded all parts of the vessel? In order to absorb it we should have to fill vessels with caustic potash and shake them incessantly. Now this substance was entirely wanting on board, and nothing could take its place.

That evening Captain Nemo was obliged to open the taps of his reservoirs and throw some columns of pure air into the interior of the *Nautilus*. Without that precaution we should never have awakened.

The next day, the 26th of March, I went on with my mining work on the fifth yard. The lateral walls and lower surface of the ice-bank thickened perceptibly. It was evident that they would come together before the *Nautilus* could be extricated. Despair came over me for an instant. My axe nearly dropped from my hands. What was the use of digging if I was to perish suffocated, crushed by the water that was turning to stone?—a death that even the ferocity of savages would not have invented. It seemed to me that I was between the formidable jaws of a monster, which were irresistibly closing.

At that moment Captain Nemo, directing the work and working himself, passed close to me. I touched him, and pointed to the walls of our prison. The port wall had advanced to within four yards of the *Nautilus*.

The captain understood me and signed to me to follow him. We re-entered the vessel. Once my diving-dress off, I accompanied him into the saloon.

"M. Aronnax," said he, "we must try some heroic means or we shall be sealed up in this freezing water as in cement."

"Yes," said I, "but what can we do?"

"Ah!" cried he, "if the *Nautilus* were but strong enough to support the pressure without being crushed!"

"What then?" I asked, not seizing the captain's idea.

"Do you not understand," he continued, "that this congelation of water will help us? Do you not see that by its solidification it will break up the ice-fields that imprison us, as in freezing it breaks up the hardest stones? Do you not see that it would be an agent of salvation instead of an agent of destruction?"

"Yes, captain, perhaps. But however capable the *Nautilus* may be of resisting pressure, it could not bear that, and would be crushed as flat as a steel plate."

"I know it, sir; therefore we must not count upon Nature for help, but upon ourselves. We must prevent this solidification. Not only are the lateral walls closing up, but there does not remain ten feet of water either fore or aft of the *Nautilus*. It is freezing on all sides of us."

"How much longer," I asked, "shall we have air to breathe on board?"

The captain looked me full in the face.

"The day after tomorrow," he said, "the reservoirs will be empty."

I broke out into a cold perspiration. And yet ought I to have been astonished at this answer? On the 22nd of March the *Nautilus* had sunk below the free waters of the Pole. We were now at the 26th. We had been living for five days on the vessel's reserves, and what remained of breathable air must be kept for the workers. Now, whilst I am writing this, my impression of it is still so acute that an involuntary terror takes possession of my whole being, and air seems wanting to my lungs.

In the meantime Captain Nemo was reflecting, silent and motionless. It was visible that his mind had grasped an idea. But he seemed to be driving it away. He answered himself in the negative. At last these words escaped from his lips:—

"Boiling water!" murmured he.

"Boiling water?" I cried.

"Yes, sir. We are inclosed in a relatively restricted space. Would not some jets of boiling water, constantly injected by the pumps of the *Nautilus*, raise the temperature of this medium, and delay its congelation?"

"It must be tried," said I resolutely.

"We will try it, professor."

The thermometer then indicated seven degrees outside. Captain Nemo took me to the kitchens, where vast distilling apparatus was at work, which furnished drinking-water by evaporation. It was filled with water, and all the electric heat of the piles was put into the serpentines, bathed by the liquid. In a few moments the water had attained 100°. It was sent to the pumps, while fresh water constantly supplied its place. The heat given off by the piles was such that the cold water taken from the sea after going through the apparatus arrived boiling in the pump.

The injection began, and three hours after the thermometer outside indicated six degrees below zero. It was one degree gained. Two hours later the thermometer only indicated four.

"We shall succeed," I said to the captain, after having followed and controlled by numerous remarks the progress of the operation.

"I think we shall," he answered. "We shall not be crushed. We have only suffocation to fear now."

During the night the temperature of the water went up to one degree below zero. The apparatus could not send it up any higher. But as sea-water does not freeze at less than two degrees, I was at last reassured against the danger of solidification.

The next day, the 27th of March, eighteen feet of ice had been taken from the trench. There still remained twelve. Another forty-eight hours' work. The air could not be renewed in the interior of the *Nautilus*. That day things went from bad to worse.

An intolerable heaviness weighed upon me. About 3 p.m. this feeling of agony became exceedingly violent. I dislocated my jaws with gaping. My lungs panted as they sought the burning fluid, indispensable for respiration, and which became more and more rarefied. A moral torpor took possession of me. I lay down without strength to move, almost without consciousness. My brave Conseil, seized by the same symptoms, suffering the same agony, did not leave my side. He took my hand, encouraged me, and I heard him murmur—

"Ah, if I could but do without breathing in order to leave more air for monsieur!"

Tears came into my eyes at hearing him speak thus.

If our situation was intolerable in the interior, with what haste and pleasure we donned our bathing-dresses to work in our turn! The pickaxes range on the frozen surface. Our arms were tired, our hands skinned, but what mattered fatigues and wounds? Our lungs had vital air. We breathed! We breathed!

And yet no one thought of prolonging his work under water beyond his allotted time. His task accomplished, each gave to his panting companion the reservoir that was to pour life into him. Captain Nemo set the example, and was the first to submit to this severe discipline. When the time came he gave up his apparatus to another, and re-entered the vitiated atmosphere on board, always calm, unflinching, and uncomplaining.

That day the usual work was accomplished with still more vigour. But six feet of ice remained. Six feet alone separated us from the open sea. But the reservoirs of air were almost empty. The little that remained must be kept for the workers. Not an atom for the *Nautilus*.

When I re-entered the vessel I was half suffocated. What a night! Such suffering could not be expressed. The next day my breathing was oppressed. Along with pains in my head came dozy vertigo that made a drunken man of me. My companions felt the same symptoms. Some of the crew had rattling in their throats.

On that day, the sixth of our imprisonment, Captain Nemo, finding the pickaxe's work too slow, resolved to crush in the bed of ice that still separated us from the water. This man kept all coolness and energy. He subdued physical pain by moral force. He thought, planned, and acted.

He ordered the vessel to be lightened—that is to say, raised from the ice by a change of specific gravity. When it floated it was towed above the immense trench dug according to its water-line. Then its reservoirs of water were filled; it sank into the hole.

At that moment all the crew came on board, and the double door of communication was shut. The *Nautilus* was then resting on a sheet of ice not three feet thick, which the bores had pierced in a thousand places.

The taps of the reservoirs were then turned full on, and a hundred cubic yards of water rushed in, increasing by 200,000lbs. the *Nautilus's* weight.

We waited and listened, forgetting our sufferings, hoping still. We had made our last effort.

Notwithstanding the buzzing in my head, I soon felt the vibrations in the hull of the *Nautilus*. A lower level was reached. The ice cracked with a singular noise like paper being torn, and the *Nautilus* sank.

"We have gone through!" murmured Conseil in my ear.

I could not answer him. I seized his hand and pressed it convulsively.

All at once, dragged down by its fearful overweight, the *Nautilus* sank like a cannon-ball—that is to say, as though it was falling in a vacuum!

Then all the electric force was put into the pumps, which immediately began to drive the water out of the reservoirs. After a few minutes our fall was stopped. Soon even the manometer indicated an ascensional movement. The screw, with all speed on, made the iron hull tremble to its very bolts, and dragged us northwards.

But how long would this navigation under the ice-bank last before we reached the open sea? Another day? I should be dead first.

Half lying on a divan in the library, I was suffocating. My face was violet, my lips blue, my faculties suspended. I saw nothing, heard nothing. All idea of time had disappeared from my mind. I could not contract my muscles.

I do not know how long this lasted. But I knew that my death-agony had begun. I saw that I was dying. Suddenly I came to myself. A few whiffs of air penetrated into my lungs. Had we, then, reached the surface of the water? Had we cleared the ice-bank?

No! Ned and Conseil, my two brave friends, were sacrificing themselves to save me. Some atoms of air had remained at the bottom of an apparatus. Instead of breathing it, they had kept it for me; and while they were suffocating, they poured me out life drop by drop! I wished to push the apparatus away. They held my hands, and for some minutes I breathed voluptuously.

My eyes fell on the clock. It was 11 a.m. It must be the 28th of March. The *Nautilus* was going at a frightful speed of forty miles an hour.

Where was Captain Nemo? Had he succumbed? Had his companions died with him?

At that moment the manometer indicated that we were only twenty feet from the surface. A simple field of ice separated us from the atmosphere. Could we not break it?

Perhaps. Anyway, the *Nautilus* was going to attempt it. I felt that it was taking an oblique position, lowering its stern, and raising its prow. An introduction of water had been sufficient to disturb its equilibrium. Then, propelled by its powerful screw, it attacked the ice-field from below like a powerful battering-ram. It broke it in slightly, then drew back, drove at full speed against the field, which broke up, and at last, by a supreme effort, it sprang upon the frozen surface, which it crushed under its weight.

The panel was opened, I might say torn up, and the pure air rushed in to all parts of the *Nautilus*.

CHAPTER XVII

From Cape Horn to the Amazon

I have no idea how I got to the platform. Perhaps the Canadian carried me there. But I was breathing, inhaling the vivifying air of the sea. My two companions were beside me, intoxicating themselves with the fresh particles. Unfortunate men, too long deprived of food, cannot throw themselves inconsiderately on the first aliments that are given to them. We, on the contrary, had no reason to restrain ourselves; we could fill our lungs with the atoms of this atmosphere, and it was the sea-breeze itself that was pouring out life to us.

"Ah," said Conseil, "how good oxygen is! Monsieur need not fear to breathe. There is enough for everyone."

Ned Land did not speak, but he opened his jaws wide enough to frighten a shark. What powerful breathing! The Canadian "drew" like a stove in full combustion.

Our strength promptly returned to us, and when I looked around me I saw that we were alone upon the platform. Not a man of the crew was there, not even Captain Nemo. The strange sailors of the *Nautilus* contented themselves with the air that circulated in the interior. Not one came to take delight in the open air.

The first words I uttered were words of thanks and gratitude to my two companions. Ned and Conseil had prolonged my existence during the last hours of this agony. All my gratitude was not too much for such self-sacrifice.

"Good, professor!" answered Ned Land; "that is not worth speaking about. What merit had we in doing that? None. It was merely a question in arithmetic. Your existence was worth more than ours, therefore it had to be preserved."

"No, Ned," I answered, "it was not worth more. No one is superior to a good and generous man, and that is what you are! And you, my brave Conseil—you have suffered much."

"Not so very much, to tell monsieur the truth. I did want for some mouthfuls of air, but I think I should have got used to it. Besides, I looked at monsieur, who was ready to die, and that did not give me the least wish to breathe. That stopped, as they say, my br——"

Conseil, confused at having fallen into such a commonplace, did not finish.

"My friends," I answered, much moved, "we are bound to one another for ever, and I am under an obligation."

"Which I shall take advantage of," replied the Canadian.

"What?" said Conseil.

"Yes," continued Ned Land, "by taking you with me when I leave this infernal *Nautilus*."

"That reminds me," said Conseil—"are we going the right way?"

"Yes," I answered, "for we are going towards the sun, and here the sun is north."

"Doubtless," said Ned Land; "but it remains to be seen if we are making for the Pacific or the Atlantic—that is to say, the frequented or solitary seas."

That I could not answer, and I feared that Captain Nemo would take us to that vast ocean that bathes the coasts both of Asia and America. He would thus complete his journey round the submarine world, and would return to those seas where the *Nautilus* found the most entire independence. But if we returned to the Pacific, far from all inhabited land, what would become of Ned Land's projects?

We were soon to be apprised of this important fact. The *Nautilus* was going at great speed. The Polar circle was soon passed, and the vessel's head directed towards Cape Horn. We were abreast of the American point on the 31st of March at 7 p.m.

Then all our past sufferings were forgotten. The remembrance of our imprisonment under the ice faded from our minds. We only thought of the future. Captain Nemo appeared no more either in the saloon or on the platform. The bearings taken each day and marked upon the planisphere by the first officer allowed me to tell the exact direction of the *Nautilus*. That evening it became evident, to my great satisfaction, that we were going up north by the Atlantic route.

I told the result of my observations to the Canadian and Conseil.

"Good news," said the Canadian; "but where is the *Nautilus* going to?"

"I cannot tell, Ned."

"Is its captain going to try the North Pole after the South, and return to the Pacific by the famous North-West Passage?"

"It would be unwise to defy him to do it," answered Conseil.

"Well," said the Canadian, "we would part company before-hand."

"In any case," added Conseil, "Captain Nemo is a great man, and we shall not regret having known him."

"Especially when we have left him!" answered Ned Land.

The next day, the 1st of April, when the *Nautilus* ascended to the surface of the sea, some minutes before noon, we sighted the west coast. It was Tierra del Fuego, to which the first navigators gave this name on seeing the quantity of smoke that was rising from the native huts. This Tierra del Fuego forms a vast agglomeration of islands which extend over a space thirty leagues long and eighty wide, between 53° and 56° of south latitude and between 67° 50' and 77° 15' of west longitude. The coast appeared low to me, but in the distance rose high mountains. I even thought I caught a glimpse of Mount Sarmiento 6,500 feet above the sea level, a pyramidical block of schist with a very sharp summit, "which, according as it is hidden by or free from mist, announces fine or bad weather," said Ned Land.

"A famous barometer, my friend."

"Yes, sir, a natural barometer that never deceived me when I was sailing amongst the passes in the Straits of Magellan."

At that moment the peak stood out clearly against the sky. It was a prophecy of good weather, and was realised.

The *Nautilus*, sunk under water, approached the shore, which it coasted at a distance of only a few miles. Through the saloon windows I saw long seaweed, gigantic fucus, and those bladder "varechs" of which the open sea at the Pole contained a few specimens; with their slimy polished filaments they measured as much as 900 feet long; veritable cases, thicker than the thumb, and very resisting; they are often used for making vessels fast. Another herb known under the name of "velp," with leaves four feet long, encrusted in coralline concretions, carpeted the bottom of the sea. They serve as nest and food to myriads of crustaceans, molluscs, crabs, and cuttle-fish. Seals and other animals make splendid meals, mixing fish and sea vegetables in the English manner.

Over these fat and luxuriant depths the *Nautilus* passed with extreme rapidity. Towards evening it approached the archipelago of the Falkland Islands, of which the next day I could recognise the steep summits. The depth of the sea was slight; I therefore thought—not without reason—that these two islands, surrounded by many islets, formerly formed part of the Magellan lands. The Falkland Islands were probably dis-covered by the celebrated John Davis, who gave them the name of South Davis Islands. Later on Richard Hawkins called them Maiden Islands. They were afterwards named the Malouines, at the beginning of the 18th century, by some Saint Malo fishermen; and, lastly, Falkland Islands by the English, to whom they now belong.

In these regions our nets brought in fine specimens of seaweed, particularly a certain fucus the roots of which were covered with mussels that are the best in the world. Wild geese and ducks came down by dozens on to the platform, and soon took their places in the pantries on board. With regard to fish I specially noticed some bony specimens of the goby species, and especially boulertos, six inches long, all over yellow and white spots.

I also admired numerous medusæ, and the finest of the genera, the crysaora, peculiar to the Falkland Islands.

371

Sometimes they formed a half-spherical parasol striped with reddish-brown lines, and ending in twelve regular festoons; sometimes they formed an overturned basket from whence gracefully escaped large leaves and long red spray. They swam agitating their over-foliated arms and let their tentacles float after them. I should like to have kept some specimens of these delicate zoophytes, but they are only clouds, shades, appearances that melt and evaporate out of their natal element.

When the last heights of the Falkland group had disappeared under the horizon, the *Nautilus* sank to a depth of from ten to fifteen fathoms, and coasted the American shore. Captain Nemo did not show himself.

Until the 3rd of April we stayed in these regions of Patagonia, sometimes under the ocean, sometimes on its surface. The *Nautilus* passed the wide estuary formed by the mouth of the La Plata, and on the 4th of April was abreast of Uruguay, but at fifty miles' distance. Its direction kept northwards, and it followed the long sinuosities of South America. We had then come 16,000 leagues since we had embarked in the seas of Japan.

About 11 a.m. we crossed the tropic of Capricorn on the 37th meridian, and passed abreast of Cape Frio. Captain Nemo, to the great displeasure of Ned Land, did not like the neighbourhood of the inhabited coasts of Brazil, for he passed them at a headlong speed. Not a fish nor a bird, however rapid, could follow us, and the natural curiosities of these seas escaped all observation.

This rapidity was kept up for several days, and on the 9th of April, in the evening, we sighted the most easterly point of South America, that forms Cape San Roque. But then the *Nautilus* went still farther out, and went to seek at greater depths a submarine valley between that cape and Sierra Leone on the African coast. This valley bifurcates at the height of the Antilles, and ends in the north by an enormous depression of five hundred fathoms. In this place the geological basin of the ocean forms, as far as the Lesser Antilles, a cliff of three and a-half miles high, very steep, and at the height of the Cape Verd

Islands, another wall no less considerable, which thus incloses all the submerged continent of Atlantis. The bottom of that immense valley is dotted with mountains that give a picturesque aspect to these submarine places. I speak from the MS. charts that were in the library of the *Nautilus*—charts evidently due to the hand of Captain Nemo, and drawn up from his personal observation.

During two days these deep and solitary waters were visited by means of the inclined planes. The *Nautilus* made long diagonal broadsides, which carried it to all elevations. But on the 11th of April it suddenly rose, and land appeared at the mouth of the Amazon River—a vast estuary through which so much water runs into the sea that it makes it less salt for a distance of several leagues.

The equator was crossed. Twenty miles to the west lay the Guianas, a French territory, on which we might have found an easy refuge. But the wind was blowing a great gale, and the furious waves would not have allowed a simple boat to survive them. Ned Land doubtless understood that, for he did not speak to me of anything. For my part I made no allusions to his schemes for flight, for I did not wish to urge him to make any attempt that must inevitably fail.

I easily consoled myself for this delay by interesting studies. During the days of the 11th and 12th of April the *Nautilus* did not leave the surface of the sea, and its nets brought in a miraculous haul of zoophytes, fish, and reptiles.

Some zoophytes had been dragged up by the chain of the nets; they were for the most part fine phyctallines, belonging to the actinidian family, and amongst other species the *Phyctalis protexta*, a native of this part of the ocean; it was a little cylindrical trunk, ornamented with vertical lines, and speckled with red dots that crowned a marvellous blossoming of tentacles. The molluscs consisted of products I had already observed, turritellas, olive porphyras, with regular intercrossed lines, with red spots standing out plainly on a background of flesh; fantastic pteroceras, like petrified scorpions, translucid hyaleas, argonauts, cuttle-fish, excellent to eat, and certain species of calmars that the naturalists of antiquity classified amongst flying-fish, and that principally serve as bait for cod-fishing.

Of the fish in these regions that I had not yet had an opportunity of studying I noticed several species. Amongst the cartilaginous fish, the petromyzons-pricka, a sort of eel, fifteen inches long, with a greenish head, violet fins, bluish-grey back and silver-brown belly, covered with bright spots, the pupil of the eye encircled with gold—curious animals that the current of the Amazon must have brought down to the sea, for they only frequent fresh water; tubercular skates with pointed snouts, a long flexible tail, and armed with a long saw; little sharks a yard long, with grey and whitish skins, whose teeth in several rows are bent back, vulgarly known as slippers; vespertilio-lophies, a sort of reddish isosceles triangle, two feet long, the pectorals of which are attached by fleshy pro-longations that make them look like bats; but whose horny appendage, near the nostrils, has caused to be named sea-unicorns; lastly, some species of balistæ, the curassavian, the spotted sides of which shine with a brilliant gold colour, and the capriscus of light violet, with *chatoyant* shades like a pigeon's throat.

I here end this somewhat dry, perhaps, but very exact catalogue, with the series of bony fish I observed; passans, belonging to the apteronotes, with snout as white as snow and very obtuse; the body a fine black, which is furnished with a very long and flexible thong; spiked odontognathes, sardines nine inches long, glittering with silver; a species of scomber, furnished with two anal fins; negro-centronotes, of blackish tints, that are fished for with torches—fish six feet long, with white, fat, and firm flesh, which, when fresh, taste like eel, and when dried like smoked salmon; reddish labres with scales only at the end of the dorsal and anal fins; chrysoptera, on which gold and silver blend their brilliancy with that of the ruby and topaz; golden-tailed spares, the flesh of which is extremely delicate, and which their phosphorescent qualities reveal in the water; gilt-heads with fine tongues and orange tints; umbra with golden caudal fins, darkish thorn-tails, anableps of Surinam, &c.

That *etcætera* shall not make me leave out a fish that Conseil will not soon forget for a very good reason.

One of our nets had hauled up a very flat skate, which, if the tail had been cut off, would have formed a perfect disc, and which weighed about 40lbs. It was white underneath, with reddish back, large, round, dark blue spot, encircled with black, very smooth skin, terminating in a bilobed fin. Laid out on the platform, it struggled, tried by convulsive movements to turn over, and made so many efforts that a last spring almost sent it into the sea. But Conseil, who wished to keep the fish, rushed to it, and, before I could prevent him, seized it with both hands.

He was immediately overthrown, with his legs in the air, and half his body paralysed, crying—

"Oh, master! my master! come to me!"

It was the first time the poor fellow had ever spoken to me otherwise than in the third person.

The Canadian and I picked him up, rubbed him vigorously, and when he came to his senses the eternal classifier murmured in a broken voice—

"Cartilaginous class, chondropterygian order, with fixed gills, sub-order of selacians, family of ray-fish, genus of torpedoes!"

"Yes, my friend," I answered, "it was an electric ray fish that put you in such a deplorable condition."

"Ah! monsieur may believe me," replied Conseil, "but I will be revenged on that animal."

"How?"

"I'll eat it."

Which he did the same evening, but for pure vengeance, for it was exceedingly tough.

The unfortunate Conseil had attacked a crampfish of the most dangerous species, the cumana. This strange animal, in a conducting medium like water, throws its electric bolts and strikes fish at several yards' distance, so great is the power of its electric organ, the two principal surfaces of which do not measure less than twenty-seven square feet.

The next day, the 12th of April, during the day the *Nautilus* approached the Dutch coast near the mouth of the Maroni. There several groups of sea-cows herded together. They were manatees, that, like the dugong and stellera, belong to the sirenian order. These fine animals, peaceable and inoffensive, from eighteen to twenty-one feet long, weight at least 8,000lbs. I told Ned Land and Conseil that foreseeing Nature had assigned an important part to these mammalia. Like seals they are destined to graze on the submarine meadows and thus destroy the agglomerations of herbs that choke up the mouth of tropical rivers.

"And do you know," I added, "what has resulted from the almost entire destruction of these useful creatures? The putrified herbs have poisoned the air, and the poisoned air is the cause of the yellow fever that desolates these beautiful countries. Venomous vegetation has been multiplied under the tropical seas, and the sickness has been irresistibly developed from the mouth of the Rio de la Plata to Florida!"

And if Toussenel is to be believed, this plague is nothing to the one that will fall upon our descendants when the seas will be depopulated of whales and seals. Then, infested with poulps, medusæ, and cuttle-fish, they will become vast hotbeds of infection, since their waters will no longer possess "those vast stomachs that God had charged to skim the surface of the sea."

However, without disdaining these theories, the crew of the *Nautilus* seized a half-dozen manatees, in order to provision the larders with excellent meat, superior to beef or veal. Their capture was not interesting. The manatees allowed themselves to be struck without defending themselves. Several thousand pounds of meat, destined to be dried, were stored on board.

That day a singular haul again increased the reserves of the *Nautilus*, so full were these seas. The net had brought up in its meshes a number of fish, the head of which terminated in an oval plate with fleshy edges. They were echeneides belonging to the third family of the subbrachian malacopterygians. Their flattened discs were composed of transverse flexible cartilaginous bones by which the animal could make a vacuum, and so adhere to any object like a cupping-glass.

The remora that I had noticed in the Mediterranean belonged to this species. But the one here was an osteochera echeneis, peculiar to this sea. Our sailors, as they took them, deposited them in buckets full of water.

The fishing ended, the *Nautilus* approached the coast. In that place a certain number of marine turtles were sleeping on the surface of the sea. It would have been difficult to take any of these precious reptiles, for the least noise wakes them, and their solid carapace is proof against the harpoon. But the echeneis causes their capture with extraordinary certainty and precision. This animal is, in fact, a living fish-hook which would delight and make the fortune of any angler.

The *Nautilus*'s men tied a ring on the tails of these fish, large enough not to impede their movements, and to this ring they fastened a long cord lashed to the side of the vessel at the other end.

The echeneids, thrown into the sea, immediately began their work and fastened themselves on to the breastplate of the turtles. Their tenacity was such that they would have torn themselves to pieces rather than let go. They were hauled on board, and with them the turtles to which they adhered.

Thus several tortoises were taken, a yard wide, that weighed 400lbs. Their carapace, covered with large horny plates, thin, transparent, and brown, with white and yellow spots, causes them to fetch a good price. Besides, they are excellent in an edible point of view, like the common turtle, which has a delicious flavour.

That day's fishing brought our stay on the shores of the Amazon to a close, and by nightfall the *Nautilus* was far out at sea.

CHAPTER XVIII

Poulps

For several days the *Nautilus* kept constantly away from the American coast. The captain evidently did not wish to frequent the waters of the Gulf of Mexico, or the seas of the Antilles. However, there would have been plenty of water, for the average depth of these seas is nine hundred fathoms; but probably these regions, strewn with islands and ploughed by steamers, did not suit Captain Nemo.

On the 16th of April we sighted Martinique and Guadaloupe, at a distance of about thirty miles. I caught a glimpse of their high peaks.

The Canadian, who counted upon putting his schemes into execution in the Gulf, either by reaching some land or hailing one of the numerous boats that coast from one island to another, was much put out. Flight would have been very practicable if Ned Land had been able to take possession of the boat without the knowledge of the captain. But in open ocean it was useless to think of it.

The Canadian, Conseil, and I had a rather long conversation on this subject. We had been prisoners on board the *Nautilus* for six months. We had come 17,000 leagues, and, as Ned Land said, there seemed no end to it. He therefore made me a proposal that I did not expect. It was to ask Captain Nemo, once and for all, if he meant to keep us indefinitely in his vessel.

Such a proceeding was very repugnant to me, and I thought it useless. It was useless to expect anything from Captain Nemo, and we could only depend upon ourselves. Besides, for some time past, this man had become graver, more retiring, less sociable. He seemed to avoid me. I only met him at rare intervals. Formerly he took some pleasure in explaining the submarine marvels to me; now he left me to my studies and came no more to the saloon.

What change had come over him? For what cause? I had nothing to reproach myself with. Perhaps our presence on board was a burden to him. However, I did not think he was a man to restore us to liberty.

I therefore begged Ned Land to reflect well before acting. If what he did had no result, it would only excite suspicion and make our situation more painful. I may add that I could in no wise complain of our health. If we except the rude shock it received under the southern ice-bank, we had never been better. The wholesome food, the salubrious atmosphere, the regular life, the uniformity of temperature, prevented illness, and for a man to whom the remembrance of earth left no regret, for a Captain Nemo in his own vessel, who goes where he likes either by mysterious means of conveyance for others and not for himself, and goes straight to his end, I understand such an existence. But we had not broken all ties that bound us to humanity. For my own part, I did not wish my curious and novel studies to be buried with me. I had now the right of writing a true account of the sea, and I wished for that account to appear sooner or later.

Then again, in these seas of the Antilles, at five fathoms below the surface, what interesting products I had to signalise in my daily notes! There were, amongst other zoophytes, those known under the name of *physalis pelagica*, a sort of large oblong bladder, with the tints of mother-of-pearl, holding out their membranes to the wind, and letting their blue tentacles float after them like threads of silk—charming medusæ to the eye, real nettles to the touch, that distil a corrosive fluid. There were also amongst the articulates annelides five feet long, armed with a pink trumpet and provided with 1,700 loco-motive organs that wind about under the water, and in passing throw out all the colours in the solar spectrum. There were in the fish category Malabar rays, enormous cartilaginous fish ten feet long and weighing 600 pounds, with a triangular pectoral fin, the middle of the back slightly humped, the eyes fixed in the extremities of the face behind the head, and which, floating like some spar from a ship, stuck on our window-pane like an opaque shutter. There were also American balistæ, that Nature has only dressed in black and white; gobies long and fleshy, with yellow fins and prominent jaws; mackerel five feet long, with shot pointed teeth, covered with little scales belonging to the albicore species. Then in swarms appeared grey mullet, clothed in gold stripes from head to tail, turning their shining fins—veritable masterpieces of jewellery formerly consecrated to Diana, particularly sought after by the rich Romans, and of which the proverb said—"He who takes them does not eat them." Lastly, golden pomacanthes, ornamented with emerald bands, dressed in velvet and silk, passed before our eyes like Veronese seigniors; spurred spars swimming away with their rapid pectoral fins; clupanodons, fifteen inches long, enveloped in their phosphorescent gleams; mullet beating the sea with their fat fleshy tails; red coregons seemed to cut the waves with their scythe-like fins; and silver selenes, worthy of their name, rose on the horizon of the water like so many moons with whitish rays.

What other marvellous and new specimens I might still have observed had not the *Nautilus* sunk into lower depths! Its inclined planes dragged it down to depths of between 1,000 and 2,000 fathoms. Then the animal life was only represented by encrines, sea-stars, charming pentacrines with medusæ heads, the straight stalk of which supports a little chalice, and littoral molluscs of a large species.

On the 20th of April we rose to an average depth of 700 fathoms. The nearest land was then the archipelago of the Bahamas, scattered like a heap of stones on the surface of the sea. There rose high submarine cliffs, straight walls of corroded blocks, amongst which were black holes that our electric rays did not light up to their depths.

These rocks were carpeted with large herbs, giant laminarisa, gigantic fucus, hydrophytes worthy of a world of Titans.

From speaking of these colossal plants, Ned, Conseil, and I naturally deviated to the gigantic animals of the sea. Some are evidently destined to serve as food to others. However, through the windows of the nearly motionless *Nautilus* I had not yet perceived in these long filaments any but the principal articulates of the brachial division peculiar to the seas of the Antilles.

It was about eleven o'clock when Ned Land attracted my attention to a formidable swarming that was going on in the large seaweed.

"Well," said I, "those are veritable caverns of poulps, and I should not be astonished to see some of those monsters."

"What!" said Conseil, "calamary, simple calamary of the cephalopod class?"

"No," said I, "poulps of very large dimensions. But friend Land is doubtless mistaken, for I see nothing."

"I am sorry for that," replied Conseil. "I should like to contemplate face to face one of those poulps I have heard so much talk about, that can drag ships down to the bottom of the sea. These animals are called krakens."

"None will ever make me believe that such animals exist," said Ned Land.

"Why not?" answered Conseil. "We all believed in monsieur's narwhal."

"We were wrong, Conseil."

"Certainly, but others believe in it still."

"That is probable, Conseil; but, for my part, I am quite decided only to admit the existence of these monsters after I have dissected one with my own hand."

"Then," asked Conseil, "monsieur does not believe in gigantic poulps?"

"Who the dickens does?" cried the Canadian.

"Many people, friend Ned."

"No fishermen. *Savants* do, perhaps."

"Excuse me, Ned, both fishers and *savants*."

"But I myself," said Conseil seriously—"I perfectly recollect having seen a large vessel being dragged under the waves by the arms of a cephalopod."

"You have seen that?" asked the Canadian.

"Yes, Ned."

"With your own eyes?"

"With my own eyes."

"And where, pray?"

"At Saint Malo," replied Conseil coolly.

"In the port?" said Ned Land ironically.

"No, in a church," answered Conseil.

"In a church!" exclaimed the Canadian.

"Yes, friend Ned. It was a picture that represented the poulp in question."

"Good!" said Ned Land, laughing. "Conseil is trying to do me."

"It is true what he says," I answered. "I have heard of the picture, but the subject it represents is taken from a legend, and you know what to think of legendary natural history. Besides, when monsters are in question imagination always takes flight. Not only has it been said that these poulps could drag down ships, but a certain Olaüs Magnus speaks of a cephalopod a mile long that looked more like an island than an animal. They relate also that the Bishop of Nidros once raised an altar on an immense rock. His mass ended, the rock set out and returned to the sea. The rock was a poulp."

"And is that all?" asked the Canadian.

"No," I replied. "Another bishop—Pontoppidan de Berghem—speaks of a poulp on which a regiment of cavalry could manœuvre."

"Bishops did not stick at much in those days," said Ned Land.

"Lastly, the naturalists of antiquity mention monsters, with mouths like a gulf, that were too large to pass through the Straits of Gibraltar."

"That's something like!" said the Canadian.

"But in all such tales what truth is there?" asked Conseil.

"None, my friends—at least, none where the limit of probability is passed and fable or legend begins. At all events, some cause or pretext must be assigned to the imagination of the story-tellers. It cannot be denied that calamary and poulps of very large size exist, but they are inferior to the cetaceans. Aristotle has stated the dimensions of a calamary as ten feet. Our fishers frequently see them six feet long. The museums of Trieste and Montpellier contain skeletons of poulps that measure six feet. Besides, according to the calculation of naturalists, one of these animals only six feet long has tentacles twenty-seven feet long. That would be enough to make a formidable monster."

"Are there any caught now?" asked the Canadian.

"If they are not caught, sailors see them. One of my friends, Captain Paul Bos, of Havre, has often affirmed to me that he had met with one of these colossal monsters in the Indian seas. But the most astonishing fact, which puts the existence of these gigantic animals beyond all doubt, occurred a few years ago—in 1861."

"What fact is that?" asked Ned Land.

"In 1861, in the north-east of Teneriffe, nearly in the same latitude as we are in now, the crew of the despatch-boat *Alecton* perceived a monstrous calamary swimming in its waters. The commander, Bouguer, approached the animal and attacked it with harpoons and cannon without much success, for cannon-balls and harpoons traversed the soft, fleshlike jelly. After several fruitless attempts the crew succeeded in throwing a running noose round the body of the mollusc; this noose slipped down to the caudal fins and there stopped. They tried to haul the monster on board, but its weight was so great that the cord cut its tail from its body, and, deprived of that ornament, it disappeared under the water."

"A fact at last," said Ned Land.

"And an indisputable fact, Ned. They proposed to call this poulp a 'Bouguer calamary.'"

"How long was it?" asked the Canadian.

"Did it not measure about eighteen feet?" said Conseil, who, posted at the window, was again examining the anfractuosities of the cliff.

"Precisely," I replied.

"Was not its head crowned with eight tentacles that moved about in the water like a nest of serpents?"

"Precisely."

"And were not its eyes prominent and very large?"

"Yes, Conseil."

"And was not its mouth a veritable parrot's beak, but a formidable beak?"

"Yes, Conseil."

"Well, then, if monsieur will please to come to the window, he will see, if not the Bouguer calamary, at least one of its brethren."

I looked at Conseil. Ned Land rushed to the window.

"The frightful animal!" he cried. I looked in my turn, and could not restrain a movement of repulsion. Before my eyes was a monster worthy to figure in teratological legends.

It was a calamary of colossal dimensions, at least thirty-two feet long. It was swimming backwards with extreme velocity in the direction of the *Nautilus*. It was staring with its enormous green eyes; its eight arms, or rather eight feet, starting from its head, which have given the name of "cephalopod" to this animal, were twice as long as its body, and twined about like the pair of the Furies. We could distinctly see the 250 blowholes on the inner side of the tentacles in the form of semi-spherical capsules. Sometimes these blowholes fastened themselves on to the pane and made a vacuum. The mouth of the monster—a horned beak made like that of a parrot—opened and shut vertically. Its tongue, a horny substance armed with several rows of sharp teeth, came quivering out of this veritable pair of shears. What a freak of Nature!—a bird's beak on a mollusc! Its body, fusiform and larger in the middle, made a fleshy mass that must have weighed from 40,000 to 50,000 lbs. Its inconstant colour, changing with extreme rapidity according to the irritation of the animal, passed successively from livid grey to reddish brown.

What had irritated this mollusc? It was doubtless the presence of this *Nautilus*, more formidable than itself, upon which its suckers or mandibles had no hold. And yet what monsters these are!—what vitality the Creator has endowed them with!—what vigour their three hearts impart to their movements!

Chance had brought us into the presence of this calamary, and I would not lose the occasion of carefully studying this specimen of cephalopods. I overcame the horror with which its aspect inspired me, and, taking a pencil, began to draw it.

"Perhaps it is the same as the *Alecton* one," said Conseil.

"No," answered the Canadian, "for this one is entire, and the other had lost its tail."

"That would not be a reason," I replied. "The arms and tail of these animals grow again by redintegration, and in seven years the tail of the Bouguer calamary has had plenty of time to grow."

"Besides," replied Ned, "if it is not this one perhaps it is one of those!"

In fact, other poulps had appeared at the port window. I counted seven. They formed a procession after the *Nautilus*, and I heard their beaks grating on the iron hull. We had plenty to choose from.

I went on with my work. These monsters kept in our vicinity with such precision that they seemed motionless, and I could have drawn their outline on the window. Besides, we were going at a moderate speed.

All at once the *Nautilus* stopped. A shock made it tremble in every joint.

"Can we be stranded?" I asked.

"Anyway," answered the Canadian, "we must be off again, for we are floating."

The *Nautilus* was certainly floating, but it was not moving onwards. The branches of its screw were not beating the waves. A minute passed. Captain Nemo, followed by his first officer, came into the saloon.

I had not seen him for some time; he looked to me very gloomy. Without speaking to us, or, perhaps, even seeing us, he went to the panel, looked at the poulps, and said a few words to his officer.

The latter went out. Soon the panels were closed. The ceiling was lighted up again.

I went towards the captain.

"A curious collection of poulps," I said in as indifferent a tone as an amateur might take before the crystal of an aquarium.

"Yes, professor," he replied, "and we are going to fight them face to face."

I looked at the captain, thinking I had not rightly heard.

"Face to face?" I echoed.

"Yes, sir. The screw is stopped. I think that the horny mandibles of one of them are caught in its branches. That prevents us moving on."

"And what are you going to do?"

"Go up to the surface and massacre all that vermin."

"A difficult enterprise."

"As you say. The electric bullets are powerless against their soft flesh, and where they do not find enough resistance to make them go off. But we will attack them with axes."

"And with harpoons, sir," said the Canadian, "if you do not refuse my aid."

"I accept it, Mr. Land."

"We will accompany you," said I, and, following Captain Nemo, we went to the central staircase.

There about ten men armed with boarding hatchets were standing ready for the attack. Conseil and I took two hatchets. Ned Land seized a harpoon.

The *Nautilus* was then on the surface of the sea. One of the sailors, placed on the lowest steps, was unscrewing the bolts of the panel. But he had hardly finished before the panel was raised with extreme violence, evidently drawn up by a blowhole in the arm of a poulp.

Immediately one of these long arms glided like a serpent through the opening, and twenty others were brandished above it. With a blow of the hatchet Captain Nemo cut off this formidable tentacle, which glided twisting down the steps.

At the moment we were crowding together to get up to the platform, two other arms stretched down to a sailor placed in front of Captain Nemo, and drew him up with irresistible violence.

Captain Nemo uttered a cry and rushed out. We followed.

What a scene! The unhappy man, seized by the tentacle and fastened to its blowholes, was balanced in the air according to the caprice of this enormous trunk. He was choking, and cried out, "*A moi! à moi!*" ("Help! help!") These French words caused me a profound stupor. Then I had a countryman on board, perhaps several! I shall hear that heart-rending cry all my life!

The unfortunate man was lost. Who would rescue him from that powerful grasp? Captain Nemo threw himself on the poulp, and with his hatchet cut off another arm. His first officer was fighting with rage against other monsters that were climbing the sides of the *Nautilus*. The crew were fighting with hatchets.

The Canadian, Conseil, and I dug our arms into the fleshy masses. A violent smell of musk pervaded the atmosphere. It was horrible.

For an instant I believed that the unfortunate man, encircled by the poulp, would be drawn away from its powerful suction. Seven of its eight arms had been cut off, one only brandishing its victim like a feather twisted about in the air. But at the very moment that Captain Nemo and his officer were rushing upon it, the animal hurled out a column of black liquid, secreted in a bag in its stomach. We were blinded by it. When this cloud was dissipated the calamary had disappeared, and with it my unfortunate countryman!

With what rage we then set upon these monsters! Ten or twelve poulps had invaded the platform and sides of the *Nautilus*. We rolled pell-mell amongst the serpents' trunks that wriggled about the platform in pools of blood and black ink. It seemed as if the viscous tentacles kept springing out again like hydra heads. Ned Land's harpoon at each stroke plunged into the green eyes of the calamary and put them out. But my brave

387

companion was suddenly thrown over by one of the tentacles of a monster which he had not been able to avoid.

Ah, how my heart beat with emotion and horror! The calamary's formidable beak opened over Ned Land. The unfortunate man was about to be cut in two. I rushed to his aid. But Captain Nemo was before me. His hatchet disappeared in the two enormous mandibles, and, miraculously preserved, the Canadian rose and plunged the whole of his harpoon into the poulp's triple heart.

"We are quits," said Captain Nemo to the Canadian.

Ned bowed without answering.

This combat had lasted a quarter of an hour. The monsters, vanquished, mutilated, and death-stricken, left the place clear at last, and disappeared under the waves.

Captain Nemo, covered with blood, stood motionless near the lantern, and looked at the sea that had swallowed one of his companions, whilst tears rolled from his eyes.

CHAPTER XIX

The Gulf Stream

We none of us can forget that terrible scene of April 20th. I wrote it under the impression of violent emotion. Since then I have revised it and read it to Conseil and the Canadian. They find it exact as to facts, but insufficient as to effect. To depict such a scene it would take the pen of the most illustrious of our poets, Victor Hugo.

I said that Captain Nemo wept as he looked at the sea. His grief was immense. It was the second companion he had lost since our arrival on board. And what a death! This friend, crushed and stifled by the formidable arm of a poulp, ground to pieces by its iron mandibles, was not destined to repose with his companions in the peaceful waters of the coral cemetery.

Amidst the struggle it was the cry of despair uttered by the unfortunate man that had wrung my heart. The poor Frenchman, forgetting his conventional language, had spoken the language of his country and his mother to utter his last appeal! Then I had a countryman amongst the crew of the *Nautilus*, associated body and soul with Captain Nemo, avoiding, like him, contact with men! Was he the only representative of France in this mysterious association, evidently composed of individuals of different nationalities? This was one more of the insoluble problems that ceaselessly came up in my mind.

Captain Nemo went back to his room, and I saw him no more for some time. But how sad, despairing, and irresolute he was, I judged by the vessel of which he was the soul, and which received all his impressions! The *Nautilus* no longer kept any determined direction. It came and went, floating like a lifeless thing on the waves. Its screw was free again, but was little used. It went about at random. But it could not tear itself away from the theatre of its last struggle—from that sea which had devoured one of its children.

Ten days passed thus. It was not till the 1st of May that the *Nautilus* frankly took a northerly direction after sighting the Bahamas at the opening of the Bahama Channel. We were then following the current of that largest sea river, which has its own banks, fish, and temperature: the Gulf Stream.

It is, in fact, a river that flows freely in the midst of the Atlantic, and its waters do not mix with those of the ocean. It is a salt river—salter than the surrounding sea. Its average depth is three thousand feet, its average breadth sixty miles. In certain places its current goes along at a speed of more than a league an hour. The invariable volume of its water is more considerable than that of all the rivers of the globe.

The veritable source of the Gulf Stream, discovered by Commander Maury, its point of departure, is situated in the Bay of Biscay. There its waters, still weak in temperature and colour, begin to form. It goes down south, coasts equatorial Africa, warms its waters in the rays of the torrid zone, crosses the Atlantic, reaches Cape San Roque on the Brazilian coast, and bifurcates into two branches, one of which goes to saturate the seas of the Antilles with its warm particles. Then the Gulf Stream, whose mission it is to re-establish equilibrium amongst different temperatures, and to mix the tropical with the boreal waters, begins its *rôle* of ponderator. Warmed to a white heat in the Gulf of Mexico, it rises north along the American coasts to Newfoundland, deviates under the propulsion of the cold current of Davis' Straits, takes up the ocean route, following one of the great circles of the globe, the loxodromic line, divides into two arms about the 43rd degree, one of which, helped by the trade wind from the north-east, comes back to the Bay of Biscay and the Azores, and the other, after having warmed the shores of Ireland and Norway, goes beyond Spitzbergen, where its temperature, fallen to four degrees, forms the open sea of the Pole.

It was upon this river that the *Nautilus* was then navigating. When it comes out of the Bahama Channel, the Gulf Stream, then fourteen leagues wide and one hundred and fifty fathoms deep, goes along at the rate of five miles an hour. This rapidity regularly decreases as it advances northward, and it is to be wished that this regularity should keep up, for it has been remarked that if its speed and direction were changed, European climates would be subject to perturbations the consequences of which could not be calculated.

About noon I was on the platform with Conseil. I was telling him the different peculiarities of the Gulf Stream. When my explanation was ended I invited him to plunge his hands into the stream.

Conseil obeyed, and was much astonished at feeling no sensation either of heat or cold.

"That comes," I said to him, "from the temperature of the Gulf Stream as it leaves the Gulf of Mexico being little different from that of blood. This Gulf Stream is a vast heating stove that gives eternal verdure to the coasts of Europe; and, if Maury is to be believed, the heat of this current, all utilised, would furnish enough caloric to hold in fusion a river of melted iron as large as the Amazon or the Missouri."

At that moment the speed of the stream was that of five feet a second. Its current is so distinct from the surrounding sea that its compressed waters rise above the level of the ocean. As it is very rich in saline particles, it is of a dark blue colour, while the waves that surround it are green. Such is the clearness of their line of demarcation that the *Nautilus*, abreast of the Carolinas, cut with its prow the waters of the Gulf Stream, whilst its screw was still beating those of the ocean.

This current carried down with it a world of living things. Argonauts, so common in the Mediterranean, travelled in it in shoals. Amongst the cartilaginous fish the most remarkable were the rays, of which the very flexible tails formed nearly a third of the body, and that were like vast lozenges twenty-five feet long; then dog-fish three feet long, with large heads, short round snouts, and pointed teeth in several rows, the bodies of which seemed covered with scales.

Amongst the bony fish I noticed some grey wrass peculiar to

these waters. Giltheads, whose eyes shone like fire; saw-fish, parakeets, veritable rainbows of the ocean that rival the finest tropical birds in colour; dipterodons with silver heads and yellow tails; different specimens of salmon; mugilomores, lithe and softly brilliant, that Lacèpéde consecrated to the amiable companion of his life; lastly, a fine fish, the American-knight, which, decorated with numberless orders and ribbons, frequents the shores of the great nation where ribbons and orders are so slightly esteemed.

I may add that during the night the phosphorescent waters of the Gulf Stream rivalled the electric brilliancy of our lantern; above all, in the stormy weather which threatened us frequently.

On the 8th of May we were still abreast of Cape Hatteras, at the height of the North Carolinas. The Gulf Stream is seventy-five miles wide there, and one hundred and five fathoms deep. The *Nautilus* continued to move about at random. All supervision seemed banished from the vessel. I acknowledge that under those circumstances an escape might succeed. In fact, the inhabited shores offered easy refuges on all sides. The sea was incessantly ploughed by numerous steamers that run between New York or Boston and the Gulf of Mexico, and night and day by little schooners that do the coasting trade on the different points of the American coast. We might hope to be picked up. It was, therefore, a favourable opportunity, notwithstanding the thirty miles that separated the *Nautilus* from the coasts of the Union.

But one vexatious circumstance thwarted the Canadian's schemes. The weather was very bad. We were approaching the regions where tempests are frequent, that country of gales and cyclones engendered by the current of the Gulf Stream. To tempt such a sea in a fragile boat was to court destruction. Ned Land agreed to that himself, and fretted his life away with nostalgia that nothing but flight could cure.

"Sir," said he to me that day, "there must be an end to this. I want to know how things stand. Your Nemo is going away from land, up north. But I declare to you that I have had enough with the South Pole, and I won't follow him to the North Pole."

"But what is to be done, Ned, as flight is impracticable just now?"

"I return to my first idea. The captain must be spoken to. You said nothing to him when he was in the seas of your country. I will speak now that we are in the seas of mine. When I think that before many days are over the *Nautilus* will be abreast of Nova Scotia, and that there, near Newfoundland, there is a wide bay, that into this bay the St. Lawrence falls, that the St. Lawrence is my river, the river of Quebec, my native town; when I think of that I am furious; my hair stands on end. I tell you, sir, I would rather throw myself into the sea! I will not stay here! I am stifled!"

The Canadian had evidently lost all patience. His vigorous nature could not get accustomed to this prolonged imprisonment. His countenance grew daily worse, his temper more sullen. I felt what he must suffer, for nostalgia had seized me too. Nearly seven months had gone by since we had heard any news of earth. What is more, Captain Nemo's isolation, his altered humour, especially since the fight with the poulps, his taciturnity, all made me see things in a different light. I no longer felt the enthusiasm of the first days. One must be a Dutchman like Conseil to accept the situation in this medium reserved for cetaceans and other inhabitants of the sea. Really if the brave fellow had gills instead of lungs I think he would make a distinguished fish.

"Well, sir?" said Ned, seeing that I did not answer.

"Well, Ned, you want me to ask Captain Nemo what his intentions are concerning us?"

"Yes, sir."

"Although he has already told them to you?"

"Yes. I want to be certain about it, once and for all. Speak for me only if you like."

"But I rarely meet him. He even avoids me."

"A greater reason for going to see him."

"I will ask him, Ned."

"When?" asked the Canadian, insisting.

"When I meet him."

"M. Aronnax, do you want me to go to him?"

"No, leave it to me. Tomorrow——"

"Today," said Ned Land.

"Very well. I will see him today," replied I to the Canadian, who would have certainly compromised all by acting on his own account.

I remained alone. Once decided to ask, I resolved to have done with it immediately. I like things better done than about to be done.

I entered my room. There I heard someone walking about in Captain Nemo's. I could not let this occasion of meeting him slip. I knocked at the door. I obtained no answer. I knocked again, and then turned the handle. The door opened.

I entered. The captain was there. Bent over his work-table, he had heard nothing. Resolved not to go out without questioning him, I approached him. He raised his head suddenly, frowned, and said rather rudely—

"You here? What do you want?"

"To speak to you, captain."

"But I am occupied, sir. I am at work. The liberty I allow you to shut yourself up, may I not enjoy it also?"

My reception was not very encouraging, but I was decided to hear everything in order to answer everything.

"Captain," said I coldly, "I have to speak to you on business that I cannot put off."

"What can that be, sir?" he replied ironically. "Have you made some discovery that has escaped me? Has the sea given up to you any fresh secret?"

We were far from the subject. Before I could answer, the captain pointed to a manuscript on the table, and said in a grave tone—

"Here is a manuscript written in several languages, M.

Aronnax. It contains the account of my studies on the sea, and, if God so please, it shall not perish with me. This manuscript, signed by my own name, completed by the history of my life, will be inclosed in an insubmersible case. The last survivor of us all on board the *Nautilus* will throw this case into the sea, and it will go where the waves will carry it."

The name of this man! His history written by himself! Then the mystery that surrounds him will be one day revealed? But at that moment I only saw in this communication an opening for me.

"Captain," I answered, "I can but approve the idea that influences you. The fruit of your studies must not be lost. But the means you employ seem to me very primitive. Who knows where the winds will carry that case, in what hands it will fall? Could you not find some better means? Could not you or one of yours——"

"Never, sir," said the captain, interrupting me.

"But I and my companions will preserve your manuscript if you will give us liberty——"

"Liberty, sir?" said Captain Nemo, rising.

"Yes, captain, and that is the subject I wished to ask you about. We have now been seven months on your vessel, and I now ask you, in the name of my companions and myself, if you mean to keep us here always?"

"M. Aronnax," said Captain Nemo, "I have only the same answer to give you that I gave you seven months ago. Whoever enters my vessel never leaves it again."

"But that is slavery!"

"Call it by what name you please."

"But everywhere a slave keeps the right of recovering his liberty! Whatever means offer he has the right to consider them legitimate."

"Who has denied you that right?" answered Captain Nemo. "Have I ever asked you to bind yourself by an oath?"

The captain looked at me and folded his arms.

"Sir," I said to him, "we shall neither of us care to return to this subject. But as we have begun it I must go on. To me study is a help, a powerful diversion, a passion that can make me forget anything. Like you, I could live ignored, obscure, in the hope of bequeathing to the future the result of my work, by means of a case confided to the mercies of waves and winds. In a word, I can admire you, follow you with pleasure in a *rôle* that I understand, up to a certain point; but there are other aspects of your life surrounded with complications and mysteries in which my companions and I alone have no part. And even when our hearts could beat for you, moved by your griefs, or stirred to the bottom by your acts of genius or courage, we are obliged to repress the least manifestation of sympathy that the sight of what is beautiful and right arouses, whether it comes from friend or enemy. It is this feeling of being strangers to everything that concerns you that makes our position unbearable, even for me, but much more for Ned Land. Every man, because he is man, is worth attention. Have you ever asked yourself what the love of liberty and hatred of slavery might arouse in a nature like that of the Canadian, what he might think or attempt—"

I was silent. Captain Nemo rose.

"It does not matter to me what Ned Land thinks or attempts. I did not take him; I do not keep him on board my vessel for my own pleasure. As to you, M. Aronnax, you are one of the few people who can understand anything, even silence. I have nothing more to answer you. This first time that you come to speak on this subject must also be the last, for I cannot even listen to you again."

I withdrew. From that day our position was clear. I related our conversation to my two companions.

"We now know," said Ned Land, "that there is nothing to expect from that man. The *Nautilus* is approaching Long Island. We will escape, no matter what the weather is."

But the sky became more and more threatening. Symptoms of a hurricane became manifest. The atmosphere became white and misty. Fine streaks of cirrus clouds were succeeded on the horizon by masses of cumulus clouds. Other low clouds swept swiftly by. The sea rose in huge billows. The birds disappeared, with the exception of petrels, those friends of the storm. The barometer fell visibly, and indicated an extreme tension of the vapours in the air. The mixture in the storm-glass was decomposed under the influence of the electricity which saturated the atmosphere. The struggle of the elements was approaching.

The tempest broke out on the 18th of May, just as the *Nautilus* was floating abreast of Long Island, at some miles from the port of New York. I can describe this struggle of the elements, for instead of avoiding it in the depths of the sea, Captain Nemo, by an inexplicable caprice, wished to dare it on the surface.

The wind was blowing from the S.W. at a speed of 45 feet a second, which became 75 before 3 p.m. That is the figure of tempests.

Captain Nemo, unshaken by the gale, had taken his place on the platform. He had fastened himself by a rope round his waist to resist the monstrous waves that swept over him. I had gone up and fastened myself too, dividing my admiration between this tempest and the incomparable man who defied it.

The sea was swept by ragged clouds that dipped into the billows. I no longer saw any of the intermediary waves that form in the large hollows—nothing but long fuliginous undulations, the crest of which did not break into foam, so compact were they. Their height increased. The *Nautilus*, sometimes lying on its side, sometimes as straight up as a mast, pitched and tossed frightfully.

About 5 p.m. rain fell in torrents, which neither beat down wind nor sea. The hurricane blew at the rate of 120 miles an hour. It is in these conditions that it blows down houses, blows in tiles and doors, breaks iron gates, and displaces twenty-four-pound cannon. And yet the *Nautilus*, amidst the torment, justified this saying of a learned engineer—"There is no well-built hull that cannot defy the sea!" It was not a resisting rock which the waves would have demolished; it was a steel spindle, obedient and mobile, without rigging or masts, which could defy their fury with impunity.

In the meantime I attentively examined these unchained billows. They were at least 45 feet high and 250 feet long, and their speed, half that of the wind, was 40 feet a second. Their volume and power increased with the depth of the water. I then understood the part these waves play, imprisoning the air and throwing it to the bottom of the seas, where they carry life with the oxygen. Their extreme force of pressure, it has been calculated, can rise to 6,000lbs. to each square foot of the surface that they beat against. They were such waves that in the Hebrides displaced a block weighing 84,000lbs., and in the tempest of December 23rd, 1864, overthrew a part of the town of Yeddo, in Japan, going at the rate of 700 kilometres an hour, and breaking the same day on the shores of America.

The intensity of the tempest increased during the night. The barometer fell as it did in 1860 at La Réunion, during a cyclone. At nightfall I saw a large ship pass on the horizon, struggling painfully. It must have been one of the steamers of the lines between New York and Liverpool or Havre. It soon disappeared in the darkness.

At 10 p.m. the sky was all on fire. The atmosphere was streaked with violent lightning. I could not support its brilliancy, whilst Captain Nemo, looking straight at it, seemed the soul of the tempest. A terrible noise filled the air, made by the waves, wind, and thunder. The wind veered to all parts of the horizon, and the cyclone, starting from the east, returned to it, passing north, west, and south in the opposite directions to the circular tempests of the austral hemisphere.

Ah! this Gulf Stream! Well did it justify its name of King of the Tempests! These formidable cyclones were its creation, caused by the difference of temperature in the strata of air above its currents.

To the shower of rain succeeded a shower of fire. The drops of water changed to fulminating sparks. One would have thought that Captain Nemo, seeking a death worthy of him, tried to get struck by lightning. With a frightful pitch the *Nautilus* threw up its steel prow into the air like a lightning-conductor, and I saw it give out sparks. Completely worn out, I crawled on all-fours towards the panel. I opened it and went down to the saloon. The tempest had then attained its maximum of intensity. It was impossible to keep on one's feet in the interior of the *Nautilus*.

Captain Nemo came in about midnight. I heard the reservoirs gradually filling, and the *Nautilus* slowly sank under the water.

Through the windows of the saloon I saw large frightened fish pass like phantoms in the fiery waters. Some were struck by lightning before my eyes.

The *Nautilus* still sank. I thought it would find calm water at a depth of eight fathoms; but no, the surface was too violently agitated. We were obliged to sink to twenty-five fathoms to find rest.

But there, what tranquillity! what silence! what a peaceful medium! Who would have said that a terrible tempest was going on upon the surface of that same ocean?

CHAPTER XX

In Latitude 47° 24' and Longitude 17° 18'

The storm had thrown us eastward once more. All hope of escaping on the shores of New York or the St. Lawrence had vanished. Poor Ned, in despair, shut himself up like Captain Nemo. Conseil and I left each other no more.

I ought rather to have given N.E. as the direction of the *Nautilus*, to be more exact. For some days it drifted about, sometimes on the surface, sometimes beneath it, amid those fogs so dreaded by sailors. What accidents are due to thick fogs! What shocks upon the reefs when the noise of the wind is louder than the breaking of the waves! What collisions between vessels, notwithstanding the fog-signals and alarm-bells!

The bottom of these seas looked like a battle-field where still lay all the ocean's victims—some already old and incrusted, some yellow and reflecting the light of our lantern on their iron and copper hulls. Amongst them lay many vessels lost with all hands—crews and emigrants—on the dangerous points signalled in their statistics, Cape Race, Saint Paul Island, Strait of Belle Isle, the estuary of the St. Lawrence. Many victims have been added to the gloomy list within several years only from the lines of the Royal Mail, Inman, and Montreal. The *Solway, Isis, Paramatta, Hungarian, Canadian, Anglo-Saxon, Humboldt, United States*, all sunk. The *Arctic, Lyonnaise*, sunk by collision. The *President, Pacific, City of Glasgow*, disappeared from unknown causes. The *Nautilus* went on amidst these gloomy remains as if passing the dead in review.

On the 15th of May we were at the southern extremity of Newfoundland Bank. This bank is formed of alluvia, or large heaps of organic matter, brought either from the equator by the Gulf Stream or from the North Pole by the counter-current of cold water that skirts the American coast. There also are piled those erratic blocks of stone carried down by the breaking up of the ice. And it is also a vast charnel-house of molluscs and zoophytes, which perish there by millions.

The depth of the sea is not great on Newfoundland Bank—a few hundred fathoms at most. But towards the south is a depression of 1,500 fathoms. There the Gulf Stream widens. It loses speed and heat and becomes a sea.

It was upon this inexhaustible Newfoundland Bank that I surprised cod in its favourite waters.

It may be said that cod are mountain-fish, for Newfoundland is only a submarine mountain. As the *Nautilus* moved through the thick shoals of them Conseil said—

"Those cod! I thought cod were as flat as soles."

"They are only flat at the grocer's," said I, "where they are open and dried. But in water they are fusiform fish, like mullet, and shaped for speed."

"What a lot of them there is!" said Conseil.

"There would be more but for their enemies—sharks and men! Do you know how many eggs there are in a single female?"

"I'll guess well," answered Conseil; "five hundred thousand!"

"Eleven millions, my friend."

"Eleven millions! I will never believe that till I count them myself."

"Count them, Conseil, but it will be quicker work to believe me. Besides, the French, English, Americans, Danes, and Norwegians catch cod by thousands. A prodigious quantity of them is consumed, and if they were not so astonishingly fertile the seas would soon be cleared of them. In England and America only, 5,000 ships, manned by 75,000 sailors, are employed in the cod fisheries. Each ship brings in an average of 40,000, which makes 25,000,000. On the coasts of Norway the same result."

"I have confidence in monsieur," said Conseil; "I will not count them."

"Count what?"

"The eleven millions of eggs. But I must make one remark."

"What?"

"Why, if all the eggs bore, four cods would be enough to feed England, America, and Norway."

Whilst we were on Newfoundland Bank I saw the long lines, armed with two hundred hooks, which each boat hangs out by dozens. Each line had a little grapline at one end, and was fastened to the surface by a buoy-rope, the buoy being made of cork. The *Nautilus* had to be skilfully steered amidst this submarine network.

However, it did not stay long in these frequented regions. It went northwards to the 42nd degree of latitude. It was abreast of Saint John's, in Newfoundland, and Heart's Content, where one extremity of the transatlantic cable touches.

The *Nautilus*, instead of keeping to its course northward, took an easterly direction as if to follow the telegraphic plateau on which the cable lies, and of which the multiplied soundings have given the exact plan.

It was on the 17th of May, at about 500 miles from Heart's Content, and at a depth of 1,400 fathoms, that I saw the cable lying on the ground. Conseil, whom I had not told about it, took it for a gigantic serpent, and prepared to classify it according to his usual method. But I consoled the worthy fellow, and by way of consolation told him various particulars about the laying down of the cable.

The first cable was laid during the years 1857 and 1858; but, after having transmitted about four hundred telegrams, it ceased to act. In 1863 the engineers manufactured a new cable, measuring 2,000 miles in length and weighing 4,500 tons, which was embarked on board the *Great Eastern*. This attempt also failed.

Now on the 25th of May the *Nautilus*, at a depth of 190 fathoms, was in the exact place where the rupture occurred that ruined the enterprise. It was at 638 miles from the Irish coast. It was perceived at 2 p.m. that communication with Europe was interrupted. The electricians on board resolved to cut the cable in order to haul it up again, and at 11 p.m. they had brought in the damaged part. They made a joint, and spliced it, and it was

402

once more submerged. But a few days later it broke, and could not be found again in the depths of the ocean.

The Americans were not discouraged. The daring Cyrus Field, the promoter of the enterprise, who had risked all his fortune in it, raised a fresh subscription. It was immediately taken up. Another cable was laid under better conditions. The conducting-wires were enveloped in gutta-percha and protected by a wadding of hemp contained in metal armour. The *Great Eastern* set out with it again on the 13th of July, 1866.

The operation went on well. However, one hitch occurred. Several times, whilst unrolling the cable, the electricians observed that nails had recently been driven into it in order to spoil the wire. Captain Anderson, his officers and engineers, met, deliberated, and caused it to be advertised that, if the culprit were caught on board, he should be thrown into the sea without further judgment. After that the criminal attempt was not repeated.

On the 23rd of July the *Great Eastern* was not more than five hundred miles from Newfoundland when the news of the armistice between Prussia and Austria, after Sadowa, was telegraphed to it. On the 27th it sighted, through the fog, the port of Heart's Content. The enterprise was happily terminated, and in the first despatch young America telegraphed to old Europe these wise words, so rarely understood:—"Glory to God in the highest, and on earth peace, goodwill towards men."

I did not expect to find the electric cable in its original state as it came from the manufactories. The long serpent, covered with *débris* of shells, bristling with foraminiferæ, was incrusted in a stony coating that protected it against perforating molluscs. It was resting tranquilly, sheltered from the movements of the sea, and under a pressure favourable to the transmission of the electric spark, which passes from America to Europe in 0.32 of a second. The duration of this cable will, doubtless, be infinite, for it has been remarked that its gutta-percha envelope is improved by the sea-water.

Besides, on this plateau, so happily chosen, the cable is never submerged at such depths as to cause it to break. The *Nautilus* followed it to its greatest depth, in about 2,200 fathoms, and there it lay without any effort of traction. Then we approached the place where the accident took place in 1863.

The bottom of the sea there formed a wide valley on which Mont Blanc might rest without its summit emerging above the waves. This valley is closed on the east by a precipitous wall 6,000 feet high. We reached it on the 28th of May, when the *Nautilus* was not more than 120 miles from Ireland.

Was Captain Nemo going north to coast the British Isles? No. To my great surprise he went southward again and returned to European seas. Whilst rounding the Emerald Isle I caught a glimpse of Cape Clear and Fastnet Beacon, which lights the thousands of vessels from Glasgow to Liverpool.

An important question then occurred to me. Would the *Nautilus* dare to enter the English Channel? Ned Land, who had reappeared since we were near land, questioned me constantly. How could I answer him? Captain Nemo remained invisible. After having allowed the Canadian a glimpse of the American shores, was he going to show me those of France?

The *Nautilus* still went southward. On the 30th of May we sighted Land's End, between the extreme point of England and the Scilly Isles, which were left to starboard.

If the vessel was going to enter the Channel it must go direct east. It did not do so.

During the whole of the 31st of May the *Nautilus* described a series of circles on the water that greatly interested me. It seemed to be seeking a spot there was some difficulty in finding. At noon Captain Nemo came to take the bearings himself. He did not speak to me, and seemed gloomier than ever. What could sadden him thus? Was it his proximity to European shores? Was it some memory of the country he had abandoned? What was it he felt, remorse or regret? For a long time this thought haunted my mind, and I felt a kind of presentiment that before long chance would reveal the captain's secreta.

The next day, the 1st of June, the *Nautilus* continued the same manœuvres. It was evidently trying to find a precise point in the ocean. Captain Nemo came to take the sun's altitude as he did the day before. The sea was calm, the sky pure. Eight miles to the east a large steamship appeared on the horizon. No flag fluttered from its mast, and I could not find out its nationality.

Some minutes before the sun passed the meridian Captain Nemo took his sextant and made his observation with extreme precision. The absolute calm of the waters facilitated the operation. The motionless *Nautilus* neither pitched nor rolled.

At that moment I was upon the platform. When the captain had taken his observation he pronounced these words:—

"It is here!"

He went down through the panel. Had he seen the ship that had tacked about, and seemed to be bearing down upon us? I cannot tell.

I returned to the saloon. The panel was shut, and I heard the water hissing into the reservoirs. The *Nautilus* began to sink vertically, its screw was stopped, and communicated no movement to it.

A few minutes later it stopped at a depth of 418 fathoms, and rested on the ground.

The luminous ceiling of the saloon was then extinguished, the panels were opened, and through the windows I saw the sea lighted up within a radius of half-a mile by our electric lantern.

I looked through the larboard window and saw nothing but an immensity of tranquil water.

On the starboard appeared a large protuberance which attracted my attention. It looked like a ruin buried under a crust of whitish shells like a mantle of snow. Whilst attentively examining this mass I thought I recognised the swollen out-lines of a ship, cleared of her masts, that must have gone down

405

prow foremost. The disaster must have taken place at a distant epoch. This wreck, incrusted with lime, had been lying many years at the bottom of the ocean.

What was this ship? Why did the *Nautilus* come to visit its tomb? Was it only a wreck that had drawn the *Nautilus* under water?

I did not know what to think, when, near me, I heard Captain Nemo say in a slow voice—

"Once that ship was called the *Marseillais*. It carried seventy-four guns, and was launched in 1762. In 1778, on the 13th of August, commanded by La Polype-Vertrieux, it fought daringly against the *Preston*. In 1779, on the 4th of July, it assisted the squadron of the Admiral d'Estaing to take Granada. In 1781, on the 5th of September, it took part in the naval battle of Chesapeake Bay. In 1794 the French Republic changed its name. On the 16th of April of the same year it joined at Brest the squadron of Villaret-Joyeuse as escort to a cargo of wheat coming from America under the command of Admiral Van Stabel. On the 11th and 12th prairial, year II., this squadron encountered the English vessels. Sir, today is the 13th prairial, the 1st of June, 1868. It is 74 years ago today, that in this same place, by 47° 4' latitude and 17° 28' longitude, this ship, after an heroic fight, dismasted, the water in her hold, the third of her crew disabled, preferred to sink with her 356 sailors than to surrender, and, nailing her colours to her stern, disappeared under the waves to the cry of 'Vive la République!'" (Carlyle says—"This enormous inspiring feat turns out to be an enormous inspiring nonentity, extant nowhere save as falsehood in the brain of Barrère!")

"The *Vengeur*!" I exclaimed.

"Yes, sir. The *Vengeur*! A glorious name!" murmured the captain as he folded his arms.

CHAPTER XXI

A Hecatomb

The unexpectedness of this scene and the way it was spoken of, the account of the patriotic ship, given coldly at first, and then the emotion with which the strange person had uttered his last words, this name of *Vengeur*, the signification of which could not escape me, all struck my imagination profoundly. My eyes no longer left the captain. He, with hands stretched out to the sea, was looking with ardent eyes at the glorious wreck. Perhaps I never was to know who he was, from whence he came, whither he was going, but I saw the man separate himself more and more from the *savant*. It was not a vulgar misanthropy that had inclosed Captain Nemo and his companions in the sides of the *Nautilus*, but a monstrous or sublime hatred that time could not quench.

Did this hatred still seek vengeance? The future was soon to tell me that.

In the meantime the *Nautilus* was slowly ascending to the surface of the sea, and I saw the confused outlines of the *Vengeur* gradually disappear. Soon a slight pitching told me we were floating in the open air.

At that moment a dull detonation was heard. I looked at the captain, but he did not stir.

"Captain?" I said.

He did not answer.

I left him and went up on to the platform. Conseil and the Canadian had preceded me there.

"What was that noise?" I asked.

"A gunshot," answered Ned Land.

I looked in the direction of the ship I had perceived before. She had neared the *Nautilus*, and was putting on more steam. Six miles separated us from her.

"What vessel is that, Ned?"

"By her rigging and the height of her low masts," answered

the Canadian, "I bet she's a warship. I hope she'll come and sink us, if necessary, along with this confounded *Nautilus*."

"What harm can she do the *Nautilus*, friend Ned?" said Conseil. "Can she attack it under the waves? Will she cannonade it at the bottom of the sea?"

"Can you tell me her nationality, friend Ned?" I asked.

The Canadian frowned, screwed up his eyes, and fixed the whole power of his eyes on to the ship.

"No, sir," he answered. "I cannot find out to what nation she belongs. Her colours are not hoisted. But I can affirm that she is a ship-of-war, for a long pendant is floating from her mainmast."

For a quarter of an hour we went on looking at the ship that was bearing down upon us. Still I did not think she had sighted the *Nautilus* at that distance, still less did she know what it was.

The Canadian soon announced that this vessel was a large warship, a two-decker, and an ironclad with a ram.

Thick black smoke was issuing from her two funnels. Her reefed sails could not be distinguished from her yards. She bore no colours. Distance prevented us making out the colour of her pendant, which streamed like a narrow ribbon.

She was rapidly approaching. If Captain Nemo allowed her to come near it would offer us a chance of escape.

"Sir," said Ned Land to me, "if that ship passes within a mile of us I shall throw myself into the sea, and I advise you to do the same."

I did not answer the Canadian's proposition, and went on looking at the ship, which grew gradually larger. Whether she were English, French, American, or Russian, she would certainly take us in if we could reach her.

"Monsieur will please to remember that we have had some experience in swimming. He can leave me the care of towing him towards the ship if it suits him to follow Ned," said Conseil.

I was going to answer when some white smoke issued from the prow of the vessel. Then, a few seconds afterwards, the water aft of the *Nautilus* was thrown up by the fall of some heavy body. In a short time we heard the report.

"Why, they are firing at us!" I exclaimed.

"Good people!" muttered the Canadian. "Then they do not take us for shipwrecked men on a raft!"

"If monsieur will allow me to say so, that's right," said Conseil, shaking off the water that another shot had sprinkled him with. "If monsieur will allow me to say so, they have sighted the narwhal, and are firing at the narwhal."

"But they must see that they have men to deal with!" I exclaimed.

"Perhaps that is the reason," answered Ned Land, looking at me.

Quite a revelation was made in my mind. They doubtless knew now what to think about the existence of the pretended monster. Doubtless Captain Farragut had found out that the *Nautilus* was a submarine boat, and more dangerous than a supernatural cetacean when it struck against the *Abraham Lincoln*.

Yes, it must be so, and they were doubtless pursuing the terrible engine of destruction in every sea.

Terrible indeed, if, as might be supposed, Captain Nemo was employing the *Nautilus* in a work of vengeance. During that night when he had imprisoned us in the cell, in the Indian Ocean, had he not attacked some ship? The man now interred in the coral cemetery, was he not a victim of the shock provoked by the *Nautilus*? Yes, I repeat, it must be so. A part of the mysterious existence of Captain Nemo was revealed. And if his identity was not found out, at least nations coalesced against him, chasing now no chimerical being, but a man who had vowed them implacable hatred!

All the formidable past appeared before my eyes. Instead of meeting with friends on the ship that was approaching, we should only find pitiless enemies.

In the meantime cannon-balls were multiplying round us. Some, meeting the liquid surface, ricochetted to considerable distances. But none reached the *Nautilus*.

The ironclad was then not more than three miles off.

Notwithstanding the violent cannonade, Captain Nemo did not make his appearance on the platform. And yet if one of these conical shots had struck the hull of the *Nautilus* in a normal line it would have been fatal to it.

The Canadian then said to me—

"Sir, we ought to attempt anything to get out of this. Let us make signals! *Mille diables!* They will perhaps understand that we are honest men!"

Ned Land took out his handkerchief to wave it in the air. But he had hardly spread it out than, floored by a grasp of iron, notwithstanding his prodigious strength, he fell on the platform.

"Wretch!" cried the captain. "Do you want me to nail you to the ram of the *Nautilus* before it rushes against that ship?"

Captain Nemo, terrible to hear, was still more terrible to behold. His face had grown pale under the spasms of his heart, which must for an instant have ceased to beat. The pupils of his eyes were fearfully contracted. His voice no longer spoke, it roared. With body bent forward, he shook the Canadian by the shoulders.

Then leaving him, and turning to the ironclad, whose shots rained round him, he said—

"Ah! you know who I am, ship of a cursed nation!" cried he in a powerful voice. "I do not need to see your colours to recognise you! Look, I will show you mine!"

And Captain Nemo spread out a black flag in the front of the platform like the one he had planted at the South Pole.

At that moment a projectile struck the hull of the *Nautilus* obliquely, and, ricochetting near the captain, fell into the sea.

Captain Nemo shrugged his shoulders. Then, speaking to me—

"Go down," he said in a curt tone—"go down, you and your companions."

"Sir," I cried, "are you going to attack that ship?"

"Sir, I am going to sink it!"

"You will not do that."

"I shall do it!" replied Captain Nemo. "Do not take upon yourself to judge me, sir. Fate has shown you what you were not to see. The attack has been made. The repulse will be terrible. Go down below."

"What is that ship?"

"You do not know? Well, so much the better! Its nationality, at least, will remain a secret to you. Go below."

The Canadian, Conseil, and I were obliged to obey. About fifteen of the *Nautilus*'s crew had surrounded the captain, and were looking with an implacable feeling of hatred at the ship that was advancing towards them. We felt that the same feeling of vengeance animated them all.

I went down as another projectile struck the *Nautilus*, and I heard its captain exclaim—

"Strike, mad vessel! Shower your useless shot! You will not escape the ram of the *Nautilus*! But this is not the place you are to perish in! Your ruins shall not mix with those of the *Vengeur*!"

I went to my room. The captain and his officer remained on the platform. The screw was put in movement. The *Nautilus* speedily put itself out of range of the ship. But the pursuit went on, and Captain Nemo contented himself with keeping his distance.

About 4 p.m. I could not contain the impatience and anxiety that devoured me, and returned to the central staircase. The panel was opened. I ventured on to the platform. The captain was walking about it still in agitation. He was looking at the vessel, which was lying five or six miles to leeward. Perhaps he hesitated to attack her.

I wished to intervene once again. But I had hardly spoken to Captain Nemo when he imposed silence on me, saying—

"I represent right and justice here! I am the oppressed, and there is the oppressor! It is through it that all I loved, cherished, and venerated—country, wife, children, father and mother—all perished! All that I hate is there! Be silent!"

I looked for the last time at the ironclad, which was putting on more steam. Then I went back to Ned and Conseil.

"We must fly!" I cried.

"Well," said Ned, "what ship is it?"

"I do not know. But whatever it is it will be sunk before night. In any case it is better to perish also than to be the accomplices of a retaliation the justice of which we cannot judge."

"I think so too," answered Ned Land coldly. "We must wait till night."

Night came. Profound silence reigned on board. The compass indicated that the *Nautilus* had not changed its direction. I heard its screw beating the waves with rapid regularity. It kept on the surface of the water, and a slight rolling sent it from side to side.

My companions and I had resolved to fly when the vessel was near enough either to hear or see us, for the moon, that would be full three days later, shone brightly. Once on board the vessel, if we could not prevent the blow that threatened her, we could at least do all that circumstances would allow us to attempt. I thought several times that the *Nautilus* was preparing for the attack. But it contented itself with allowing its adversary to approach, and a short time afterwards fled away again.

A part of the night passed without incident. We were awaiting an occasion to act. We spoke little, being too much excited. Ned Land wanted to throw himself into the sea. I made him wait. I thought the *Nautilus* would attack the two-decker on the surface of the sea, and then it would not only be possible but easy to escape.

At 3 a.m., being uneasy, I went up on to the platform. Captain Nemo had not left it. He was standing near his flag, which a slight breeze was waving over his head. He did not lose sight of the vessel. His look, of extraordinary intensity, seemed to attract her, fascinate her, and draw her onward more surely than if he had been towing her.

The moon was then passing the meridian. Jupiter was rising in the east. Sky and ocean were equally tranquil, and the sea offered to the Queen of Night the clearest mirror that had ever reflected her image.

And when I compared the profound calm of the elements with the anger that was smouldering in the *Nautilus* I felt myself shudder all over.

The ship kept at two miles' distance from us. She kept approaching the phosphorescent light that indicated the presence of the *Nautilus*. I could see her green and red lights and white lantern hung from her mainstay. An indistinct reflection lighted up her rigging and showed that the fires were heated to the uttermost. Sparks and flames were escaping from her funnels and starring the atmosphere.

I remained thus till 6 a.m. without Captain Nemo appearing to perceive me. The vessel was a mile and a-half off, and with the break of day her cannonade began again. The moment could not be distant when, the *Nautilus* attacking its adversary, my companions and I would for ever leave this man whom I dared not judge.

I was about to go down to tell them about it when the offices came up on the platform. Several sailors accompanied him. Captain Nemo either did not or would not see them. Certain precautions were taken, which might be called the clearing up for the fight. They were very simple. The iron balustrade was lowered. The lantern and pilot-cages were sunk into the hull until they were on a level with the deck. The surface of the long steel-plated cigar no longer offered a single salient point that could hinder its manœuvres.

I returned to the saloon. The *Nautilus* was still above the water. Some morning beams were filtering through their liquid bed. Under certain undulations of the waves the windows were lighted up with the red beams of the rising sun. The dreadful 2nd of June had dawned.

At 5 a.m. the log showed me that the speed of the *Nautilus* was slackening. I understood that it was letting the ship approach. Besides, the firing was more distinctly heard, and the projectiles, ploughing up the surrounding water, were extinguished with a strange hissing noise.

"My friends," said I, "the time is come. One grasp of the hand,

and may God help us!"

Ned Land was resolute, Conseil calm, I nervous, scarcely able to contain myself.

We all passed into the library. As I was opening the door that gave on to the cage of the central staircase I heard the upper panel shut with a bang.

The Canadian sprang up the steps, but I stopped him. A well-known hissing sound told me that they were letting water into the reservoirs. In a few minutes' time the *Nautilus* sank a few yards below the surface of the sea.

I now understood its manœuvre. It was too late to do anything. The *Nautilus* did not think of striking the two-decker in her impenetrable armour, but below her water-line, where her metal covering no longer protected her.

We were again imprisoned, unwilling witnesses to the fatal drama that was preparing. We had hardly time to reflect. Taking refuge in my room, we looked at each other without speaking a word. A profound stupor took possession of my mind. My thoughts seemed to stand still. I was in that painful state of expectation that precedes a dreadful crash. I waited and listened. I was all ear.

In the meantime the speed of the *Nautilus* visibly increased. It was taking a spring. All its hull vibrated.

Suddenly I uttered a cry. A shock had taken place, but a relatively slight one. I felt the penetrating force of the steel ram. I heard a grating, scraping sound. But the *Nautilus*, carried along by its force of propulsion, passed through the mass of the ship like a needle through sailcloth.

I could stand it no longer. I rushed like a madman into the saloon.

Captain Nemo was there. Mute, sombre, implacable, he was looking through the port panel.

An enormous mass was sinking through the water, and, in order to lose nothing of its agony, the *Nautilus* was sinking with it. At thirty feet from me I saw the broken hull, into which the water was rushing with a noise like thunder, then the double line of guns and bulwarks. The deck was covered with black moving shades.

The water rose. The unfortunate creatures were crowding in the ratlines, clinging to the masts, struggling in the water. It was a human ant-hill inundated by the sea!

Paralysed, stiffened with anguish, my hair standing on end, eyes wide open, panting, breathless, voiceless, I looked too. An irresistible attraction glued me to the window.

The enormous ship sank slowly. The *Nautilus*, following her, watched all her movements. All at once an explosion took place. The compressed air blew up the decks of the ship as though her magazines had been set fire to. The water was so much disturbed that the *Nautilus* swerved.

Then the unfortunate ship sank more rapidly. Her tops, loaded with victims, appeared; then her spars, bending under the weight of men; then the summit of her mainmast. Then the dark mass disappeared, and with it the dead crew, drawn down by a formidable eddy.

I turned to Captain Nemo. That terrible avenger, a perfect archangel of hatred, was still looking. When all was over he went to the door of his room, opened it, and went in. I followed him with my eyes.

On the end panel, below his heroes, I saw the portrait of a woman still young, and two little children. Captain Nemo looked at them for a few moments, held out his arms to them, and, kneeling down, burst into sobs.

CHAPTER XXII

Captain Nemo's Last Words

The panels were closed on this frightful vision, but light had not been restored to the saloon. In the interior of the *Nautilus* reigned darkness and silence. It was leaving this place of desolation, a hundred feet under the water, at a prodigious speed. Where was it going—north or south? Where was the man flying to after this horrible retaliation?

I went back to my room, where Ned and Conseil had silently stopped. I felt an insurmountable horror of Captain Nemo. Whatever he may have suffered he had no right to punish thus. He had made me, if not his accomplice, at least the witness of his vengeance! That was too much!

At eleven o'clock the electric light reappeared. I went into the saloon and consulted the different instruments. The *Nautilus* was flying north at a speed of twenty-five miles an hour, sometimes on the surface of the sea, sometimes thirty feet below it.

By taking our bearings on the chart I saw that we were passing the entrance to the English Channel, and that we were going to the North seas at a frightful speed.

I could hardly see in their rapid passage the long-nosed dogfish, hammer-fish, and rougettes that frequent these waters; large sea-eagles, hippocamps like chess-knights, eels twisting about like fiery serpents, armies of crabs flying obliquely, folding their claws across their shells; lastly, shoals of herrings rivalling the *Nautilus* in speed. But there was no question of observing, studying, and classifying then.

In the evening we had traversed two hundred leagues of the Atlantic. Night came, and the sea was dark till the moon rose.

I went to my room, but could not sleep. I was assailed by nightmare. The horrible scene of destruction was repeated in my mind.

From that day who could tell where the *Nautilus* took us in this North Atlantic basin? Always with inappreciable speed. Always amidst the hyperborean mists. Did it touch at Spitzbergen or the shores of Nova Zembla? Did we explore the unknown White Sea, Kara Sea, Gulf of Obi, Archipelago of Liarrov, and the unknown coast of Asia? I cannot tell. I do not even know how the time went. The clocks on board had stopped. It seemed as if night and day, as in polar countries, no longer followed their regular course. I felt myself carried into that region of the strange where the overridden imagination of Edgar Poe roamed at will. At each instant I expected to see, like the fabulous Gordon Pym, "that veiled human face, of much larger proportions than that of any inhabitant of the earth, thrown across the cataract that defends the approach to the Pole!"

I estimate—but perhaps I am mistaken—that this adventurous course of the *Nautilus* lasted fifteen or twenty days, and I do not know how long it would have lasted but for the catastrophe that ended this voyage. Captain Nemo never appeared, nor his officer. Not a man of the crew was visible for an instant. The *Nautilus* kept below the water almost incessantly. When it went up to the surface to renew the air, the panels opened and shut mechanically. The bearings were no longer reported on the chart. I did not know where we were.

I must say also that the Canadian, out of all patience, did not appear either. Conseil could not get a word out of him, and feared that in an access of delirium, and under the influence of dreadful nostalgia, he might kill himself. He watched over him, therefore, with constant devotion.

It will be understood that under such circumstances the situation was no longer bearable.

One morning—I do not know its date—I had fallen into an uneasy slumber at early dawn. When I woke I saw Ned Land bending over me, and heard him whisper—

"We are going to fly!"

I sat up.

"When?" I asked.

"Tonight. All supervision seems to have disappeared from the *Nautilus*. Stupor seems to reign on board. Shall you be ready, sir?"

"Yes. Where are we?"

"In sight of land that I have just sighted through the mist, twenty miles to the east."

"What land is it?"

"I do not know, but whatever it is we will seek refuge on it."

"Yes! Ned—yes, we will go tonight, even should the sea swallow us up!"

"The sea is rough, the wind violent, but twenty miles in that light boat of the *Nautilus* do not frighten me. I have put some provisions and a few bottles of water in it without the knowledge of the crew."

"I will follow you."

"Besides," added the Canadian, "if I am caught, I shall defend myself and get killed."

"We will die together, friend Ned."

I had made up my mind to anything. The Canadian left me. I went up on the platform, where I could scarcely stand against the waves. The sky was threatening, but as land lay there in those thick mists, we must fly. We must not lose a day nor an hour.

I went down to the saloon both fearing and wishing to meet Captain Nemo, both wanting and not wanting to see him. What could I say to him? Could I hide from him the involuntary horror he inspired me with? No! It was better not to find myself face to face with him! Better to forget him! And yet——

What a long day was the last I had to pass on board the *Nautilus*! I remained alone. Ned Land and Conseil avoided me, so as not to betray ourselves by talking.

At 6 p.m. I dined, but without appetite. I forced myself to eat notwithstanding my repugnance, wishing to keep up my strength.

At half-past six Ned Land entered my room. He said to me—

"We shall not see each other again before our departure. At ten o'clock the moon will not yet be up. We shall take advantage of the darkness. Come to the boat. Conseil and I will be waiting for you there."

Then the Canadian went out without giving me time to answer.

I wished to verify the direction of the *Nautilus*. I went to the saloon. We were going N.N.E. with frightful speed, at a depth of twenty-five fathoms.

I looked for the last time at all the natural marvels and riches of art collected in this museum, in this unrivalled collection destined one day to perish in the depths of the sea with the man who had made it. I wished to take a supreme impression of it in my mind. I remained thus for an hour, bathed in the light of the luminous ceiling, and passing in review the shining treasures in their glass cases. Then I went back to my room.

There I put on my solid sea-garments. I collected my notes together and placed them carefully about me. My heart beat loudly. I could not check its pulsations. Certainly my agitation would have betrayed me to Captain Nemo.

What was he doing at that moment? I listened at the door of his room. I heard a noise of footsteps: Captain Nemo was there. He had not gone to bed. At every movement that he made I thought he was going to appear and ask me why I wanted to escape! I was constantly on the alert. My imagination magnified everything. This impression became so poignant that I asked myself if I had not better enter the captain's room, see him face to face, dare him with look and gesture!

It was a madman's inspiration. Happily I restrained myself, and lay down on my bed to stay the agitation of my body. My nerves gradually grew calmer, but in my excited brain I passed in review my whole existence on board this *Nautilus*, all the happy or unfortunate incidents that had occurred since my disappearance from the *Abraham Lincoln*, the submarine hunts, Torres Straits, the Papuan savages, the stranding, the coral cemetery, the Suez tunnel, Santorin Island, the Cretan plunger, Vigo Bay, Atlantis, the ice-bank, the South Pole, the imprisonment in ice, the fight with the poulps, the tempest of the Gulf Stream, the *Vengeur*, and that horrible scene of the sunken ship and her crew! All these events passed through my mind like the background to a scene at the theatre. Then Captain Nemo grew out of all proportion in this strange medium. He was no longer a man like me, but the genius of the sea. It was then half-past nine. I held my head in my hands to prevent it bursting. I closed my eyes, and was determined to think no more. Another half-hour to wait! Another half-hour's nightmare would drive me mad!

At that moment I heard the vague chords of the organ, a sad harmony under an indefinable melody, veritable wails of a soul that wished to break all terrestrial ties. I listened with all my senses, hardly breathing, plunged, like Captain Nemo, in one of those musical ecstasies which took him beyond the limits of this world.

Then a sudden thought terrified me. Captain Nemo had left his room. He was in the saloon that I was obliged to cross in my flight. There I should meet him for the last time. He would see me, perhaps speak to me. A gesture from him could annihilate me, a single word could chain me to his vessel.

Ten o'clock was on the point of striking. The moment had come to leave my room and rejoin my companions.

I could not hesitate should Captain Nemo stand before me. I opened my door with precaution, and yet it seemed to make a fearful noise. Perhaps that noise only existed in my imagination.

I felt my way along the dark waist of the *Nautilus*, stopping at every step to suppress the beatings of my heart.

I reached the corner door of the saloon and opened it softly. The saloon was quite dark. The tones of the organ were feebly sounding. Captain Nemo was there. He did not see me. I think that in a full light he would not have perceived me, he was so absorbed.

I dragged myself over the carpet, avoiding the least contact, lest the noise should betray my presence. It took me five minutes to reach the door into the library.

I was going to open it when a sigh from Captain Nemo nailed me to the place. I understood that he had got up. I even saw him, for some rays from the lighted library reached the saloon. He came towards me with folded arms, silent, gliding rather than walking, like a ghost. His oppressed chest heaved with sobs, and I heard him murmur these words—the last I heard:—

"Almighty God! Enough! Enough!"

Was it remorse that was escaping thus from the conscience of that man?

Desperate, I rushed into the library, went up the central staircase, and, following the upper waist, reached the boat through the opening that had already given passage to my two companions.

"Let us go! Let us go!" I cried.

"At once," answered the Canadian.

The orifice in the plates of the *Nautilus* was first shut and bolted by means of a wrench that Ned Land had provided himself with. The opening in the boat was also closed, and the Canadian began to take out the screws that still fastened us to the submarine vessel.

Suddenly a noise was heard in the interior. Voices answered one another quickly. What was the matter? Had they discovered our flight? I felt Ned Land glide a dagger into my hand.

"Yes!" I murmured, "we shall know how to die!"

The Canadian had stopped in his work. But one word, twenty times repeated, a terrible word, revealed to me the cause of the agitation on board the *Nautilus*. It was not we the crew were anxious about.

"The Maëlstrom! the Maëlstrom!" they were crying.

The Maëlstrom! Could a more frightful word in a more frightful situation have sounded in our ears? Were we then on the most dangerous part of the Norwegian shore? Was the

Nautilus being dragged into a gulf at the very moment our boat was preparing to leave its side?

It is well known that at the tide the pent-up waters between the Feroë and Loffoden Islands rush out with irresistible violence. They form a whirlpool from which no ship could ever escape. From every point of the horizon rush monstrous waves. They form the gulf justly called "Navel of the Ocean," of which the power of attraction extends for a distance of ten miles. There not only vessels but whales and bears from the boreal region are sucked up.

It was there that the *Nautilus* had been voluntarily or involuntarily run by its captain. It was describing a spiral, the circumference of which was lessening by degrees. Like it, the boat fastened to it was whirled round with giddy speed. I felt it. I felt the sick sensation that succeeds a long-continued movement of gyration. We were horror-stricken with suspended circulation, annihilated nervous influence, covered with cold sweat like that of death! What noise surrounded our fragile boat! What roaring, which echo repeated at a distance of several miles! What an uproar was that of the water breaking on the sharp rocks at the bottom, where the hardest bodies are broken, where the trunks of trees are worn away, and are "made into fur," according to a Norwegian saying!

What a situation! We were frightfully tossed about. The *Nautilus* defended itself like a human being. Its steel muscles cracked. Sometimes it stood upright, and we with it!

"We must hold on and screw down the bolts again," said Ned Land. "We may still be saved by keeping to the *Nautilus*——"

He had not finished speaking when a crash took place. The screws were torn out, and the boat, torn from its groove, sprang like a stone from a sling into the midst of the whirlpool.

My head struck on its iron framework, and with the violent shock I lost all consciousness.

CHAPTER XXIII

Conclusion

So ended this voyage under the sea. What happened during that night, how the boat escaped the formidable eddies of the Maëlstrom, how Ned Land, Conseil, and I got out of the gulf, I have no idea. But when I came to myself I was lying in the hut of a fisherman of the Loffoden Isles. My two companions, safe and sound, were by my side pressing my hands. We shook hands heartily.

At this moment we cannot think of going back to France. Means of communication between the north of Norway and the south are rare. I am, therefore, obliged to wait for the steamer that runs twice a month to Cape North.

It is here, therefore, amidst the honest folk who have taken us in, that I revise the account of these adventures. It is exact. Not a fact has been omitted, not a detail exaggerated. It is a faithful narrative of an incredible expedition in an element inaccessible to man, and to which progress will one day open up a road.

Shall I be believed? I do not know. After all, it matters little. All I can now affirm is my right to speak of the seas under which, in less than ten months, I journeyed twenty thousand leagues during that submarine tour of the world that has revealed so many marvels of the Pacific, the Indian Ocean, Red Sea Mediterranean, Atlantic, and the austral and boreal seas!

But what has become of the *Nautilus*? Has it resisted the pressure of the Maëlstrom? Is Captain Nemo still alive? Is he still pursuing his frightful retaliations under the ocean, or did he stop at that last hecatomb? Will the waves one day bring the manuscript that contains the whole history of his life? Shall I know at last the name of the man? Will the ship that has disappeared tell us by its nationality the nationality of Captain Nemo?

I hope so. I also hope that his powerful machine has conquered the sea in its most terrible gulf, and that the

Nautilus has survived where so many other ships have perished! If it is so, if Captain Nemo still inhabits the ocean, his adopted country, may hatred be appeased in his savage heart! May the contemplation of so many marvels extinguish in him the desire of vengeance! May the judge disappear, and the *savant* continue his peaceful exploration of the sea! If his destiny is strange, it is sublime also. Have I not experienced it myself? Have I not lived ten months of this unnatural life? Two men only have a right to answer the question asked in the Ecclesiastes 6,000 years ago, "That which is far off and exceeding deep, who can find it out?" These two men are Captain Nemo and I.

20,000 Leagues under the Sea first appeared in serialised form in 1869. Since that date, the *Nautilus* and its captain have entered folklore. It was the seventh of the *Voyages extraordinaires* which Jules Verne had contracted to produce for the publisher Hetzel, first by individual volume and then at the rate of three books a year. The first of these, *Five Weeks in a Balloon* (1863), founded the genre of science fiction. In 1864 came *Voyage to the Centre of the Earth* and in 1865 Verne's moonshot, *From the Earth to the Moon*. These books were immensely successful. The first edition of *Five Weeks in a Balloon* was 76,000; *20,000 Leagues* was a more modest 50,000, and *Round the World in Eighty Days* (1873) attained 108,000. Verne was read throughout the world. In Russia and Spain works by other authors were passed off as his to guarantee sales.

His world combines the empiricism of the Industrial Revolution and the fantastical imagery of late Romanticism. Though Captain Nemo aspires to the status of a Nietzschean hero, psychology tends to be lacking; Vernian heroes do not develop. A scholar is invariably present in the *Voyages,* since didacticism, sometimes leavened with humour, is the order of the day. Verne was not a scientist, though he took trouble to establish his facts. His error concerning Captain Nemo's diving-suits is not untypical (note to page 110). But it is his gift for anticipating future developments that is the most extraordinary aspect of the *Voyages*. In *20,000 Leagues*, Captain Nemo sails under the Antarctic ice-cap in a submarine powered by a mysterious form of electricity. Under the ice-cap lies a continent, so this feat is permanently impossible. Performance of an equivalent feat had to wait until 1958, when the U.S.S *Nautilus*, the first nuclear-powered submarine, sailed under the ice-cap of the North Pole. Verne was 89 years ahead of his time. In Simon Vierne's estimate, Nemo's *Nautilus* sailed some 41,500 miles in less than ten months, with many a pause on the way. In 1960, the U.S.S. *Triton* sailed around the world without surfacing, and did so in 84 days at an average speed of 18 knots. Nemo's *Nautilus* is capable of fifty miles an hour and descends to some 14,600 metres, in this operating at or beyond the limits of today's technology. His attacks on shipping are a sombre prediction of the submarine warfare of the First and Second World Wars.

The figure of Captain Nemo, ambiguously compassionate, a man of heroic capacities, was variously conceived by Verne. We have no doubt of Nemo's liberationist politics, and his dream of absolute freedom governed only by its own moral law is as old as philosophy. Verne first imagined him as a Pole whose wife and children had been raped and massacred by Russian troops, but relations between France and Russia were fraught and Hetzel was afraid that his profitable translation contracts would be imperilled. Nemo the enemy of the slave trade was also ruled out by Hetzel, though some marks of this incarnation have been retained, notably in references to John Brown.

The mythological status that Nemo attains as a "presiding spirit of the sea" in *20,000 Leagues* is not really compatible with a solution to the mystery of his existence. His *Nautilus* is a kind of Utopia in a capsule. Its library of 12,000 volumes has (unsurprisingly) not yet been equalled in a submarine; its art collections would require the resources of the Getty Museum and some useful sales by national galleries if it were to be assembled today. Its "aquarium" windows were imitated by the aesthete des Esseintes in Huysman's *A Rebours* as the *nec plus ultra* of luxury. Jules Verne was an enthusiastic sailor who often wrote aboard his yacht. He was also a man of somewhat anarchist views. He would have been delighted to enjoy the freedom offered by Nemo's vessel in Verne's own favoured element, the sea.

Nemo returns to life in Verne's *The Mysterious Island* (1874–1875). There he is revealed as Prince Dakkar, the "spirit of Lincoln island" as he had been the "spirit of the sea". His father was an Indian Rajah who ruled the independent state of Bundelkund; Nemo was sent to Europe at ten to be educated for the sole purpose of liberating his occupied country from the oppression of the East India Company. Returning to Bundelkund in 1849, he set out to subvert the company's rule, and when the Indian Mutiny broke out in 1857 he led the sepoys in battle. His parents, wife and children paid for his insurgency before he was aware of the danger that they ran. And the Mutiny failed; for the East India Company was substituted the full might of the British state. This is indeed a tragic destiny, comparable to that of such heroes of Indian resistance as Subhas Chandra Bose. Disgusted with politics, Nemo decided on a life of scholarship and had the *Nautilus* built on a desert island. But over the years, his crew died, leaving Nemo sole survivor. One of his ports was on Lincoln Island, and there he awaited death until a balloon carrying escapees from a Union prison landed there. Their talk of the American Civil War and of the liberation of slaves won his heart. Now read on. For the British reader, the comparison between Russian occupation of Poland and British occupation of India is not a flattering one. Verne's admiration for the technological confidence and enterprise of the Anglo-Saxon world was eventually matched by his hatred of imperialism.

Recent study of Verne has focused on the possibility that the powerful imagery of his novels disguises initiatory rites; an example in *20,00 Leagues* is the confinement of Aronnax and company in a kind of "limbo" before they are allowed contact with the world of Nemo. Verne's gift for tableaux of resonant simplicity and sublimity lends itself to symbolic interpretation, and initiatory rites, themselves the product of an occult tradition, can easily be made to match Verne's imagery. Though Verne's co-editor on Hetzel's *Magasin illustré* was Jean Macé, a prominent Freemason whom Verne described in a letter to Hetzel as "my master...I owe him more even than I owe you", the case for Verne's fictions having a masonic architecture is not proven. His images have, perhaps, no architectonic. They were written for children, but please any age. This contemporary translation used in the present edition has much of the flavour of the original – not least its transparent haste of composition. Published in 1917 by James Nisbet & Co., then of Berners Street, London, it did not name the translator; the present publishers would be grateful for any information that could help with his or her identification. In the notes that follow, which are necessarily selective, words found in any good dictionary are not glossed.   *Ed.*

p. 9   *Cuvier, Lacépède, M. Dumeril, M. de Quatrefages*: Etienne Lacépède, Comte de la Ville-sur-Illon (1756–1825), was Keeper of the Cabinet du Roi, which eventually became the Paris Museum of Natural History. Lacépède wrote the sections of Buffon's *Natural History* on fish and *cetaceae*. Baron Georges Cuvier (1769–1823) was Professor at the Paris Museum of Natural History and a pioneer of palaeontology and comparative anatomy. André-Marie-Constant Dumeril (1774–1860) succeeded Lacépède in the Chair of Herpetology and Ichthyology at the Museum. Jean-Louis de Quatrefages de Bréau (1810–1892), was also a Professor at the Museum, and a specialist in *Annelida*. Verne is establishing the scholarly lineage of his hero Aronnax, who is Assistant Professor of the Paris Museum of Natural History.

p. 11   *Moby Dick*: the novel of this name by Herman Melville (1819–181) was published in 1851 but not translated into French until 1941. Verne's source here was an article on the white whale in the magazine *Musée des Familles* (vol. 4, pp. 97–104, January 1837), a journal to which he occasionally contributed.

p. 11   *Aristotle, Pliny, Bishop Pontoppidan, Paul Hegedde, Mr. Harrington*: Aristotle (384–322 B.C.), one of the greatest philosophers of all times and tutor to Alexander the Great, was a systematizer of the knowledge of his time, for example in the *Historia animalium.* Pliny the Elder (A.D. 23/24–79) wrote the *Naturalis historia*, which, in

430

his own words, collected 20,000 useful facts from 100 principal authors; he describes a giant polyp at IX.30 and serpents at VIII.14. His account of a cephalopod climbing a tree may be unique. Bishop Pontopiddan [sic] (1698–1764) wrote a *Natural History of Norway* (translated 1755). Verne may have used this as a source, since Pontopiddan cites Olaus Magnus, Pliny and Egede. Hans Egede (1686–1758), a Norwegian missionary to Greenland, saw a "most dreadful Monster, that shewed itself upon the Surface of the Water in the Year 1734 [Pontopiddan gives the date as 6 July], off our new Colony in 64 degrees. The Monster was of so huge a Size, that, coming out of the Water, its Head reached as high as the Masthead; its Body was as bulky as the Ship, and three or four Times as long. It had a long pointed Snout, and spouted like a Whale-Fish; great, broad Paws, and the Body seemed covered with Shell-Work, its Skin very rugged and uneven. The Under Part of its Body was shaped like an enormous huge Serpent, and when it dived again under Water, it plunged backwards into the Sea, and so raised its Tail aloft, which seemed a Whole Ship's Length distant from the bulkiest Part of its Body" (Egede: *Description of Greenland*, 1741, English translation 1745). It should be noted that Egede, as the rest of the *Description* makes clear, is a competent naturalist. His son, Poul Egede (1708–1789), succeeded his father as superintendent of the mission, and published a journal in 1788. Pontopiddan's reference is to "Mr. Rev. Egede's *Journal of the Greenland Mission* and his *New Survey of Old Greenland*"; the latter is presumably the *Description* above. It seems likely that Verne mistook Hans for Poul [sic] Egede when reading Pontopiddan's account, but Poul's publications may also include monsters. Captain Harrington's sea-serpent is less remote from reality, in that it appeared in *The Times* of London on 4 February 1858. The letter gives an extract of the meteorological log of the *Castilian* for 12 December 1857, 6.30 p.m. The ship was then off the N.E. end of Saint Helena. The ship's crew and officers saw a sea-serpent 7-8 foot in diameter and 200–500 foot long some 20 yards from the ship. The letter of 16 February (cited by Peter Costello in his well-informed edition of *20,000 Leagues*) is a reaffirmation of this sighting. Another sea-serpent had been seen in August 1848 by the officers of the HMS *Daedalus* under Captain M'Quhae, and this sighting had been disputed by a ship on a similar course which had winched in a vast "serpent" of seaweed; the same number of *The Times* carries a reaffirmation of the latter sighting.

p. 11   *Le Constitutionnel*: a liberal, anti-clerical paper founded in 1851, was said to have invented the sea-serpent as part of a campaign of journalistic hoaxes.

p. 11   *Linnaeus*: Carl von Linné (1707–1778), the founder of modern taxonomic botany. The remark parodied is "Nature did not make monsters".

p. 12   *Hippolytus*: in Greek legend, Theseus cursed his son Hippolytus when under the illusion that Hippolytus had made advances to Hippolytus's step-mother Phaedra; in fact, the reverse was the case. A sea-monster was sent by Poseidon in answer to Theseus's curse. In the version of the myth given by the French dramatist Jean Racine (1639–1699), to which Verne's words implicitly refer, Hippolytus kills the monster (Act V, sc. 6); its dying throes frighten the horses of Hippolytus's chariot, and he is dragged to his death.

p. 17   *chassepot ... torpedoes ... submarine rams*: Antoine-Alphonse Chassepot (1774–1905) invented a breech-loading rifle known as the 1866 model or *fusil Chassepot*; it was issued to the French army in that year. The torpedo was invented by Alfred Whitehead in 1862. Underwater rams had been in use since classical times on surface ships. Peter Costello, in his edition of *20,000 Leagues*

(London, 1993), believes that Horace Huntley's 'David' submarines used rams against Union warships. In fact, they used "spar-torpedoes", effectively a mine on a long pole attached to the fore of the boat. The CSS *H.L. Huntley* destroyed the *Housatonic*, a sloop, with this device on 17 February 1864, but predictably perished in the attempt. On 18 April 1864 a 'David' successfully attacked the Union vessel *Minnesota*.

p. 17 *monitor*: the invention of John Ericsson (1803–1889), a Swedish-born U.S. naval engineer, monitors are not submarines, but screw-propelled warships with an armoured superstructure at near-water-level and an armoured revolving gun-turret. One of these, the *Monitor*, fought a battle (9 March, 1862) with the armoured frigate *Merrimack*, renamed *Virginia* at Hampton Roads on the James River during the American Civil War (1861–1865). The battle was inconclusive but influenced all subsequent warship design.

p. 18 *narwhal*: in fact, the narwhal (*Monocedon monoceros*) is confined to Arctic waters and does not use its horn in combat or hunting.

p. 20 *Captain Farragut*: Verne borrowed this name from Admiral David Farragut (1801–1870), who won a series of naval victories for the Confederates during the American Civil War.

p. 22 *Jardin des Plantes*: the site of the Paris Museum of Natural History.

p. 22 *Conseil*: Verne's servant takes his name from Jacques-François Conseil, who had been working on a steam-driven submarine at Le Tréport, near Verne's seaside residence at Le Crotoy. Conseil the servant forms the second part of the Verne team, which, as in *Five Weeks in a Balloon* and *Round the World in 80 Days*, comprises master-and-intellectual, sceptical companion, and able-bodied servant.

433

p. 24   *babiroussa*: the babirussa (sic) is a horned hog.

p. 26   *thirty-nine stars*: the thirteen stripes of the 'Stars and Stripes' symbolize the original states; each new star indicated a further accession. At this date, there were in fact only thirty-seven.

p. 27   *Dieudonné de Gozon*: elected Grand Master of the Hospitallers of Rhodes in 1346, he is said to have slain a dragon on Rhodes in 1342, after returning to France to train his dogs and horses to attack a fake dragon in preparation for this event. Hospitallers had been forbidden to attack the monster after many had been killed, and de Gozon's reward was to be temporarily expelled from the Order.

p. 28   *Rabelais*: it was thought that old French (Rabelais's *Gargantua* was published in 1532/3) was preserved unchanged in the speech of some Canadian provinces.

p. 31   *iron plate eight inches thick*: the character of Ned Land is occasionally used to voice Verne's dramatic irony. See p. 50.

p. 35   *aneurism*: sac formed by abnormal dilation of blood vessel.

p. 35   *erethismus*: more commonly "erethism". An abnormal degree of irritability or sensitivity in any part of the body.

p. 40   *gymnotus*: now known as electrophorus, the "electric eel", in fact an eel-like fish.

p. 47   *Byron or Edgar Poe*: the poet Lord Byron (1788–1924) famously swam the Hellespont in 1810 while on a tour of the Mediterranean. Edgar Allan Poe (1809–1849), American short-story writer and poet, claimed to have swum six miles against a strong tide. The claim is made in the *Southern Literary Messenger* (May 1835, p. 9) and in his letter of April 30, 1835 to Thomas H. White (*The Letters of E.A. Poe*, ed. John Ward Ostrom, vol. I, p. 57).

p. 52   *far-off chords*: these add a touch of Gothic to Verne's science-fiction. For the explanation, see pp. 164–5.

p. 56 *the language of Arago nor Faraday*: François Arago (1786–1853), French physicist, greatly advanced the study of electromagnetism, as did Michael Faraday (1791–1867), English physicist. In short, neither English nor French.

p. 57 *kitchen*: the Latin of the Roman orator Cicero (106–43 B.C.) is considered a model of style; the same cannot be said of the translator, who has failed to convey Verne's reference to "dog Latin" (*Latin de cuisine* or "kitchen Latin").

p. 58 *Tortoise liver*: again, Ned Land is a (fairly) accurate prophet. See p. 72.

p. 63 *secret*: there is no evidence in the conduct of the *Nautilus* toward the *Abraham Lincoln* of a concern for secrecy.

p. 63 *half a Frenchman*: Verne refers to the French saying "Impossible is not French".

p. 71 *Captain Nemo*: The name the Captain gives is the Latin word for "no one", and associates him with another famous mariner, Odysseus, who gives his name to the Cyclops Polyphemus as *outis*, the Greek for "no one". (The name of Nemo's submarine is the Greek for 'sailor' and "ship".) Verne mythologises Captain Nemo by such associations and by emphasising his moral ambiguity.

p. 73 *The sea does not belong to despots*: this is our first clue to the political nature of Nemo's alienation.

p. 76 *Homer … Madame Sand*: Madame Sand has a special title to a place in the *Nautilus's* library. In July 1865, she wrote to thank Jules Verne for sending her two novels, probably *Voyage to the Centre of the Earth* and *From the Earth to the Moon:* "I hope that you will soon take us down into the depths of the sea and have your characters travel in diving suits, which you will allow your knowledge of science and your imagination to perfect". The finest things in literature and history are mostly, it seems, Greek or French.

p. 76 *Humboldt ... Agassis*: the authors who appear again are individually annotated. Jean-Bernard Foucault (1819–1868), French physicist, invented a technique for measuring the absolute velocity of light, and gave his name to the Foucault pendulum. Henri-Etienne Sainte-Claire Deville (1818–1881), French chemist, discovered the first economical process for the extraction of aluminium. Michel Chasles (1793–1880), French mathematician, was a Professor at the Sorbonne. John Tyndall (1820–1893), British physicist, demonstrated why the sky is blue. Marcellin Berthelot (1827–1907) was an organic and physical chemist and historian of science. Pietro Angelo Secchi (1818–1878), an Italian Jesuit priest, was an astrophysicist, who pioneered spectral classification of the stars. August Petermann (d. 1878) was a German geographer and cartographer. Louis Agassiz (1807–1873), Swiss-born and naturalized American, was a naturalist and geologist, who studied fossil fish, molluscs, and glaciation. He was opposed to the theory of evolution. The work by Joseph Bertrand (1822–1900), mathematician and educator, is a real one.

p. 78 *Raphael ... Holbein*: this collection would be the envy of many national museums, more especially in its original form (the translator took it upon himself to abridge this passage), which brings it up to the time of Verne himself, with works by Delacroix, Decamps and Daubigny.

p. 78 *Weber ... Gounod*: Verne had already reviewed the literature and music of his time in *Paris in the 20th Century (Paris au XXe siècle)*, a work set in 1961, rejected by Verne's publisher Hetzel in 1863 and first published in 1994. Meyerbeer, Hérold, Gounod and Auber are nineteenth-century composers whose music is now no longer as highly esteemed as it was in its own time.

p. 82   *barometer ... storm-glass*: these instruments would, of course, be unable to function in the controlled environment of the *Nautilus*.

p. 82   *electricity*: the first submarine to use electricity for underwater propulsion was the *Narval* (1898) designed by the French engineer Labœuf.

p. 87   *Bunsen...Ruhmkorff*: Robert Wilhelm Bunsen (1811–1899), a pioneer of spectrum analysis, invented the carbon-zinc electric cell. Heinrich Daniel Rühmkorff (1803–1877) invented the induction coil that bears his name.

p. 93   *The Dutchman Jansen*: presumably Jan Janszoon (Jansonius, c. 1588–1664), the Dutch cartographer.

p. 95   *myriametre*: 10,000 metres.

p. 97   *Galileo ... Maury*: Galileo Galilei (1564–1642), mathematician, astronomer, physician and founder of the experimental method, was arrested by the Inquisition for his exposition of heliocentrism in *Dialogue concerning the Two Chief World Systems* (1633), and forced to retract his views. Matthew Maury (1807–1873), a pioneer of hydrography and founder of oceanography, had his career interrupted by the American Civil War, in which he took the part of the Confederates.

p. 100 *What a spectacle!*: it must be remembered that, when Verne wrote, no one had ever seen this spectacle. Our own familiarity with films of underwater scenes can lead us to underestimate Verne's imaginative achievement.

p. 100 *Ehremberg*: Christian Ehrenberg [sic] (1795–1876), biologist, microscopist and scientific explorer, was a pioneer of micropaleontology and identified planktonic phosphorescence.

p. 102 *six orders*: the classification of fish, which is taken from Cuvier, has changed, and Ned Land's distinctions may be the more reliable. Verne's didactism is ingeniously leavened with humour.

p. 107 *I began the account of these adventures*: Verne contrives in this way to reinforce the appearance of authenticity given to Aronnax's account.

p. 110 *The Rouquayrol-Denayrouze apparatus*: invented in 1865, it was the predecessor of Cousteau's aqualung (1943); it allowed the diver to refill his pressurized tank at a air-pipe projecting down from the surface. Nemo's modification, far from perfecting the apparatus, would be fatal; the pressure of water would drive the blood into the only part of the body protected from that pressure, the head.

p. 115 *Words are powerless...*: again, Verne's description is of events very rarely experienced at that date: *20,000 Leagues* appeared only five years after the invention of the Rouquayrol-Denayrouze apparatus.

p. 123 *extinct*: this is the first of several observations which might be described as ecological in spirit. Such observations never prevent the death of the animal in question.

p. 125 *chalut*: trawl- or drag-net.

p. 128 *infusoria*: an obsolete term for microscopic organisms such as protozoa found in infusions of organic material.

p. 130 *Athenæus...Galen*: Athanaeus of Attaleia practised medicine under the Roman Emperor Claudius A.D. 441–54. He founded a school of Pneumatists, for whom pneuma (breath) was a fifth element. He was admired by Galen of Pergamum (A.D.129–?199), a gladiator-physician who rose to become court physician to the Emperor Marcus Aurelius. An anatomist and physiologist who compiled the medical information of the schools of his time, Galen is regarded as one of the fathers of modern medicine.

p. 131 *Orbigny*: Alcide Dessalines d'Orbigny (1802–1857) came to the notice of the Museum of Natural History with a study of *Foraminifera*; he then went on an important study trip in South America for the Museum, which he wrote up in many volumes.

p. 131 *Jean Macé*: Jean Macé (1815–1868) was a friend and colleague of Jules Verne and a prominent Freemason; the latter point is important for those who, like Simone Vierne, a leading French Verne scholar, believe Verne's imagery is based on initiatory rites such as those practised by the Freemasons. Verne worked with him on the *Magasin d'éducation et récréation*, which was published by Verne's own publisher, Hetzel. Macé's principal title to fame is as founder of the Ligue française de l'enseignement, but he also wrote books for children about science. The mention is a wink to Macé and Hetzel of a kind that Verne had unsuccessfully attempted in his *Paris au XXe siècle*, where they had been rejected by Hetzel as "puerile".

p. 133 *Mr. Milne-Edwards*: Henry Milne-Edwards (1800–1805) was born in Belgium of English stock and replaced Cuvier in the Académie des Sciences. He continued Buffon's project in writing the *Natural History of Crustaceans* in three volumes and a *Natural History of Polyps*. His identification as Aronnax's master is of interest in that the age of the world is among the scientific topics raised by Verne, and Milne-Edwards was a creationist. Milne-Edwards was one of the first naturalists to advance his science by diving.

p. 134 *Darwin*: Charles Darwin (1809–1882), author of *On the Origin of the Species* (1859), reflects on these phenomena in the twenty-second chapter of *The Voyage of the Beagle* (1831–1836) and in *The Structure and Distribution of Coral Reefs* (1842).

p. 135 *La Pérouse*: Jean-François de Galaud, Comte de La Pérouse (1741–1788), French explorer. The story of his death is recounted in the pages that follow.

p. 136 *Tasman, Torricelli*: Abel Janszoon Tasman (1603–probably before 1659), Dutch navigator and explorer, "discovered" Tasmania, New Zealand and the Tonga and Fiji islands. Evangelista Torricelli (1608–1647),

Italian physicist and mathematician, invented the barometer; he was assistant to Galileo in the last three months of the latter's life.

p. 136 *Cook, D'Entrecasteaux, Dumont d'Urville*: James Cook (1728–1779), navigator, captained the *Endeavour* on the Royal Society expedition to Tahiti. He circumnavigated Antarctica on his second voyage. On his third voyage, he unsuccessfully sought a passage around the north coast of America (the North West Passage) from the Pacific, and was killed by natives of Hawaii after turning back. Joseph-Antoine Bruni d'Entrecasteaux (1737–1793) took part in the American War of Independence before sailing in 1786 from India to China against the prevailing monsoon. In 1791, he set out with two ships, *Recherche* and *Esperance*, to search for La Pérouse, as Verne describes; he died of a fever at sea on this voyage. Jules Dumont d'Urville (1790–1842) commanded expeditions to the South Pacific (1826–9) and Antarctic (1837–40), where he discovered Joinville Island and Adélie Land. He was killed in a railway disaster while returning from an excursion to Versailles. His description of the Venus of Milo was largely responsible for its joining the collections of the Musée du Louvre.

p. 136 *Seneca*: Lucius Anneus Seneca (the Younger), born between 4 B.C. and A.D. 1, forced to commit suicide in 65 A.D.. Stoic philosopher and author of influential verse tragedies, he used his *Epistulae Morales* as a vehicle for Stoic teachings. The reference here is *Epistulae Morales* 78.23, where an ill person is not, in Seneca's view, to be pitied for lacking such luxuries as Lucrine oysters opened at the table.

p. 136 *Bougainville*: Louis-Antoine de Bougainville (1729–1814), naval officer, sent in 1776 to establish a colony in the Falkland Islands; he circumnavigated the globe and wrote a *Round-the-World Voyage* in 1771.

p. 139 *Bazin m'a fait*: (French) "Bazin made me": a standard formula for hand-produced work.

p. 145 *M. de Rienzi*: Louis Grégoire Domeny de Rienzi (c. 1759–?) made voyages to the Orient, to China and the South Sea Islands. He wrote two works on the latter, from one of which this quote presumably comes.

p. 146 *Luis Vaez de Torres*: Vaez de Torres left Callao in 1605 and reached the New Hebrides in 1606, after which he navigated the Torres Strait, which bears his name, "discovering" New Guinea, but unaware that the "undiscovered" continent of Australia was relatively close by. The narrative of his voyage was kept in Manila as an official secret and only came to light in 1762, after Manila was captured by the English.

p. 155 *If you don't return to the charge*: the anonymous translator is excessively literal. The expression "revenir à la charge" literally means "return to the attack" and here suggests "ask for more".

p. 164 *Besides, those you call savages, are they worse than the others?*: the anti-colonial implications of Nemo's remark are more characteristic of Verne's later work. In *Five Weeks in a Balloon*, published in 1863 in book form, cannibals are found eating their freshly-killed antagonists raw, and one of them is gratuitously shot for this as a lesson in civilization.

p. 174 *Ægri somnia*: (Latin) "morbid dreams". It refers to the hallucinations experienced by Aronnax at the end of the chapter.

p. 174 *holy ark*: Verne steadily works toward the mythologization of Nemo and his vessel.

p. 184 *Gratiolet, Moquin-Tandon*: in the French text, Gratiolet is first mentioned on Nemo's appearance. Louis-Pierre Gratiolet (1815–1865) was the author of *Comparative Anatomy of the Nervous System Considered in its Relations to Intelligence*, and began his career as a *préparateur* at the Paris Museum. Horace-Bénédict-

Alfred Moquin-Tandon (1804–1863) qualified as a doctor before, appropriately enough, studying leeches. His *World of the Sea*, originally titled *Natural History of the Sea*, was published posthumously in 1864.

p. 187 *the Marseillais Peysonnel*: Joseph-Antoine Peysonnel (1694–1757) was a doctor of medicine who co-founded the Académie de Marseilles. He published his *Observations on Coral* in 1756.

p. 188 *serpentines*: the word is used here of the coil of the Rühmkorff induction coil by which their way is lit.

p. 199 *Remington*: Eliphalet Remington (1793–1861), a manufacturer of small-arms who supplied the U.S. army with its first breech-loading rifle, the Jenks carbine, in 1847. For Chassepot, see note to page 17.

p. 200 *Mr. Darwin and Captain Fitz-Roy*: Keeling Island is the subject of Chapter 22 of *The Voyage of the Beagle*. Captain FitzRoy of the *Beagle* had expressed a desire for the presence of "some scientific person"; he "got" Charles Darwin, who, over the course of this voyage, formed impressions that led him to the theory of evolution.

p. 202 *Oppian*: Oppian of Cilicia wrote Greek poems about hunting (the *Cynegetika*) and fishing (the *Halieutika*) in the late 2nd century A.D.. References to argonauts would be in the latter. For Aristotle and Pliny see note to p. 11; for Athenaeus, see note to p. 130.

p. 203 *Argonaut*: Conseil's joke about the differences between argonauts and nautili is enhanced by the fact that the Argonauts of myth were the sailors on the ship *Argo* who accompanied Jason in his quest for the Golden Fleece. Verne is again mythologizing the *Nautilus* and its commander.

p. 206 *a book giving an account of this island*: in the original, Aronnax finds such a book in Nemo's library: H.C. Sirr's *Ceylon and the Cinghalese* (1850). Verne often cites his sources in his narrative. The running joke about sharks

is a characteristic means for Verne to make his didacticism more acceptable.

p. 207 *Percival*: Robert Percival (1765–1826), British sailor and
explorer, published his *An Account of Ceylon, with the
Journal of an Embassy to Candy*; it includes (Chapter
III) a detailed account of the Manaar pearl-fishery, of
which Verne seems to have made extensive use.

p. 213 *Servilia*: Servilia, the half-sister of Cato and mother of
Brutus, was the most famous of the mistresses of Julius
Caesar (100–44 B.C.) after Cleopatra.

p. 219 *ten nails long*: a nail is an obsolete measure for cloth:
2.25 inches, or a sixth of a yard. It is used to translate the
French "decimètre".

p. 220 *really inexhaustible*: this is one of Verne's more
optimistic statements of the relation of man to the
maritime world.

p. 225 *with a vigorous kick*: vigorous indeed; the diving suits
would have to have been weighted to allow the divers to
walk on the bottom of the sea, and Nemo could not
therefore spring to the surface.

p. 229 *Edrisi*: or Al Idrisi, Arab geographer born c. 1100 in
Ceuta; he died in 1164. He created a world map in 70
sheets, and his circular representation of the earth
served as a basis for most subsequent world maps.

p. 233 *Strabo*: Strabo (64/3 B.C.–at least A.D. 21), a Greek
historian and geographer from Pontus. His *Geographia*
has survived in 17 books, of which the last deals with
Egypt.

p. 234 *Arrian, Agatharchides, and Artemidorus*: Flavius
Arrianus (2nd century A.D.) defeated the Alan invasion
of 134 as a governor of Bithynia under the Emperor
Hadrian. A pupil of Epictetus, he wrote a history of
Alexander the Great entitled *Anabasis*. Agatharchides, a
Greek grammarian and Peripatetic from Cnidos, was
guardian to a young Ptolemy of Egypt around 116 B.C..
Extracts from his work survive in Diodorus Siculus,

Book 3, which gives a vivid description of the fate suffered by sailors stranded in the Red Sea while transporting elephants by boat. Artemidorus (fl. 104–101 B.C.) wrote eleven geographical books, much quoted by subsequent authors.

p. 235 *En signe de cette merveille/Devint la mer rouge et vermeille/Non puis ne surent la nommer/Autrement que la rouge mer*: the chronicler tells us that the drowning of the Egyptian host pursuing Moses and the Israelites was commemorated by the sea turning red. "In token of this wonder/The sea became red and scarlet/ Then could they name it/No other than red sea".

p. 236 *Sesostris*: a canal joining the Bitter Lakes and Red Sea was first attempted around 1800 B.C. It was extended by the Romans and known as Trajan's Canal. This was finally filled in by the Ottomans as late as 1775. Sesostris is a mythical king of Egypt, who is discussed in Herodotus 2.102–111.

p. 237 *Lesseps*: Ferdinand de Lesseps (1805–1894), French engineer and diplomat, directed the building of the Suez Canal and went on to begin the Panama Canal before being convicted of breach of trust in relation to the management of the latter.

p. 238 *Aures habient et non audient*: (Latin) "They have ears and will not hear".

p. 247 *fellies*: segments or the whole circumference of a wooden wheel.

p. 248 *twenty minutes*: the Suez Canal is 114 miles long. Assuming the underground tunnel to be of the same length, the *Nautilus* attains a speed of 342 m.p.h.. Nemo is indeed a skilled helmsman. In *Journey to the Centre of the Earth*, the protagonists are carried along on a sea similarly emptying its waters down a tunnel, this time in an open boat, and again without accident.

p. 254 *Est in Carpathio Neptuni gurgite vates/ Caeruleus*

Proteus. Virgil's *Georgics*, IV, 387–8: "There is in the Carpathian sea a prophet of Neptune's, sea-blue Proteus". In Greek mythology, Proteus is the herdsman of Neptune's seal-flocks. His prophecies could be extracted from him only by seizing him when he was asleep; he would then change shape in an attempt to escape, but if held fast, would resume his own shape and prophesy. He seems to have been dear to the heart of Verne, who cites him again in *20,000 Leagues* and at the heart of *Voyage to the Centre of the Earth*. There Proteus appears with the spurious quotation "Immanis pecoris custos, immanior ipse", which also appears in *Paris au XXe siècle* (1863) and *Une Ville Idéale* of 1875. It seems to be a conflation of *Georgics*, IV, 394–5 ("immania cuius/armenta"), and *Eclogues* V, 44 "Formosi pecoris custos, formosior ipse". In both 1863 and 1875 it is cited in the context of mistranslation; perhaps a joke is intended about the inversion "formosus/immanis" (handsome/monstruous)? Carpathos is the southernmost island of the Aegean with the exception of Crete, and the Carpathian sea is that south of the isle.

p. 255 *Vitellius*: this is Aulus Vitellius (A.D. 15–69), hailed as Emperor in 69 by his troops on the death of Galba. History has recorded him as an incompetent and a glutton. We know about him from the "life" in *Lives of the Caesars* by the Roman historian Suetonius (b. c. A.D. 69).

p. 256 *modern Greek characters*: a man of Aronnax's distinction can hardly have been unaware that, though the Greek language has changed, the Greek alphabet has not.

p. 258 *Cassiodorus*: Flavius Cassiodorus (c. A.D. 490–c. 583) author of histories of Rome and of the Goths, organised a religious community on his own estate whose *Institutiones* served as a model for later monastic

445

institutions. He is one of the founders of Western medieval civilization.

p. 260 *Michelet*: Jules Michelet (1798–1874), French historian, wrote a 17-volume *History of France* (to 1867), one of the most celebrated achievements of Romantic historiography. The 'Picture of France' constituting Volume 2 suggests how geographical features may influence character.

p. 262 *Lucullus*: Lucius Lucullus, Consul of Rome in 74 B.C., retired after a highly active political and military career to the Epicurean existence for which he is famed.

p. 264 *Arachne*: in legend, a skilful weaver who challenged the goddess Athene. Athene could no find no fault with Arachne's handiwork, and tore it to pieces. Arachne hanged herself in despair, but Athene saved her life by turning her into a spider.

p. 268 *tartan*: single-masted Mediterranean vessel, usually with lateen sail.

p. 269 *Avienus*: Avianus or Avienus (fl. c. A.D. 400), a Roman fabulist who wrote forty-two fables in elegiac metre, is a strange authority to cite.

p. 275 *Kosciusko, etc.*: the "one great humane idea" here is national liberation. Tadeusz Kosciuszko [sic] (1746–1817), Polish patriot, took an active part in the American War of Independence and led the Polish Insurrection of 1794 against Russian occupation. Kosciuszko's inadequately armed troops were eventually defeated at Macejowice, and he was forced into exile. It is not clear where Verne thinks that he "fell". Markos Botsaris (c. 1788–1823), an important leader of the early part of the Greek War of Independence against Ottoman occupation, was killed in battle at Karpaision. Daniel O'Connell (1775–1847), nicknamed "The Liberator", formed the Catholic Association to fight elections against landlords. His election as M.P. for County Clare forced Wellington's government to grant Catholic Emancipation

(1829). He agitated for the end of Union with Britain, and suffered imprisonment for his pains. George Washington (1732–99), Commander of American forces in the American War of Independence, was the first U.S. President (1789–1797). Daniele Manin (1804–1857) was the Venice leader of the Risorgimento against Austrian rule in Italy. He was forced into exile when the Austrians recaptured Venice in 1849. Abraham Lincoln (1809–1865), 16th President of the United States, freed the slaves of the separatist states during the American Civil War, and was assassinated by J. Wilkes Booth in Ford's Theatre during his second term. John Brown (1800–1859), a militant abolitionist, attempted to set up a liberationist state. He led a raid on a federal armoury in Virginia in 1859. It was recaptured by Marines, and he was hanged for treason. The song 'John Brown's body' was popular with Union soldiers in the American Civil War. One of Verne's sources here may be the poem by Victor Hugo that he cites. Hugo's poem is *L'Année Terrible* [1872]: *Décembre: III: Le Message de Grant,* 23–28, in which Brown's gallows are presented as casting a shadow over the world "like a second Golgotha". This section of the poem also mentions Kosciuszko and Lincoln, and elsewhere, in *La Voix de Guernesey,* III, 11–3, Hugo associates Brown with Giuseppe Garibaldi, one of the principal leaders of the Risorgimento.

p. 279 *the Incas and Ferdinand Cortez' conquered peoples*: Hernan Cortés (1485–1547), the Spanish Conquistador, overthrew the Aztec Empire (1519–1521) using cavalry among a people to whom horses were unknown, and won Mexico for Spain. The treasure of Vigo was topical in 1869 when *20,000 Leagues* was appearing in serial form, as Bazin had discovered traces of the galleons and an expedition had been mounted to retrieve it. This forms part of Verne's up-to-the-minute factual background to his fantastic narrative.

p. 283 *an iron spiked stick*: Verne's "bâton ferré" is a charming indication of how much the conventions of his underwater world have come to resemble those of the terrestrial world. His walking stick, unless tipped with a great deal of iron, would, of course, be buoyant, and therefore somewhat unserviceable.

p. 288 *like the eruption of Vesuvius on another Torre del Greco*: Torre del Greco lies on the Bay of Naples and was two-thirds destroyed by the eruption of the volcano Vesuvius in 1631.

p. 288 *Atlantis*: Plato describes Atlantis in the *Timaeus* 24e-26b and in the *Critias*. He tells of a land that stood before the Pillars of Hercules and was "larger than Libya and Asia put together"; it had "a great and wonderful empire". Atlantis launched an attack on the Mediterranean basin, and Athens alone held out. But in a cataclysm the island of Atlantis sank to the bottom of the sea, taking with it the Athenian armies. Verne's source for this review of the literature is probably Henri Martin's *Etude sur le Timée* of 1840. The *Timaeus* is open to allegorical interpretation, the option of Iamblichus (c. A.D. 250-c. 325), a Neo-Platonist who wrote commentaries on Plato and Aristotle, and of Origen (c. 185-c. 284), the Alexandrian theologian and biblical critic who castrated himself to assist his aspiration to chastity. Strabo (2, 102) tells us that Posidonius (c. 135-c. 51-50 B.C.), philosopher and historian, acknowledged the possibility of Atlantis, given that Solon (the historical character presented in Plato's dialogue) consulted the Egyptian priesthood on the subject. Tertullian (c. 160-c. 220), Carthaginian Church father, admits that the world has changed, and gives ironic credence to Plato in *De Pallio* II, 3. The reference in Ammianus Marcellinus is ambiguous. Theopompus (b. c. 370 B.C.), the Greek historian, of whose work only fragments survive, is recorded by

Claudius Aelianus (c. A.D. 170–235) in his *Varia Historia*, a collection of anecdotes, III.18. as recounting words spoken by the satyr and prophet Silenus to King Midas. At one time, Silenus said, there were two towns in a country outside the known world, Eusebes, a peace-loving place much frequented by the gods, where the golden age reigned, and Machimos, a warlike city; Machimos invaded the known world, but hearing from the Hyperboreans that they were its happiest inhabitants, thought it not worth their while to go further. He also spoke of men called Meropians (Ethiopians, or humans), through whose country flowed the rivers of Pleasure and Pain. By the courses of these rivers grew respectively Pleasure and Pain trees. A man who ate their fruit wasted away in grief and died (Pain) or retraced life through youth to babyhood and thus perished. Aelian dismisses this as rubbish. Jean-Baptiste d'Anville (1697–1782) was a French geographer, cartographer and classical scholar. Conrad Malte-Brun (1775–1826), the author of several geographical works, was the founder of the first modern geographical society (1810–1829). Alexander von Humboldt (1769–1859), German naturalist and explorer, laid the foundations of meteorology during his intensive voyages of discovery in South and Central America. Joseph Tournefort (1656–1708) was a French botanist and physician who pioneered binomial botanical nomenclature; he worked at the Jardin des Plantes, the site of the Paris Natural History Museum. Tournefort followed Diodorus Siculus in believing that the accumulated waters of the "lake" of the Mediterranean had burst forth through the Pillars of Hercules and overwhelmed Atlantis. Samuel Engel (1702–1784) was a Swiss geographer, geologist and economist. Sherer is presumably the English geographer John Sherer. Georges-Louis Leclerc, Comte de Buffon (1707–1788),

449

the "first modern writer to translate the facts of nature into a history", was curator of the Jardin du Roi (Jardin des Plantes) and wrote a *Histoire naturelle* in 44 volumes, the most famous being perhaps those on the geological periods of the earth, the *Epoques de la nature*, of which some propositions were condemned by the Sorbonne. Buffon located Atlantis in Armenia. Pascal d'Avezac de Castera-Macaya (1800–1875) wrote on historical geography and particularly on the discoveries of the 15th and 16th centuries.

p. 290 *Makhimos ... Eusebius*: see preceding note, Machimos and Eusebes.

p. 290 *ignivome*: vomiting fire, i.e. volcanic.

p. 292 *Bailly*: Jean-Sylvain Bailly (1736–1793), French astronomer and first Mayor of Paris in 1789, died at the guillotine. His *Letters on Atlantis* were addressed to Voltaire; he placed Atlantis in Mongolia.

p. 293 *balloon journey*: this had, of course, been the subject of Verne's first great success, the *Five Weeks in a Balloon*, a part of the drama of whose narrative is precisely the impossibility of steering a balloon.

p. 295 *tundish*: "a wooden dish or shallow vessel with a tube at the bottom fitting into the bung-hole of a tun or cask" (*Shorter Oxford English Dictionary*): in short, a funnel. A tundish is used in brewing.

p. 302 *Walter Scott's hero*: this is presumably Sir Arthur Wardour and his daughter, caught by the tide when walking the sands between Knockwinnock and Monkbarns in *The Antiquary* (1816) by Sir Walter Scott (1771–1832).

p. 304 *Sargazzo*: the Spanish word is "sargazo".

p. 309 *McClintock*: Sir Francis McClintock (1819–1907) undertook four voyages in the attempt to establish the fate of the Arctic explorer Sir John Franklin (1786–1847), who had set out to discover the North West Passage. On the fourth voyage he discovered Franklin's journal and the graves of some of his men. Franklin's expedition had been stranded in thick ice in the Victoria Straits.

p. 310 *8,000 fathoms*: a fathom is six foot, so this depth is 14, 630 metres. For comparison, in 1961, coincidentally the year in which Verne's *Paris au XXe siècle* is set, the bathyscape *Archimedes* dived to 11,000 metres, the greatest depth yet explored by man.

p. 317 *They are taken for islands*: this is the story preserved in Olaus Magnus (1490-1557), who speaks of sailors planting stakes in whales, mooring their ships to them, and lighting fires. The whale then feels the fire and submerges. Or again sailors seeking refuge in a storm drop anchor and take refuge on the sandy back of the whale, which submerges dragging down men and ships. The story is given in *Historia de gentibus septentrionalibus*, Bk 10, Chapter 25, and cited by Pontopiddan. Cf. note to p. 11.

p. 320 *The barbarous and inconsiderate greed*: Verne/Nemo's prediction is now close to fulfilment.

p. 321 *Frédol:* Alfred Frédol was a pseudonym of Moquin-Tandon. Cf. note to p. 184.

p. 328 *Hansten ... Duperrey:* Christopher Hansteen [sic] (1784-1873), Norwegian astronomer and physicist specialising in geomagnetism, who published the first reliable chart of magnetic intensities. His work was refined by Louis-Isidore Duperrey (1786-1865), a celebrated explorer and geographer who published several works on geomagnetism; his voyage in *La Coquille* (departed 1822) is cited by Darwin in *The Voyage of the Beagle*.

p. 331 *If a continent emerges at the Pole*: the Antarctic is indeed a continent, and the *Nautilus's* voyage an impossibility. The obliging reader will transfer it to the Arctic for the purposes of feasibility.

p. 339 *James Ross*: Sir John [sic] Ross (1777-1856) made two Arctic expeditions in search of the North West Passage. He made a third voyage in search of Sir John Franklin in

1850. Ross made substantial contributions to oceanography.

p. 339 *quebrante-huesos*: the name is Spanish for "bone-
breaker".

p. 342 *congener*: animal of the same species.

p. 347 *in spite of its name*: the name "balaenopteron" is a
compound of "balenus" (whale) and "pteron" (feather/
wing).

p. 371 *Davis ... Hawkins*: John Davis (c. 1550–1605), English
navigator, discovered the Falkland Islands on 9 August
1592, when seeking a passage through the Strait of
Magellan. He died at the hands of Japanese pirates. Sir
Richard Hawkins (c. 1560–1622), English navigator,
sighted what was probably the Falkland Islands, and
named them Hawkins Maidenland. Not long afterwards
he was captured in a battle with Spanish ships and
ransomed. He published *Observations on his Voyage to
the South Seas* in 1622.

p. 376 *Toussenel*: this is presumably Alphonse Toussenel, one
of two brothers who were both littérateurs. Alphonse, a
Fouriériste journalist, published some natural history
writings. But it is not clear that he was expert on whales
and manatees. The theory Toussenel advances is highly
ecological, and the result the usual one; the manatees
are killed all the same.

p. 378 *Poulp*: octopus.

p. 381 *calamary*: squid.

p. 382 *Saint Malo*: this *ex voto* in the seamen's church in Saint-
Malo was cited by the French naturalist Denys de
Montfort in his *Natural History of Molluscs* (1802) as
evidence of the existence of giant octopuses.

p. 382 *Pontoppidan*: Pontopiddan believed the kraken to be
an enormous cephalopod. Some of those he mentions
are the size of small islands, and one of them is one and
a half English miles in circumference.

p. 383 *Bouguer*: Bouguer is in fact Frédéric Bouyer, the

452

commander of the *Alecton*, which hunted down a "giant octopus" and lost it as it was being hauled aboard. Bouyer reported it as being 15-18 foot long. This creature was an *Architeuthis* or giant squid, of which specimens have been washed ashore over 35 foot long, and which the *Encyclopaedia Britannica* declares can grow to 20 metres in length.

p. 384 *teratological*: relating to the study of freaks or monsters real or legendary.

p. 389 *Victor Hugo*: Verne is acknowledging his inspiration for the battle of the *Nautilus* and the octopuses: a battle between a fisherman and a giant octopus that takes place in Hugo's *The Toilers of the Sea* (1866), Part II, Section IV, 1-3. In the Gazette Littéraire of *Le Figaro*, 21 August 1871, Fernand de Rodays complained of Verne's misspelling of Frédéric Bouyer's name and noted Bouyer's attachment to "his" octopus, which had, Bouyer felt, been "spoilt" by Hugo in his "stupid" novel.

p. 390 *Gulf Stream*: here Verne is particularly indebted to Arthur Mangin: *Les Mystères de l'océan* (1864) Bk III, Chapter 3.

p. 402 *Great Eastern*: the *Great Eastern*, the masterpiece of the British engineer Isambard Kingdom Brunel (1806-1859), and the largest ship in the world at the time of its construction (1853-1858), had long fascinated Verne; he had visited it on his first trip to Great Britain, and vowed to sail on her as soon as he could afford it. The Verne brothers travelled on the first transatlantic voyage of the ship after it had been converted back from cable-laying.

p. 403 *Cyrus Field*: Cyrus Field (1819-1892) worked his way from errand boy to mogul. He made a fortune in paper, risked it in the Atlantic cable scheme, and created the 'L', the elevated railway system in New York, which was the probable inspiration for Verne's overhead railway in *Paris au XX*ᵉ *siècle*.

p. 403 *Sadowa*: tensions over Prussian hegemony within the German Confederation led to war between Prussia and the rest of the Confederation. The Prussians under von Moltke won a decisive victory over the Hanoverian armies at Sadowa on 3 July 1866. The armistice was in fact signed on July 26.

p. 406 *Carlyle*: the parenthesis is an interpolation by the translator, who is clearly more attentive to national honour than idiom. Barrère is Bertrand Barrère de Vieuzac (1755–1841), the Conventionnel, who reported to the Convention on the heroic loss of the *Vengeur*. Basing himself on the reports of a witness on the British side, one Lt. Griffiths, the historian Thomas Carlyle (1795–1881) disputed the French account in his *The French Revolution: A History* (1837, Book V, Chapter VI) as "the largest, most inspiring piece of *blague* manufactured for some centuries, by any man or nation". At issue is whether the *Vengeur* went down with all hands; it seems that some of its crew escaped into English hands, but that a fair proportion of the crew did indeed go down with their ship.

p. 415 *portrait of a woman*: Nemo's motives remain obscure in *20,000 Leagues*, but all is revealed in *The Mysterious Island*. See pp. 428–9 above.

p. 417 *Gordon Pym*: *The Narrative of Arthur Gordon Pym of Nantucket* by Edgar Allan Poe (1809–1849) in fact ends with these words: "And now we rushed into the embraces of the cataract, where a chasm threw itself open to receive us. But there arose in our pathway a shrouded human figure, very far larger in its proportions than any dweller among men. And the hue of the skin of the figure was of the perfect whiteness of snow". Verne would have depended on the translation by Charles Baudelaire (1821–1867) published in 1858. Verne's *Le Sphinx des glaces* (1897) is a continuation of Poe's novel.

p. 421 *The Maëlstrom*: Verne here relies somewhat upon the source that he has just acknowledged, that is, Edgar Allan Poe. Poe's story 'A Descent into the Maelström', first published in *Graham's Magazine* in 1841, was slightly revised for the *Tales* of 1845. Verne would again have been relying on Baudelaire's translations of the *Tales,* which were published in two volumes in 1856 and 1857 respectively. The maelstrom is a real phenomenon, though both Poe and Verne exaggerate its strength and size.